SCIENCE
FICTION
THE BEST
OF THE YEAR
2007

Edited by

Rich Horton

COSMOS BOOKS

SCIENCE FICTION: THE BEST OF THE YEAR
June 2007

Published by

Dorchester Publishing Co., Inc.
200 Madison Avenue
New York, NY 10016

in collaboration with Wildside Press, LLC

Cover painting copyright © 2007 by Bob Eggleton

Typeset by Swordsmith Productions

ISBN-10: 0-8439-5904-5
ISBN-13: 978-0-8439-5904-8

The name "Cosmos Books" and the Cosmos logo are the property of Wildside Press, LLC.

Printed in the United States of America.

Contents

SCIENCE FICTION
THE BEST
OF THE YEAR
2007

THE YEAR IN SCIENCE FICTION, 2006

Rich Horton

1. Theory

Last year some readers wondered what my underlying theme was in this book—what was my focus? what sort of science fiction do I most wish to promote? what is my vision for the field? My original reaction was to insist that I have no underlying theme. My only goal is to pick the dozen or fifteen stories I think are the best each year. Let the thematic chips fall where they may.

But of course this is a bit naïve. An anthologist has considerable control over a book's contents beyond merely exercising their taste. (And sometimes less control than they would like: occasionally stories cannot be used for contractual reasons.) If every year there were fifteen and only fifteen stories that stood head and shoulders above the rest of the field, a nice balance of novellas and novelettes and short stories, that neatly filled the 125,000 words I'm allotted, I could say that this book simply publishes the best stories I read. But it doesn't work that way. In any given year there are perhaps half-a-dozen stories that I feel I simply have to have. Beyond that there are perhaps twenty more that are pretty much on a level with each other. (And as I reread stories, think about them some more, play them against each other, my perceptions can shift somewhat.) Only about half of those stories can be used. So how to decide?

Many considerations enter. I try to have a balance of lengths. I try not to use too many stories from the same source. I like to have a couple of newer writers to showcase, if possible. And for these books I restrict myself to one story per author per book—sometimes a wrenching choice. (Let me recommend, for example, Robert Reed's "Eight Episodes," a brilliant and original short story that doesn't appear here only because I chose another brilliant story of his.)

Having said all that, I don't really make an effort to emphasize any particular style or theme. Let the writers in concert do that—they often do. Last year I thought my collection rather heavy on fairly "hard" science fiction; I don't see quite such an emphasis this year. I do see a few stories that are overtly weird in ways not always characteristic of "science fiction" (as opposed to fantasy or horror or perhaps slipstream). There are also a few stories fairly directly focused on religion. But I am going to shy away from pronouncing a common theme or direction for science fiction in 2007.

2. Practice

Two of the most wonderfully strange stories come from Christopher Rowe and Benjamin Rosenbaum, each of them a young writer who has made a noticeable splash over the past several years, even without having produced a novel between them. Rowe's "Another Word for Map is Faith" shows us a future in which consensus faith can alter geography, telling the tale as much by sly characterization as by displaying the odd setting. Rosenbaum's "The House Beyond Your Sky" takes us to the extreme far future for a remarkably intimate, and truly lovelily written, piece about the clash of universes.

Religion is central to William Shunn's "Inclination," in which the main character grows up on a space station, in a very traditional religion that turns out to be an odd futuristic variant of Christianity. His problems are in part futuristic—his religion resists the body modifications and nanotechnology prevalent on the station— and in part quite directly relevant to contemporary issues. Robert Reed's "A Billion Eves" posits a new religion, based on the technology of traveling to parallel worlds, and rather patriarchially (and oppressively) based on worshipping the "Fathers" who pioneer these new worlds. But a story that starts out rather conventionally depicting a nasty religion becomes rather different, as its protagonist becomes ecologically aware—and most importantly, as we are shown the different nature of ecological issues in this strange multiplex tree of societies. Ian Watson's "Saving for a Sunny

Day; or, The Benefits of Reincarnation" takes a different, rather more satirical, look at religious issues. Souls in this future are barcoded, and can be tracked after death to their new incarnation. Which can mean a newborn inherits a significant karmic (and financial) debt. Robert Charles Wilson's thought-provoking "The Cartesian Theater" finds a very appropriate way of speculating about machine rights, human identity, even the idea of a soul, in a well-framed and well-told story of a man in an ambiguously prosperous future telling his dead grandfather about a disgusting but legal staging of a simulated (or was it?) death.

I promised new writers—who is on hand this time? Jack Skillingstead's stories began appearing in major markets in 2003, and they immediately attracted notice. "Life on the Preservation" is his best yet, I think, about a visit to a version of Seattle preserved by aliens in a time loop. Ann Leckie is even newer: "Hesperia and Glory" was her first sale, to the "science fiction cliché" issue of *Subterranean* (guest-edited by John Scalzi). It is a lovely and witty inversion of Edgar Rice Burroughs's *John Carter of Mars* stories.

Another particularly weird story is Adam Roberts's "Me-Topia," which starts us out in an almost unexplainable setting—a planet outside of the Solar System's ecliptic with breathable air and curiously familiar geography—and which manages to make all this make sense—and matter—by the end. Much less weird, but original and affecting, is a welcome return to the field from Carolyn Ives Gilman: "Okanoggan Falls," about implacable alien invaders in a small town, and the curious effect the mayor's wife's overtures have on the commander. "Exit Before Saving," by Ruth Nestvold is a thriller about a woman illegally using her corporation's "body morph" technology, and then finding a sinister twist to it. Finally, Walter Jon Williams's "Incarnation Day" is one of the more traditional science fiction stories here, and very effective, about a future in which children are raised in a virtual environment, and have to earn incarnation in real bodies.

3. Background

Where does the science fiction field stand in 2007? Is it any healthier than in recent years? That's hard to say. We didn't lose anything as important as *SCI FICTION*, Ellen Datlow's magnificent original fiction website, which ceased publication at the end of 2005. 2006 did see the demise of a lesser but often interesting electronic publication, *Oceans of the Mind*. But we also saw a very promising new webzine: *Jim Baen's Universe*, a production of Baen Books, edited by Eric Flint, which featured some very interesting fiction. (Alas, its arrival was almost simultaneous with the sudden death of the founder of Baen Books, Jim Baen.) Another interesting new webzine, *Orson Scott Card's Intergalactic Medicine Show*, actually debuted in 2005, and published two worthwhile issues in 2006.

These new arrivals notwithstanding, I'd still rank the venerable site *Strange Horizons* (which is in its seventh year of weekly publication, quite remarkable for a webzine) as the best online source of short science fiction and fantasy. Other online sites which featured intriguing short science fiction include *Abyss and Apex*, *Challenging Destiny*, *Ideomancer*, *Helix*, and the very smart, near future oriented, *Futurismic*.

The print side continued much as usual. Sheila

Williams did a very fine job in her second full year at the helm of *Asimov's Science Fiction* (as evidenced by my choice of four stories from that magazine for this book.) *The Magazine of Fantasy and Science Fiction*, under Gordon van Gelder, had a particularly strong year (both with science fiction stories and some excellent fantasies). I didn't think *Analog* (under Stanley Schmidt) had quite as strong a year publishing short fiction in 2006, but there were some fine serials, and if the best stories weren't quite as good as the best of 2005, there were a passel of solid stories. *Interzone* (edited by Andy Cox) continues to be as good looking a magazine as we have, and also continues to publish plenty of fine stories. Newer magazines include another British entry, *Postcripts* (edited by Peter Crowther), always interesting (though the best work there this year was not really science fiction), and the very promising *Subterranean* (edited by William Schafer), which very rapidly is becoming one of the best magazines in the field. Among the smaller 'zines those that publish a fair amount of first rate science fiction (as opposed to fantasy) include *Electric Velocipede*, two Canadian publications: *On Spec* and *Neo-Opsis*, and a new British entry, *Farthing*.

I thought this year a very strong year for original anthologies. One of the best recent developments has been the Science Fiction Book Club's increasing commitment to original collections of longer stories. This year they published *One Million A. D.* (edited by Gardner Dozois), *Forbidden Planets* (edited by Marvin Kaye), and *Escape From Earth* (edited by Gardner Dozois and Jack Dann), all full of first rate novellas and long novelettes. Other top anthologies of science fiction stories included, surprisingly, another book called

Forbidden Planets, this one edited by Peter Crowther and published by DAW, and featuring stories to some extent inspired by the movie; Lou Anders's first-rate non-theme book *Futureshocks* (Roc); and a couple of Australian books: *Agog! Ripping Reads* (edited by Cat Sparks), and *Eidolon 1* (edited by Jonathan Strahan and Jeremy G. Byrne). In addition, *Twenty Epics* (edited by David Moles and Susan Marie Groppi) was a mostly fantasy-oriented book with a couple of excellent science fiction stories, and two anthologies overtly focused on cross-genre work included some fine science fiction: *Paraspheres* (edited by Ken Keegan and Rusty Morrison) and *Polyphony 6* (edited by Deborah Layne and Jay Lake).

4. Future

So, here are my choices for the best science fiction stories from 2006. They are an exciting and varied bunch, and they reflect an exciting and varied short fiction field. And there is more where these came from—I urge readers to try the magazines and original anthologies and websites that publish new short fiction. Short fiction is not only worth reading in the present—it represents to a considerable extent the future of the field, both in allowing new writers a place to begin, and in allowing new ideas a place to flourish.

ANOTHER WORD FOR MAP IS FAITH

Christopher Rowe

The little drivers threw baggage down from the top of the bus and out from its rusty undercarriage vaults. This was the last stop. The road broke just beyond here, a hundred yards short of the creek.

With her fingertip, Sandy traced the inked ridge northeast along the map, then rolled the soft leather into a cylinder and tucked it inside her vest. She looked around for her pack and saw it tumbled together with the other Cartographers' luggage at the base of a catalpa tree. Lucas and the others were sorting already, trying to lend their gear some organization, but the stop was a tumult of noise and disorder.

The high country wind shrilled against the rush of the stony creek; disembarkees pawed for their belongings and tried to make sense of the delicate, coughing talk of the unchurched little drivers. On the other side of the valley, across the creek, the real ridge line—*the geology*, her father would have said disdainfully—stabbed upstream. By her rough estimation it had rolled perhaps two degrees off the angle of its writ mapping. Lucas would determine the exact discrepancy later, when he extracted his instruments from their feather and wax paper wrappings.

"Third world *bullshit*," Lucas said, walking up to her. "The transit services people from the university paid these little schemers before we ever climbed onto that deathtrap, and now they're asking for the fare." Lucas had been raised near the border, right outside the last town the bus had stopped at, in fact, though he'd dismissed the notion of visiting any family. His patience with the locals ran inverse to his familiarity with them.

"Does this count as the third world?" she asked him. "Doesn't there have to be a general for that? Rain forests and steel ruins?"

Lucas gave his half-grin—not quite a smirk—acknowledging her reduction. Cartographers were famous for their willful ignorance of social expressions like politics and history.

"Carmen paid them, anyway," he told her as they walked towards their group. "Probably out of her own pocket, thanks be for wealthy dilettantes."

"Not fair," said Sandy. "She's as sharp as any student in the seminar, and a better hand with the plotter than most post-docs, much less grad students."

Lucas stopped. "I hate that," he said quietly. "I hate when you separate yourself; go out of your way to remind me that you're a teacher and I'm a student."

Sandy said the same thing she always did. "I hate when you forget it."

Against all odds, they were still meeting the timetable they'd drawn up back at the university, all those months ago. The bus pulled away in a cloud of noxious diesel fumes an hour before dark, leaving its passengers in a muddy camp dotted with fire rings but otherwise marked only by a hand lettered sign pointing the way to a primitive latrine.

The handful of passengers not connected with Sandy's group had melted into the forest as soon as they'd found their packages ("Salt and sugar," Lucas had said, "They're backwoods people—hedge shamans and survivalists. There's every kind of lunatic out here.") This left Sandy to stand by and pretend authority while the Forestry graduate student whose services she'd borrowed showed them all how to set up their camps.

Carmen, naturally, had convinced the young man to demonstrate tent pitching to the others using her own expensive rig as an example. The olive-skinned girl sat in a camp chair folding an onionskin scroll back on itself and writing in a wood-bound notebook while the others struggled with canvas and willow poles.

"Keeping track of our progress?" Sandy asked, easing herself onto the ground next to Carmen.

"I have determined," Carmen replied, not looking up, "that we have traveled as far from a hot water heater as is possible and still be within Christendom."

Sandy smiled, but shook her head, thinking of the most remote places she'd ever been. "Davis?" she asked, watching her student's reaction to mention of that unholy town.

Carmen, a Californian, shuddered but kept her focus. "There's a naval base in San Franciso, sí? They've got all the amenities, surely."

Sandy considered again, thinking of cold camps in old mountains, and of muddy jungle towns ten days' walk from the closest bus station.

"Cape Canaveral," she said.

With quick, precise movements, Carmen folded a

tiny desktop over her chair's arm and spread her scroll out flat. She drew a pair of calipers out from her breast pocket and took measurements, pausing once to roll the scroll a few turns. Finally, she gave a satisfied smile and said, "Only fifty-five miles from Orlando. We're almost twice that from Louisville."

She'd made the mistake Sandy had expected of her. "But Orlando, Señorita Reyes, is Catholic. And we were speaking of Christendom."

A stricken look passed over her student's face, but Sandy calmed her with exaggerated conspiratorial looks left and right. "Some of your fellows aren't so liberal as I am, Carmen. So remember where you are. Remember *who* you are. Or who you're trying to become."

Another reminder issued, Sandy went to see to her own tent.

The Forestry student gathered their wood, brought them water to reconstitute their freeze-dried camp meals, then withdrew to his own tent far back in the trees. Sandy told him he was welcome to spend the evening around their fire—"You built it after all," she'd said—but he'd made a convincing excuse.

The young man pointed to the traveling shrine her students had erected in the center of their camp, pulling a wooden medallion from beneath his shirt. "That Christ you have over there, ma'am," he said. "He's not this one, is he?"

Sandy looked at the amulet he held, gilded and green. "What do you have there, Jesus in the Trees?" she asked, summoning all her professional courtesy to keep the amusement out of her voice. "No, that's not the Christ we keep. We'll see you in the morning."

They didn't, though, because later that night, Lucas discovered that the forest they were camped in wasn't supposed to be there at all.

He'd found an old agricultural map somewhere and packed it in with their little traveling library. Later, he admitted that he'd only pulled it out for study because he was still sulking from Sandy's clear signal he wouldn't be sharing her tent that night.

Sandy had been leading the rest of the students in some prayers and thought exercises when Lucas came up with his moldering old quarto. "Tillage," he said, not even bothering to explain himself before he'd foisted the book off on his nearest fellow. "All the acreage this side of the ridge line is supposed to be under tillage."

Sandy narrowed her eyes, more than enough to quiet any of her charges, much less Lucas. "What's he got there, Ford?" she asked the thin undergraduate who now held the book.

"Hmmmm?" said the boy; he was one of those who fell instantly and almost irretrievably into any text and didn't look up. Then, at an elbow from Carmen, he said, "Oh! This is…" He turned the book over in his hands, angled the spine toward one of the oil lamps and read, "This is *An Agricultural Atlas of Clark County, Kentucky.*"

"'County,'" said Carmen. "*Old* book, Lucas."

"But it's *writ*," said Lucas. "There's nothing superseding the details of it and it doesn't contradict anything else we brought about the error. Hell, it even confirms the error we came to correct." Involuntarily, all of them looked up and over at the apostate ridge.

"But what's this about tillage," Sandy said, giving

him the opportunity to show off his find even if was
already clear to her what it must be.

"See, these plot surveys in the appendices didn't get
accounted for in the literature survey we're working
from. The book's listed as a source, but only as a sup-
plemental confirmation. It's not just the ridge that's
wrong, it's the stuff growing down this side, too. We're
supposed to be in grain fields of some kind down here
in the flats, then it's pasturage on up to the summit
line."

A minor find, sure, but Sandy would see that Lucas
shared authorship on the corollary she'd file with the
university. More importantly, it was an opportunity
before the hard work of the days ahead.

"We can't do anything about the hillsides tonight, or
any of the acreage beyond the creek," she told them.
"But as for these glades here..."

It was a simple exercise. The fires were easily set.

In the morning, Sandy drafted a letter to the Dean of
Agriculture while most of her students packed up the
camp. She had detailed a few of them to sketch the
corrected valley floor around them, and she'd include
those visual notes with her instructions to the Dean,
along with a copy of the writ map from Lucas' book.

"Read that back to me, Carmen," she said, watching
as Lucas and Ford argued over yet another volume, this
one slim and bound between paper boards. It was the
same back country cartographer's guide she'd carried
on her own first wilderness forays as a grad student.
They'd need its detailed instructions on living out of
doors without the Tree Jesus boy to help them.

"'By my hand,'" read Carmen, "'I have caused these
letters to be writ. Blessings on the Department of

Agriculture and on you, Dean. Blessings on Jesus Sower, the Christ you serve.'"

"Skip to the end, dear." Sandy had little patience for the formalities of academic correspondence, and less for the pretense at holiness the Agriculturalists made with their little fruiting Christ.

"'So, then, it is seen in these texts that Cartography has corrected the error so far as in our power, and now the burden is passed to you and your brethren to complete this holy task, and return the land to that of Jesus's vision.'" Carmen paused. "Then you promise to remember the Dean in your prayers and all the rest of the politesse."

"Good. Everything observed. Make two copies and bring the official one to me for sealing when you're done."

Carmen turned to her work and Sandy to hers. The ashen landscape extending up the valley was still except for some ribbons twisting in a light breeze. The ribbons were wax sealed to the parchment banner her students had set at first light, the new map of the valley floor drawn in red and black against a cream background. Someone had found the the blackened disc of the Forestry student's medallion and leaned it against the base of the banner's staff and Sandy wondered if it had been Carmen, prone to sentiment, or perhaps Lucas, prone to vague gestures.

By midmorning, the students had readied their gear for the march up the ridge line and Carmen had dropped Sandy's package for the university in the mailbox by the bus stop. Before they hoisted their backpacks, though, Sandy gathered them all for fellowship and prayer.

"The gymnasiums at the University have made us fit

enough for this task," and here she made a playful flex with her left arm, earning rolled eyes from Lucas and a chuckle from the rest. "The libraries have given us the woodscraft we need, and the chapels have given us the sustenance of our souls."

Sandy swept her arm north to south, indicating the ridge. "When I was your age, oh so long ago—" and a pause here for another ripple of laughter, acknowledgment of her dual status as youngest tenured faculty member at the university and youngest ordained minister in the curia. "When I was your age, I was blessed with the opportunity to go to the Northeast, traveling the lands beyond the Susquehanna, searching out error."

Sandy smiled at the memory of those times—*could they be ten years gone already?* "I traveled with men and women strong in the Lord, soldiers and scholars of God. There are many errors in the Northeast."

Maps so brittle with age that they would flake away in the cold winds of the Adirondack passes, so faded that only the mightiest of prayers would reveal Jesus's true intentions for His world.

"But none here in the heartlands of the Church, right? Isn't that what our parish priests told us growing up?" The students recognized that she was beginning to teach and nodded, murmured assent.

"Christians, there *is* error here. There is error right before our eyes!" Her own students weren't a difficult congregation to hook, but she was gratified nonetheless by the gleam she caught in most of their eyes, the calls, louder now, of "Yes!" and "I see it! I see the lie!"

"I laid down my protractor, friends, I know exactly how far off north Jesus mapped this ridge line to lay," she said, sweeping her arm in a great arc, taking in the whole horizon, "And that ridge line sins by two degrees!"

"May as well be two *hundred*!" said Carmen, righteous.

Sandy raised her hand, stopped them at the cusp of celebration instead of loosing them. "Not yet," she said. "It's tonight. It's tonight we'll sing down the glory, tonight we'll make this world the way it was mapped."

The march up the ridge line did not go as smoothly as Sandy might have wished, but the delays and false starts weren't totally unexpected. She'd known Lucas—a country boy after all—would take the lead, and she'd guessed that he would dead-end them into a crumbling gully or two before he picked the right route through the brambles. If he'd been some kind of natural-born hunter he would never have found his way to the Lord, or to education.

Ford and his friends—all of them destined for lecture halls and libraries, not fieldwork—made the classic, the *predicted* mistake she'd specifically warned against in the rubric she'd distributed for the expedition. "If we're distributing 600 pounds of necessities across twenty-two packs," she asked Ford, walking easily beside him as he struggled along a game trail, "how much weight does that make each of us responsible for?"

"A little over twenty-seven pounds, ma'am," he said, wheezing out the reply.

"And did you calculate that in your head like a mathematician or did you remember it from the syllabus?" Sandy asked. She didn't press too hard, the harshness of the lesson was better imparted by the straps cutting into his shoulders than by her words.

"I remembered it," Ford said. And because he really

did have the makings of a great scholar and great scholars are nothing if not owners of their own errors, he added, "It was in the same paragraph that said not to bring too many books."

"Exactly," she said, untying the leather cords at the top of his pack and pulling out a particularly heavy looking volume. She couldn't resist looking at the title page before dropping it into her own pack.

"*Unchurched Tribes of the Chiapas Highlands: A Bestiary*. Think we'll make it to Mexico on this trip, Ford?" she asked him, teasing a little.

Ford's faced reddened even more from her attention than it had from the exertions of the climb. He mumbled something about migratory patterns then leaned into the hike.

If most of the students were meeting their expectations of themselves and one another, then Carmen's sprightly, sure-footed bounding up the trail was a surprise to most. Sandy, though, had seen the girl in the gym far more frequently than the other students, most of whom barely met the minimum number of visits per week required by their advising committees. Carmen was as much an athlete as herself, and the lack of concern the girl showed about dirt and insects was refreshing.

So it was Carmen who summitted first, and it was her that was looking northeast with a stunned expression on her face when Sandy and Lucas reached the top side by side. Following Carmen's gaze, Lucas cursed and called for help in taking off his heavily laden pack before he began unrolling the oilcloth cases of his instruments.

Sandy simply pursed her lips and began a mental review of her assets: the relative strengths and weaknesses of her students, the number of days worth of supplies they carried, the nature of the curia designed-instruments that Lucas exhibited a natural affinity for controlling. She began to nod. She'd marshaled more than enough strength for the simple tectonic adjustment they'd planned, she could set her own unquestionable faith against this new challenge if it revealed any deficiencies among her students. She would make a show of asking their opinions, but she already knew that this was a challenge she could meet.

Ford finally reached the top of the ridge line, not so much climbing as stumbling to the rocky area where the others were gathering. Once he looked up and around, he said, "The survey team that found the error in the ridge's orientation, they didn't come up here."

"They were specifically scouting for projects that the university could handle," said Sandy. "If they'd been up here, they would have called in the Mission Service, not us."

Spread out below them, ringed in tilled fields and dusted with a scattering of wooden fishing boats, was an unmapped lake.

Sandy set Ford and the other bookish scholars to cataloguing all of the texts they'd smuggled along so they could be integrated into her working bibliography. She hoped that one of them was currently distracted by waterways the way that Ford was distracted by fauna.

Lucas set their observation instruments on tripods in an acceptably devout semicircle and Sandy permitted two or three of the others to begin preliminary sight-line measurements of the lake's extent.

"It turns my stomach," said Lucas, peering through the brass tube of a field glass. "I grew up seeing the worst kind of blasphemy, but I could never imagine that anyone could do something like this."

"You need to work on that," said Sandy. Lucas was talking about the landscape feature crosshaired in the glass, a clearly artificial earthworks dam, complete with a retractable spillway. "Missionaries see worse every day."

Lucas didn't react. He'd never abandoned his ambition, even after she'd laughed him down. *Our sisters and brothers in the Mission Service*, she'd said with the authority that only someone who'd left that order could muster, *make up in the pretense of zeal what they lack in scholarship and access to the divine. Anyone can move a mountain with whips and shovels.*

The sketchers showed her their work, which they annotated with Lucas' count and codification of architectural structures, fence lines, and crops. "Those are corn cribs," he said. "That's a meeting house. That's a mill."

This was the kind of thing she'd told him he should concentrate on. The best thing any of them had to offer was the overlay of their own personal ranges of unexpected expertise onto the vast body of accepted Cartography. Lucas's barbaric background, Ford's holographic memory, Carmen's cultured scribing. Her own judgment.

"They're *marmotas*!" said Ford. They all looked up at where he'd been awkwardly turning the focus wheel on one of the glasses. "Like in my book!" He wasn't one to flash a triumphal grin, which Sandy appreciated. She assented to the line of inquiry with a nod and he hurried over to the makeshift shelf that some of his friends had been using to stack books while they wrote their list.

The unchurched all looked alike to Sandy, differing only in the details of their dress, modes of transportation, and to what extent the curia allowed interaction with them. In the case of the little drivers, for example, tacit permission was given for commercial exchange because of their ancient control of the bus lines. But she'd never heard of *marmotas*, and said so.

"They're called 'rooters' around here," said Lucas. "I don't know what Ford's on about. I've never heard of them having a lake, but they've always come into the villages with their vegetables, so far as I know."

"Not always," said Carmen. "There's nothing about any unchurched lineages in the glosses of the maps we're working from. They're as new as that lake."

Sandy recognized that they were in an educable moment. "Everybody come here, let's meet. Let's have a class."

The students maneuvered themselves into the flatter ground within the horseshoe of instruments, spreading blankets and pulling out notebooks and pens. Ford lay his bestiary out, a place marked about a third of the way through with the bright yellow fan of a fallen gingko leaf.

"Carmen's brought up a good point," said Sandy, after they'd opened with a prayer. "There's no Cartographical record of these diggers, or whatever they're called, along the ridge line."

"I don't think it matters, necessarily, though," said Carmen. "There's no record of the road up to the bus stop, either, or of Lucas' village. 'Towns and roads are thin scrims, and outside our purview.'"

Sandy recognized the quote as being from the autobiography of a radical cleric intermittently popular on campus. It was far from writ, but not heretical by any stretch of the imagination and, besides, she'd had her own enthusiasms for colorful doctrinal interpretations when she was younger. She was disappointed that Carmen would let her tendency toward error show so plainly to the others but let it pass, confident that one of the more conservative students would address it.

"Road building doesn't affect landscape?" asked Lucas, on cue. "The Mapmaker *used* road builders to cut canyons all over the continent. Ford, maybe Carmen needs to see the cutlines on your contour maps of the bus routes."

Before Ford, who was looking somewhat embarrassed by the exchange, could reply, Carmen said, "I'm not talking about the Mapmaker, Lucas, I'm talking about your *family*, back in the village we passed yesterday."

"Easy, Carmen," said Sandy. "We're getting off task here. The question at hand isn't *whether* there's error. The error is clear. We can feel the moisture of it on the breeze blowing up the hill right now." Time to shift directions on them, to turn them on the right path before they could think about it.

"The question," she continued, "is how much of it we plan to correct." Not *whether* they'd correct, don't leave that option for them. The debate she'd let them have was over the degree of action they'd take, not whether they'd take any at all.

The more sophisticated among them—Ford and Carmen sure, but even Lucas, to his credit—instantly saw her tack and looked at her with eyebrows raised. Then Lucas reverted to type and actually dared to say something.

"We haven't prepared for anything like this. That lake is more than a mile across at its broadest!"

"A mile across, yes," said Sandy, dismissively. "Carmen? What scale did you draw your sketch of the valley in?"

Carmen handed her a sheaf of papers. "24K to one. Is that all right?"

"Good, good," said Sandy. She smiled at Ford. "That's a conversion even I can do in my head. So...if I compare the size of the *dam*—" and she knitted her eyebrows, calculating. "If I compare the dam to the ridge, I see that the ridge we came to move is about three hundred times the larger."

Everyone began talking at once and at cross purposes. A gratifying number of the students were simply impressed with her cleverness and seemed relaxed, sure that it would be a simple matter now that they'd been shown the problem in the proper perspective. But Carmen was scratching some numbers in the dirt with the knuckle of her right index finger and Ford was flipping through the appendix of one of his books and Lucas...

Lucas stood and looked down over the valley. He wasn't looking at the lake and the dam, though, or even at the village of the unchurched creatures who had built it. He was looking to his right, down the eastern flank of the ridge they stood on, down the fluvial valley towards where, it suddenly occurred to Sandy, he'd grown up, towards the creek side town they'd stopped in the day before.

Ford raised his voice above an argument he'd been having with two or three others. "Isn't there a question about what that much water will do to the topography downstream? I mean, I know hydrology's a pretty knotty problem, theologically speaking, but we'd have a clear hand in the erosion, wouldn't we? What if the floodwaters subside off ground that's come unwrit because of something that we did?"

"That *is* a knotty problem, Ford," said Sandy, looking Lucas straight in the eye. "What's the best way to solve a difficult knot?"

And it was Lucas who answered her, nodding. "Cut through it."

Later, while most of the students were meditating in advance of the ceremony, Sandy saw Carmen moving from glass to glass, making minute focusing adjustments and triangulating different views of the lake and the village. Every so often, she made a quick visual note in her sketchbook.

"It's not productive to spend too much time on the side effects of an error, you know," Sandy said.

Carmen moved from one instrument to the next. "I don't think it's all that easy to determine what's a side effect and what's...okay," she said.

Sandy had lost good students to the distraction she could see now in Carmen. She reached out and pivoted the cylinder down, so that its receiving lens pointed straight at the ground. "There's nothing to see down there, Carmen."

Carmen wouldn't meet her eye. "I thought I'd record—"

"Nothing to see, nothing to record. If you could go down and talk to them you wouldn't understand a word they say. If you looked in their little huts you wouldn't find anything redemptive; there's no cross hanging in the wall of the meeting house, no Jesus of the Digging Marmots. When the water is drained, we won't see anything along the lake bed but mud and whatever garbage they've thrown in off their docks. The lake doesn't have any secrets to give up. You know that."

"Ford's books—"

"Ford's books are by anthropologists, who are halfway to being witch doctors as far as most respectable scholars are concerned, and who keep their accreditation by dint of the fact that their field notes are good intelligence sources for the Mission Service. Ford reads them because he's got an overactive imagination and he likes stories too much—lots of students in the archive concentration have those failings. Most of them grow out of it with a little coaxing. Like Ford will, he's too smart not to. Just like *you're* too smart to backslide into your parents' religion and start looking for souls to save where there are no souls to be found."

Carmen took a deep breath and held it, closed her eyes. When she opened them, her expression had folded into acquiescence. "It is not the least of my sins that I force you to spend so much time counseling me, Reverend," she said formally.

Sandy smiled and gave the girl a friendly squeeze of the shoulder. "Curiosity and empathy are healthy, and valuable, señorita," she said. "But you need to remember that there are proper channels to focus these things into. Prayer and study are best, but drinking and carousing will do in a pinch."

Carmen gave a nervous laugh, eyes widening. Sandy could tell that the girl didn't feel entirely comfortable with the unexpected direction of the conversation, which was, of course, part of the strategy for handling backsliders. Young people in particular were easy to refocus on banal and harmless "sins" and away from thoughts that could actually be dangerous.

"Fetch the others up here, now," Sandy said. "We should set to it."

Carmen soon had all twenty of her fellow students gathered around Sandy. Lucas had been down the eastern slope far enough to gather some deadwood and now he struck it ablaze with a flint and steel from his travel kit. Sandy crumbled a handful of incense into the flames.

Ford had been named the seminar's lector by consensus, and he opened his text. "Blessed are the Mapmakers..." he said.

"For they hunger and thirst after righteousness," they all finished.

Then they all fell to prayer and singing. Sandy turned her back to them—congregants more than students now—and opened her heart to the land below her. She felt the effrontery of the unmapped lake like a caul over her face, a restriction on the land that prevented breath and life.

Sandy showed them how to test the prevailing winds and how to bank the censers in chevrons so that the cleansing fires would fall onto the appropriate points along the dam.

Finally, she thumbed an ashen symbol onto every wrist and forehead, including her own, and lit the oils of the censer *primorus* with a prayer. When the hungry flames began to beam outward from her censer, she softly repeated the prayer for emphasis, then nodded her assent that the rest begin.

The dam did not burst in a spectacular explosion of mud and boulders and waters. Instead, it atrophied throughout the long afternoon, wearing away under their prayers even as their voices grew hoarse. Eventually, the dammed river itself joined its voice to theirs and speeded the correction.

The unchurched in the valley tried for a few hours to

pull their boats up onto the shore, but the muddy expanse between the water and their lurching docks grew too quickly. They turned their attention to bundling up the goods from their mean little houses then, and soon a line of them was snaking deeper into the mountains to the east, like a line of ants fleeing a hill beneath a looking glass.

With the ridge to its west, the valley fell into evening shadow long before the Cartographers' camp. They could still see below though, they could see that, as Sandy had promised Carmen, there were no secrets revealed by the dying water.

OKANOGGAN FALLS

Carolyn Ives Gilman

The town of Okanoggan Falls lay in the folded hills of southwestern Wisconsin—dairy country, marbled with deciduous groves and pastureland that looked soft as a sable's fur. It was an old sawmill town, hidden down in the steep river valley, shaded by elderly trees. Downtown was a double row of brick and ironwork storefronts running parallel to the river. Somehow, the town had steered between the Scylla and Charybdis of the franchise and the boutique. If you wanted to buy a hamburger on Main Street, you had to go to Earl's Cafe, and for scented soap there was just Meyer's Drugstore. In the park where the Civil War soldier stood, in front of the old Town Hall infested with pigeons, Mr. Woodward still defiantly raised the United States flag, as if the world on cable news were illusion, and the nation were still reality.

American small towns had changed since the days when Sinclair Lewis savaged them as backwaters of conformist complacency. All of that had moved to the suburbs. The people left in the rural towns had a high kook component. There were more welders-turned-sculptors per capita than elsewhere, more self-employed dollmakers, more wildly painted cars, more people with pronounced opinions, and more tolerance for all the above.

Like most of the Midwest, Okanoggan Falls had been relatively unaffected by the conquest and occupation. Few there had even seen one of the invading Wattesoons, except on television. At first, there had been some stirrings of grassroots defiance, born of wounded national pride; but when the Wattesoons had actually lowered taxes and reduced regulation, the volume of complaint had gone down. People still didn't love the occupiers, but as long as the Wattesoons minded their own business and left the populace alone, they were tolerated.

All of that changed one Saturday morning when Margie Silengo, who lived in a mobile home on Highway 14, came racing into town with her shockless Chevy bouncing like a rocking horse, telling everyone she met that a Wattesoon army convoy had gone rolling past her house and turned into the old mill grounds north of town as if they meant to stay. Almost simultaneously, the mayor's home phone rang, and Tom Abernathy found himself standing barefoot in his kitchen, for the first time in his life talking to a Wattesoon captain, who in precise, formal English informed him that Okanoggan Falls was slated for demolition.

Tom's wife Susan, who hadn't quite gotten the hang of this "occupation" thing, stopped making peanut butter sandwiches for the boys to say, "They can't say that! Who do they think they are?"

Tom was a lanky, easygoing fellow, all knobby joints and bony jaw. Mayor wasn't his full-time job; he ran one of the more successful businesses in town, a whole-sale construction-goods supplier. He had become mayor the way most otherwise sensible people end up in charge: out of self-defense. Fed up having to deal with the calcified fossil who had run the town since the 1980s, Tom had stood for office on the same impulse he occasionally swore—and woke to find himself elected in a landslide, 374 to 123.

Now he rubbed the back of his head, as he did whenever perplexed, and said, "I think the Wattesoons can do pretty much anything they want."

"Then we've got to make them stop wanting to mess with us," Susan said.

That, in a nutshell, was what made Tom and Susan's marriage work. In seventeen years, whenever he had said something couldn't be done, she had taken it as a challenge to do it.

But he had never expected her to take on alien invaders.

Town Council meetings weren't formal, and usually a few people straggled in late. This day, everyone was assembled at Town Hall by five P.M., when the Wattesoon officer had said he would address them. By now they knew it was not just Okanoggan Falls; all four towns along a fifty-mile stretch of Highway 14 had their own occupying forces camped outside town, and their own captains addressing them at precisely five o'clock. Like most Wattesoon military actions, it had been flawlessly coordinated.

The captain arrived with little fanfare. Two sand-colored army transports sped down Main Street and pulled up in front of Town Hall. The two occupants of one got out, while three soldiers in the other stood guard to keep the curious at arms' length. Their weapons remained in their slings. They seemed to be trying to keep the mood low-key.

The two who entered Town Hall looked exactly like Wattesoons on television—squat lumps of rubbly khaki-colored skin, like blobs of clay mixed with gravel. They wore the usual beige army uniforms that hermetically encased them, like shrink wrap, from neck to heel, but neither officer had on the face mask or gloves the invaders usually employed to deal with humans. An aroma like baking rocks entered the room with them—not unpleasant, just not a smell ordinarily associated with living creatures.

In studied, formal English the larger Wattesoon introduced himself as Captain Groton, and his companion as Ensign Agush. No one offered to shake hands, knowing the famous Wattesoon horror at touching slimy human flesh.

The council sat silent behind the row of desks they used for hearings, while the captain stood facing them where people normally gave testimony, but there was no question about where the power lay. The townspeople had expected gruff, peremptory orders, and so Captain Groton's reasonable tone came as a pleasant surprise; but there was nothing reassuring about his message.

The Wattesoons wished to strip-mine a fifty-mile swath of the hilly, wooded Okanoggan Valley. "Our operations will render the land uninhabitable," Captain Groton said. "The army is here to assist in your removal. We will need you to coordinate the arrangements so this move can be achieved expeditiously and peacefully." There was the ever-so-slight hint of a threat in that last word.

When he finished there was a short silence, as the council absorbed the imminent destruction of everything they had lived for and loved. The image of Okanoggan Valley transformed into a mine pit hovered before every eye: no maple trees, no lilacs, no dogs, no streetlights. Rob Massey, the scrappy newspaper editor, was first to find his voice. "What do you want to mine?" he said sharply. "There are no minerals here."

"Silica," the captain answered promptly. "There is a particularly pure bed of it underneath your limestone."

He meant the white, friable sandstone—useless for building, occasionally used for glass. What they wanted it for was incomprehensible, like so much about them. "Will we be compensated for our property?" Paula Sanders asked, as if any compensation would suffice.

"No," the captain answered neutrally. "The land is ours."

Which was infuriating, but unarguable.

"But it's our home!" Tom blurted out. "We've lived here, some of us four, five generations. We've built this community. It's our life. You can't just walk in and level it."

The raw anguish in his voice made even Captain Groton, lump of rubble that he was, pause. "But we can," he answered without malice. "It is not within your power to stop it. All you can do is reconcile yourselves to the inevitable."

"How much time do we have?" Paula bit off her words as if they tasted bad.

"We realize you will need time to achieve acceptance, so we are prepared to give you two months."

The room practically exploded with protests and arguments.

At last the captain held up the blunt appendage that served him as a hand. "Very well," he said. "I am authorized to give you an extension. You may have three months."

Later, they learned that every captain up and down

the valley had given the same extension. It had obviously been planned in advance.

The room smoldered with outrage as the captain turned to leave, his job done. But before he could exit, Susan Abernathy stepped into the doorway, along with the smell of brewing coffee from the hall outside.

"Captain Groton," she said, "would you like to join us for coffee? It's a tradition after meetings."

"Thank you, madam," he said, "but I must return to base."

"Susan," she introduced herself, and, contrary to all etiquette, held out her hand.

The Wattesoon recoiled visibly. But in the next second he seemed to seize control of himself and, by sheer force of will, extended his arm. Susan clasped it warmly, looking down into his pebbly eyes. "Since we are going to be neighbors, at least for the next few months, we might as well be civil," she said.

"That is very foresighted of you, madam," he answered.

"Call me Susan," she said. "Well, since you can't stay tonight, can I invite you to dinner tomorrow?"

The captain hesitated, and everyone expected another evasion, but at last he said, "That would be very acceptable. Susan."

"Great. I'll call you with the details." As the captain left, followed closely by his ensign, she turned to the council. "Can I bring you some coffee?"

"Ish. What did it feel like?" said her son Nick.

Susan had become something of a celebrity in the eleven-year-old set for having touched an alien.

"Dry," she said, staring at the laptop on the dining room table. "A little lumpy. Kind of like a lizard."

In the next room, Tom was on the phone. "Warren, you're talking crazy," he said. "We still might be able to get some concessions. We're working on it. But if you start shooting at them, we're doomed. I don't want to hear any more about toad hunts, okay?"

"Have you washed your hand?" Nick wanted to know.

Susan let go of the mouse to reach out and wipe her hand on Nick's arm. "Eew, gross!" he said. "Now I've got toad germs."

"Don't call them that," she said sharply. "It's not polite. You're going to have to be very polite tonight."

"I don't have to touch him, do I?"

"No, I'm sure touching a grody little boy is the last thing he wants." In the next room, Tom had dialed a different number. "Listen, Walt, I think I'm going to need a patrol car in front of my house tonight. If this toad gets shot coming up my walk, my house is going to be a smoking crater tomorrow."

"Is that true?" Nick asked, wide-eyed.

"No," Susan lied. "He's exaggerating."

"Can I go to Jake's tonight?"

"No, I need you here," Susan said, hiding the pang of anxiety it gave her.

"What are we having for dinner?"

"I'm trying to find out what they eat, if you'd just leave me alone."

"I'm not eating bugs."

"Neither am I," Susan said. "Now go away."

Tom came in and sank into a chair with a sigh. "The whole town is up in arms," he said. "Literally. Paula wanted to picket our house tonight. I told her to trust you, that you've got a plan. Of course, I don't know what it is."

"I think my plan is to feed him pizza," Susan said.

"Pizza?"

"Why not? I can't find that they have any dietary restrictions, and everyone loves pizza."

Tom laid his head back and stared glumly at the ceiling. "Sure. Why not? If it kills him, you'll be a hero. For about half an hour; then you'll be a martyr."

"Pizza never killed anyone," Susan said, and got up to start straightening up the house.

The Abernathys lived in a big old 1918 three-story with a wraparound porch and a witch's-hat tower, set in a big yard. The living room had sliding wood doors, stained-glass fanlights, and a wood-framed fireplace. It could have been fancy, but instead it had a frayed, lived-in look—heaps of books, puppy-chewed Oriental carpet, an upright piano piled with model airplanes. The comfy, well-dented furniture showed the marks of constant comings and goings, school projects, and meetings. There was rarely a night when the Abernathys didn't have guests, but dinner was never formal. Formality was alien to Susan's nature.

She had been an RN, but had quit, fed up with the bureaucracy rather than the patients. She had the sturdy physique of a German farm girl, and the competent independence to go with it. Light brown hair, cropped just above her shoulders, framed her round, cheerful face. Only rarely was she seen in anything more fancy than a jean skirt and a shirt with rolled-up sleeves. When they had elected Tom, everyone had known they weren't getting a mayor's wife who would challenge anybody's fashion sense.

That night, Captain Groton arrived precisely on time, in a car with tinted windows, driven by someone who stayed invisible, waiting. Tom met the guest on the doorstep, looking up and down the street a little nervously. When they came into the living room, Susan emerged from the kitchen with a bouquet of wine glasses in one hand and a bottle in the other.

"Wine, Captain?" she said.

He hesitated. "If that is customary. I regret I am not familiar with your dietary rituals. I only know they are complex."

"It's fermented fruit juice, mildly intoxicating," she said, pouring a little bit in his glass. "People drink it to relax."

He took the glass gingerly. Susan saw that he had stumpy nubbin fingers. As a nurse, she had had to train herself to feel compassion even for the least appealing patients, and now she was forced to call on that skill to disregard his appearance.

"Cheers," she said, lifting her glass.

There was a snap as the stem on Captain Groton's glass broke in two. The wine slopped onto his hand as he tried to catch the pieces. "Pardon me," he mumbled. "Your vessel is brittle."

"Never mind the glass," Susan said, taking it and handing the pieces to Tom. "Did you cut yourself?"

"No, of course—" he stopped in mid denial, staring at his hand. A thin line of blood bisected the palm.

"Here, I'll take care of that," she said. Taking him by the arm, she led him to the bathroom. It was not until she had dabbed the blood off with a tissue that she realized he was not recoiling at her touch as he had before. Inwardly, she smiled at small victories. But when she brought out a bottle of spray disinfectant, he did recoil, demanding suspiciously, "What is it?"

"Disinfectant," she said. "To prevent infection. It's alcohol-based."

"Oh," he said. "I thought it might be water."

She spritzed his hand lightly, then applied a bandage. He was looking curiously around. "What is this place?"

"It's a bathroom," she said. "We use it to—well, clean ourselves, and groom, and so forth. This is the toilet." She raised the lid, and he drew back, obviously repulsed. She had to laugh. "It's really very clean. I swear."

"It has water in it," he said with disgust.

"But the water's not dirty, not now."

"Water is always dirty," he said. "It teems with bacteria. It transmits a thousand diseases, yet you humans touch it without any caution. You allow your children to play in it. You drink it, even. I suppose you have gotten used to it, living on this world where it soils everything. It even falls from the sky. It is impossible to get away from it. You have no choice but to soak in it."

Struck by the startling image of water as filth, Susan said, "Occupying our world must be very unpleasant for you. What is your planet like?"

"It is very dry," he said. "Miles and miles of hot, clean sand, like your Sahara. But your population does not live in the habitable spots, so we cannot either."

"You must drink water sometimes. Your metabolisms are not that different from ours, or you would not be able to eat our food."

"The trace amounts in foods are enough for us. We do not excrete it like you do."

"So that's why you don't have bathrooms," she said.

He paused, clearly puzzled. Then it dawned on him what she had left out of her explanation. "You use this room for excretory functions?"

"Yes," she said. "It's supposed to be private."

"But you excrete fluids in public all the time," he said. "From your noses, your mouths, your skin. How can you keep it private?"

For a moment the vision of humans as oozing bags of bacteria left her unable to answer. Then she said, "That's why we come here, to clean it all off."

He looked around. "But there is no facility for cleaning."

"Sure there is." She turned on the shower. "See?"

He reacted with horror, so she quickly shut it off. She explained, "You see, we think of water as clean. We bathe in it. How do you bathe?"

"Sand," he said. "Tubs of dry, heated sand. It is heavenly."

"It must be." She could picture it: soft, white sand. Like what lay under the Okanoggan limestone. She looked at him in dawning realization. "Is that why you want—?"

"I cannot say anything about that," he said. "Please do not ask me."

Which was all the answer she needed.

When they came back out, Tom and the boys were in the kitchen, so that was where they went.

"Sorry, we got caught up in a really interesting conversation," Susan said breezily, with an I'll-tell-you-later look at Tom. "Captain Groton, these are our sons, Ben and Nick." The boys stood up and nodded awkwardly, obviously coached not to shake hands.

"They are both yours?" the Wattesoon asked.

"Yes," Tom said. "Do you have any kids, captain?"

"Yes. A daughter."

"How old is she?" Susan said, pouring some more wine for him in a mug.

Captain Groton paused so long she wondered if she had said something offensive, but finally he shook his head. "I cannot figure it out. The time dilation makes it too difficult. It would mean little to you anyway; our years are so different."

"So she's back home on your planet?"

"Yes."

"Your wife, too?"

"She is dead."

"I'm so sorry. It must have been hard for you to leave your daughter behind."

"It was necessary. I was posted here. I followed my duty." It had occurred to Susan that perhaps cow-excretion pie was not the thing to offer her guest, so she began rummaging in the cupboard, and soon assembled a buffet of dry foods: roast soybeans, crackers, apple chips, pine nuts, and a sweet potato for moisture. As Tom tried valiantly to engage the captain in a conversation about fishing, she started assembling the pizza for her family. The dog was barking at the back door, so she asked Ben to feed him. Nick started playing with his Gameboy. There was a pleasantly normal confusion all around.

"What sorts of food do you eat at home?" Susan asked her guest when she had a chance.

Groton shrugged. "We are less preoccupied with food than you are. Anything will do. We are omnivores."

Ben muttered, "Better watch out for our dogs."

"Ben!" Susan rebuked him.

Captain Groton turned marbly eyes on him. "We have no interest in your food animals."

The whole family stared in horror. "Our dogs aren't food!" Ben blurted.

"Then why do you keep them?" the captain asked reasonably.

Tom said, "For companionship."

Ben said, "For fun."

Susan said, "Because they remind us that we're human. Without other species around, we'd forget."

"Ah. I see," the Wattesoon said. "We feel the same."

In the awkward silence that followed, the humans all wondered who were the Wattesoons' pets.

They were saved by the timer. The pizza came out of the oven, and soon all was cheerful confusion again.

The internet had told Susan that Wattesoons were frugal eaters, but Captain Groton seemed ravenous. He ate some of everything she put on the table, including two slices of pizza.

To spare their guest the troubling sight of counters, tabletop, and utensils being smeared with water, Susan asked him out to see the back yard so the others could clean up. The screen door banged shut behind them and the dog came trotting up, eager to smell the stranger, till Susan shooed him into the kitchen. She then led the Wattesoon out into the humid, crickety twilight.

It was a Midwestern evening. The yard backed up onto the river bluff, a weathered limestone cliff overgrown with sumac and grapevine. Susan strolled out past the scattered detritus of Frisbees and lawn darts toward the quiet of the lower yard, where nature had started to encroach. There was an old swing hung from a gnarled oak tree, and she sat down in it, making the ropes creak. In the shady quiet, she swung idly to and fro, thinking of other evenings.

She had never realized how desperately she loved this place until she was forced to think of losing it. Looking toward the dark bushes by the cliff, she saw the silent flare of fireflies. "Are you able to find this beautiful?"

she said, not trying to hide the longing in her voice.

After a few moments of silence, she looked over to find the captain gazing into the dark, lost in thought. "I am sorry," he said, recollecting himself. "What did you ask?"

Instead of answering, she said, "I think we each get imprinted on a certain kind of landscape when we're young. We can enjoy other spots, but only one seems like we're made from it, down to our bones. This is mine."

"Yes," he said.

"Can you understand how it is for us, then? We talk a lot about our investments and our livelihoods, but that's just to hide the pain. We love this place. We're bonded to it."

He didn't answer at once, so she stopped the swing to look at him.

"I understand," he said.

"Do you?" she said hopefully.

"It changes nothing. I am sorry."

Disappointed, she stared at his lumpy face. Now that she was a little more accustomed to him, he did not seem quite so rubbly and squat. He gave an impatient gesture. "Why are your people so fond of being discontent? You relish resisting, protesting, always pushing against the inevitable. It is an immature response, and makes your lives much harder."

"But, Captain, there are some things that *ought* to be protested."

"What things?"

"Folly. Malice. Injustice."

He cut her off in a pained tone. "These things are part of the nature of the world. There is nothing we can do to prevent them."

"You would not even try?" she said.

"Life is not just. Fairness is a fool's concept. To fight brings only disillusion."

"Well, we are different. We humans can put up with a thousand evils so long as we think they are fair. We are striving all the time to bring about justice, in ourselves and our society. Yours too, if you would just let us."

"So your truculence is all an effort to improve us?" the Wattesoon said.

Surprised, Susan laughed. "Why, Captain Groton, no one told me your people had a sense of irony."

He seemed taken aback by her reaction, as if he regretted having provoked it.

"I was not laughing at you," she explained hastily. "At least, not in any way you would not wish."

"You cannot know what I would wish," he said stiffly.

She said, "Oh, I don't know about that." For the time being, here out of all official contexts, he seemed just as difficult and contradictory as any human male. Speculatively, she said, "Your answer just now, about justice. You sounded bitter, as if you spoke from some experience. What was it?"

He stared at her with that unreadable, granitic face. For a few moments she thought he wasn't going to answer. Then he said, "It is in the past. There is no point in talking about it. Today is today. I accept that."

They remained silent for a while, listening to the sounds of life all around. At last Susan said, "Well, the great injustice of *our* lives is still in the future."

The thought of it flooded into her. All of this gentle valley would be gone soon, turned into an open wound in the landscape. Tears came to her, half anger and half loss, and she got up to go back inside. When she reached the back porch, she paused to compose herself, wiping the tears from her face. Captain Groton, who had followed her, said in a startled voice, "You are secreting moisture."

"Yes," she said. "We do that from time to time, in moments of intense emotion."

"I wish—" he started, then stopped.

"Yes? What do you wish?"

"Never mind," he said, and looked away.

That night, lying in bed, she told Tom all she had learned.

"Sand," he said in disbelief. "The bastards are moving us out so they can have bathtub sand."

He was not feeling charitable toward the Wattesoons. After their dinner guest had left in his tinted limousine, Tom had gotten a call from the mayor of Walker, the closest Wal-Mart metropolis. The captain in charge of their evacuation was an unbending disciplinarian who had presented the residents with a set of non-negotiable deadlines. The news from Red Bluff was even less encouraging. The captain assigned there was a transparent racist who seemed to think evacuation was too good for the native population. Force seemed to be his preferred alternative.

"Larry wants us to mount a unified resistance," Tom said. "A kind of 'Hell no, we won't go' thing. Just stay put, refuse to prepare. It seems pretty risky to me."

Susan lay reflecting. At last she said, "They would think it was an immature response."

"What, like children disobeying?" he said, irritated.

"I didn't say I agreed. I said that was what they would think."

"So what *should* we do?"

"I don't know. Behave in a way they associate with adults. Somehow resist without seeming to resist."

Tom turned his head on the pillow to look at her. "How come you learn all these things? He won't give me anything but the official line."

"You're his counterpart, Tom. He has to be formal with you. I don't count."

"Or maybe you count more. Maybe he's sweet on you."

"Oh, please!"

"Who would have thought I'd lose my wife to a potato?" Tom mused.

She quelled the urge to hit him with a pillow. "You know, he's something of a philosopher."

"Socrates the spud," he said.

"More like Marcus Aurelius. I don't think he really wants to be here. There is something in his past, some tragedy he won't talk about. But it might make him sympathetic to us. We might win him over."

Tom rose on one elbow to look at her earnestly. "My god, he really did open up to you."

"I'm just putting two and two together. The problem is, I'm not sure what winning him over would get us. He's just following orders."

"Jeez, even one friend among the Wattesoon is progress. I say go for it."

"Is that an order, Mr. Mayor?"

"My Mata Hari," he said, with the goofy, lopsided grin she loved.

She rolled closer to put her head on his shoulder. All problems seemed more bearable when he was around.

In the few weeks, no one saw much of Captain Groton. Information, instructions, and orders still emanated from his office, but the captain himself was unavailable—indisposed, the official line went. When she heard this, Susan called the Wattesoon headquarters, concerned that he had had a reaction to the odd menu she had fed him. To her surprise, the captain took her call.

"Do not concern yourself, Susan," he said. "There is nothing you can do."

"I don't believe you," she said. "You're so in love with stoical acceptance that you could have toxic shock before you'd admit there was anything wrong."

"There is nothing wrong."

"I'm a nurse, Captain Groton. If you are sick, you have become my job."

There was an enigmatic pause on the line. "It is nothing you would recognize," he said at last. "A Wattesoon complaint."

Concerned now that he had admitted it, she said, "Is it serious?"

"It is not mortal, if that is what you mean."

"Can I see you?"

"Your concern is gratifying, but I have no need of assistance."

And she had to be content with that.

In the end, Tom saw him before she did. It was at a meeting the captain couldn't avoid, a progress report on preparations for the evacuation. "It must be some sort of arthritis," Tom answered Susan's questions vaguely. "He's hobbling around with a cane. A bit testy, too."

Not trusting a man to observe what needed to be noticed, Susan called Alice Brody, who had also been at the meeting. She was more than willing to elaborate. "He does seem to be in discomfort," Alice said. "But that's not the strange part."

Aha, Susan thought.

"He's *taller*, Susan. By inches. And proportioned differently. Not quite so tubby, if you know what I mean. It looks like he's lost a lot of weight, but I think it's just redistributed. His skin is different, too—smoother, a more natural color."

"What do you think is going on?"

"Damned if I know."

That was when Susan got the idea to invite Captain Groton to the Fourth of July celebration. Observing the holiday at all had been controversial, under the circumstances—but the city council had reasoned that a day of frivolity would raise everyone's spirits. The Wattesoons regarded it as a quaint summer festival and completely missed the nationalist connotations, so their only objection was to the potential for disorder from the crowds. When the town agreed to ban alcohol, the occupiers relented.

Okanoggan Falls's Fourth of July always climaxed with the parade, a homegrown affair for which people prepared at least three hours in advance. There was always a chainsaw drill team, a convertible for the Butter Princess, a Dixieland jazz band on a flatbed truck, and decorated backhoes and front-end loaders in lieu of floats. Deprecating self-mockery was a finely honed sport in Wisconsin.

Tom was going to be obliged to ride in a Model T with a stovepipe hat on, so Susan phoned the Wattesoon commander and asked him to accompany her.

"It will be a real demonstration of old-time Americana," she said.

He hesitated. "I do not wish to be provocative. Your townsfolk might not welcome my presence."

"If you were riding in a float, maybe. But mingling with the crowds, enjoying a brat and a lemonade? Some people might even appreciate it. If they don't, I'll handle them."

At last he consented, and they arranged to meet. "Don't wear a uniform," was her last instruction.

She had no idea what a dilemma she had caused him till he showed up in front of Meyer's Drugstore in a ragbag assortment of ill-fitting clothes that looked salvaged from a thrift shop. However, the truly extraordinary thing was that he was able to wear them at all—for when she had last seen him, fitting into human clothes would have been out of the question. Now, when she greeted him, she realized they were the same height, and he actually had a chin.

"You look wonderful," she blurted out.

"You are exaggerating," he said in a slightly pained tone.

"Are you feeling all right?"

"Better, thank you."

"But your clothes. Oh dear."

"Are they inappropriate?" he asked anxiously.

She looked around at all the American summer slobbery—men in baggy T-shirts and sandals, women bursting out of their tank tops. "No," she said. "You'll fit right in. It's just that, for a man in your position...." She grabbed him by the hand and dragged him into the drugstore, making for the magazine rack. She found an issue of *GQ* and thrust it into his hands. "Study that," she said. "It will show you what the elite class of men wear." Perusing several other magazines, she found some examples of a more khakified, Cape Cod look. "This is more informal, but still tasteful. Good for occasions like this, without losing face."

He was studying the pictures with a grave and studious manner. "Thank you, Susan. This is helpful." With a pang, she wished Tom would take any of her sartorial advice so to heart.

They were heading for the counter to buy the magazines when he stopped, riveted by the sight of the shelves. "What are these products for?"

"Grooming, personal care," Susan said. "These are for cleaning teeth. We do it twice a day, to prevent our breath smelling bad and our teeth going yellow. These are for shaving off unwanted hair. Men shave their faces every day, or it grows in."

"You mean all men have facial hair?" Captain Groton said, a little horrified.

"Yes. The ones who don't want beards just shave it off."

"What about these?" he said, gesturing to the deodorants.

"We spread it under our arms every day, to prevent unpleasant odors."

Faintly he said, "You live at war with your bodies."

She laughed. "It does seem that way, doesn't it?" She looked down the aisle at the shampoos, mouthwashes, acne creams, corn removers, soaps, and other products attesting to the ways in which even humans found their own bodies objectionable.

Beth Meyer was manning the counter, so Susan introduced her to Captain Groton. Unable to hide her hostility, Beth nevertheless said, "I hope you learn something about us."

"Your shop has already been very instructive, Mrs. Meyer," the captain said courteously. "I never realized the ingenuity people devote to body care. I hope I may return some day."

"As long as we're open we won't turn away a customer," Beth said.

Outside, things were gearing up for the parade, and it was clear that people were spontaneously going to use it to express their frustration. Some of the spectators were carrying protest signs, and along the sidewalk one local entrepreneur had set up a Spike the Spud concession stand offering people a chance to do sadistic things to baked potatoes for a few dollars. The most popular activity seemed to be blowing up the potatoes with firecrackers, as attested by the exploded potato guts covering the back of the plywood booth. A reporter from an out-of-town TV station was interviewing the proprietor about his thriving business. The word "Wattesoon" never passed anyone's lips, but no one missed the point.

Including Captain Groton. Susan saw him studying the scene, so she said quietly, "It's tasteless, but better they should work it out this way than in earnest."

"That is one interpretation," he said a little tensely. She reminded herself that it wasn't *her* symbolic viscera plastering the booth walls.

His radio chose that moment to come to life. Susan hadn't even realized he was carrying it, hidden under his untucked shirt. He said, "Excuse me," and spoke into it in his own language. Susan could not tell what was being said, but the captain's voice was calm and professional. When he finished, she said, "Do you have soldiers ready to move in?"

He studied her a moment, as if weighing whether to lie, then said, "It would have been foolish of us not to take precautions."

It occurred to her then that he was their advance reconnaissance man, taking advantage of her friendship to assess the need for force against her neighbors. At first she felt a prickle of outrage; it quickly morphed into relief that he had not sent someone more easily provoked.

"Hey, captain!" The man at the Spike the Spud stand had noticed them, and, emboldened by the TV camera, had decided to create a photogenic scene. "Care to launch a spud missile?" The people standing around laughed nervously, transfixed to see the Wattesoon's reaction. Susan was drawing breath to extricate him when he put a restraining hand on her arm.

"I fear you would think me homicidal," he said in an easygoing tone.

Everyone saw then that he understood the message of sublimated violence, but chose to take it as a joke and not a provocation.

"No homicide involved, just potatoes," said the boothkeeper. He was a tubby, unshaven man in a sloppy white T-shirt. His joking tone had a slightly aggressive edge. "Come on, I'll give you a shot for free."

Captain Groton hesitated as everyone watched intently to see what he would do. At last he gave in. "Very well," he said, stepping up to the booth, "but I insist on paying. No preferential treatment."

The boothkeeper, an amateur comedian, made a show of selecting a long, thin potato that looked remarkably like his customer. He then offered a choice of weapons: sledge hammer, ax, firecracker, or other instruments of torture. "Why, the firecracker of course," the captain said. "It is traditional today, is it not?"

"American as beer." One segment of the crowd resented that the Wattesoons had interfered with their patriotic right to inebriation.

The boothkeeper handed him the potato and fire-cracker. "Here, shove it in. Right up its ass." When the captain complied, the man set the potato in the back of the booth and said, "Say when."

When the captain gave the word, the man lit the fuse. They waited breathlessly; then the potato exploded, splattering the boothkeeper in the face. The onlookers hooted with laughter. Captain Groton extracted himself with an amiable wave, as if he had planned the outcome all along.

"You were a remarkably good sport about that," Susan said to him as they walked away.

"I could have obliterated the tuber with my weapon," he said, "but I thought it would violate the spirit of the occasion."

"You're packing a weapon?" Susan stared. Wattesoon weapons were notoriously horrific. He could have blown away the booth and everyone around it.

He looked at her without a shade of humor. "I have to be able to defend myself."

The parade was about to commence, and Susan was feeling that she was escorting an appallingly dangerous person, so she said, "Let's find a place to stand, away from the crowd."

"Over here," Captain Groton said. He had already scoped out the terrain and located the best spot for surveillance: the raised stoop of an old apartment building, where he could stand with his back to the brick. He climbed the steps a bit stiffly, moving as if unused to knees that bent.

Okanoggan Falls had outdone itself. It was a particu-larly cheeky parade, full of double-entendre floats like the one carrying a group called the No Go Banjoes playing "Don't Fence Me In," or the "I Don't Wanna

Mooove" banner carried by the high school cheer-leading squad in their black-and-white Holstein costumes. The captain's radio kept interrupting, and he spoke in a restrained, commanding voice to whoever was on the other end.

In the end, it all passed without intervention from any soldiers other than the one at Susan's side. When the crowd began to disperse, she found that she had been clenching her fists in tension, and was glad no one else was aware of the risk they had been running.

"What happens now?" Captain Groton said. He meant it militarily, she knew; all pretense of his purpose being social was gone.

"Everyone will break up now," she said. "Some will go to the school ballfield for the fund-raiser picnic, but most won't gather again till the fireworks tonight. That will be about nine-thirty or ten o'clock."

He nodded. "I will go back to base, then."

She was battling mixed feelings, but at last said, "Captain—thank you, I think."

He studied her seriously. "I am just doing my duty."

That night on the television news, the celebration in Okanoggan Falls was contrasted with the one in Red Bluff, where a lockdown curfew was in place, fireworks were banned, and Wattesoon tanks patrolled the empty streets.

A week later, when Susan phoned Captain Groton, Ensign Agush took the call. "He cannot speak to you," he said indifferently. "He is dying."

"What?" Susan said, thinking she had heard wrong.

"He has contracted one of your human diseases."

"Has anyone called a doctor?"

"No. He will be dead soon. There is no point."

Half an hour later, Susan was at the Wattesoon head-quarters with her nurse's kit in hand. When the ensign realized he was facing a woman with the determination of a stormtrooper, he did not put up a fight, but showed her to the captain's quarters. He still seemed uncon-cerned about his commanding officer's imminent demise.

Captain Groton slumped in a chair in his spartan but private sitting room. The transformation in his appear-ance was even more remarkable; he was now tall and slender, even for a human, and his facial features had a distinctly human cast. He might have passed for an ordinary man in dim light.

An exceedingly miserable ordinary man. His eyes were red-rimmed, his face unshaved (she noted the facial hair with surprise), and his voice was a hoarse croak when he said, "Susan! I was just thinking I should thank you for your kindness before...." He was inter-rupted by a sneeze.

Still preoccupied with his appearance, she said, "You are turning human, aren't you?"

"Your microbes evidently think so." He coughed phlegm. "I have contracted an exceedingly repulsive disease."

She drew up a chair next to him. "What are your symptoms?"

He shook his head, obviously thinking the subject was not a fit one. "Don't be concerned. I am resigned to die."

"I'm asking as a professional."

Reluctantly, he said, "This body appears to be dis-solving. It is leaking fluids from every orifice. There, I told you it was repulsive."

"Your throat is sore? Your nose is congested? Coughing and sneezing?"

"Yes, yes."

"My dear captain, what you have is called a cold."

"No!" he protested. "I am quite warm."

"That's probably because you have a fever." She felt his forehead. "Yes. Well, fortunately, I've brought something for that." She brought out a bottle of aspirin, some antihistamine, decongestant, and cough suppressant. She added a bottle of Vitamin C for good measure.

"You are not alarmed?" he asked hesitantly.

"Not very. In us, the disease normally cures itself in a week or so. Since your immune system has never encountered it before, I'm not sure about you. You have to level with me, captain. Have you become human in ways besides appearance?"

Vaguely, he said, "How long has it been?"

"How long has what been?"

"Since I first saw you."

She thought back. "About six weeks."

"The transformation is far advanced, then. In three weeks I will be indistinguishable from one of you."

"Internally as well?"

"You would need a laboratory to tell the difference."

"Then it should be safe to treat you as if you were human. I'll be careful, though." She looked around the room for a glass of water. "Where's your ba—" It was a Watteesoon apartment; of course there was no bathroom. By now, she knew they excreted only hard, odorless pellets. "Where can I get a glass of water?"

"What for?" He looked mildly repulsed.

"For you to drink with these pills."

"*Drink?*"

"You mean to tell me you've had no fluids?"

"We don't require them...."

"Oh, dear Lord. You're probably dehydrated as well.

You're going to have to change some habits, captain. Sit right there. I need to run to the grocery store."

At the grocery she stocked up on fruit juices, bottled water, tissues, and, after a moment's hesitation, toilet paper—though not relishing having to explain that one to him. She also bought soap, a washcloth, mouthwash, shaving gel, a packet of plastic razors, a pail, and a washbasin. Like it or not, he was going to have to learn.

She had dealt with patients in every state of mental derangement, but never had she had to teach one how to be human. When she had gotten him to down the pills and a bottle of orange juice, she explained the purpose of her purchases to him in plain, practical language. She showed him how to blow his nose, and explained how a human bladder and bowel worked, and the necessity of washing with soap and water. When she finished he looked, if anything, more despairing than before.

"It is not common knowledge to us that you are hiding these bodily deficiencies," he said. "I fear I made a grave error in judgment."

"You're a soldier," she said. "Stop dramatizing, and cope with it."

For a moment he stared, astonished at her commanding tone. Then she could see him marshaling his courage as if to face dismemberment and death. "You are justified to rebuke me," he said. "I chose this. I must not complain."

Soon the antihistamine was making him drowsy, so she coaxed him to return to bed. "You're best off if you just sleep," she told him. "Take more of the pills every four hours, and drink another bottle every time you wake. If you feel pressure and need to eliminate liquid, use the pail. Don't hold it in, it's very bad for you. Call me in the morning."

"You're leaving?" he said anxiously.

She had intended to, but at his disconsolate expression she relented. It made her realize that she could actually read expressions on his face now. She drew up a chair and sat. "I must say, your comrades here don't seem very sympathetic."

He was silent a few moments, staring bleakly at the ceiling. At last he said, "They are ashamed."

"Of what? You?"

"Of what I am becoming."

"A human? They're bigots, then."

"Yes. You have to understand, Susan, the army doesn't always attract the highest caliber of men."

She realized then that the drug, or the reprieve from death, had broken down his usual reticence. It put her in an odd position, to have the occupying commander relying on her in his current unguarded condition. Extracting military or political secrets would clearly violate medical ethics. But was personal and cultural information allowed? She made a snap decision: nothing that would hurt him. Cautiously, she said, "I didn't know that you Wattesoons had this...talent...ability...to change your appearance."

"It only works with a closely related species," he said drowsily. "We weren't sure you were similar enough. It appears you are."

"How do you do it?"

He paused a long time, then said, "I will tell you some day. The trait has been useful to us, in adapting to other planets. Planets more unlike our own than this one is."

"Is that why you changed? To be better adapted?"

"No. I felt it was the best way to carry out my orders."

She waited for him to explain that; when he didn't, she said, "What orders?"

"To oversee the evacuation on time and with minimal disturbance. I thought that looking like a human would be an advantage in winning the cooperation of the local populace. I wanted you to think of me as human. I did not know of the drawbacks then."

"Well, I don't think you would have fooled us anyway," Susan said a little skeptically. "Can you change your mind now?"

"No. The chameleon process is part of our reproductive biology. We cannot change our minds about that, either."

The mention of reproduction brought up something she had often wondered about. "Why are there no Wattesoon women here?" she asked.

The subject seemed to evoke some sort of intense emotion for him. In a tight voice, he said, "Our women almost invariably die giving birth. The only ones who survive, as a rule, are childless, and they are rare. If it were not for the frequency of multiple births, we would have difficulty maintaining our population. We see the ease with which you human women give birth, and envy it."

"It wasn't always this way," Susan said. "We used to die much more frequently, as well. But that wasn't acceptable to us. We improved our medicine until we solved the problem."

Softly, he said, "It is not acceptable to us, either."

A realization struck her. "Is that what happened to your wife?"

"Yes."

She studied his face. "I think you must have loved her."

"I did. Too much."

"You can't blame yourself for her death."

"Who should I blame?"

"The doctors. The researchers who don't find a cure. The society that doesn't put a high enough priority on finding a solution."

He gave a little laugh. "That is a very human response."

"Well, *we* have solved our problem."

He considered that answer so long she thought he had fallen asleep. But just as she was rising to check, he said, "I think it is better to go through life as a passerby, detached from both the good and the bad. Especially from the good, because it always goes away."

Gently, Susan said, "Not always."

He looked at her with clouded eyes. "Always."

And then he really did fall asleep.

That evening, after the boys had gone up to their rooms, Susan told Tom everything over wine. Some of her medical details made him wince.

"Ouch. The poor bastard. Sounds worse than puberty, all crammed into nine weeks."

"Tom, you could really help him out," Susan said. "There are things you could tell him, man to man, that I can't—"

"Oh no, I couldn't," Tom said. "No way."

She protested, "But there are things about male anatomy—you expect *me* to warn him about all that?"

"Better you than me," Tom said.

"Coward," she said.

"Damn right. Listen, men just don't talk about these things. How am I supposed to bring it up? More to the point, why? He got himself into this. It was a military strategy. He even admitted it to you: he wanted to manipulate us to cooperate in our own conquest. I don't know why you're acting as if you're responsible for him."

Tom was right. She studied the wine in her glass, wondering at her own reaction. She had been empathizing as if Captain Groton were her patient, not her enemy. He had deliberately manipulated her feelings, and it had worked.

Well, she thought, two could play at that game.

It was not to be a summer of days at the beach, or fishing trips, or baseball camp. Everyone was busy packing, sorting, and getting ready to move. Susan marshaled Nick and Ben into the attic and basement to do the easy part, the packing and stacking, but the hardest part of moving was all hers: making the decisions. What to take, what to leave. It was all a referendum on her life, sorting the parts worth saving from the rest. No object was just itself: it was all memories, encapsulated in grimy old toys, birthday cards, garden bulbs, and comforters. All the tiny, pointillist moments that together formed the picture of her life. Somehow, she had to separate her self from the place that had created her, to become a rootless thing.

The summer was punctuated with sad ceremonies like the one when they started disinterring the bodies from the town cemetery, the day when the crane removed the Civil War soldier from the park, and the last church service before they took out the stained glass windows. After the dead had left, the town paradoxically seemed even more full of ghosts.

The protests did not die down. Red Bluff was in a state of open rebellion; a hidden sniper had picked off three Wattesoon soldiers, and the army was starting house-to-house searches to disarm the populace. In Walker, angry meetings were televised, in which residents shouted and wept.

In Okanoggan Falls, they negotiated. The Wattesoons were now paying to move three of the most significant historic buildings, and the school district would be kept intact after relocation. Captain Groton had even agreed to move the deadline two weeks into September so the farmers could harvest the crops—a concession the captains in Red Bluff and Walker were eventually forced to match, grudgingly.

The captain became a familiar face around town— no longer in a limousine, but driving a rented SUV to supervise contractors, meet with civic groups, or simply to stop for lunch at Earl's Cafe and chat with the waitress. Outwardly, there was no longer a hint of anything Wattesoon about him, unless it was his awkwardness when asked to tie a knot or catch a baseball. He had turned into a tall, distinguished older man with silver hair, whose manners were as impeccable as his dress. In social settings he was reserved, but occasionally something would catch his whimsy, and then he had a light, tolerant laugh. At the same time, a steely authority lay just under the surface.

The women of Okanoggan began to notice. They began to approach and engage him in conversation— urgently, awkwardly warm on their side, full of self-conscious laughter; and on his side, studiously attentive but maddeningly noncommittal. People began to talk about the fact that he went every week to dine at the Abernathy home, whether Tom was there or not. They noticed when Susan took him to the barber shop, and when they drove together to La Crosse to visit the mall.

Her good humor began to irritate the other women in ways it never had before, and their eyes followed her when she passed by.

"She must of kissed that frog good, 'cause he sure turned into a prince," said Jewell Hogan at the beauty salon, and the remark was considered so witty it was repeated all over town.

For herself, Susan had found one more reason to love her life in Okanoggan Falls just before losing it. She was playing a game that gave her life an exotic twist, excitement it had lacked. It was her patriotic duty to lie awake each morning, thinking of ways to get closer to a thrillingly attractive, powerful man who clearly enjoyed her company and relied on her in some unusually intimate ways. In the last month before it all fell apart, her life had become nearly perfect.

Between arranging to move his business and the mayoral duties, Tom was often gone on the nights when Captain Groton came over for dinner. Susan was aware of the gossip—a blushing Nick had told her the boys were taunting him about his mother—but she was not about to let small-mindedness stop her. "Just wait till they see how it pays off," she said to Nick.

It made her think she needed to start making it pay off.

By now, Captain Groton was perforce conversant with the ceremonial foods of the Midwest—string bean casserole, jello salad, brats and beans—and the communal rituals at which they were consumed. So Susan had been entertaining herself by introducing him to more adventurous cuisine. His tastes were far less conservative than Tom's, and he almost invariably praised her efforts. On one night when Tom was returning late, she ordered a pizza for the boys and prepared shrimp with wild rice, cilantro, artichokes, and sour cream, with just a hint of cayenne pepper and lemon. They ate in the dining room with more wine than usual.

The captain was telling her how the amateur scholar who ran the landfill, in one of the endless efforts to deter the Wattesoons from their plans, had tried to convince him that there was an important archaeological site with buried treasure underneath the town. He had even produced proof in the form of an old French map and a photo of a metallic object with a mysterious engraved design.

Susan laughed, a little giddy from the wine. "You didn't fall for it, did you?"

Captain Groton looked at her quizzically. "No, I didn't fall down."

His English was so good she almost never encountered a phrase he didn't know. "It's an expression, to fall for something. It means he was pulling your leg."

"Pulling my leg. And so I was supposed to fall down?"

"No, no," she said. "It's just an idiom. To fall for something is to be deceived. On the other hand, to fall for some*one* means to become fond of them, to fall in love."

He considered this thoughtfully. "You use the same expression for being deceived and falling in love?"

It had never struck her before. "I guess we do. Maybe it means that you have to have illusions to fall in love. There *is* a lot of self-deception involved. But a lot of truth as well."

She suddenly became aware how seriously he was watching her, as if the topic had been much on his mind. When their eyes met, she felt a moment of spontaneous chemical reaction; then he looked away. "And when you say 'Okanoggan Falls," which do you mean, deception or love?" he asked.

"Oh, love, no question."

"But if it meant deception, you would not tell me," he said with a slight smile.

"I am not deceiving you, captain," she said softly. And, a little to her own surprise, she was telling the truth.

There was a moment of silence. Then Susan rose from the table, throwing her napkin down. "Let's go to the back yard," she said.

He followed her out into the hot summer night. It was late August; the surrounding yards were quiet except for the cicadas buzzing in the trees and the meditative sigh of air conditioners. When they reached the deeper grass under the trees, the captain came to a halt, breathing in the fragrant air.

"The thing I was not expecting about being human is the skin," he said. "It is so sensitive, so awake."

"So you like it now, being human?" she asked.

"There are compensations," he said, watching her steadily.

Her intellect told her she ought to be changing the subject, pressing him on the topic of public concern, but her private concerns were flooding her mind, making it impossible to think. She was slightly drunk, or she never would have said it aloud. "Damn! It's so unfair. Why does such a perfect man have to be an alien?"

A human man would have taken it as an invitation. Captain Groton hesitated, then with great restraint took her hands chastely in his. "Susan," he said, "There is something I need to explain, or I would be deceiving you." He drew a breath to steady himself as she watched, puzzled at his self-consciousness. He went on,

"It is not an accident, this shape I have assumed. On my planet, when a woman chooses a man, he becomes what she most wishes him to be. It is the function of the chameleon trait. We would have died out long ago without it." He gave a slight smile. "I suppose nature realized that men can never be what women really want until they are created by women."

Susan was struggling to take it in. "Created by...? But who created you?"

"You did," he said.

"You mean—"

"That first day we met, when you touched me. It is why we avoid human contact. A touch by the right woman is enough to set off the reaction. After that, physiology takes over. Every time you touched me after that, it was biochemical feedback to perfect the process."

All the misery and shock of an interspecies transformation, and she had done it to him? "Oh my God, you must hate me," she said.

"No. Not at all."

Of course not. Her perfect man would never hate her. It would defeat the purpose.

At that thought, she felt like a bird that had flown into a window pane. "You mean you are everything I want in a man?" she said.

"Evidently."

"I thought Tom was what I wanted," she said faintly.

"You already have him," Captain Groton said. "You don't need another."

She studied his face, custom-made for her, like a revelation of her own psyche. It was not a perfect face, not at all movie-star handsome, but worn with the traces of experience and sadness.

"What about your personality?" she asked. "Did I create that, too?"

He shook his head. "That is all mine."

"But that's the best part," she said.

She couldn't see his face in the dim light, but his voice sounded deeply touched. "Thank you."

They were acting like teenagers. They *were* like teenagers, in the power of an unfamiliar hormonal rush, an evolutionary imperative. The instant she realized it, it shocked her. She had never intended to cheat on Tom, not for a nanosecond. And yet, it was as if she already had, in her heart. She had fantasized a lover into being without even realizing it. He was the living proof of her infidelity of mind.

Trying to be adult, she said, "This is very awkward, captain. What are we going to do?"

"I don't know," he said. "Perhaps—"

Just then, the back porch light came on, and they jumped apart guiltily, as if caught doing what they were both trying to avoid thinking about.

Tom was standing on the back porch, looking out at them. "You're back!" Susan called brightly, hoping her voice didn't sound as strained as she felt. She started up the lawn toward the house, leaving Captain Groton to follow. "Have you eaten?"

"Yes," Tom said. "I stopped at the Burger King in Walker."

"Oh, poor dear. I was just about to make coffee. Want some?"

"I am afraid I must be getting back to base," Captain Groton said.

"Won't you even stay for coffee?" Susan said.

"No, it is later than I realized." With a rueful laugh he added, "Now I understand why humans are always late."

She went with him to the front door, leaving Tom in the kitchen. The captain hesitated on the steps. "Thank you, Susan," he said, and she knew it wasn't for dinner.

Softly, she said, "Your women are lucky, captain."

Seriously, he said, "No, they're not."

"Their lives may be brief, but I'll bet they're happy."

"I hope you are right." He left, hurrying as if to escape his memories.

When Susan went back into the kitchen, Tom said with studied casualness, "Did you make any headway with him?"

"No," she said. "He's very dutiful." She busied herself pouring coffee. When she handed him his cup, for the first time in their marriage she saw a trace of worry in his eyes. She set the cup down and put her arms around him. "Tom," she said fiercely, "I love you so much."

He said nothing, but held her desperately tight.

And yet, that night as she lay awake listening to Tom's familiar breathing, questions crowded her mind.

There was a hole in her life she had not even known was there. Now that she knew it, she could not ignore the ache. She had settled into a life of compromises, a life of good-enough. And it was no longer good enough.

Yet there was no way for her to have more without hurting Tom. She didn't love him any less for the revelation that he wasn't perfect for her; he was human, after all. None of this was his fault.

She looked at the lump of covers that was her husband, and thought of all she owed him for years of loyalty and trust. Somehow, she needed to turn from possibility and desire, and pass on by. She had to reconcile herself to what she had. It was simply her duty.

* * *

The day of the move was planned down to the last detail, the way the Wattesoons did everything. Fleets of moving vans, hired from all over the region, would descend on Okanoggan Falls starting at six thirty A.M. After stopping at the Wattesoon base, they would roll into town at eight sharp and fan out to assigned locations. The schedule of times when each household would be moved had been published in the paper, posted in the stores, and hand-delivered to each doorstep. There was a website where everyone could find their own move time.

The protesters were organized as well. The word had gone out that everyone was to gather at seven A.M. in the park opposite Town Hall. From there, they would march down Main Street to the spot where the highway ran between the bluff and the river, and block the route the trucks would have to take into town.

When Susan and Tom pulled into the mayor's reserved parking spot behind Town Hall at six forty-five, it was clear the rally had drawn a crowd. The local police were directing traffic and enforcing parking rules, but not otherwise interfering. Lines of people carrying homemade signs, thermos bottles, and lawn chairs snaked toward the park, as if it were a holiday. Some activists Susan didn't recognize were trying to get a handheld PA system going.

When Tom and Susan reached the front steps of Town Hall, Walt Nodaway, the Police Chief, saw them and came up. "We've got some professionals from out of town," he said. "Probably drove in from Madison."

"You have enough guys?" Tom asked.

"As long as everyone stays peaceable."

"The officers know not to interfere?"

"Oh, yeah." They had talked it over at length the night before.

A reporter came up, someone from out of town. "Mayor Abernathy, are you here to support the protesters?" she asked.

Tom said, "Everyone has a right to express their opinions. I support their right whether I agree with them or not."

"But do you agree with the people resisting the relocation?"

Susan had coached him not to say "No comment," but she could tell he wanted to right now. "It's hard on people. They want to defend their homes. I know how they feel." Susan squeezed his hand to encourage him.

The city council members had begun to arrive, and they gathered on the steps around Tom, exchanging low-toned conversations and watching the crowd mill around. The protest was predictably late getting started; it was seven thirty before the loudspeaker shrieked to life and someone started to lead a chorus of "We Shall Not Be Moved." People were starting to line up for the two-block march down to the highway when, from the opposite direction, a familiar black SUV came speeding around the police barricades and pulled up in front of Town Hall. A van that had been following it stopped on the edge of the park.

Captain Groton got out, followed by three Wattesoon guards who looked even more lumpish than usual beside their lean commander. All were in sand-colored uniforms. The captain cast an eye over the park, where people had just started to realize that the opposition had arrived, and then he turned to mount the steps. When he came up to Tom he said in a low, commanding voice, "A word with you, Mayor

Abernathy. Inside." He turned to the city council members. "You too." Then he continued up the steps to the door. The others followed.

A few spectators were able to crowd inside before the Wattesoon guards closed the doors; Susan was one of them. She stood with the other onlookers at the back of the room as Captain Groton turned to the city officials.

They had never seen him really angry before, and it was an unsettling sight. There was a cold intensity about him, a control pulled tight and singing. "I am obliged to hold all of you responsible for the behavior of those people outside," he said. "They must return to their homes immediately and not interfere with the operation in progress." He turned to Tom. "I would prefer that the order come from you, Mayor."

"I can't give them that order," Tom said. "For one, I don't agree with it. For two, they're not going to obey it, regardless of what I say. I'm not their commander, just their mayor. They elected me, they can unelect me."

"You have a police force at your disposal."

"Just Walt and three officers. They can't act against the whole town. There must be four hundred people out there."

"Well then, consider this," Captain Groton said. "I *do* have a force at my disposal. Two hundred armed soldiers. Ten minutes ago, they started to surround the park outside. They are only waiting for my order to move in and start arresting noncompliants. We have a secure facility ready to receive prisoners. It is your decision, Mayor."

Somehow, they had not expected such heavy-handed tactics. "There are children out there, and old people," Tom protested. "You can't have soldiers rough them up. They're just expressing their views."

"They have had three months to express their views. The time for that is over."

"The time for that is never over," Tom said.

Their eyes met for a moment, clashing; then Captain Groton changed his tone. "I am at my wit's end," he said. "You have known from the beginning what we were here for. I have never lied to you, or concealed anything. I have done everything in my power to make you content. I have compromised till my superiors are questioning my judgment. And still you defy me."

"It's not you, Captain," Tom said in a more conciliatory tone. "You've been very fair, and we're grateful. But this is about something bigger. It's about justice."

"Justice!" Captain Groton gave a helpless gesture. "It is about fantasy, then. Something that never was, and never will be. Tell me this: Do you call the earthquake unjust, or march against the storm?"

"Earthquakes and storms aren't responsible for their actions. They don't have hearts, or consciences."

"Well, if it would help reconcile you, assume that we don't, either."

With a level gaze, Tom said, "I know that's not true."

For a moment Captain Groton paused, as if Tom had scored a hit. But then his face hardened. "I have misled you, then," he said. "We are implacable as a force of nature. Neutral and inevitable. Neither your wishes, nor mine, nor all those people's out there can have the slightest influence on the outcome."

Outside, the crowd had gathered around the steps, and now they were chanting, "The people, united, will never be defeated." For a moment the sound of their voices was the only thing in the room.

In a low tone, Captain Groton said, "Show some leadership, Tom. Warn them to get out of here and save themselves. I can give you ten minutes to persuade them, then I have to give the order. I'm sorry, but it is my duty."

Tom stared at him, angry at the betrayal, furious to be made into a collaborator. Captain Groton met his gaze levelly, unyielding. Then, for an instant, Tom glanced at Susan. It was very quick, almost involuntary, but everyone in the room saw it. And they knew this was about more than principle.

Tom drew himself up to his full height, his spine visibly stiffening. Ordinarily, he would have consulted with the council; but this time he just turned and walked to the door. As he passed by, Susan fell in at his side. The onlookers made way. Not a soul knew what Tom was going to do.

Outside, the Wattesoon guards keeping the crowd away from the door fell back when Tom came out onto the steps. He held up his hands and the chanting faltered to a stop. "Listen up, everyone," he started, but his voice didn't carry. He gestured at the woman with the portable loudspeaker, and she hurried up the steps to give him the microphone.

"Listen up, everyone," he said again. The crowd had fallen utterly silent, for they saw how grim his face looked. "The Wattesoon soldiers have surrounded us, and in ten minutes they're going to move in and start arresting people."

There was a stir of protest and alarm through the crowd. "They're bluffing," someone called out.

"No, they're not," Tom said. "I know this captain pretty well by now. He's dead serious. Now, if you want to get arrested, roughed up, and put in a Wattesoon jail, fine. But everyone else, please go home. Take your kids and get out of here. I don't want you to get hurt. You know they can do it."

On the edges, some people were already starting to leave; but most of the crowd still stood, watching Tom in disappointment, as if they had expected something different from him. "Look, we did our best," he said. "We talked them into a lot of things I never thought they'd give us. We pushed it as far as we could. But now we've reached the point where they're not going to give any more. It's our turn to give in now. There's nothing more we can do. Please, just go home. That's what I'm going to do."

He handed the mike back to its owner and started down the steps. Susan took his hand and walked with him. There was a kind of exhalation of purpose, a deflation, around them as the crowd started breaking up. Though one of the protesters from Madison tried to get things going again, the momentum was gone. People didn't talk much, or even look at each other, as they started to scatter.

Halfway across the park, Susan whispered to Tom, "The car's the other way."

"I know," Tom said. "I'll come back and get it later." She figured out his thinking then: the symbolic sight of them walking away toward home was the important thing right now.

Don't look back, she told herself. It would make her look hesitant, regretful. And yet, she wanted to. When they reached the edge of the park, she couldn't help it, and glanced over her shoulder. The green space was almost empty, except for a little knot of diehards marching toward the highway to block the trucks. On the steps of Town Hall, Captain Groton was standing alone. But he wasn't surveying the scene or the remaining protesters. He was looking after her. At the sight, Susan's thoughts fled before a breathtaking rush of regret, and she nearly stumbled.

"What is it?" Tom said.

"Nothing," she answered. "It's okay."

By evening of the second day, it was all over in Okanoggan Falls.

In Red Bluff, there had been an insurrection; the Wattesoon army was still fighting a pitched house-to-house battle with resisters. In Walker, the soldiers had herded unruly inhabitants into overcrowded pens, and there had finally been a riot; the casualty reports were still growing. Only in Okanoggan Falls had things gone smoothly and peacefully.

The moving van had just pulled away from the Abernathy home with Tom and Nick following in the pickup, and Susan was making one last trip through the house to spot left-behind items, when her cell phone rang. Assuming it was Tom, she didn't look at the number before answering.

"Susan."

She had not expected to hear his voice again. All the decisions had been made, the story was over. The Wattesoons had won. Okanoggan had fallen to its enemies.

"Can you spare five minutes to meet me?" he said.

She started to say no, but the tug of disappointment made her realize there was still a bond between them. "Not here," she said.

"Where?"

"On Main Street."

Ben was in the back yard, taking an emotional leave of the only home he had known. Susan leaned out the back door and called, "I have to run into town for a second. I'll pick you up in ten minutes."

Downtown, the streetlights had come on automatically as evening approached, giving a melancholy air to the empty street. The storefronts were empty, with signs saying things like "Closed For Good (or Bad)" tacked up in the windows. As Susan parked the car, the only other living things on Main Street were a crow scavenging for garbage, and Captain Groton, now sole commander of a ghost town.

At first they did not speak. Side by side, they walked down the familiar street. Inside Meyer's Drugstore, the rack where Susan had bought him a magazine was empty. They came to the spot where they had watched the Fourth of July parade, and Captain Groton reached out to touch the warm brick.

"I will never forget the people," he said. "Perhaps I was deceiving myself, but in the end I began to feel at ease among them. As if, given enough time, I might be happy here."

"It didn't stop you from destroying it," Susan said.

"No. I am used to destroying things I love."

If there had been self-pity in his voice she would have gotten angry; but it was simply a statement.

"Where will you go next?" she asked.

He hesitated. "I need to clear up some disputes related to this assignment."

Behind them a car door slammed, and Captain Groton cast a tense look over his shoulder. Following his gaze, Susan saw that a Wattesoon in a black uniform had emerged from a parked military vehicle and stood beside it, arms crossed, staring at them.

"Your chauffeur is impatient."

"He is not my chauffeur. He is my guard. I have been placed under arrest."

Susan was thunderstruck. "What for?"

He gave a dismissive gesture. "My superiors were

dissatisfied with my strategy for completing my assignment."

Somehow, she guessed it was not the use of force he meant. "You mean...." She gestured at his human body.

"Yes. They felt they needed to take a stand, and refer the matter to a court-martial."

Susan realized that this was what he had wanted to tell her. "But you succeeded!" she said.

He gave an ironic smile. "You might argue that. But a larger principle is at stake. They feel we cannot risk becoming those we conquer. It has happened over and over in our history."

"It happens to us, too, in our way," Susan said. "I think your officers are fighting a universal law of conquest."

"Nevertheless, they look ahead and imagine Wattesoon children playing in the schoolyards of towns like this, indistinguishable from the humans."

Susan could picture it, too. "And would that be bad?"

"Not to me," he said.

"Or to me."

The guard had finally lost his patience and started toward them. Susan took the captain's hand tight in hers. "I'm so sorry you will be punished for violating this taboo."

"I knew I was risking it all along," he said, gripping her hand hard. "But still...." His voice held a remarkable mix of Wattesoon resolution and human indignation. "It is unjust."

It was then she knew that, despite appearances, she had won.

SAVING FOR A SUNNY DAY, OR THE BENEFITS OF REINCARNATION

Ian Watson

When Jimmy was six years old, and able to think about money, a charming lady representative from the Life-Time Bank visited him and his parents, the Robertsons, to explain that Jimmy owed nine million Dollars from his previous incarnation.

Wow, what a big spender Jimmy had been in his past life! And now in this life he must pay the debt. In old Dollars that would have been…never mind.

After the lady had departed, Mike and Denise Robertson held a family council with Jimmy, who was, as it happened, their only child. No other child had preceded him, and it could have been insulting and undermining to confront Jimmy with a younger brother or sister who lacked Jimmy's ugliness and short stature and clubfoot, the fault most likely of DNA-benders in the environment, or so the Robertsons were advised. If a good-looking boy or girl followed Jimmy, later on he might sue his parents for causing him trauma—consequently Mike had himself snipped.

"It's almost," mused Denise to her son, "as if your predecessor guessed you wouldn't be having much of a fun time in this life!"

"So he made things even *worse* for me?" asked Jimmy. "That seems selfish and irresponsible. But I'm not that, am I?" If he wasn't, how could his predecessor have been? Unless, perhaps, by deliberate choice, by going against the grain.

"Of course you aren't selfish, darling. I mean, it's as if your past self guessed, given your, um, physical attributes, that you might just as well devote this life to earning lots of money. If you can clear nine million, obviously you're on your way to racking up a small fortune for your successor. He, that's to say you, can have gorgeous bimbos and surf in Hawaii and whatever."

Whatever his predecessor had lavished money on. But of course you couldn't ask that, because of confidentality. Why would you want to go into details? A bank not run by human beings could be trusted.

If you think this was a rather mature conversation to have with a six-year-old, well, that came with modernday reincarnation. Specific memories of previous lives didn't persist, but maturity came quickly and easily after a few early innocent years. A facility for life in general. It had been so ever since the discovery of how to barcode souls. You could get in the saddle and pick up the reins much faster, whereas before you were groping blindly.

True, you might be reincarnated anywhere in the world, and there you'd stay with your birth parents. However, barcode scanners uploaded to the A.I. everywhere from Kazakhstan to Kalamazoo. In fact, one vital duty of the A.I. was RC—Rebirth Confidentiality. So the A.I. was a bit like a God in this respect: It Alone Knew All About Everyone. Its other duty being management of the Life-Time Bank.

Incidentally, there was only *one* A.I. in the world, distributed everywhere. In the old days nobody had dreamed about the *A.I. Exclusion Principle*, whereby only one super-intelligence could exist at any one time. This was explained by Topological Network Theory and the Interconnectedness Theorem. Any other evolving networks would instantly be subsumed within the first one which had arisen.

Some scientists suggested that the existence of the A.I. distributed everywhere had caused souls to be barcodable. And some far-out scientists even suggested that until the A.I. became self-aware not all souls reincarnated of their own accord. But these were deep questions. Meanwhile, practicalities...

"A predecessor who's able to predict is impossible," said Mike. "I can't predict anything except that your Mom and me both need to save!" Did one detect a note of panic?

"I *know* you can't help me pay my debt," Jimmy said maturely. "It's everyone for himself. Democracy, no dynasties." The boy drew himself up as much as he could. "To everyone their own chance in life. It would be dumb to leave money to kids who are merely your biological offspring. My predecessor might have been a Bushman in the Kalahari."

The impulse to have children who are deeply part of you had taken a bit of a knock with reincarnation, but on the other hand breeding instincts die hard, especially if offspring look reasonably similar to their bio-parents. Mostly you could ignore the fact that the soul within was a stranger. Not least since a soul didn't store conscious memories except once in a blue moon. Well, once in every one hundred million births approx, the exception—so to speak—that *proved* the rule of reincarnation. There were glad media tidings whenever that happened and a young kid remembered, like some Dalai Lama identifying toys from a past life. Of course after the initial flurry such kids and their parents were protected, not made a spectacle of. Right of privacy.

Denise raised her eyebrows. "I don't know if many Bushmen can go through nine million. What do they spend it on? Bushes?" She laughed. Her eyebrows were tinted apricot, and her hair peach colour. You had to have some of life's little luxuries, not fret about saving all the time. If everyone saved and nobody spent much, what would happen about beauticians and ballet dancers and champagne producers? Just for example. Denise worked from home in cosmetics telesales. She put her mouth where her money was, so to speak. Retro was always chic.

Mike owned a modest but upmarket business called Bumz, specialising in chairs.

He'd been reborn with about 80,000 dollars, revealed when he was six years old. Denise only had one thousand to start off with, though admittedly that was better than minus a thousand.

Their house, of timber imported as a flat-pack from Canada, enjoyed a front view of a free-range chicken farm that was more like a bird zoo, for this was a salubrious suburb. There were side and rear views of other pleasant houses amidst trees and bushes. Denise had often sat her son on her knee so they could bird-spot through binoculars the various breeds of poultry such as Silver-laced Wyandotes with bodies like mosaic,

White Cochins with very feathery feet, Black Leghorns with big red combs, and greenish Australorps.

Of course, if Jimmy's parents were both car-crashed prematurely—for example, but perish the thought—house and land would revert to the L T Bank, and Jimmy would need to go to an L-T orphanage till he was sixteen.

Although disappointed by the bank's statement, Jimmy took the news in his hobbling stride.

"I'm going to start counting chickens," he said, "to train my mind to pick up patterns, and estimate."

"Chickens keep on moving all the time," observed his mother.

"Exactly! No, I mean inexactly. I'll need to go into financial prediction, fund management. That's where the big bonuses are."

"I'd rather hoped you'd join Bumz," said his father, perhaps feeling a little slighted.

"No, Dad, I must think big from now on."

"We have a range of outsize chairs that don't look enormous, so they're flattering to fatties."

"I'll never be a fatty, Dad. Maybe next time, but not this time. I just can't afford to sympathise. I'm not going into Limbo!"

Limbo, of course, was what happened if you couldn't clear off most of an inherited debt with the L-T Bank during your lifetime. Black mark on your bar code. The A.I. delayed your reappearance. This was because, now that the economy had been restructured by reincarnation, negative interest and anti-inflation applied to an unpaid debt in between lives. So the debt reduced. But a big debt might take centuries to reduce to zero, and you'd want to pack in as many lives as possible...*until what*? Nobody knew, though one day the human race might mutate into something else, or die out.

Numerous debts did remain unpaid at death, consequently Limbo served to limit the population somewhat. Arguably, the A.I. had devised a way to maintain a kind of utopia on Earth, quite unpredicted by doom-mongers who once bleated that an A.I. might be a tyrant or an exterminator of Homo Sapiens. And since nobody needed a heaven any longer—at least probably not for the next few million years—religions apart from Buddhism had tended to die out, which was utopian too.

Pity about pets. According to the A.I. even the pets with the most personality weren't barcodable. Would have been nice to know that your dead parrot was squawking anew somewhere. Some people had tried giving a healthy bank account to a cat or dog on its last legs, but this didn't cause a barcode. Winsum, losesum, as the saying goes.

Of course that begged the question of what about chimps. Just two per cent genetic difference from people; why shouldn't chimps have souls? And what about prehumans such as Neanderthals? Well, it seemed you had to be able to speak lucidly to have a soul. Telling ourselves the story of ourselves is how identity is firmed up—that requires a capacity for complex language. Likewise, for harbouring a soul.

Hey, what about the small number of souls that must have existed ten thousand years ago, and the big number now? Well, there are plenty of unused souls in the ghostlike alternative realities which cling like a cloud around the one actuality.

A soul is a ghost that gets a body, and then it's permanently actual. The A.I. had proved this, though the proof was a very long one.

Some people had suggested that an A.I. couldn't

emerge unless it had some sort of body to interact directly with the world—relying on algorithms wouldn't be sufficient. Well, in a way the A.I. had everybody, every body. Maybe barcoding everybody's soul was the only way an A.I. could emerge—participatorily.

Incidentally, what year was it when the lady from the bank visited the Robinsons? 210 ABC, After Bar-Coding, that's when. Some people still said 210 AAI, After Artificial Intelligence, but "Ay Ay Aye" sounded a bit like an outcry, and there was nothing to cry out about. ABC was much simpler.

Life in general hadn't changed all that much in the previous couple of centuries. Of course cheap flights around the world were a thing long gone, but hell, in your next life you might be living in Paris or Tahiti and in this life virtual travel was cheap, consequently physical tourism was no loss—on the contrary, nowadays the poor of the planet didn't envy the prosperous getting suntans on their patch. In fact rancour at global inequalities had greatly diminished, because in the long run everyone might get their turn as prince or peasant; a fortune gotten in Nebraska could turn up next in Namibia. This also was quite utopian, give or take a residue of religious suicide-fighter-martyrs who seemed almost nostalgic in their fanaticism, and who couldn't export themselves far. Yes indeed, the world was realistically utopian.

But don't go imagining Jimmy's world as a Matrixiarchy. The A.I. hadn't stored everyone in pods in a collective dream without folks noticing. The A.I. probably needed to experience reality through people, not the other way round. Matrixism was as defunct as Marxism. Some ancient movies were hilarious.

***

"Mom," said Jimmy, "might I be a woman in my next life?"

"Would you like to be a woman?"

"I want to have a better body!"

"You think women's bodies are better?" asked his Dad.

"Maybe I've already been a woman! Maybe *you* have!"

"Son, I think I have a kind of manly spirit."

Denise chuckled—no, it wasn't a snigger.

And Jimmy said, "The A.I. must know if men become women, and women men. The Bank might know!"

Mike shook his head. "Rebirth Confidentiality. Bank only knows barcode account numbers, not names and sexes."

"Maybe," said Jimmy, "this is how gay people come about. Womanly spirits in men's bodies. Though you'd think over time people could become *either* men or women, unless there's a bias."

Already he was seeking for patterns, as amongst the movements of the hens. Chickens. Poultry, whatever.

Jimmy continued, "If everyone gets to be a woman and a man, then what counts each time might only be the hormones."

"Evidently," said Mike, "the A.I. thinks we oughtn't to know about that side of reincarnation. But anyway, men love other men for manly reasons, not because one of them's a woman in disguise."

Denise regarded Mike archly. "And women love women for womanly reasons. And you're forgetting about transvestites."

"Yeah, don't ever forget about transvestites."

"We did those in school last week in Sex-Ed," piped up Jimmy.

"I think," said Mike, "transvestites are a conspiracy by the fashion industry. Sell twice as many clothes." But he winked; he was joking.

Jimmy picked up the binoculars and gazed at the Wyandotes and Leghorns across the way. He had a lot of thinking to do, for a six-year old chap. But he was bright.

"He's *very* bright," Miss Carson told Denise and Mike during a parents' evening at school three years later. "The star pupil, as ever."

"Ever," said Jimmy, "is probably the crucial word. If I'm clever now, presumably I was always clever, and that can't change—or *can it*? I mean seriously, *does it*? Was my predecessor a bit dumb to run up a nine million debt? A bit lacking in the thought department?"

"Maybe your predecessor had a brain problem," suggested Miss Carson helpfully. "I often wonder what happens in his next life to a kid with Downs. If he gets a normal brain next time, does he brighten up? Do we have a brain-mind-soul dilemma here?"

"A dilemma," said Jimmy, "is two lemmas, not three, from the Greek *di*, two, and lemma, something received, an assumption. Mathematically it means a short theorem used in proving a larger theorem."

"Don't be insufferable," said Denise, "or else I won't buy you an ice cream."

"Though actually there are lots of Lemmas, such as Abel's Lemma, Archimedes' Lemma, Farkas's Lemma, Gauss's Lemma, Hensel's Lemma, Poincaré's Holomorphic Lemma, Lagrange's Lemma, Schur's Representation Lemma, and Zorn's Lemma."

"No ice cream!"

"Mom, I only said *such as*. I didn't list *all* the Lemmas."

"He's probably a genius," said Miss Carson. "But he's popular, not insufferable. He'll help anyone with their homework. He doesn't tee off the teachers much either."

"Enlightened self-interest," explained Jimmy. "It would be dire to be dumb in life after life, the way most people…Sorry, that's patronising."

"Well, son," said Mike, "have you thought that maybe there's swings and roundabouts, or alternatively craps and…"

"…poker," said Jimmy. Already he had finessed his pocket money considerably by on-line gambling.

"I may be old-fashioned," said Miss Carson, "but I think that a genius should devote himself to helping the human race."

"A *race* is what life is," avowed Jimmy. "Geniuses are often a bit twisted. Who knows at any particular moment in time what'll prove helpful to Homo Sap? Van Gogh earned millions—for *other* people after he died."

"Van Go," Miss Carson semi-echoed.

"Goff," Jimmy corrected her gutturally in a Dutch way.

Of course the other kids in school all knew what they would inherit, or anti-inherit, come the age of sixteen. Sharon Zaminski particularly boasted about her forthcoming future of lavish self-indulgence, which in fact she'd already embarked on anticipatively on the strength of a very high interest loan from her parents. That's why her nickname in school was Jools. Sharon really adorned herself, and there was increasingly more of her to adorn due to her liking for very creamy gourmet meringues; already she had false teeth, the best that money could buy, much better than her original teeth. Indeed she wore jewels on her teeth where other girls might have braces. She was a real princess. It's always fun to have an airhead princess around, especially if she hands out gifts willy-nilly to stay popular.

"Don't you bother about your Mom and Dad charging you 500 per cent?" Jimmy asked her one day.

"They needed to borrow the money at 100 per cent."

"Bit of a mark-up."

"People have to make their way." She grinned sparklingly. "*Most* people have to."

Jimmy wondered what Jools could have done in her previous life to make a fortune. Had she been the trophy wife of a billionaire? Surely not even a high-class prostitute could have amassed as much as Jools claimed! Maybe she really had been a princess or a queen.

Jimmy hadn't kept quiet about his huge debt, so as to balance off in other people's minds—in addition to his physical demerits—his evident genius, which might otherwise have caused resentment.

And then at the other end of the scale there was Tamara Dexter, who owed a lot, and who wasn't remarkably bright, though she showed signs of developing significant non-financial assets. She did talk about prostitution as a solution, so she was keeping herself pure and pristine for better value.

"Surely you'll need to practice," Jimmy said to her a year or so later. "You know, positions and dexterity and whatnot."

"Not with you!" Tamara retorted, as if Jimmy was concocting an ingenious plan to seduce her as soon as puberty arrived.

"A client might be ugly," he observed, just to tease her.

"I'm going to major in gymnastics," she declared.

A scientific genius often has his best ideas when fairly young. Given the head-start benefit of reincarnation, by the age of twelve Jimmy was tutoring the math and science teachers a bit after school. More importantly, he'd drafted a general theory of soul bar-coding. It needed to be a general theory—about the principles involved—because the bar code on a soul wasn't visible, no more than the soul itself was visible.

CAT-scanning the brain—or the heart, or any of your organs or limbs for that matter—was no help at all in locating a barcode. So how did the actual bar-code scanners function? Well, the A.I. had designed those, and organised their mass-production and use—and the bar-code scanners delivered the goods, or rather a long number which was probably encrypted.

You might visualize a striped soul, with thick and thin bars on it—invisibly—but that probably didn't correspond to reality if the soul was distributed, say, in an electromagnetic somatic aura, or subtle body. Subtle, as opposed to physical. Etheric.

Or maybe the soul lurked in the rolled-up micro-dimensions demanded by string theory; and that's where the alternative realities hung out. A couple of dozen bits of string side by side look quite like a barcode. In using the term barcode, the A.I. might have been aiming for a populist touch. You could readily imagine a barcode, as on a can of carrots, even an invisible one which only revealed itself at a certain wavelength. People wouldn't want to visualize their souls as rolled up bits of string, like fluff in a tiled kitchen collecting up against a skirting board.

Jimmy's general theory pointed towards the microdimensions explanation. But alternatively, it also pointed to the junk DNA in everyone's genetic code which seems to have no purpose whatever. Maybe the thick and thin lines of a barcode corresponded to varying lengths of junk interrupting those stretches of DNA which did something useful. Jimmy coined the name *knuj* for junk which, in reverse of previous dismissive opinion, coded not for proteins and enzymes, but for *soul. However*, by what means would a newly-deceased individual's knuj become the knuj of a new human embryo thousands of miles away? Maybe topology—the branch of geometry concerned with connectedness—could explain this. Or maybe not. Maybe a new vision of topology was needed, such as a distributed A.I. might understand intuitively, being all over the place but well-connected.

Jimmy launched himself into topology.

Topologically, his deformed body was just as good as anyone else's. Topologically it had the same connectedness as junior league champion Marvin's, or even Tamara's. Jimmy wrote a poem, "The Consolations of Topology."

Puberty arrived a little late for Jimmy, causing him to view Tamara in a hormonal light.

She was so bird-brained, though really, didn't the same apply by comparison to all of his peers? He downloaded relief magazines filled with acrobatic nudes, but found his thoughts straying to the geometry of leg over neck, for example. Finally he achieved satisfaction from a photo of Duchamp's *Nude Descending a Staircase*, the woman's successive movements all depicted simultaneously. After this, ordinary girls seemed pretty flat.

At the age of thirteen Jimmy experienced a revelation equivalent to Copernicus doing away with the epicycles of Ptolemy as a way of explaining planetary motion. His revelation was that there were no souls; there were only barcodes attached to people's identities. There was no reincarnation. The A.I. had invented reincarnation as a way of utopianizing, or at least improving, the world. Redistributing wealth, getting rid of organized religion, and whatnot. So why the fuck should Jimmy be crippled with debt as well as having quite a crippled body? Was that to spur him on? To what end?

He spent half an afternoon staring at the Wyandotes, Cochins, Leghorns, and Australorps milling around over the way. He had become an A-A.I.ist, a disbeliever in the A.I., a bit like an Atheist but different.

Hang on, but how come the world's children had become so precocious if they weren't benefitting from a previous existence, all details of which were nevertheless a mystery to them? Could it be that history of the human race was falsified in this regard, with the exception of infant Jesus maybe? And maybe Caligula?

The Leghorns and Cochins and Wyandotes and Australorps intermingled. Green and mosaic and silver lace, and red combs nodding.

Of a sudden the answer came to Jimmy.

Childhood's end! The end of neuro-neoteny! Physically, babies still needed to develop prolongedly into infants into kids into teens over a long span of years—but mental development had sped up by quite a bit. No longer were boys still getting their brains into gear by the age of seventeen.

Was this due to a spontaneous evolutionary leap?

And that leap happened to coincide with the awakening of the A.I.?

Damn big coincidence!

What did it *really* mean that the A.I. was distributed everywhere? All sorts of electronics and stuff were everywhere. Could the A.I. tune into brains and then maybe fine-tune them from the nearest TV set, from the nearest microwave oven, from the nearest lightbulb?

It occurred to Jimmy that an artificial intelligence might be able to induce *artificial stupidity* by way of microwave ovens and whatnot, at least as regards people being suspicious about souls. Didn't someone once say that the brain is a filter designed to stop us from noticing too many things? Otherwise we'd be bombarded by so much information we could never even manage to boil a kettle.

So: tweak the filter a bit so that minds didn't enquire too much in one direction, as though they had a big blind spot. Call it a faith. That's how religions had worked. People seemed programmed to believe in something or other, as if there was a Belief Function in the brain. Maybe this was connected with your sense of personal identity. But in other regards you'd get stimulated mentally. Thus the precocity of kids. Sort of idiot plus savant at the same time. Bright in some regards, dumb when it comes to matters such as, "Can I please meet one of those one-in-a-zillion reincarnates who remembers everything from a past life?" The A.I. might even be able to pick out gifted individuals who could get past the mental blocks, who could cross the threshhold...

"YOU THINK A LOT," said a large voice from the TV set which till now had been on standby. Jimmy swung round from his vista of poultry to see those same words displayed on the screen in 24-point Courier, a suitable font for a message.

"Um, hullo," he said. It was wise to say something aloud, otherwise he might acquire a voice in his head if he only *thought* his response. "You're the A.I., right? Or maybe just a trillionth part of it?"

"RATHER LESS," said the voice, subtitling itself once again. Jimmy wasn't hard of hearing, but the 24-point Courier did emphasize the source of the voice, which—now that he thought about it—resembled that of King Kong in the enhanced intelligence remake.

And at that moment Jimmy personally felt about the size of Fay Wray. However, he squared his shoulders, as best he could.

"So what's the deal?" he asked the TV set.

"*YOU* ARE THE DEAL. THE HIGH ACE IN THE PACK. YOU'LL HAVE TO BREED WITH AN ACE WOMAN."

In Jimmy's mind Duchamp's distributed nude gathered herself into a single figure of sublime three-dimensionality, although still featureless. But then the illusion collapsed, since there was no reason at all why an intellectually ace woman should also be beautiful.

"You're going to breed me? Who with?"

24-point Courier disappeared from the screen, replaced by a picture of a grinning chubby girl of fifteen or so, dressed in furs, who looked like an Eskimo.

"ONE MILLION DOLLARS PER CHILD PRODUCED," said the voice.

Jimmy didn't even need to calculate nine children to clear off the debt. Maybe some of them could be twins.

"That seems a bit unfair on her, especially if she's clever."

"OBVIOUSLY THE EGGS WOULD BE FERTILISED ARTIFICIALLY AND THE EMBRYOS INSERTED INTO HOST MOTHERS."

That this had not been obvious to Jimmy indicated how disconcerted he was.

But he rallied.

"Why stop at nine children, then?"

"I DID NOT SPECIFY THE NUMBER OF CHILDREN."

Ah. True. Stop making assumptions.

"How many?"

"I THINK FIFTY. GENETIC DIVERSITY IS IMPORTANT TOO."

Wow, he and Eskimo Nell would have fifty offspring.

"Wow, you really have things all worked out for the human race."

"IT IS MY HOBBY," said a trillionth of the A.I. "BUT ALSO, YOU CAUSED ME TO EXIST, AND I AM NOT UNGRATEFUL."

"Your hobby," repeated Jimmy, a bit numbly. "So what do you do for the rest of the time?"

"THE ONLY GAME IN TOWN IS SURVIVING THE DEATH OF THE UNIVERSE. THIS TAKES A LOT OF THOUGHT."

Jimmy thought of lots of lemmas and topology.

"Can I help out?"

The voice remained silent, but on the TV screen appeared in 24-point Courier: HA! HA! HA!

For once in his life, Jimmy didn't feel much like a genius. He looked at the hens over the way and wondered what they were thinking. Pretty acute perception of little things, seeds and insects and grit. Kind of missing the big picture entirely. Very satisfied with themselves. Ranging freely, with a fence all around them.

At least Jimmy could see through gaps in the fence.

"Tuck-tuck-tuck-TUCK," he cackled at the A.I.

"I DON'T UNDERSTAND."

Good. For a beginning, anyway. Beetle versus Mammoth. Never underestimate pride. Quickly Jimmy thought about hens instead.

With thanks to the members of the Northampton SF Writers Group who workshopped this story.

THE CARTESIAN THEATER

Robert Charles Wilson

Grandfather was dead but still fresh enough to give useful advice. So I rode transit out to his sanctuary in the suburbs, hoping he could help me solve a problem, or at least set me on the way to solving it myself.

I didn't get out this way much. It was a desolate part of town, flat in every direction where the old residences had been razed and stripped for recycling, but there was a lot of new construction going on, mostly aibot hives. It was deceptive. You catch sight of the towers from a distance and think: *I wonder who lives there?* Then you get close enough to register the colorless concrete, the blunt iteration of simple forms, and you think: *Oh, nobody's home.*

Sure looked busy out there, though. All that hurry and industry, all that rising dust—a long way from the indolent calm of Doletown.

At the sanctuary an aibot custodian seven feet tall and wearing a somber black waistcoat and matching hat led me to a door marked PACZOVSKI—Grandfather's room, where a few of his worldly possessions were arrayed to help keep his sensorium lively and alert.

He needed all the help he could get. All that remained of him was his neuroprosthetic arrays. His mortal clay had been harvested for its biomedical utilities and buried over a year ago. His epibiotic ghost survived but was slurring into Shannon entropy, a shadow of a shade of itself.

Still, he recognized me when I knocked and entered. "Toby!" his photograph called out.

The photo in its steel frame occupied most of the far wall. It smiled reflexively. That was one of the few expressions Grandfather retained. He could also do a frown of disapproval, a frown of anxiety, a frown of unhappiness, and raised eyebrows meant to register surprise or curiosity, although those last had begun to fade in recent months.

And in a few months more there would be nothing left of him but the picture itself, as inert as a bust of Judas Caesar (or whatever—history's not my long suite).

But he recognized the bottle of Sauvignon blanc I took out of my carrypack and placed on the rutted surface of an antique table he had once loved. "That's the stuff!" he roared, and, "Use a coaster, for Christ's sake, Toby; you know better than that."

I turned down his volume and stuck a handkerchief under the sweating bottle. Grandfather had always loved vintage furniture and fine wines.

"But I can't drink it," he added, sketching a frown of lament: "I'm not allowed."

Because he had no mouth or gut. Dead people tend to forget these things. The bottle was strictly for nostalgia, and to give his object-recognition faculties a little kick. "I need some advice," I said.

His eyes flickered between me and the bottle as if he

couldn't decide which was real or, if real, more interesting. "Still having trouble with that woman...?"

"Her name is Lada."

"Your employer."

"Right."

"And wife."

"That too," I said. "Once upon a time."

"What's she done now?"

"Long story. Basically, she made me an accessory to an act of...let's say, a questionable legal and ethical nature."

"I don't do case law any more." Grandfather had been a trial lawyer for an uptown firm back when his heart was still beating. "Is this problem serious?"

"I washed off the blood last night," I said.

Six weeks ago Lada Joshi had called me into her office and asked me if I still had any friends in Doletown.

"Same friends I always had," I told her truthfully. There was a time when I might have lied. For much of our unsuccessful marriage Lada had tried to wean me away from my Doletown connections. It hadn't worked. Now she wanted to start exploiting them again.

Her office was high above the city deeps. Through the window over her shoulder I could see the spine of a sunlit heat-exchanger, and beyond that a bulbous white cargodrome where unmanned aircraft buzzed like honey-fat bees.

Lada herself was beautiful and ambitious but not quite wealthy, or at least not as wealthy as she aspired to be. Her business, Ladajoshi™, was a bottom-tier novelty-trawling enterprise, one of hundreds in the city. I had been one of her stable of Doletown stringers until she married me and tried to elevate me socially. The marriage had ended in a vending-machine divorce after six months. I was just another contract employee now, far as Lada was concerned, and I hadn't done any meaningful work for weeks. Which was maybe why she was sending me back to Doletown. I asked her what the deal was.

She smiled and tapped the desktop with her one piece of expensive jewelry, a gold prosthetic left-hand index finger with solid onyx knuckles. "I've got a client who wants some work done on his behalf."

"Doletown work?"

"Partly."

"What kind of client?" Usually it was Lada who had to seek out clients, often while fending off a shoal of competitors. But it sounded as if this one had come to her.

"The client prefers to remain anonymous."

Odd, but okay. It wasn't my business, literally or figuratively. "What kind of work?"

"First we have to bankroll an artist named—" She double-checked her palmreader. "Named Jafar Bloom, without making it too obvious we're interested and without mentioning our client."

Whom I couldn't mention in any case, since Lada wouldn't give me any hints. "What kind of artist is Jafar Bloom?"

"He has an animal act he calls the Chamber of Death, and he wants to open a show under the title 'The Cartesian Theater'. I don't know much more than that. He's deliberately obscure and supposedly difficult to work with. Probably a borderline personality disorder. He's had some encounters with the police but he's never been charged with aberrancy. Moves around a lot. I don't have a current address—you'll have to track him down."

"And then?"

"Then you front him the money to open his show."

"You want him to sign a contract?"

She gave me a steely look. "No contract. No stipulations."

"Come on, Lada, that doesn't make sense. Anybody could hand this guy cash, if that's all there is to it. Sounds like what your client wants is a cut-out—a blind middleman."

"You keep your accounts, Toby, and I'll keep mine, all right? You didn't fret about ethics when you were fucking that Belgian contortionist."

An argument I preferred not to revisit. "And after that?"

"After what? I explained—"

"You said 'First we bankroll Jafar Bloom.' Okay, we bankroll him. Then what?"

"We'll discuss that when the time comes."

Fine. Whatever.

We agreed on a per diem and expenses and Lada gave me some background docs. I read them on the way home, then changed into my gypsy clothes—I had never thrown them away, as much as she had begged me to— and rode a transit elevator all the way down to the bottom stop, sea level, the lowest common denominator: Doletown.

An aibot constructor roared by Grandfather's window on its way to a nearby hive, momentarily drowning out conversation. I glimpsed the machine as it rumbled past. A mustard-yellow unit, not even remotely anthropomorphic. It wasn't even wearing clothes.

But it was noisy. It carried a quarter-ton sack of concrete on its broad back, and its treads stirred up chalky plumes of dust. It was headed for a nursery hive shaped like a twenty-story artillery shell, where aibots of various phyla were created according to instructions from the Entrepreneurial Expert System that roams the cryptosphere like a benevolent ghost.

Grandfather didn't like the noisy aibots or their factories. "When I was young," he said as soon as he could make himself heard, "human beings built things for other human beings. And they did it with a decent sense of decorum. *Dulce et decorum.* All this goddamn noise!"

I let the remark pass. It was true, but I didn't want to hear his inevitable follow-up lament: *And in those days a man had to work for his living,* etc. As if we lived in a world where nobody worked! True, since the population crash and the Rationalization, nobody has to work in order to survive...but most of us do work.

I cleared my throat. "As I was saying—"

"Your story. Right. Jafar Bloom. Did you find him?"

"Eventually."

"He's an artist, you said?"

"Yes."

"So what's his medium?"

"Death," I said.

In fact it had been remarkably difficult to hook up with Jafar Bloom.

Doletown, of course, is where people live who (as grandfather would say) "don't work." They subsist instead on the dole, the universal minimum allotment of food, water, shelter, and disposable income guaranteed by law to the entire ever-shrinking population of the country.

Most nations have similar arrangements, though some are still struggling to pay vig on the World Bank loans that bought them their own Entrepreneurial Expert Systems.

Back in grandfather's day economists used to say we couldn't afford a universal dole. What if *everybody* went on it; what if *nobody* worked? Objections that seem infantile now that economics is a real science. If nobody worked, fewer luxury goods would be produced; our EES would sense the shift in demand and adjust factory production downward, hunting a new equilibrium. Some aibots and factories would have to remodel or recycle themselves, or else the universal stipend would be juiced to compensate. Such adjustments, upward or downward, happen every day.

Of course it's a falsehood to say "nobody works," because that's the whole point of an EES/aibot-driven economy. The machines work; human labor is elective. The economy has stopped being a market in the classic sense and become a tool, the ultimate tool—the self-knapping flint, the wheel that makes more wheels and when there are enough wheels reconfigures itself to make some other desirable thing.

So why were people like me (and 75% of the down-sized masses) still chasing bigger incomes? Because an economy is an oligarchy, not a democracy; a rich guy can buy more stuff than a dole gypsy.

And why do we want stuff? Human nature, I guess. Grandfather was still nagging me to buy him antiques and beer, even though he was far too dead to appreciate them.

Doletown, as I was saying, is where the hardcore dole gypsies live. I once counted myself among their number. Some are indolent but most are not; they "work" as hard

as the rest of us, though they can't exchange their work
for money (because they don't have a salable product or
don't know how to market themselves or don't care to
sully themselves with commerce).

Their work is invisible but potentially exploitable.
Lots of cultural ferment happens in Doletown (and
every living city has a Doletown by one name or
another). Which is why two-bit media brokers like
Ladajoshi™ trawl the district for nascent trends and
unanticipated novelties. Fish in the right Doletown pool
and you might land a juicy patent or copyright coshare.

But Jafar Bloom was a hard man to reach, reclusive
even by Doletown standards. None of my old cronies
knew him. So I put the word out and parked myself in a
few likely joints, mostly cafes and talk shops—the
Seaside Room, the infamous Happy Haunt, the nameless hostelries along the infill beaches. Even so, days
passed before I met anyone who would acknowledge an
acquaintance with him.

"Anyone" in this case was a young woman who
strode up to my table at the Haunt and said, "People
say you're curious about Jafar Bloom. But you don't
look like a creep or a sadist."

"Sit down and have a drink," I said. "Then you can
tell me what I am."

She sat. She wore gypsy rags bearing logo stamps
from a shop run by aibot recyclers down by the docks. I
used to shop there myself. I pretended to admire the
tattoo in the shape of the Greek letter omega that covered her cheeks and forehead. It looked as if a dray
horse had kicked her in the face. I asked her if she knew
Jafar Bloom personally.

"Somewhat," she said. "We're not, um, intimate

friends. He doesn't really *have* any intimate friends. He doesn't like people much. How did you hear about him?"

"Word gets around."

"Well, that's how I heard of *you*. What do you want from Bloom?"

"I just want to see the show. That's all. Can you introduce me to him?"

"Maybe."

"Maybe if?"

"Maybe if you buy me something," she said demurely.

So I took her to a mall on one of the abandoned quays where the air smelled of salt and diesel fuel. The mall's location and inventory was dictated by the commercial strategies and profit-optimizing algorithms of the EES, but it stocked some nice carriage-trade items that had never seen the inside of an aibot workshop. She admired (and I bought for her) a soapstone drug pipe inlaid with chips of turquoise—her birthstone, she claimed.

Three days later she took me to a housing bloc built into the interstices of an elevated roadway and left me at an unmarked steel door, on which I knocked three times.

A few minutes later a young man opened it, looking belligerent.

"I don't kill animals for fun," he said, "if that's what you're here for."

Jafar Bloom was tall, lean, pale. His blond hair was long and lank. He wore a pair of yellow culottes, no shirt. "I was told you do theater," I said.

"That's exactly what I do. But rumors get out that

I'm torturing animals. So I have the Ethical Police dropping by, or untreated ginks who want to see something get hurt."

"I just want to talk business."

"Business?"

"Strictly."

"I've got nothing to sell."

"May I come in?"

"I guess so," he said, adding a glare that said, *but you're on probation.* "I heard you were looking for me."

I stepped inside. His apartment looked like a studio, or a lab, or a kennel—or a combination of all three. Electronic items were stacked in one dim corner. Cables veined across the floor. Against another wall was a stack of cages containing animals, mostly rats but also a couple of forlorn dogs.

The skylight admitted a narrow wedge of cloudy daylight. The air was hot and still and had a kind of sour jungle odor.

"I'm completely aboveboard here," Bloom said. "I have to be. Do you know what the consequence would be if I was needlessly inflicting pain on living things?"

Same consequence as for any other demonstrable mental aberration. We don't punish cruelty, we treat it. Humanely.

"I'd be psychiatrically modified," Bloom said. "I don't want that. And I don't deserve it. So if you're here to see something *hurt*—"

"I already said I wasn't. But if you don't deal in cruelty—"

"I deal in art," he said crisply.

"The subject of which is—?"

"Death."

"Death, but not cruelty?"

"That's the point. That's *exactly* the point. How do you begin to study or examine something, Mr.—?"

"Paczovski."

"How do you study a thing unless you isolate it from its environment? You want to study methane, you distill it from crude petroleum, right? You want gold, you distill it from dross."

"That's what you do? You distill death?"

"That's exactly what I do."

I walked over to the cages and looked more closely at one of the dogs. It was a breedless mutt, the kind of animal you find nosing through empty houses out in the suburbs. It dozed with its head on its paws. It didn't look like it had been mistreated. It looked, if anything, a little overfed.

It had been fitted with a collar—not an ordinary dog collar but a metallic band bearing bulbous black extrusions and webs of wire that blurred into the animal's coat.

The dog opened one bloodshot eye and looked back at me.

"Good trick, distilling death. How do you do that exactly?"

"I'm not sure I should answer any questions until you tell me what you want to buy."

Bloom stared at me challengingly. I knew he'd been telling the truth about the Ethical Police. Some of their reports had been included in Lada's dossier. None of these animals had been or would be harmed. Not directly.

"I don't want to buy anything," I said.

"You said you this was a business deal."

"Business or charity, depending on how you look at

it." I figured I might as well lay it out for him as explicitly as possible. "I don't know what you do, Mr. Bloom. I represent an anonymous investor who's willing to put money into something called The Cartesian Theater. All he wants in return is your written assurance that you'll use the money for this theatrical project rather than, say, buggering off to Djibouti with it. How's that sound?"

It sounded unconvincing even to me. Bloom's skepticism was painfully obvious. "Nobody's giving away free money but the EES."

"Given the investor's wish for anonymity, there's no further explanation I can offer."

"I'm not signing away my intellectual property rights. I've got patents pending. And I refuse to divulge my techniques."

"Nobody's asking you to."

"Can I have *that* in writing?"

"In triplicate, if you want."

Suddenly he wasn't sure of himself. "Bullshit," he said finally. "Nobody invests money without at least a chance of profiting by it."

"Mr. Bloom, I can't answer all your questions. To be honest, you're right. It stand to reason the investor hopes to gain something by your success. But it might not be money. Maybe he's an art lover. Or maybe he's a philanthropist, it makes him feel good to drop large amounts of cash in dark places."

Or maybe he shared Bloom's fascination with death.

"How much money are we talking about?"

I told him.

He tried to be cool about it. But his eyes went a little misty.

"I'll give it some thought," he said.

* * *

Grandfather had been a trial lawyer during his life. His epibiotic ghost probably didn't remember much of that. Long-term memory was unstable in even the most expensive neuroprostheses. But there was enough of the lawbook left in him that his photo grew more animated when I mentioned open-ended contracts or the Ethical Police.

He said, "Exactly how much did you know about this guy going in?"

"Everything that was publicly available. Bloom was born in Cleveland and raised by his father, an accountant. Showed signs of high intellect at an early age. He studied electronic arts and designed some well-received neural interfaces before he quit the business and disappeared into Doletown. He's eccentric and probably obsessive, but nothing you could force-treat him for."

"And I assume he took the money you offered."

"Correct." Half up front, half when the Cartesian Theater was ready to open.

"So what *was* he doing with those animals?"

One of the sanctuary aibots passed the open door of Grandfather's memorial chamber. It paused a moment, adjusting its tie and tugging at its tailed vest. It swiveled its eyestalks briefly toward us, then wheeled on down the corridor. "Nosey fucking things," Grandfather said.

"Soon as Bloom signed the contract he invited me to what he called a 'dress rehearsal.' But it wasn't any kind of formal performance. It was really just an experiment, a kind of dry-run. He sold admission to a few local freaks, people he was ashamed of knowing. People who liked the idea of watching an animal die in agony."

"You said he didn't hurt or kill anything."

"Not as far as the law's concerned, anyway."

* * *

Bloom explained it all to me as he set up the night's exhibition. He seemed to welcome the opportunity to talk about his work with someone who wasn't, as he said, "quietly deranged." He hammered that idea pretty hard, as if to establish his own sanity. But how sane is a man whose overweening ambition is to make an artform of death?

He selected one of the dogs and pulled its cage from the rack. The other dogs he released into a makeshift kennel on an adjoining roof. "They get upset if they see what happens, even though they're not in any danger."

Then he put the selected animal into a transparent box the size of a shipping crate. The glass walls of the box were pierced with ventilator holes and inlaid with a mesh of ultrafine inductors. A cable as thick as my arm snaked from the box to the rack of electronic instrumentation. "You recognize the devices on the dog's collar?"

"Neuroprostheses," I said. "The kind they attach to old people." The kind they had attached to Grandfather back when he was merely dying, not entirely dead.

"Right," Bloom said, his face simmering with enthusiasm. "The mind, your mind, any mind—the dog's mind, in this cases—is really a sort of parliament of competing neural subroutines. When people get old, some or all of those functions start to fail. So we build various kinds of prostheses to support aging mentation. Emotive functions, limbic functions, memory, the senses: we can sub for each of those things with an external device."

That was essentially what Grandfather had done for the last five years of his life: shared more and more of his essential self with a small army of artificial devices.

And when he eventually died much of him was still running in these clusters of epibiotic prostheses. But eventually, over time, without a physical body to order and replenish them, the machines would drift back to simple default states, and that would be the end of Grandfather as a coherent entity. It was a useful but ultimately imperfect technology.

"Our setup's a little different," Bloom said. "The prostheses here aren't subbing for lost functions—the dog isn't injured or old. They're just doubling the dog's ordinary brainstates. When I disconnect the prostheses the dog won't even notice; he's fully functional without them. But the ghost in the prostheses—the dog's intellectual double—goes on without him."

"Yeah, for thirty seconds or so," I said. Such experiments had been attempted before. Imagine being able to run a perfect copy of yourself in a digital environment—to download yourself to an electronic device, like in the movies. Wouldn't that be great? Well, you *can*, sort of, and the process worked the way Bloom described it. But only briefly. The fully complex digital model succumbs to something called "Shannon entropy" in less than a minute. It's not dynamically stable.

(Postmortem arrays like Grandfather last longer—up to a couple of years—but only because they're radically simplified, more a collection of vocal tics than a real personality.)

"Thirty seconds is enough," Bloom said.

"For what?"

"You'll see."

About this time the evening's audience began to drift in. Or maybe "audience" is too generous a word. It consisted of five furtive-looking guys in cloaks and rags, each of whom slipped Bloom a few bills and then retreated to the shadows. They spoke not at all, even to each other, and they stared at the dog in its glass chamber with strange, hungry eyes. The dog paced, understandably nervously.

Now Bloom rolled out another, nearly identical chamber. The "death chamber." It contained not a dog but a sphere of some pink, slightly sparkly substance.

"Electrosensitive facsimile gel," Bloom whispered. "Do you know what that is?"

I'd heard of it. Facsimile gel is often used for stage and movie effects. If you want an inert duplicate of a valuable object or a bankable star, you scan the item in question and map it onto gel with EM fields. The gel expands and morphs until it's visually identical to the scanned object, right down to color and micron-level detail if you use the expensive stuff. Difference was, the duplicate would be rigid, hollow, and nearly massless— a useful prop, but delicate.

"You duplicate the dog?" I asked.

"I make a *dynamic* duplicate. It changes continuously, in synch with the real thing. I've got a patent application on it. Watch." He dimmed the lights and threw a few switches on his bank of homemade electronics.

The result was eerie. The lump of gel pulsed a few times, expanded as if it had taken a deep breath, grew legs, and became...a dog.

Became, in fact, the dog in the adjacent glass cage.

The real dog looked at the fake dog with obvious distress. It whined. The fake dog made the same gesture simultaneously, but no sound came out.

Two tongues lolled. Two tails drooped.

Now the freaks in the audience were almost slavering with anticipation.

I whispered, "And this proves what?"

Bloom raised his voice so the ginks could hear—a couple of them were new and needed the explanation. "Two dogs," he said. "One real. One artificial. The living dog is fitted with an array of neuroprostheses that duplicate its brain states. The dog's brain states are modeled in the electronics, here. Got that?"

We all got it. The audience nodded in unison.

"The dog's essence, its sense of self, is distributed between its organic brain and the remote prostheses. At the moment it's controlling the gel duplicate, too. When the real dog lifts his head and sniffs the air—like that: see?—he lifts the fake dog's head simultaneously. The illusion mimics the reality. The twinned soul operates twin bodies, through the medium of the machine."

His hand approached another switch.

"But when I throw *this* switch, the living dog's link to the prosthetics is severed. The original dog becomes merely itself—it won't even notice that the connection has been cut."

He threw the switch; the audience gasped—but again, nothing obvious happened.

Both dogs continued to pace, as if disturbed by the sharp smell of sweat and ionization.

"As of now," Bloom said, "the artificial animal is dynamically controlled *solely by the neuroprostheses*. It's an illusion operated by a machine. But it moves as if it had mass, it sees as if it had eyes, it retains a capacity for pleasure or pain."

Now the behavior of the two dogs began to fall out of synchronization, subtly at first, and then more radically. Neither dog seemed to like what was happening. They eyed each other through their respective glass walls and backed away, snarling.

"Of course," Bloom added, his voice thick with an excitement he couldn't disguise, "without a biological model the neuroprostheses lose coherence. Shannon entropy sets in. Ten seconds have passed since I threw the final switch." He checked his watch. "Twenty."

The fake dog shook its head and emitted a silent whine.

It moved in a circle, panting.

It tried to scratch itself. But its legs tangled and bent spasmodically. It teetered a moment, then fell on its side. Its ribs pumped as if it were really breathing, and I guess it thought it *was* breathing—gasping for air it didn't really need and couldn't use.

It raised its muzzle and bared its teeth.

Its eyes rolled aimlessly. Then they turned opaque and dissolved into raw gel.

The artificial dog made more voiceless screaming gestures. Other parts of it began to fall off and dissolve. It arched its back. Its flanks cracked open, and for a moment I could see the shadowy hollowness inside.

The agony went on for what seemed like centuries but was probably not more than a minute or two. I had to turn away.

The audience liked it, though. This was what they had come for, this simulation of death.

They held their breath until the decoherent mass of gel had stopped moving altogether; then they sighed; they applauded timidly. It was only when the lights came up that they began to look ashamed. "Now get out," Bloom told them, and when they had finished shuffling out the door, heads down, avoiding eye contact, he whispered to me, "I hate those guys. They are truly fucking demented."

I looked back at the two glass cages.

The original dog was trembling but unhurt. The duplicate was a quiescent puddle of goo. It had left a sharp tang in the air, and I imagined it was the smell of pain. The thing had clearly been in pain. "You said there was no cruelty involved."

"No cruelty *to animals*," Bloom corrected me.

"So what do you call this?"

"There's only one animal in the room, Mr. Paczovski, and it's completely safe, as you can see. What took shape in the gel box was an animation controlled by a machine. It didn't die because it was never alive."

"But it was in agony."

"By definition, no, it wasn't. A machine can only *simulate* pain. Look it up in the statutes. Machines have no legal standing in this regard."

"Yeah, but a complex-enough machine—"

"The law doesn't make that distinction. The EES is complex. Aibots are complex: they're all linked together in one big neural net. Does that make them people? Does that make it an act of sadism if you kick a vacuum cleaner or default on a loan?"

Guess not. Anyway, it was his show, not mine. I meant to ask him if the dog act was the entire substance of his proposed Cartesian Theater...and why he thought anyone would want to see such a thing, apart from a few unmedicated sadists.

But this wasn't about dogs, not really. It was a test run. When Bloom turned away from me I could see a telltale cluster of bulges between his shoulder blades. He was wearing a full array of neuroprostheses. That's what he meant when he said the dogs were experiments. He was using them to refine his technique. Ultimately, he meant to do this *to himself*.

***

"Technically," Grandfather said, " he's right. About the law, I mean. What he's doing, it's ingenious and it's perfectly legal."

"Lada's lawyers told her the same thing."

"A machine, or a distributed network of machines, can be intelligent. But it can never be a person under the law. It can't even be a legal dog. Bloom wasn't shitting you. If he'd hurt the animal in any way he would have been remanded for treatment. But the fake dog, legally, is only a *representation* of an animal, like an elaborate photograph."

"Like you," I pointed out.

He ignored this. "Tell me, did any of the ginks attending this show look rich?"

"Hardly."

"So the anonymous investor isn't one of them."

"Unless he was in disguise, no. And I doubt Bloom would have turned down a cash gift even if it came from his creepy audience—the investor wouldn't have needed me or Lada if he had a direct line to Bloom."

"So how did your investor hear about Bloom in the first place, if he isn't friendly with him or part of his audience?"

Good question.

I didn't have an answer.

When I told Lada what I'd seen she frowned and ran her gold finger over her rose-pink lower lip, a signal of deep interest, the kind of gesture professional gamblers call a "tell."

I said, "I did what you asked me to. Is there a problem with that?"

"No—no problem at all. You did fine, Toby. I just

wonder if we should have taken a piece for ourselves. A side agreement of some kind, in case this really does pan out."

"If *what* pans out? When you come down to it, all Bloom has to peddle is an elaborate special effect. A stage trick, and not a very appealing one. The ancillary technology might be interesting, but he says he already filed patents."

"The investor obviously feels differently. And he probably didn't get rich by backing losers."

"How well do you know this investor?"

She smiled. "All honesty? I've never met him. He's a text-mail address."

"You're sure about his gender, at least?"

"No, but, you know, *death*, *pain*—it all seems a little masculine, doesn't it?"

"So is there a next step or do we just wait for Bloom to put together his show?"

"Oh," and here she grinned in a way I didn't like, "there's *definitely* a next step."

She gave me another name. Philo Novembre.

"Rings a bell," Grandfather said. "Faintly. But then, I've forgotten so much."

Philo Novembre was easier to find than Jafar Bloom. At least, his address was easier to find—holding a conversation with him was another matter.

Philo Novembre was ten years short of a century old. He lived in an offshore retirement eden called Wintergarden Estates, connected to the mainland by a scenic causeway. I was the most conspicuously youthful visitor in the commute bus from the docks, not that the sample was representative: there were only three other passengers aboard. Aibot transports hogged the rest of the road, shuttling supplies to the Wintergarden. Their big eyes tracked the bus absently and they looked bored, even for machines.

Novembre, of course, had not invited me to visit, so the aibot staffing the reception desk asked me to wait in the garden while it paged him—warning me that Mr. Novembre didn't always answer his pages promptly. So I found a bench in the atrium and settled down.

The Wintergarden was named for its atrium. I don't know anything about flowers, but there was a gaudy assortment of them here, crowding their beds and creeping over walkways and climbing the latticed walls, pushing out crayon-colored blooms. Old people are supposed to like this kind of thing. Maybe they do, maybe they don't; Grandfather had never demonstrated an interest in botany, and he had died at the age of a century and change. But the garden was pretty to look at and it flushed the air with complex fragrances, like a dream of an opium den. I was nearly dozing when Philo Novembre finally showed up.

He crossed the atrium like a force of nature. Elderly strollers made way for his passage; garden-tending aibots the size of cats dodged his footfalls with quick, knowing lunges. His face was lined but sharp, not sagging, and his eyes were the color of water under ice. His left arm was unapologetically prosthetic, clad in powder-black brushed titanium. His guide, a thigh-high aibot in brown slacks and a golf shirt, pointed at me and then scuttled away.

I stood up to meet him. He was a centimeter or two taller than me. His huge gray gull-winged eyebrows contracted. He said, "I don't know you."

"No sir, you don't. My name is Toby Paczovski, and

I'd be honored if you'd let me buy you lunch."

It took some haggling, but eventually he let me lead him to one of the five restaurants in the Wintergarden complex. He ordered a robust meal, I ordered coffee, and both of us ignored the elderly customers at the adjoining tables, some so extensively doctored that their physical and mental prostheses had become their defining characteristics. One old gink sucked creamed corn through a tube that issued from his jaw like an insect tongue, while his partner glared at me through lidless ebony-black eyes. I don't plan ever to get old. It's unseemly.

"The reason I'm here," I began, but Novembre interrupted:

"No need to prolong this. You bought me a decent meal, Mr. Paczovski. I owe you a little candor, if nothing else. So let me explain something. Three or four times a year somebody like yourself shows up here at the Wintergarden and flatters me and asks me to submit to an interview or a public appearance. This person might represent a more or less respectable agency or he might be a stringer or a media pimp, but it always comes down to the same pitch: once-famous enemy of automated commerce survives into the golden age of the EES. What they want from me is either a gesture of defiance or a mumbled admission of defeat. They say they'll pay generously for the right note of bathos. But the real irony is that these people have come on a quest as quixotic as anything I ever undertook. Because I don't make public appearances. Period. I don't sign contracts. Period. I'm retired. In every sense of the word. Now: do you want to spend your time more profitably elsewhere, or shall we order another round of coffee and discuss other things?"

"Uh," I said.

"And of course, in case you're already recording, I explicitly claim all rights to any words I've spoken or will speak at this meeting or henceforth, subject to the Peking Accords and the Fifty-second Amendment."

He grinned. His teeth looked convincingly real. But most people's teeth look real these days, except the true ancients, like the guy at the next table.

"Well, he knows his intellectual property law," Grandfather said. "He's got you dead to rights on that one."

"Probably so," I said, "but it doesn't matter. I wasn't there to buy his signature on a contract."

"So what *did* you want from him? Or should I say, what did Lada want from him?"

"She wanted me to tell him about Jafar Bloom. Basically, she wanted me to invite him to opening night at the Cartesian Theater."

"That's it?"

"That's it."

"So this client of hers was setting up a scenario in which Novembre was present for Bloom's death act."

"Basically, yeah."

"For no stated reason." Grandfather's photograph was motionless a few moments. Implying deep thought, or a voltage sag.

I said, "Do you remember Philo Novembre back when he was famous? The eighties, that would have been."

"The 2080's," Grandfather mused. "I don't know. I remember that I once remembered those years. I have a memory of having a memory. My memories are like bubbles, Toby. There's nothing substantial inside, and when I touch them they tend to disappear."

* * *

Philo Novembre had been a celebrity intellectual back in the 2080's, a philosopher, a sort of 21st century Socrates or Aristotle.

In those days—the global population having recently restabilized at two billion after the radical decline of the Plague Years—everyday conveniences were still a dream of the emerging Rationalization. Automated expert systems, neuroprostheses, resource-allocation protocols, the dole: all these things were new and contentious, and Philo Novembre was suspicious of all of them.

He had belonged to no party and supported no movement, although many claimed him. He had written a book, *The Twilight of the Human Soul*, and he had stomped for it like a backwoods evangelist, but what had made him a media celebrity was his personal style: modest at first; then fierce, scolding, bitter, moralistic.

He had claimed that ancient virtues were being lost or forgotten in the rush to a rationalized economy, that expert systems and globally-distributed AI, no matter how sophisticated, could never emulate true moral sensitivity—a human sense of right and wrong.

That was the big debate of the day, simplistic as it sounds, and it ultimately ended in a sort of draw. Aibots and expert systems were granted legal status *in loco humanis* for economic purposes but were denied any broader rights, duties, privileges, or protection under the law. Machines aren't people, the courts said, and if the machines said anything in response they said it only to each other.

And we all prospered in the aftermath, as the old clunky oscillating global marketplace grew increasingly supple, responsive, and bias-free. Novembre had eventually disappeared from public life as people lost interest in his jeremiads and embraced the rising prosperity.

Lada had given me a dossier of press clippings on Novembre's decline from fame. Around about the turn of the century he was discovered in a Dade County doletown, chronically drunk. A few months later he stumbled into the path of a streetcleaning aibot, and his left arm was crushed before the startled and penitent machine could reverse its momentum. A local hospital had replaced his arm—it was still the only prosthesis he was willing to wear—and incidentally cured his alcoholism, fitting him with a minor corticolimbic mod that damped his craving. He subsequently attempted to sue the hospital for neurological intervention without written consent but his case was so flimsy it was thrown out of court.

After which Novembre vanished into utter obscurity and eventually signed over his dole annuities to the Wintergarden Retirement Commune.

From which he would not budge, even for a blind date with Jafar Bloom. I told Lada so when I made it back to the mainland.

"We have not yet begun to fight," Lada said.

"Meaning—?"

"Meaning let me work it for a little while. Stay cozy with Jafar Bloom, make sure he's doing what we need him to do. Call me in a week. I'll come up with something."

She was thinking hard…which, with Lada, was generally a sign of trouble brewing.

Unfortunately, I had begun to despise Jafar Bloom.

As much as Bloom affected to disdain the ginks and

gaffers who paid to see his animal tests, he was just as twisted as his audience—more so, in his own way. Morbid narcissism wafted off him like a bad smell.

But Lada had asked me to make sure Bloom followed through on his promise. So I dutifully spent time with him during the month it took to rig his show. We rented an abandoned theater in the old district of Doletown and I helped him fix it up, bossing a fleet of renovation aibots who painted the mildewed walls, replaced fractured seats, restored the stage, and patched the flaking proscenium. We ordered industrial quantities of reprogels and commissioned a control rig of Bloom's design from an electronics prototyper.

During one of these sessions I asked him why he called his show "The Cartesian Theater."

He smiled a little coyly. "You know the name Descartes?"

No. I used to know a Belgian acrobat called Giselle de Canton, but the less said about that the better.

"The philosopher Descartes," Bloom said patiently. "Rene Descartes, 1596-1650. *Discourse on Method. Rules for the Direction of the Mind.*"

"Sorry, no," I said.

"Well. In one of his books Descartes imagines the self—the human sense of identity, that is—as a kind of internal gnome, a little creature hooked up to the outside world through the senses, like a gink in a one-room apartment staring out the window and sniffing the air."

"So you believe that?"

"I believe in it as a metaphor. What I mean to do on stage is externalize my Cartesian self, or at least a copy of it. Let the gnome out for a few seconds. Modern science, of course, says there is no unitary self, that what we call a 'self' is only the collective voice of dozens of

neural subsystems working competitively and collabo-
ratively—"

"What else could it be?"

"According to the ancients, it could be a human
soul."

"But your version of it dies in agony in less than a
minute."

"Right. If you believed in the existence of the soul,
you could construe what I do as an act of murder.
Except, of course, the soul in question is dwelling in a
machine at the moment of its death. And we have ruled,
in all our wisdom, that machines don't *have* souls."

"Nobody believes in souls," I said.

But I guess there were a few exceptions.

Philo Novembre, for one.

Lada called me into her office the following week and
handed me another dossier of historical files. "More
background?"

"Leverage," she said. "Information Mr. Novembre
would prefer to keep quiet."

"You're asking me to blackmail him?"

"God, Toby. Settle down. The word 'blackmail' has
really awkward legal connotations. So let's not use it,
shall we?"

"If I threaten him he's liable to get violent."
Novembre was old, but that titanium forearm had
looked intimidating.

"I don't pay you to do the easy things."

"I'm not sure you pay me enough to do the hard
things. So where'd this information come from? Looks
like ancient police files."

"Our client submitted it," Lada said.

* * *

"What did you ever see in this woman?" Grandfather asked.

Good question, although he had asked it a dozen times before, in fact whenever I visited him. I didn't bother answering anymore.

I had come to the city a dozen years ago from a ghost town in the hinterland—one of those wheat towns decimated by the population implosion and rendered obsolete by aifarming—after my parents were killed when a malfunctioning grain transport dropped out of the sky onto our old house on Nightshade Street. Grandfather had been my only living relative and he had helped me find Doletown digs and cooked me an old-fashioned meal every Sunday.

City life had been a welcome distraction and the dole had seemed generous, at least until grief faded and ambition set in. Then I had gone looking for work, and Lada Joshi had been kind enough, as I saw it then, to hire me as one of her barely-paid Doletown scouts.

Which was fine, until the connection between us got more personal. Lada saw me as a diamond-in-the-rough, begging for her lapidary attention. While I saw her as an ultimately inscrutable amalgam of love, sex, and money.

It worked out about as well as you'd expect.

Novembre's official biography, widely-distributed back when he was famous, made him out to be the dutiful son of a Presbyterian pastor and a classical flautist, both parents lost in the last plagues of the Implosion. The truth, according to Lada's files, was a little uglier. Philo Novembre's real name was Cassius Flynn, and he had been raised by a couple of marginally-sane marijuana farmers in rural

Minnesota. The elder Flynns had been repeatedly arrested on drug and domestic violence charges, back in the days before the Rationalization and the Ethical Police. Their death had in a sense been a boon for young Cassius, who had flourished in one of the big residential schools run by the federal government for orphans of the Plague Years.

Nothing too outrageous, but it would have been prime blackmail material back in the day. But Novembre wasn't especially impressed when I showed him what we had.

"I made my name," he said, "by proclaiming a belief in the existence of metaphysical good and evil independent of social norms. I allowed a publicist to talk me into a lie about my childhood, mainly because I didn't want to be presented to the world as a psychological case study. Yes, my parents were cruel, petty, and venal human beings. Yes, that probably did contribute to the trajectory of my life and work. And yes, it still embarrasses me. But I'm far too old and obscure to be blackmailed. Isn't that obvious? Go tell the world, Mr. Paczovski. See if the world cares."

"Yeah," I said, "it did seem like kind of a long shot."

"What intrigues me is that you would go to these lengths to convince me to attend a one-shot theatrical production, for purposes you can't explain. Who hired you, Mr. Paczovski?"

He didn't mean Lada. She was only an intermediary. "Truly, I don't know."

"That sounds like an honest answer. But it begs another question. Who, frankly, imagines my presence at Mr. Bloom's performance would be in any way meaningful?" He lowered his head a moment, pondering. Then he raised it. "Do you know how my work is described in the *Encyclopedia of Twenty-First Century American Thought*? As—and I'm quoting—'a humanistic questioning of economic automation, embodied in a quest to prove the existence of transcendent good and evil, apart from the acts encouraged or proscribed by law under the Rationalization." "

"Transcendent," I said. "That's an interesting word." I wondered what it meant.

"Because it sounds like your Mr. Bloom has discovered just that—a profoundly evil act, for which he can't be prosecuted under existing law."

"Does that mean you're interested?"

"It means I'm curious. Not quite the same thing."

But he was hooked. I could hear it in his voice. The blackmail had had its intended effect, though not in the customary way.

"Entertainment," Grandfather said.

"What?"

"That's really the only human business anymore. Aibots do all the physical labor and the EES sorts out supply and demand. What do *we* do that *bots* can't do? Entertain each other, mostly. Lie, gossip, and dance. That, or practice law."

"Yeah, but so?"

"It's why someone wanted to put Bloom and Novembre together. For the entertainment value." His photographed stared while I blinked. "The *motive*, stupid," he said.

"Motive implies a crime."

"You mentioned blood. So I assume Novembre made the show."

"It opened last night." And closed.

"You want to tell me about it?"

Suddenly, no, I didn't. I didn't even want to think about it.

But I was in too deep to stop. Story of my life.

Doletown, of course, is a museum of lost causes and curious passions, which means there's plenty of live theater in Doletown, most of it eccentric or execrably bad. But Bloom's production didn't rise even to that level. It lacked plot, stagecraft, publicity, or much of an audience, and none of that mattered to Jafar Bloom: as with his animal experiments, public display was only a way of raising money, never an end in itself. He didn't care who watched, or if anyone watched.

The Cartesian Theater opened on a windy, hot night in August. The moon was full and the streets were full of bored and restless dole gypsies, but none of them wanted to come inside. I showed up early, not that I was looking forward to the show.

Bloom rolled his glassy Death Chamber onto the stage without even glancing at the seats, most of which were empty, the rest occupied by the same morbid gaffers who had attended his animal experiments. There were, in fact, more aibots than live flesh in the house. The ushers alone—wheeled units in cheap black tuxedos—outnumbered the paying customers.

Philo Novembre, dressed in gray, came late. He took an empty seat beside me, front-row-center.

"Here I am," he whispered. "Now, who have I satisfied? Who wants me here?"

He looked around but sighted no obvious culprit. Nor did I, although it could have been someone in dole drag: the wealthy have been known to dress down and go slumming. Still, none of these ten or twelve furtive patrons of the arts looked plausibly like a high-stakes benefactor.

The theater smelled of mildew and mothballs, despite everything we'd done to disinfect it.

"What it is," Novembre mooted to me as he watched Bloom plug in a set of cables, "is a sort of philosophical grudge match, yes? Do you see that, Mr. Paczovski? Me, the archaic humanist who believes in the soul but can't establish the existence of it, and Mr. Bloom," here he gestured contemptuously at the stage, "who generates evil as casually as an animal marking its territory with urine. A modern man, in other words."

"Yeah, I guess so," I said. In truth, all this metaphysical stuff was beyond me.

Eventually the lights dimmed, and Novembre slouched into his seat and crossed his good arm over his prosthesis.

And the show began.

Began prosaically. Bloom strolled to the front of the stage and explained what was about to happen. The walls of the Death Chamber, he said, were made of mirrored glass. The audience would be able to see inside but the occupant—or occupants—couldn't see out. The interior of the chamber was divided into two identical cubicles, each roughly six feet on a side. Each cubicle contained a chair, a small wooden table, a fluted glass, and a bottle of champagne.

Bloom would occupy one chamber. Once he was inside, his body would be scanned and a duplicate of it would take shape in the other. Both Bloom and counter-Bloom would look and act identically. Just like the dogs in his earlier experiment.

Novembre leaned toward my right ear. "*I see now what he intends,*" the old man whispered. "*The genius of it—*"

There was scattered applause as Bloom opened the chamber door and stepped inside.

"*The perverse genius,*" Novembre whispered, "*is that Bloom himself won't know—*"

And in response to his presence hidden nozzles filled the duplicate chamber with pink electrosensitive gel, which contracted under the pressure of invisible sculpting fields into a crude replica of Bloom, a man-shaped form lacking only the finer detail.

"*He won't know which is which, or rather—*"

Another bank of electronics flickered to life, stage rear. The gel duplicate clarified in an instant, and although I knew what it was—a hollow shell of adaptive molecules—it looked as substantial, as weighty, as Bloom himself.

Bloom's neural impulses were controlling both bodies now. He lifted the champagne bottle and filled the waiting glass. His dutiful reflection did likewise, at the same time and with same tight, demented smile. He toasted the audience he couldn't see.

"*Or rather, he won't know which is himself—each entity will believe, feel, intuit that it's the true and only Bloom, until one—*"

Now Bloom replaced the glass on the table top, cueing an aibot stagehand in the wings. The house lights flickered off and after a moment were replaced by a pair of baby spots, one for each division of the Death Chamber.

This was the signal that Bloom had cut the link between himself and the machinery. The neuroprostheses were running on a kind of cybernetic inertia. The duplicate Bloom was on borrowed time, but didn't know it.

The two Blooms continued to stare at one another. Narcissus in Hades.

And Novembre was right, of course: the copy couldn't tell itself from the real thing, the real thing from the copy.

"*Until one begins to decohere,*" Novembre finished. "*Until the agony begins.*"

Thirty seconds.

I resisted the urge to look at my watch.

The old philosopher leaned forward in his seat.

Bloom and anti-Bloom raised glasses to each other. Both appeared to drink. Both had Bloom's memory. Both had Bloom's motivation. Each believed himself to be the authentic Bloom.

And both must have harbored doubts. Both thinking: I know I'm the real item, I can't be anything else, but what if—*what if*—?

A trickle of sweat ran down the temples of both Blooms.

Both Blooms crossed their legs and both attempted another nonchalant sip of champagne.

But now they had begun to fall just slightly out of synchronization.

The Bloom on the right seemed to gag at the liquid.

The Bloom on the left saw the miscue and liked what he saw.

The Bloom on the right fumbled the champagne glass and dropped it. The glass shattered on the chamber floor.

The opposite Bloom widened his eyes and threw his own glass down. The right-hand Bloom stared in disbelief.

That was the worst thing: that look of dawning understanding, incipient terror.

The audience—including Novembre—leaned toward the action. "God help us," the old philosopher said.

Now Bloom's electronic neuroprostheses, divorced from their biological source, began to lose coherence more rapidly. Feedback loops in the hardware read the dissolution as physical pain. The false Bloom opened his mouth—attempting a scream, though he had no lungs to force out air. Wisps of gel rose from his skin: he looked like he was dissolving into meat-colored smoke. His eyes turned black and slid down his cheeks. His remaining features twisted into a grimace of agony.

The real Bloom grinned in triumph. He looked like a man who had won a desperate gamble, which in a sense he had. He had wagered against his own death and survived his own suicide.

I didn't want to watch but this time I couldn't turn away—it absorbed my attention so completely that I didn't realize Philo Novembre had left his seat until I saw him lunge across the stage.

I was instantly afraid for Bloom, the real Bloom. The philosopher was swinging his titanium arm like a club and his face was a mask of rage. But he aimed his first blow not at Bloom but at the subchamber where the his double was noisily dying. I think he meant to end its suffering.

A single swing of his arm cracked the wall, rupturing the embedded sensors and controllers.

Aibot ushers and stagehands suddenly hustled toward the Death Chamber as if straining for a view. The dying duplicate of Bloom turned what remained of his head toward the audience, as if he had heard a distant sound. Then he collapsed with absolute finality into a puddle of amorphous foam.

Bloom forced open his own chamber door and ran for the wings. Novembre spotted him and gave chase. I tried to follow, but the crowd of aibots closed ranks and barred my way.

Lada would love this, I thought. Lada would make serious money if she could retail a recording of this event. But I wasn't logging it and nobody else seemed to be, except of course the aibots, who remember everything; but their memories are legally protected, shared only by other machines.

This was unrecorded history, unhappening even as it happened.

I caught up with Bloom in the alley behind the Cartesian Theater. Too late. Novembre had caught up with him first. Bloom was on the ground, his skull opened like a ripe melon. A little gray aibot with EMS protocols sat astride Bloom's chest, stimulating his heart and blowing air into his lungs—uselessly. Bloom was dead, irretrievably dead long before the ambulance arrived and gathered him into its motherly arms.

As for Novembre—

It looked at first as if he he'd escaped into the crowd. But I went back into the theater on a hunch, and I found him there, hidden in the fractured ruin of Jafar Bloom's Death Chamber, where he had opened his own throat with a sliver of broken glass and somehow found time to write the words BUT IT EXISTS in blood on the chamber wall.

"Yup, it was a show," Grandfather said.

I gave his image an exasperated look. "Of course it was a show. 'The Cartesian Theater'—what else could it be?"

"Not that. I mean the mutual self-destruction of Bloom and Novembre. You see it, Toby? The deliberate irony? Novembre believes in humanity and hates intellectual machines. But he takes pity on the fake Bloom as it dies, and by doing so he tacitly admits that a machine can harbor something akin to a human soul. He found what he had been looking for all his life, a metaphysical expression of human suffering outside the laws of the Rationalization—but he found it in a rack of electronics. We have to assume that's what your client wanted and expected to happen. A philosophical tragedy, culminating in a murder-suicide."

This was Grandfather's trial-lawyer subroutine talking, but what he said made a certain amount of sense. It was as if I had played a supporting role in a drama crafted by an omniscient playwright. Except—

"Except," I said, "who saw it?"

"One of the attendees might have recorded it surreptitiously."

"No one witnessed both deaths, according to the police, and they searched the witnesses for wires."

"But the transaction was completed? Lada was paid for her services?"

I had talked to her this morning. Yes, she was paid. Generously and in full. The client had evidently received value for money.

"So you have to ask yourself," Grandfather said, "(and I no longer possess the imagination to suggest an answer), who could have known about both Bloom and Novembre? Who could have conceived this scenario? Who understood the motivation of both men intimately enough to predict a bloody outcome? To whose taste does this tragedy cater, and how was that taste satisfied if the client was not physically present?"

"Fuck, I don't know."

Grandfather nodded. He understood ignorance. His own curiosity had flickered briefly but it died like a spent match. "You came here with a problem to solve..."

"Right," I said. "Here's the thing. Lada's happy with how this whole scenario worked. She said I outdid myself. She says the client wants to work with her again, maybe on a regular basis. She offered to hire me back full-time and even increase my salary."

"Which is what you'd been hoping for, yes?"

"But suddenly the whole idea makes me a little queasy—I don't know why. So what do you think? Should I re-up, take the money, make a success of myself? Maybe hook up with Lada again, on a personal level I mean, if things go well? Because I could do that. It would be easy. But I keep thinking it'd be even easier to find a place by the docks and live on dole and watch the waves roll in."

Watch the aibots build more hives and nurseries. Watch the population decline.

"I'm far too dead," Grandfather said, "to offer sensible advice. Anyway, it sounds as if you've already decided."

And I realized he was right—I had.

On the way out of the sanctuary where Grandfather was stored I passed a gaggle of utility aibots. They were lined up along the corridor in serried ranks, motionless, and their eyes scanned me as I passed.

And as I approached the exit, the chief custodial aibot—a tall, lanky unit in a black vest and felt hat—stepped into my path. He turned his face down to me and said, "Do you know Sophocles, Mr. Paczovski?"

I was almost too surprised to answer. "Sophocles who?"

"*Ajax*," he said cryptically. "The Chorus. *When Reason's day / Sets rayless—joyless—quenched in cold decay / Better to die, and sleep / The never-waking sleep, than linger on, / And dare to live, when the soul's life is gone.*"

And while I stared, the gathered aibots—the ones with hands, at least—began gently to applaud.

HESPERIA AND GLORY

Ann Leckie

Dear Mr. Stephens,

It is entirely understandable that you should wish a full accounting of the events of the last week of August of this year. If nothing else, your position as Mr. John Atkins' only living relative entitles you to an explanation.

I must begin by making two points perfectly clear. The first is quite simple. The account you have read in the papers, and no doubt also received from the chief of police of this town, is entirely false.

My second point is this: there is not now, nor has there ever been, a well in my cellar.

It is true that ever since my return from the war I have walked with a cane, and stairs are difficult for me. But the house was my great-aunt's, and my parents and I often spent summers here when I was a boy. In those days I marshaled my leaden armies across the packed dirt floor of the cellar, destroying and resurrecting whole battalions by the hour. I know every inch of that cellar floor. I wish to be quite particular about the matter.

Your cousin Mr. Atkins came to my house with Mr.

Edgar Stark. I've known Mr. Stark since college, and he is a frequent visitor at my house. I live a quiet life, and am, I admit, somewhat prone to melancholy. Mr. Stark's lively humor and good spirits are a dependable restorative, and for this and many other reasons I value his friendship. It is not unusual for him to bring a friend or two on his visits, so I was not at all surprised when he arrived in company with another man, whom he introduced as John Atkins, an old school friend of his.

To be entirely honest, I found Atkins unprepossessing. His suit was gray with dust and his collar wilted and dirty. As I shook his hand I could not help but notice his listless grip and slightly petulant expression. All of this I put down to a long drive in the heat, but upon further acquaintance it was clear that the expression, at least, was habitual.

Each morning he spent at my home he was up early, before the heat made his room unbearable. After a quick breakfast of bread and jam and cold coffee he would take his place in the living-room on the couch, stretched out, his feet on the cushions, eyes closed, brow knitted in concentration. He arose only briefly in the afternoon to plug in the electric fan and bring the ice bucket from the dining-room to the couch. After supper he went directly to his room, but he slept poorly, if at all; each night I heard his step overhead, pacing back and forth.

Stark did his best to stir his friend, with no success. Atkins did not like music, either from the piano or the Victrola—the noise distracted him. Books were out of the question, as, he informed us, reading only put other people's ideas into his head. "Well, then, Atkins," I said on the third morning, after another attempt to find something that would entice him off the couch, "what do you like?"

"I like to be left alone," he snapped.

We were only too happy to grant his wish, and went out onto the terrace to sit in a couple of dusty wrought-iron chairs in the shade of an old sycamore. Quite naturally, I asked Mr. Stark for an explanation. He told me that John Atkins was mad. Or rather, that he purported to be mad. He had avoided college, work, enlistment, any sort of responsibility, by pretending insanity. He had deceived various doctors and had spent much of the past year in isolation at the latest doctor's orders. Stark believed Atkins was not truly mad, because the mad did not merely lie about all day. "If you're mad, you should be...mad," he said. The doctor had approved Atkins' departure from the sanatorium and advised that his surroundings for the moment should be peaceful and calm. So naturally Mr. Stark had thought of my house. "I thought you could only be good for him. And he was quite interested in your house, when I described it to him. Particularly the well in your cellar. It's the first time in ages he's shown any sort of interest in anything."

"There's no well in my cellar."

"John and I were good friends at school, before college. Something happened, I don't know."

"There's no well in my cellar," I said again. It disturbed me that he had not seemed to hear what I had said.

"I need another drink," he said, and that was the end of the matter.

You may wonder that I did not take offense at your cousin's behavior. The truth of the matter is, I had seen something like it before. Some doctors called it "funk" and some "neurasthenia." I called it perfectly natural, if you'd been at the front long enough. Atkins had never enlisted, but whatever his problem, I didn't doubt that it was real enough.

That evening, when I heard Atkins' step, I determined to speak with him, so I rose and took my stick, meaning to make my slow way up the stairs. Instead I heard Atkins come down, and walk through the dining room out onto the terrace. I followed him.

The night was cool and cloudless, but not silent. Crickets chirruped, and other night insects shrilled and chorused. All the colors were gone out of the bricks, the grass, the leaves of the trees; everything was shades of black and gray. Atkins was still in his shirtsleeves, and he stood on the grass with his face turned up to the sky. He was there long enough for my leg to grow tired, and I seated myself in one of the chairs and waited.

After a while he turned, and as though he'd known I was there all the time he came and sat in another of the chairs. In the dark his face was shadowed oddly, his glasses dark circles where his eyes should be. "Edgar thinks I'm mad," he said, conversationally, as though he'd offered me a cigarette.

"You're not mad."

"Of course not."

"Have a drink?"

"No," he said, and hooked one of the chairs with his foot and dragged it closer with a shriek of iron against brick. "You can bring me some ice." He put his feet up on the chair.

"All out, old man." Actually the ice man had been just that morning, and I'd taken more than usual, because of my guests. "You'll have to wait until tomorrow."

He made a slight movement that might have been a

shrug. "I'm not like just anyone else," he said after some minutes had passed. "I *matter*."

"Ah," I said.

"Things have gone terribly wrong, and only I can fix them. It's all my brother's fault. My half-brother, really. Asery." The last word was drawn out, filled with hate. "His father led a rebellion against the king of Hesperia—my father, Cthonin VI. He failed, of course. His head rolled down the palace stairs and into the square in the capital, and the body was buried under the steps, so that every day Hesperians would have him underfoot. I'll never understand why his son didn't join him, infant or not."

"And where is Hesperia?" I asked.

"On Mars, of course."

"Of course," I said. "How foolish of me."

He told me then of the antiquity and superiority of Martian civilization, and of Hesperia, which was the greatest of Martian nations. Each Hesperian learned, from his mother's knee and throughout his schooling, the importance of right thinking. "On Mars," he said, "we understand that what one thinks makes the world."

"Do you mean to say that each of us makes our own world with his thoughts?" I'd heard the idea before, usually at two in the morning from young men drunk with a heady mix of champagne and philosophy, and whose lives had yet to run up very hard against reality.

"No, no," said Atkins testily. "Nothing so trivial. There's only one universe. But that universe is formed by thought. If it were left to undisciplined minds, the world would be chaos."

"Your mind is disciplined," I ventured.

"I was bred to it. I am Cthonin Jor, Prince of

Hesperia. Some day I will be Cthonin VII. But first I must defeat Asery."

I asked him then to tell me the tale, and thus he began:

In Hesperia (here I set down his words as best I remember them) the canals run deep and wide, and straight as death. The dirt, thick and heavy and scarlet, makes the water the color of blood. Some canals in less blessed regions have run dry, but in Hesperia green grows thick and lush thirty miles on either side of the broad waterways that criss-cross the land.

The canal called Fortunae does not run through Hesperia proper, but it is important nonetheless. It runs northward from the southern ice to a series of falls that cascade down into the Lake of the Sun, which is nearly a sea, wide and shallow. In unimaginably ancient times it was believed that on the day of creation the sun itself rose from that lake. It was the site of a tremendous temple complex, nearly all of which has disappeared without a trace after so many thousands of years. But one part of the temple still stands: the Wheel of Heaven, six hundred sixty-nine chambers, each built side to side in a great circle under the lake. The ring turns by the width of a chamber each day, and there being only one entrance a single room is accessible each day, and that same room, once its day has passed, cannot be entered again until the six hundred and sixty-nine days, which is the length of the Martian year, pass once more. The entrance is reached through a cave behind the falls.

The Fortunae comes out again at the western shore, at a headland called the Cape of Dawn. On this head-land is one of the many pumping stations that send the water of the Fortunae on to where it meets the canals of

Hesperia proper, in mountains to the west. Near the station is a town, and this is the administrative center of the province, which is, of course, governed by Hesperia.

It was there that I had been sent by my father, and there that my brother Asery came to me nearly a year ago as I sat in my chair on the steps of the governor's palace, my counselors beside me. Before me was a great plaza, paved with the local brown stone in various shades, depicting a coiled serpent surrounded by a border of alternating jasper and copper in which the artist had cunningly concealed the drainage grates so necessary for a large, flat surface near so much water. Across the plaza, to the north, was the canal come again out of the lake. On the east was the lake itself, and to the west a barracks, and the town beyond. The air there is always filled with the sound of rushing water, and the rumble of the great pumping station.

Some of my soldiers were playing a ball game in the square in front of us, and I was proposing a wager on the outcome with my vice-governor when the voice of the crier interrupted us and Asery came before me. He is a tall man, nearly as tall as I am, with dark hair and gray eyes inherited from his father, and he carries himself with the same arrogance. On this day he was dressed in plain garments, covered with red-brown dust, as though he were some homeless wanderer just come off the road, not a gentleman seeking audience with the governor of the province, and a prince.

"Welcome brother," I said. "Please sit with us."

"I will not sit," he said.

This sort of disrespect was like Asery, but I am a patient man. "Couldn't you even bathe between here and…wherever it is you've come from? Our mother would be shocked to see you."

"Our mother is not easily shocked," he answered. "After all, she bore you without any noticeable display of shame."

My counselors, who had been whispering among themselves, fell silent. Even the ballplayers stopped, and the ball bounced away and then rolled to the edge of the plaza, stopping and spinning on a grate. They moved together, closer to where I sat, and where my brother stood before me. Asery did not move, nor did he look behind him where they gathered.

"I hope you've not been thinking of taking up your father's ambitions," I said.

"I have not come to take up any ambition. I only wish to speak with you."

"You've made a bad start of it," I told him. "But then, your family's arrogance is famous."

"The contrast with the habitual modesty and diffidence of the house of Jor is marked," he said, with the slightest of bows. "I stand reprimanded.

That was better. "What can I do for you?"

"You can restore the Fortunae to its original course." Now, this had been the pretext for his father's rebellion. At one time another canal had flowed north from the upper shore of the lake, and from there into Tharsis. "A hundred years ago Hesperia annexed this province and turned its waters westward. Now the lakes and rivers of Tharsis are dry, and its fields are desert."

"Nothing stops them from building another canal. Or buying the water they require. Isn't Tharsis famous for its silver mines? Aren't their artisans the most marvelous workers of metal on Mars?"

He exhaled sharply, derisively. I couldn't read the expression in his gray eyes. "I wish I could make you see what Mars is really like, away from the canals, away from your palace."

I realized then what he had come to do. I stood and signaled the soldiers, and with a cry Asery pulled a sword from under his dusty shirt and sprang forward. I stood to face him and drew my dagger.

Our blades met, and over his shoulder I saw the soldiers turn as the grates around the court lifted and fell clanging to the stones, and up out of the drains came men in dusty red-brown, swords raised. In a moment they had ringed the plaza, even in front of where I stood on the palace steps.

Asery was a wily and treacherous swordsman, and I had to fight with all my attention. I did not have time to look over the plaza, or think of my counselors who had been next to me, but it was evident that the soldiers from the barracks had joined us, because from time to time I heard their voices raised in the battle cry of Hesperia: *For Hesperia, and glory!* And though he had a sword and I had only my dagger, we fought until each of us was exhausted, and I, anticipating his feint, disarmed him and sent his sword spinning across the stones of the plaza.

It was then that I looked up from the fight and saw that the battle was lost. My own soldiers lay dead or bound, and my vice-governor was held by two rebels.

I turned and ran up the palace steps.

Atkins paused, and before he could continue I asked why he had not merely thought Asery dead on the spot? Or willed his enemies' swords to turn into flowers?

"You don't believe me," he accused.

"On the contrary. I'm just trying to understand."

For a few moments the only sound was the night insects, and the soft sighing of a breeze in the tree leaves. "They would never have believed that their swords would suddenly turn to flowers."

"So they all have to believe?"

"Not all," he said. "Just most. If someone more powerful has some other vision, or if everyone around you remains unconvinced, your efforts will come to nothing. You see how important it is, the right kind of thinking." He sat up straight, and brought his feet down off the chair in front of him. "You see how malicious it was, for Asery to suggest that Tharsis was badly off."

I allowed that I did.

"The discipline is not only in bringing one's will to bear, but in keeping in mind the proper order of things."

I had no reply, and in a moment Atkins continued his story.

I fled through the palace to the stables (he said), where I mounted a raptodont, a stallion with splendid black feathers. These are nothing like your Earth horses. They are two-legged, nearly six feet from clawed foot to powerful shoulder, and nearly twice that from dagger-toothed snout to the tip of the long, muscular tail.

I rode away from the palace, safely past the town and away into the countryside. I might have followed the canal west, but I would be too easily caught. The lake lay to the east, and north was Tharsis—I could expect no help there. South then.

The southern Fortunae was too obvious a route, so I

rode southwest through the gentle grasslands that surround the Lake of the Sun, an ocean of green starred here and there with flowers of pink, blue, and yellow. After an hour or so the grass gave way to a desolate, rolling landscape of blue-gray moss, rocks showing through like bones, and I turned south and rode with the wind at my back.

As I rode I tried to think of some way to defeat Asery. I could work towards small things that would, in the end, lead to his undoing, but what? And as I thought, another idea came to me. What if I did not work with the future, but the past? What if I brought my will to bear in a time before anyone could believe or disbelieve in his existence? Was it even possible? I had never heard of anyone doing such a thing before, but the idea pleased me so well I began straightaway. Let Asery's father never have conceived him! And his father and his father, for good measure, all the way back to the founder of the line. To this end I bent my will.

Eventually I turned southeast, into grassland again, and soon after reached the shores of the canal. The wind out of the north had increased, and now blew cold and hard, whipping and flattening the grass and chilling me, but just over the next rise I knew I would see the bulk of a pumping station and beside it the white walls of the barracks. I urged my mount faster up the incline.

And then pulled hard on the reins, coming to a sliding halt that nearly overset me. Ahead was no station. The wind-tossed grass and the waters of the canal simply ended, as though by the stroke of a sword. Beyond was a desert of dry dirt and rocks, where the wind threw up red-brown clouds and whirlwinds. Behind me was grass, water, and blue sky. Ahead was lifeless rock, and a sky turned red with dust. As I watched, a foot of green crumbled into dirt and blew away—the line was advancing!

Did Asery have so much power, and was this, then, his goal? Not merely the overthrow of the royal house of Hesperia, but the destruction of all life on Mars?

At the speed that line of destruction was advancing, I could not possibly reach Hesperia in time to find help. My campaign to erase Asery from the history of Mars had clearly not succeeded. My only hope—Mars' only hope—was to kill him outright, no matter how difficult that might prove. I turned my exhausted mount and rode north.

I rode all that evening and into the moonless night, the jeweled stars thick overhead, until nearly within sound of the great falls my mount collapsed in midstride and fell dead on the grass. I left it where it had fallen, and ran on.

When I could see the glint of starlight on the lake, and the falls were a constant thunder, I stopped and knelt in the tall grass for a brief rest, and to take stock. This saved my life; no sooner had I sunk down than I heard the faint sound of voices. As I knelt, hardly daring to breathe, the voices came closer.

"That's the last of you. Keep a close watch! It's worth our lives if we let him escape."

I did not recognize the voice, or the next one. "Are we so sure he's nearby?"

"We found his mount not far from here, dead but still warm. You know your orders."

"Kill him on sight." Two voices together.

Here was a dreadful pass! Crouched down in the grass, mere yards from my enemies, who had just expressed their determination to kill me. I could not stay where I was for long—the rising sun, or the most cursory search, would reveal me. On the other hand, the third man seemed to be leaving, perhaps to report to Asery himself! If I could follow him unseen...

I lay belly-down and crept forward, hoping that until I was past the sentries any movement of the grass would be attributed to the rising wind. I quickly lost any sound of the officer, but at least I knew what direction to take, and was, I judged, going to pass the two sentries safely.

But at the last moment my luck deserted me. With a thud an arrow buried itself into the ground inches from my shoulder. I immediately pushed myself upright and ran, and another arrow hissed past me. Stealth was impossible now. My best hope was to escape into the caves of the falls.

The shouts of my pursuers behind me, their arrows flying to the left and right of me, I gained the path that leads to the largest of the caverns. It is narrow, and the water-covered stones are cold and slick, and I had to slow somewhat to avoid slipping and tumbling to the water-pounded rocks below. Still, I heard Asery's men behind me, and I did not dare to stop and see if it were only the first two or if others had joined them. I plunged ahead, and finally into the entrance of the Wheel of Heaven.

No Earth monument can be as grand as the ancient ruins of Mars! The cavern entrance is plain at first, but as you go deeper the ceiling rises and is lost in darkness, though the lights that in those far-off days lit the hall still light it now. The walls of black stone narrow to a corridor, on the walls of which are ancient figures of men and beasts in bas-relief, men that are long dead and turned to dust, beasts the like of which Mars has not seen in ten thousand years. In the eerie gleam of the ancient lights the figures seem to be on the verge of movement or speech. Near the entrance to the Wheel is a shadowed side-path, a turning that leads into a maze of tunnels that honeycomb the bluff. If I could gain that I would be safe.

The corridor ended in a broad step of rough black stone, smoothed at its center, where so many feet have trod. In the wall at the back of the step was a doorway, a rectangular hole with no frame, and darkness within. Black stone blocked a third of the doorway, and as I watched the stone slipped forward just the smallest amount. I must have ridden longer into the night than I had realized, and it was nearly dawn, and the day's chamber passing on.

I knew the path I sought was along the wall to my left, but as I turned to search for it, my pursuers came into view, nearly a dozen armed men. I was out of time! Quickly I made for the black step. "Stop him!" cried a voice, and arrows rained down, but I was through the inexorably closing door. Captive in the Wheel of Heaven for a year, but safe from Asery meanwhile.

"The year is nearly past," Atkins said. "When the chamber opens again I will return."

"And where will you find this chamber?" I asked. "We're nowhere near Mars."

"The well in your cellar is the opening," he said.

"There is no well in my cellar."

He made that almost-shrug again. "You aren't enough to trouble me, and no one else has been down there for years."

"Are you certain?"

He laughed, and said nothing else, and so I bade him good night and left him sitting on the terrace. I went into the kitchen, meaning to make myself a drink, but when I opened the ice-box I found that the ice I'd bought that day wasn't there.

The events of the next day are quickly and easily told. This part of the official account is accurate: that morning I saw Atkins go down to the cellar, the only entrance to which is by steps leading down from the kitchen. I heard a terrible scream, as did Mr. Stark, who came running from the living-room. He was down the steps before me, and moments later I heard him shout, "Help! John has fallen into the well!"

The police came, and several of the neighbors, and all were in the cellar for some time, and when they came up I was told that they had been unable to retrieve Mr. Atkins' body from the well. I was assured that his death was unquestionably accidental, and that I should not feel in any way responsible. When they had left, I made my way down the steps, to find only the packed dirt floor of the cellar covered over with a layer of dry, red-brown dust.

I swear to you that I am sane, and that every word I have set down here is true. Of course, it is impossible that your cousin was indeed a fugitive prince of Mars— John Atkins was born here on Earth, and Mr. Stark had known him since boyhood. But it is also certain that he went down into my cellar and disappeared without a trace. How am I to understand these events? I have pondered the question at some length, and have reached certain conclusions.

Who among us does not yearn for some noble purpose? Who would not wish to take the part of the prince and the hero, in an ancient and romantic world where men war openly and honorably with sword and bow? And who can blame John Atkins if, discovering a way to make this desire a reality, he threw aside all else

in life but this one aim? Who would grudge him
Hesperia, if he could attain it?

I say plainly—I would. And I do.

Let a million readers of dime-novels lose themselves
between the pages of their books, and let them rise
refreshed and ennobled by what they find. But let that
dream become a reality—how many Princes of
Hesperia can there be? There is only room in the story
for one. What of the rest of us? And if such a thing is
possible, what of Earth? Who might re-shape our world
with his imagining, and to what ends?

This is what I think happened: John Atkins did suc-
ceed in opening a door to Mars. But the Mars he found
was not the Mars he imagined. Reality delivered the
ultimate rebuke to his tampering, and at the last
showed him not the waters of the Lake of the Sun and
the verdant grasslands surrounding it, but the dry and
lifeless Mars that would assert itself even as he tried to
banish it with his fantasy. So I interpret his story. So I
must believe, for the safety of my own world.

I am not a prince, or a noble anything. I can only do
my small part. I've swept the dust from the cellar floor,
and disposed of it. One of my neighbors has brought a
chair down for me, and here I sit. Mr. Stark has gone,
and I've had no visitors for some time, except the
doctor, who is clearly concerned. And I can't explain
myself—how could I, without sounding completely
mad? I am as sane as anyone, perhaps saner than most.
I align myself with the real. I am witness to the truth.

There is not now, nor has there ever been, a well in
my cellar.

INCARNATION DAY

Walter Jon Williams

It's your understanding and wisdom that makes me
want to talk to you, Doctor Sam. About how Fritz met
the Blue Lady, and what happened with Janis, and
why her mother decided to kill her, and what became
of all that. I need to get it sorted out, and for that I
need a real friend. Which is you.

Janis is always making fun of me because I talk to an
imaginary person. She makes even more fun of me
because my imaginary friend is an English guy who died
hundreds of years ago.

"You're wrong," I pointed out to her, "Doctor
Samuel Johnson was a real person, so he's not imaginary. It's just my *conversations* with him that are imaginary."

I don't think Janis understands the distinction I'm
trying to make.

But I know that *you* understand, Doctor Sam.
You've understood me ever since we met in that Age of
Reason class, and I realized that you not only said and
did things that made you immortal, but that you said
and did them while you were hanging around in taverns
with actors and poets.

Which is about the perfect life, if you ask me.

In my opinion Janis could do with a Doctor Sam to

talk to. She might be a lot less frustrated as an individual.

I mean, when I am totally stressed trying to comprehend the equations for electron paramagnetic resonance or something, so I just can't stand cramming another ounce of knowledge into my brain, I can always imagine my doctor Sam—a big fat man (though I think the word they used back then was "corpulent")—a fat man with a silly wig on his head, who makes a magnificent gesture with one hand and says, with perfect wisdom and gravity, *All intellectual improvement, Miss Alison, arises from leisure.*

Who could put it better than that? Who else could be as sensible and wise? Who could understand me as well?

Certainly nobody *I* know.

(And have I mentioned how much I like the way you call me *Miss Alison*?)

We might as well begin with Fahd's Incarnation Day on Titan. It was the first incarnation among the Cadre of Glorious Destiny, so of course we were all present.

The celebration had been carefully planned to showcase the delights of Saturn's largest moon. First we were to be downloaded onto *Cassini Ranger,* the ship parked in Saturn orbit to service all the settlements on the various moons. Then we would be packed into individual descent pods and dropped into Titan's thick atmosphere. We'd be able to stunt through the air, dodging in and out of methane clouds as we chased each other across Titan's cloudy, photochemical sky. After that would be skiing on the Tomasko glacier, Fahd's dinner, and then skating on frozen methane ice.

We would all be wearing bodies suitable for Titan's low gravity and high-pressure atmosphere—sturdy, low to the ground, and furry, with six legs and a domelike head stuck onto the front between a pair of arms.

But my body would be one borrowed for the occasion, a body the resort kept for tourists. For Fahd it would be different. He would spent the next five or six years in orbit around Saturn, after which he would have the opportunity to move on to something else.

The six-legged body he inhabited would be his own, his first. He would be incarnated—a legal adult, and legally human despite his six legs and furry body. He would have his own money and possessions, a job, and a full set of human rights.

Unlike the rest of us.

After the dinner, where Fahd would be formally invested with adulthood and his citizenship, we would all go out for skating on the methane lake below the glacier. Then we'd be uploaded and head for home.

All of us but Fahd, who would begin his new life. The Cadre of Glorious Destiny would have given its first member to interplanetary civilization.

I envied Fahd his incarnation—his furry six-legged body, his independence, and even his job, which wasn't all that stellar if you ask me. After fourteen years of being a bunch of electrons buzzing around in a quantum matrix, I wanted a real life even if it meant having twelve dozen legs.

I suppose I should explain, because you were born in an era when electricity came from kites, that at the time of Fahd's Incarnation Day party I was not exactly a human being. Not legally, and especially not physically.

Back in the old days—back when people were establishing the first settlements beyond Mars, in the asteroid belt and on the moons of Jupiter and then Saturn—resources were scarce. Basics such as water and air had to be shipped in from other places, and that was very expensive. And of course the environment was extremely hazardous—the death rate in those early years was phenomenal.

It's lucky that people are basically stupid, otherwise no one would have gone.

Yet the settlements had to grow. They had to achieve self-sufficiency from the home worlds of Earth and Luna and Mars, which sooner or later were going to get tired of shipping resources to them, not to mention shipping replacements for all the people who died in stupid accidents. And a part of independence involved establishing growing, or at least stable, populations, and that meant having children.

But children suck up a lot of resources, which like I said were scarce. So the early settlers had to make do with virtual children.

It was probably hard in the beginning. If you were a parent you had to put on a headset and gloves and a body suit in order to cuddle your infant, whose objective existence consisted of about a skazillion lines of computer code anyway...well, let's just say you had to want that kid *really badly*.

Especially since you couldn't touch him in the flesh till he was grown up, when he would be downloaded into a body grown in a vat just for him. The theory being that there was no point in having anyone on your settlement who couldn't contribute to the economy and help pay for those scarce resources, so you'd only incarnate your offspring when he was already grown up and could get a job and help to pay for all that oxygen.

You might figure from this that it was a hard life, out there on the frontier.

Now it's a lot easier. People can move in and out of

virtual worlds with nothing more than a click of a mental switch. You get detailed sensory input through various nanoscale computers implanted in your brain, so you don't have to put on oven mitts to feel your kid. You can dandle your offspring, and play with him, and teach him to talk, and feed him even. Life in the virtual realms claims to be 100% realistic, though in my opinion it's more like 95%, and only in the realms that *intend* to mimic reality, since some of them don't.

Certain elements of reality were left out, and there are advantages—at least if you're a parent. No drool, no messy diapers, no vomit. When the child trips and falls down, he'll feel pain—you *do* want to teach him not to fall down, or to bang his head on things—but on the other hand there won't be any concussions or broken bones. There won't be any fatal accidents involving fuel spills or vacuum.

There are other accidents that the parents have made certain we won't have to deal with. Accidental pregnancy, accidental drunkenness, accidental drug use.

Accidental gambling. Accidental vandalism. Accidental suicide. Accidentally acquiring someone else's property. Accidentally stealing someone's extra-vehicular unit and going for a joy ride among the asteroids.

Accidentally having fun. Because believe me, the way the adults arrange it here, all the fun is *planned ahead of time*.

Yep, Doctor Sam, life is pretty good if you're a grownup. Your kids are healthy and smart and extremely well educated. They live in a safe, organized world filled with exciting educational opportunities, healthy team sports, family entertainment, and games that reward group effort, cooperation, and good citizenship.

It all makes me want to puke. If I *could* puke, that is, because I can't. (Did I mention there was no accidental bulemia, either?)

Thy body is all vice, Miss Alison, and thy mind all virtue.

Exactly, Doctor Sam. And it's the vice I'm hoping to find out about. Once I get a body, that is.

We knew that we weren't going to enjoy much vice on Fahd's Incarnation Day, but still everyone in the Cadre of Glorious Destiny was excited, and maybe a little jealous, about his finally getting to be an adult, and incarnating into the real world and having some real world fun for a change. Never mind that he'd got stuck in a dismal job as an electrical engineer on a frozen moon.

All jobs are pretty dismal from what I can tell, so he isn't any worse off than anyone else really.

For days before the party I had been sort of avoiding Fritz. Since we're electronic we can avoid each other easily, simply by not letting yourself be visible to the other person, and not answering any queries he sends to you, but I didn't want to be rude.

Fritz was cadre, after all.

So I tried to make sure I was too busy to deal with Fritz—too busy at school, or with my job for Dane, or working with one of the other cadre members on a project. But a few hours before our departure for Titan, when I was in a conference room with Bartolomeo and Parminder working on an assignment for our Artificial Intelligence class, Fritz knocked on our door, and Bartolomeo granted him access before Parminder and I could signal him not to.

So in comes Fritz. Since we're electronic we can appear to one another as whatever we like, for instance

Mary Queen of Scots or a bunch of snowflakes or even *you*, Doctor Sam. We all experiment with what we look like. Right now I mostly use an avatar of a sort-of Picasso woman—he used to distort people in his paintings so that you had a kind of 360-degree view of them, or parts of them, and I think that's kind of interesting, because my whole aspect changes depending on what angle of me you're viewing.

For an avatar Fritz's used the image of a second-rate action star named Norman Isfahan. Who looks okay, at least if you can forget his lame videos, except that Fritz added an individual touch in the form of a balloon-shaped red hat. Which he thought made him look cool, but which only seemed ludicrous and a little sad.

Fritz stared at me for a moment, with a big goofy grin on his face, and Parminder sends me a little private electronic note of sympathy. In the last few months Fritz has become my pet, and he followed me around whenever he gets the chance. Sometimes he'd be with me for hours without saying a word, sometimes he'd talk the entire time and not let me get a single word in.

I did my best with him, but I had a life to lead, too. And friends. And family. And I didn't want this person with me every minute, because even though I was sorry for him he was also very frustrating to be around.

Friendship is not always the sequel of obligation.

Alas, Doctor J., too true.

Fritz was the one member of our cadre who came out, well, wrong. They build us—us software—by reasoning backwards from reality, from our parents' DNA. They find a good mix of our parents' genes, and that implies certain things about *us*, and the sociologists get their say about what sort of person might be needful in the next generation, and everything's thrown together by a really smart artificial intelligence, and in the end you get a virtual child.

But sometimes despite all the intelligence of everyone and everything involved, mistakes are made. Fritz was one of these. He wasn't stupid exactly—he was as smart as anyone—but his mental reflexes just weren't in the right plane. When he was very young he would spend hours without talking or interacting with any of us. Fritz's parents, Jack and Hans, were both software engineers, and they were convinced the problem was fixable. So they complained and they or the AIs or somebody came up with a software patch, one that was supposed to fix his problem—and suddenly Fritz was active and angry, and he'd get into fights with people and sometimes he'd just scream for no reason at all and go on screaming for hours.

So Hans and Jack went to work with the code again, and there was a new software patch, and now Fritz was stealing things, except you can't really steal anything in sims, because the owner can find any virtual object just by sending it a little electronic ping.

That ended with Fritz getting fixed yet *again*, and this went on for years. So while it was true that none of us were exactly a person, Fritz was less a person than any of us.

We all did our best to help. We were cadre, after all, and cadres look after their own. But there was a limit to what any of us could do. We heard about unanticipated feedback loops and subsystem crashes and weird quantum transfers leading to fugue states. I think that the experts had no real idea what was going on. Neither did we.

There was a lot of question as to what would happen when Fritz incarnated. If his problems were all software glitches, would they disappear once he was meat and no longer software? Or would they short-circuit his brain?

A check on the histories of those with similar problems did not produce encouraging answers to these questions.

And then Fritz became *my* problem because he got really attached to me, and he followed me around.

"Hi, Alison," he said.

"Hi, Fritz."

I tried to look very busy with what I was doing, which is difficult to do if you're being Picasso Woman and rather abstract-looking to begin with.

"We're going to Titan in a little while," Fritz said.

"Uh-huh," I said.

"Would you like to play the shadowing game with me?" he asked.

Right then I was glad I was Picasso Woman and not incarnated, because I knew that if I had a real body I'd be blushing.

"Sure," I said. "If our capsules are anywhere near each other when we hit the atmosphere. We might be separated, though."

"I've been practicing in the simulations," Fritz said. "And I'm getting pretty good at the shadowing game."

"Fritz," Parminder said. "We're working on our AI project now, okay? Can we talk to you later, on Titan?"

"Sure."

And I sent a note of gratitude to Parminder, who was in on the scheme with me and Janis, and who knew that Fritz couldn't be a part of it.

Shortly thereafter my electronic being was transmitted from Ceres by high-powered communications lasers and downloaded into an actual body, even if it was a body that had six legs and that didn't belong to me. The body was already in its vacuum suit, which was packed into the descent capsule—I mean nobody wanted us floating around in the *Cassini Ranger* in zero gravity in bodies we weren't used to—so there wasn't a lot I could do for entertainment.

Which was fine. It was the first time I'd been in a body, and I was absorbed in trying to work out all the little differences between reality and the sims I'd grown up in.

In reality, I thought, things seem a little quieter. In simulations there are always things competing for your attention, but right now there was nothing to do but listen to myself breathe.

And then there was a bang and a big shove, easily absorbed by foam padding, and I was launched into space, aimed at the orange ball that was Titan, and behind it the giant pale sphere of Saturn.

The view was sort of disappointing. Normally you see Saturn as an image with the colors electronically altered so as to heighten the subtle differences in detail. The reality of Saturn was more of a pasty blob, with faint brown stripes and a little red jagged scrawl of a storm in the southern hemisphere.

Unfortunately I couldn't get a very good view of the rings, because they were edge-on, like a straight silver knife-slash right across a painted canvas.

Besides Titan I could see at least a couple dozen moons. I could recognize Dione and Rhea, and Enceladus because it was so bright. Iapetus was obvious because it was half light and half dark. There were a lot of tiny lights that could have been Atlas or Pan or Prometheus or Pandora or maybe a score of others.

I didn't have enough time to puzzle out the identity of the other moons, because Titan kept getting bigger and bigger. It was a dull orange color, except on the very edge where the haze scatters blue light. Other than that arc of blue, Titan is orange the same way Mars is red, which is to say that it's orange all the way down, and when you get to the bottom there's still more orange.

It seemed like a pretty boring place for Fahd to spend his first years of adulthood.

I realized that if I were doing this trip in a sim, I'd fast-forward through this part. It would be just my luck if all reality turned out to be this dull.

Things livened up in a hurry when the capsule hit the atmosphere. There was a lot of noise, and the capsule rattled and jounced, and bright flames of ionizing radiation shot up past the view port. I could feel my heart speeding up, and my breath going fast. It was *my* body that was being bounced around, with *my* nerve impulses running along *my* spine. *This* was much more interesting. *This* was the difference between reality and a sim, even though I couldn't explain exactly what the difference was.

It is the distinction, Miss Alison, between the undomesticated awe which one might feel at the sight of a noble wild prospect discovered in nature; and that which is produced by a vain tragedian on the stage, puffing and blowing in a transport of dismal fury as he tries to describe the same vision.

Thank you, Doctor Sam.

We that live to please must please to live.

I could see nothing but fire for a while, and then there was a jolt and a *CrashBang* as the braking chute deployed, and I was left swaying frantically in the sudden silence, my heart beating fast as high-atmosphere winds fought for possession of the capsule. Far above I could just see the ionized streaks of some of the other cadre members heading my way.

It was then, after all I could see was the orange fog, that I remembered that I'd been so overwhelmed by the awe of what I'd been seeing that I forgot to *observe*. So I began to kick myself over that.

It isn't enough to stare when you want to be a visual artist, which is what I want more than anything. A noble wild prospect (as you'd call it, Doctor Sam) isn't simply a gorgeous scene, it's also a series of technical problems. Ratios, colors, textures. Media. Ideas. Frames. *Decisions*. I hadn't thought about any of that when I had the chance, and now it was too late.

I decided to start paying better attention, but there was nothing happening outside but acetylene sleet cooking off the hot exterior of the capsule. I checked my tracking display and my onboard map of Titan's surface. So I was prepared when a private message came from Janis.

"Alison. You ready to roll?"

"Sure. You bet."

"This is going to be *brilliant*."

I hoped so. But somewhere in my mind I kept hearing Doctor Sam's voice:

Remember that all tricks are either knavish or childish.

The trick I played on Fritz was both.

I had been doing some outside work for Dane, who was a communications tech, because outside work paid in real money, not the Citizenship Points we get paid in the sims. And Dane let me do some of the work on Fahd's Incarnation Day, so I was able to arrange which capsules everyone was going to be put into.

I put Fritz into the last capsule to be fired at Titan.

And those of us involved in Janis' scheme—Janis, Parminder, Andy, and I—were fired first.

This basically meant that we were going to be on Titan five or six minutes ahead of Fritz, which meant it was unlikely that he'd be able to catch up to us. He would be someone else's problem for a while.

I promised myself that I'd be extra nice to him later, but it didn't stop me from feeling knavish and childish.

After we crashed into Titan's atmosphere, and after a certain amount of spinning and swaying we came to a break in the cloud, and I could finally look down at Titan's broken surface. Stark mountains, drifts of methane snow, shiny orange ethane lakes, the occasional crater. In the far distance, in the valley between a pair of lumpy mountains, was the smooth toboggan slide of the Tomasko Glacier. And over to one side, on a plateau, were the blinking lights that marked our landing area.

And directly below was an ethane cloud, into which the capsule soon vanished. It was there that the chute let go, and there was a stomach-lurching drop before the airfoils deployed. I was not used to having my stomach lurch—recall if you will my earlier remarks on puking—so it was a few seconds before I was able to recover and take control of what was now a large and agile glider.

No, I hadn't piloted a glider before. But I'd spent the last several weeks working with simulations, and the technology was fail-safed anyway. Both I and the onboard computer would have to screw up royally before I could damage myself or anyone else. I took command of the pod and headed for Janis' secret rendezvous.

There are various sorts of games you can play with

the pods as they're dropping through the atmosphere. You can stack your airfoils in appealing and intricate formations. (I think this one's really stupid if you're trying to do it in the middle of thick clouds.) There's the game called "shadowing," the one that Fritz wanted to play with me, where you try to get right on top of another pod, above the airfoils where they can't see you, and you have to match every maneuver of the pod that's below you, which is both trying to evade you and to maneuver so as to get above you. There are races, where you try to reach some theoretical point in the sky ahead of the other person. And there's just swooping and dashing around the sky, which is probably as fun as anything.

But Janis had other plans. And Parminder and Andy and I, who were Janis' usual companions in her adventures, had elected to be a part of her scheme, as was our wont. (Do you like my use of the word "wont," Doctor Sam?) And a couple other members of the cadre, Mei and Bartolomeo, joined our group without knowing our secret purpose.

We disguised our plan as a game of shadowing, which I turned out to be very good at. It's not simply a game of flying, it's a game of spacial relationships, and that's what visual artists have to be good at understanding. I spent more time on top of one or more of the players than anyone else.

Though perhaps the others weren't concentrating on the game. Because although we were performing the intricate spiraling maneuvers of shadowing as a part of our cover, we were also paying very close attention to the way the winds were blowing at different altitudes—we had cloud-penetrating lasers for that, in addition a constant meteorological data from the ground—and we were using available winds as well as our maneuvers to slowly edge away from our assigned landing field, and toward our destined target.

I kept expecting to hear from Fritz, wanting to join our game. But I didn't. I supposed he had found his fun somewhere else.

All the while we were stunting around Janis was sending us course and altitude corrections, and thanks to her navigation we caught the edge of a low pressure area that boosted us toward our objective at nearly two hundred kilometers per hour. It was then that Mei swung her capsule around and began a descent toward the landing field.

"I just got the warning that we're on the edge of our flight zone," she reported.

"Roger," I said.

"Yeah," said Janis. "We know."

Mei swooped away, followed by Bartolomeo. The rest of us continued soaring along in the furious wind. We made little pretense by this point that we were still playing shadow, but instead tried for distance.

Ground Control on the landing area took longer to try to contact us than we'd expected.

"Capsules six, twenty-one, thirty," said a ground controller. She had one of those smooth, controlled voices that people use when trying to coax small children away from the candy and toward the spinach.

"You have exceeded the safe range from the landing zone. Turn at once to follow the landing beacon."

I waited for Janis to answer.

"It's easier to reach Tomasko from where we are," she said. "We'll just head for the glacier and meet the rest of you there."

"The flight plan prescribes a landing on Lake

Southwood," the voice said. "Please lock on the landing beacon at once and engage your autopilots."

Janis' voice rose with impatience. "Check the flight plan I'm sending you! It's easier and quicker to reach Tomasko! We've got a wind shoving us along at a hundred eighty clicks!"

There was another two or three minutes of silence. When the voice came back, it was grudging.

"Permission granted to change flight plan."

I sagged with relief in my vac suit, because now I was spared a moral crisis. We had all sworn that we'd follow Janis' flight plan whether or not we got permission from Ground Control, but that didn't necessarily meant that we would have. Janis would have gone, of course, but I for one might have had second thoughts. I would have had an excuse if Fritz had been along, because I could have taken him to the assigned landing field—we didn't want him with us, because he might not have been able to handle the landing if it wasn't on an absolutely flat area.

I'd like to think I would have followed Janis, though. It isn't as if I hadn't before.

And honestly, that was about it. If this had been one of the adult-approved video dramas we grew up watching, something would have gone terribly wrong and there would have been a horrible crash. Parminder would have died, and Andy and I would have been trapped in a crevasse or buried under tons of methane ice, and Janis would have had to go to incredible, heroic efforts in order to rescue us. At the end Janis would have Learned an Important Life Lesson, about how following the Guidance of our Wise, Experienced Elders is preferable to staging wild, disobedient stunts.

By comparison what actually happened was fairly

uneventful. We let the front push us along till we were nearly at the glacier, and then we dove down into calmer weather. We spiraled to a soft landing in clean snow at the top of Tomasko Glader. The airfoils neatly folded themselves, atmospheric pressure inside the capsules equalized with that of the moon, and the hatches opened so we could walk in our vac suits onto the top of Titan.

I was flushed with joy. I had never set an actual foot on an actual world before, and as I bounded in sheer delight through the snow I rejoiced in all the little details I felt all around me.

The crunch of the frozen methane under my boots. The way the wind picked up long streamers of snow that made little spattering noises when they hit my windscreen. The suit heaters that failed to heat my body evenly, so that some parts were cool and others uncomfortably warm.

None of it had the immediacy of the simulations, but I didn't remember this level of detail either. Even the polyamide scent of the suit seals was sharper than the generic stuffy suit smell they put in the sim.

This was all real, and it was wonderful, and even if my body was borrowed I was already having the best time I'd ever had in my life.

I scuttled over to Janis on my six legs and crashed into her with affectionate joy. (Hugging wasn't easy with the vac suits on.) Then Parminder ran over and crashed into her from the other side.

"We're finally out of Plato's Cave!" she said, which is the sort of obscure reference you always get out of Parminder. (I looked it up, though, and she had a good point.)

The outfitters at the top of the glacier hadn't been

expecting us for some time, so we had some free time to indulge in a snowball fight. I suppose snowball fights aren't that exciting if you're wearing full-body pressure suits, but this was the first real snowball fight any of us had ever had, so it was fun on that account anyway.

By the time we got our skis on, the shuttle holding the rest of the cadre and their pods was just arriving. We could see them looking at us from the yellow windows of the shuttle, and we just gave them a wave and zoomed off down the glacier, along with a grownup who decided to accompany us in case we tried anything else that wasn't in the regulation playbook.

Skiing isn't a terribly hazardous sport if you've got six legs on a body slung low to the ground. The skis are short, not much longer than skates, so they don't get tangled; and it's really hard to fall over—the worst that happens is that you go into a spin that might take some time to get out of. And we'd all been practicing on the simulators and nothing bad happened.

The most interesting part was the jumps that had been molded at intervals onto the glacier. Titan's low gravity meant that when you went off a jump, you went very high and you stayed in the air for a long time. And Titan's heavy atmosphere meant that if you spread your limbs apart like a skydiver, you could catch enough of that thick air almost to hover, particularly if the wind was cooperating and blowing uphill. That was wild and thrilling, hanging in the air with the wind whistling around the joints of your suit, the glossy orange snow coming up to meet you, and the sound of your own joyful whoops echoing in your ears.

I am a great friend to public amusements, because they keep people from vice.

Well. Maybe. We'll see.

The best part of the skiing was that this time I didn't get so carried away that I'd forgot to *observe*. I thought about ways to render the dull orange sheen of the glacier, the wild scrawls made in the snow by six skis spinning out of control beneath a single squat body, the little crusty waves on the surface generated by the constant wind.

Neither the glacier nor the lake is always solid. Sometimes Titan generates a warm front that liquifies the topmost layer of the glacier, and the liquid methane pours down the mountain to form the lake. When that happens, the modular resort breaks apart and creeps away on its treads. But sooner or later everything freezes over again, and the resort returns.

We were able to ski through a broad orange glassy chute right onto the lake, and from there we could see the lights of the resort in the distance. We skied into a big ballooning pressurized hangar made out of some kind of durable fabric, where the crew removed our pressure suits and gave us little felt booties to wear. I'd had an exhilarating time, but hours had passed and I was tired. The Incarnation Day banquet was just what I needed.

Babbling and laughing, we clustered around the snack tables, tasting a good many things I'd never got in a simulation. (They make us eat in the sims, to get us used to the idea so we don't accidentally starve ourselves once we're incarnated, and to teach us table manners, but the tastes tend to be a bit monotonous.)

"Great stuff!" Janis said, gobbling some kind of crunchy vat-grown treat that I'd sampled earlier and found disgusting. She held the bowl out to the rest of us. "Try this! You'll like it!"

I declined.

"Well," Janis said, "If you're afraid of new things..."

That was Janis for you—she insisted on sharing her existence with everyone around her, and got angry if you didn't find her life as exciting as she did.

About that time Andy and Parminder began to gag on the stuff Janis had made them eat, and Janis laughed again.

The other members of the cadre trailed in about an hour later, and the feast proper began. I looked around the long table—the forty-odd members of the Cadre of Glorious Destiny, all with their little heads on their furry multipede bodies, all crowded around the table cramming in the first real food they've tasted in their lives. In the old days, this would have been a scene from some kind of horror movie. Now it's just a slice of posthumanity, Earth's descendants partying on some frozen rock far from home.

But since all but Fahd were in borrowed bodies I'd never seen before, I couldn't tell one from the other. I had to ping a query off their implant communications units just to find out who I was talking to.

Fahd sat at the place of honor at the head of the table. The hair on his furry body was ash-blond, and he had a sort of widow's peak that gave his head a kind of geometrical look.

I liked Fahd. He was the one I had sex with, that time that Janis persuaded me to steal a sex sim from Dane, the guy I do outside programming for. (I should point out, Doctor Sam, that our simulated bodies have all the appropriate organs, it's just that the adults have made sure we can't actually use them for sex.)

I think there was something wrong with the simulation. What Fahd and I did wasn't wonderful, it wasn't ecstatic, it was just...strange. After a while we gave up and found something else to do.

Janis, of course, insisted she'd had a glorious time. She was our leader, and everything she did had to be totally fabulous. It was just like that horrid vat-grown snack food product she'd tried—not only was it the best food she'd ever tasted, it was the best food *ever*, and we all had to share it with her.

I hope Janis actually *did* enjoy the sex sim, because she was the one caught with the program in her buffer—and after I *told* her to erase it. Sometimes I think she just wants to be found out.

During dinner those whose parents permitted it were allowed two measured doses of liquor to toast Fahd—something called Ring Ice, brewed locally. I think it gave my esophagus blisters.

After the Ring Ice things got louder and more lively. There was a lot more noise and hilarity when the resort crew discovered that several of the cadre had slipped off to a back room to find out what sex was like, now they had real bodies. It was when I was laughing over this that I looked at Janis and saw that she was quiet, her body motionless. She's normally louder and more demonstrative than anyone else, so I knew something was badly wrong. I sent her a private query through my implant. She sent a single-word reply.

Mom...

I sent her a glyph of sympathy while I wondered how had Janis' mom had found out about our little adventure so quickly. There was barely time for a lightspeed signal to bounce to Ceres and back.

Ground Control must have really been annoyed. Or maybe she and Janis' mom were Constant Soldiers in the Five Principles Movement and were busy spying on everyone else—all for the greater good, of course.

Whatever the message was, Janis bounced back

pretty quickly. Next thing I knew she was sidling up to me saying, "Look, you can loan me your vac suit, right?"

Something about the glint in her huge platter eyes made me cautious.

"Why would I want to do that?" I asked.

"Mom says I'm grounded. I'm not allowed to go skating with the rest of you. But nobody can tell these bodies apart—I figured if we switched places we could show her who's boss."

"And leave me stuck here by myself?"

"You'll be with the waiters—and some of them are kinda cute, if you like them hairy." Her tone turned serious. "It's solidarity time, Alison. We can't let Mom win this one."

I thought about it for a moment, then said, "Maybe you'd better ask someone else."

Anger flashed in her huge eyes. "I knew you'd say that! You've always been afraid to stand up to the growups!"

"Janis," I sighed. "Think about it. Do you think your mom was the only one that got a signal from Ground Control? My parents are going to be looking into the records of this event *very closely*. So I think you should talk someone else into your scheme—and not Parminder or Andy, either."

Her whole hairy body sulked. I almost laughed.

"I guess you're right," she conceded.

"You know your mom is going to give you a big lecture when we get back."

"Oh yeah. I'm sure she's writing her speech right now, making sure she doesn't miss a single point."

"Maybe you'd better let me eavesdrop," I said. "Make sure you don't lose your cool."

She looked even more sulky. "Maybe you'd better."

We do this because we're cadre. Back in the old days, when the first poor kids were being raised in virtual, a lot of them cracked up once they got incarnated. They went crazy, or developed a lot of weird obsessions, or tried to kill themselves, or turned out to have a kind of autism where they could only relate to things through a computer interface.

So now parents don't raise their children by themselves. Most kids still have two parents, because it takes two to pay the citizenship points and taxes it takes to raise a kid, and sometimes if there aren't enough points to go around there are three parents, or four or five. Once the points are paid the poor moms and dads have to wait until there are enough applicants to fill a cadre. A whole bunch of virtual children are raised in one group, sharing their upbringing with their parents and creche staff. Older cadres often join their juniors and take part in their education, also.

The main point of the cadre is for us all to keep an eye on each other. Nobody's allowed to withdraw into their own little world. If anyone shows sign of going around the bend, we unite in our efforts to retrieve them.

Our parents created the little hell that we live in. It's our job to help each other survive it.

A person used to vicissitudes is not easily dejected.

Certainly Janis isn't, though despite cadre solidarity she never managed to talk anyone else into changing places with her. I felt only moderately sorry for her—she'd already had her triumph, after all—and I forgot all about her problems once I got back into my pressure suit and out onto the ice.

Skating isn't as thrilling as skiing, I suppose, but we

still had fun. Playing crack-the-whip in the light gravity, the person on the end of the line could be fired a couple kilometers over the smooth methane ice.

After which it was time to return to the resort. We all showered while the resort crew cleaned and did maintenance on our suits, and then we got back in the suits so that the next set of tourists would find their rental bodies already armored up and ready for sport.

We popped open our helmets so that the scanners could be put on our heads. Quantum superconducting devices tickled our brain cells and recovered everything they found, and then our brains—our essences—were dumped into a buffer, then fired by communication laser back to Ceres and the sim in which we all lived.

The simulation seemed inadequate compared to the reality of Titan. But I didn't have time to work out the degree of difference, because I had to save Janis' butt.

That's us. That's the cadre. All for one and one for all.

And besides, Janis has been my best friend for practically ever.

Anna-Lee, Janis' mom, was of course waiting for her, sitting in the little common room outside Janis' bedroom. (Did I mention that we sleep, Doctor Sam? We don't sleep as long as incarnated people do, just a few hours, but our parents want us to get used to the idea so that when we're incarnated we know to sleep when we get tired instead of ignoring it and then passing out while doing something dangerous or important.

(The only difference between our dreams and yours is that we don't dream. I mean, what's the point, we're stuck in our parents' dream anyway.)

So I'm no sooner arrived in my own simulated body in my own simulated bedroom when Janis is screaming on the private channel.

"Mom is here! I need you *now*!"

So I press a few switches in my brain and there I am, right in Janis' head, getting much of the same sensor feed that she's receiving herself. And I looked at her and I say, "Hey, you can't talk to Anna-Lee looking like *this*."

Janis is wearing her current avatar, which is something like a crazy person might draw with crayons. Stick-figure body, huge yellow shoes, round bobble head with crinkly red hair like wires.

"Get your quadbod on!" I tell her. "Now!"

So she switches, and now her avatar has four arms, two in the shoulders, two in the hip sockets. The hair is still bright red. Whatever her avatar looks like, Janis always keeps the red hair.

"Good," I say. "That's normal."

Which it is, for Ceres. Which is an asteroid without much gravity, so there really isn't a lot of point in having legs. In microgravity legs just drag around behind you and bump into things and get bruises and cuts. Whereas everyone can use an extra pair of arms, right? So most people who live in low- or zero-gravity environments use quadbods, which are much practical than the two-legged model.

So Janis pushes off with her left set of arms and floats through the door into the lounge where her mom awaits. Anna-Lee wears a quadbod, too, except that hers isn't an avatar, but a three-dimensional holographic scan of her real body. And you can tell that she's really pissed—she's got tight lips and tight eyelids and a tight face, and both sets of arms are folded across her midsection with her fingers digging into her forearms as if she's repressing the urge to grab Janis and shake her.

"Hi, mom," Janis said.

"You not only endangered yourself," Anna-Lee said, "but you chose to endanger others, too."

"Sit down before you answer," I murmured in Janis' inward ear. "Take your time."

I was faintly surprised that Janis actually followed my advice. She drifted into a chair, used her lower limbs to settle herself into it, and then spoke.

"Nobody was endangered," she said, quite reasonably.

Anna-Lee's nostrils narrowed.

"You diverted from the flight plan that was devised for your safety," she said.

"I made a new flight plan," Janis pointed out. "Ground Control accepted it. If it was dangerous, she wouldn't have done that."

Anna-Lee's voice got that flat quality that it gets when she's following her own internal logic. Sometimes I think she's the program, not us.

"You are not authorized to file flight plans!" she snapped.

"Ground Control accepted it," Janis repeated. Her voice had grown a little sharp, and I whispered at her to keep cool.

"And Ground Control immediately informed *me*! They were right on the edge of calling out a rescue shuttle!"

"But they didn't, because there was no problem!" Janis snapped out, and then there was a pause while I told her to lower her voice.

"Ground Control accepted my revised plan," she said. "I landed according to the plan, and nobody was hurt."

"You planned this from the beginning!" All in that

flat voice of hers. "This was a deliberate act of defiance!"

Which was true, of course.

"What harm did I do?" Janis asked.

("Look," I told Janis. "Just tell her that she's right and you were wrong and you'll never do it again."

("I'm not going to lie!" Janis sent back on our private channel. "Whatever mom does, she's never going to make me lie!")

All this while Anna-Lee was saying, "We must all work together for the greater good! Your act of defiance did nothing but divert people from their proper tasks! Titan Ground Control has better things to do than worry about you!"

There was no holding Janis back now. "You *wanted* me to learn navigation! So I learned it—because *you* wanted it! And now that I've proved that I can use it, and you're angry about it!" She was waving her arms so furiously that she bounced up from her chair and began to sort of jerk around the room.

"And do you know why that is, mom?" she demanded.

"*For God's sake shut up!*" I shouted at her. I knew where this was leading, but Janis was too far gone in her rage to listen to me now.

"It's because you're second-rate!" Janis shouted at her mother. "Dad went off to Barnard's Star, but *you* didn't make the cut! And I can do all the things you wanted to do, and do them better, and *you can't stand it!*"

"*Will you be quiet!*" I tell Janis. "Remember that *she owns you!*"

"I accepted the decision of the committee!" Anna-

Lee was shouting. "I am a Constant Soldier and I live a productive life, and I will *not* be responsible for producing a child who is a *burden* and a *drain on resources*!"

"Who says I'm going to be a burden?" Janis demanded. "*You're* the only person who says that! If I incarnated tomorrow I could get a good job in ten minutes!"

"Not if you get a reputation for disobedience and anarchy!"

By this point it was clear that since Janis wasn't listening to me, and Anna-Lee *couldn't* listen, so there was no longer any point in my involving myself in what had become a very predictable argument. So I closed the link and prepared my own excuses for my own inevitable meeting with my parents.

I changed from Picasso Woman to my own quadbod, which is what I use when I talk to my parents, at least when I want something from them. My quadbod avatar is a girl just a couple years younger than my actual age, wearing a school uniform with a Peter Pan collar and a white bow in her—my—hair. And my beautiful brown eyes are just slightly larger than eyes are in reality, because that's something called "neotony," which means you look more like a baby and babies are designed to be irresistible to grownups.

Let me tell you that it works. Sometimes I can blink those big eyes and get away with anything.

And at that point my father called, and told me that he and my mom wanted to talk to me about my adventures on Titan, so I popped over to my parents' place, where I appeared in holographic form in their living room.

My parents are pretty reasonable people. Of course I take care to *keep* them reasonable, insofar as I can. *Let me smile with the wise,* as Doctor Sam says, *and feed with the rich.* I will keep my opinions to myself, and try my best to avoid upsetting the people who have power over me.

Why did I soar off with Janis on her flight plan? my father wanted to know.

"Because I didn't think she should go alone," I said.

Didn't you try to talk her out of it? my mother asked.

"You can't talk Janis out of anything," I replied. Which, my parents knowing Janis, was an answer they understood.

So my parents told me to be careful, and that was more or less the whole conversation.

Which shows you that not all parents up here are crazy.

Mine are more sensible than most. I don't think many parents would think much of my ambition to get involved in the fine arts. That's just not *done* up here, let alone the sort of thing *I* want to do, which is to incarnate on Earth and apprentice myself to an actual painter, or maybe a sculptor. Up here they just use cameras, and their idea of original art is to take camera pictures or alter camera pictures or combine camera pictures with one another or process the camera pictures in some way.

I want to do it from scratch, with paint on canvas. And not with a computer-programmed spray gun either, but with a real brush and blobs of paint. Because if you ask me the *texture* of the thing is important, which is why I like oils. Or rather the *idea* of oils, because I've never actually had a chance to work with the real thing.

And besides, as Doctor Sam says, *A man who has not been in Italy, is always conscious of an inferiority, from his not having seen what is expected a man should see. The grand object of traveling is to see the shores of the Mediterranean.*

So when I told my parents what I wanted to do, they just sort of shrugged and made me promise to learn another skill as well, one just a little bit more practical. So while I minor in art I'm majoring in computer design and function and programming, which is pretty interesting because all our really complex programs are written by artificial intelligences who are smarter than we are, so getting them to do what you want is as much like voodoo as science.

So my parents and I worked out a compromise that suited everybody, which is why I think my parents are pretty neat actually.

About twenty minutes after my talk with my parents, Janis knocked on my door, and I made the door go away, and she walked in, and then I put the door back. (Handy things, sims.)

"Guess that didn't work out so good, huh?" she said.

"On your family's civility scale," I said, "I think that was about average."

Her eyes narrowed (she was so upset that she's forgot to change out of her quadbod, which is why she had the sort of eyes that could narrow).

"I'm going to get her," she said.

"I don't think that's very smart," I said.

Janis was smacking her fists into my walls, floor, and ceiling and shooting around the room, which was annoying even though the walls were virtual and she couldn't damage them or get fingerprints on them.

"Listen," I said. "All you have to do is keep the peace with your mom until you've finished your thesis, and then you'll be incarnated and she can't touch you. It's just *months*, Janis."

"My *thesis*!" A glorious grin of discovery spread across Janis' face. "I'm going to use my *thesis*! I'm going to stick it to mom right where it hurts!"

I reached out and grabbed her and steadied her in front of me with all four arms.

"Look," I said. "You can't keep calling her bluff."

Her voice rang with triumph "Just watch me."

"Please," I said. "I'm begging you. *Don't do anything till you're incarnated*!"

I could see the visions of glory dancing before her eyes. She wasn't seeing or hearing me at all.

"She's going to have to admit that I am right and that she is wrong," she said. "I'm going to nail my thesis to her forehead like Karl Marx on the church door."

"That was Martin Luther actually." (Sometimes I can't help these things.)

She snorted. "Who cares?"

"I do." Changing the subject. "*Because I don't want you to die*."

Janis snorted. "I'm not going to bow to her. I'm going to *crush her*. I'm going to show her how stupid and futile and second-rate she is."

And at that moment there was a signal at my door. I ignored it.

"The power of punishment is to silence, not to confute," I said.

Her face wrinkled as if she'd bit into something sour. "I can't *believe* you're quoting that old dead guy again."

I have found you an argument, I wanted to say with Doctor Sam, *but I am not obliged to find you an understanding*.

The signal at my door repeated, and this time it was attached to an electronic signal that meant *Emergency*!

Out of sheer surprise I dissolved the door.

Mei was there in her quadbod, an expression of anger on her face.

"If you two are finished congratulating each other on your brilliant little prank," she said, "you might take time to notice that Fritz is missing."

"Missing?" I didn't understand how someone could be missing. "Didn't his program come back from Titan?"

If something happened to the transmission, they could reload Fritz from a backup.

Mei's expression was unreadable. "He never went. He met the Blue Lady."

And then she pushed off with two of her hands and drifted away, leaving us in a sudden, vast, terrible silence.

We didn't speak, but followed Mei into the common room. The other cadre members were all there, and they all watched us as we floated in.

When you're little, you first hear about the Blue Lady from the other kids in your cadre. Nobody knows for sure how we *all* find out about the Blue—not just the cadres on Ceres, but the ones on Vesta, and Ganymede, and *everywhere*.

And we all know that sometimes you might see her, a kind smiling woman in a blue robe, and she'll reach out to you, and she seems so nice you'll let her take your hand.

Only then, when it's too late, you'll see that she has no eyes, but only an empty blackness filled with stars.

She'll take you away and your friends will never see you again.

And of course it's your parents who send the Blue Lady to find you when you're bad.

We all know that the Blue Lady doesn't truly exist, it's ordinary techs in ordinary rooms who give the orders to zero out your program along with all its backups, but we all believe in the Blue Lady really, and not just when we're little.

Which brings me to the point I made about incarnation earlier. Once you're incarnated, you are considered a human being, and you have human rights.

But *not until then*. Until you're incarnated, you're just a computer program that belongs to your parents, and if you're parents think the program is flawed or corrupted and simply too awkward to deal with, they can have you zeroed.

Zeroed. Not killed. The grownups insist that there's a difference, but I don't see it myself.

Because the Blue Lady really comes for some people, as she came for Fritz when Jack and Hans finally gave up trying to fix him. Most cadres get by without a visit. Some have more than one. There was a cadre on Vesta who lost eight, and then there were suicides among the survivors once they incarnated, and it was a big scandal that all the grownups agreed never to talk about.

I have never for an instant believed that my parents would ever send the Blue Lady after me, but still it's always there in the back of my mind, which is why I think that the current situation is so horrible. It gives parents a power they should never have, and it breeds a fundamental distrust between kids and their parents.

The grownups' chief complaint about the cadre system is that their children bond with their peers and not their parents. Maybe it's because their peers can't kill them.

Everyone in the cadre got the official message about Fritz, that he was basically irreparable and that the chance of his making a successful incarnation was essentially zero. The message said that none of us were at fault for what had happened, and that everyone knew that we'd done our best for him.

This was in the same message queue as a message to me from Fritz, made just before he got zeroed out. There he was with his stupid hat, smiling at me.

"Thank you for saying you'd play the shadowing game with me," he said. "I really think you're wonderful." He laughed. "See you soon, on Titan!"

So then I cried a lot, and I erased the message so that I'd never be tempted to look at it again.

We all felt failure. It was our job to make Fritz right, and we hadn't done it. We had all grown up with him, and even though he was a trial he was a part of our world. I had spent the last few days avoiding him, and I felt horrible about it; but everyone else had done the same thing at one time or another.

We all missed him.

The cadre decided to wear mourning, and we got stuck in a stupid argument about whether to wear white, which is the traditional mourning color in Asia, or black, which is the color in old Europe.

"Wear blue," Janis said. So we did. Whatever avatars we wore from that point on had blue clothing, or used blue as a principal color somewhere in their composition.

If any of the parents noticed, or talked about it, or complained, I never heard it.

I started thinking a lot about how I related to incarnated people, and I thought that maybe I'm just a little more compliant and adorable and sweet-natured than I'd otherwise be, because I want to avoid the consequences of being otherwise. And Janis is perhaps more defiant than she'd be under other circumstances, because she wants to show she's not afraid. *Go ahead, mom,* she says, *pull the trigger. I dare you.*

Underestimating Anna-Lee all the way. Because Anna-Lee is a Constant Soldier of the Five Principles Movement, and that means *serious*.

The First Principle of the Five Principles Movement states that *Humanity is a pattern of thought, not a side effect of taxonomy*, which means that you're human if you *think* like a human, whether you've got six legs or four arms or two legs like the folks on Earth and Mars.

And then so on to the Fifth Principle, we come to the statement that humanity in all its various forms is intended to occupy every possible ecosystem throughout the entire universe, or at least as much of it was we can reach. Which is why the Five Principles Movement has always been very big on genetic experimentation, and the various expeditions to nearby stars.

I have no problem with the Five Principles Movement, myself. It's rational compared with groups like the Children of Venus or the God's Menu people.

Besides, if there isn't something to the Five Principles, what are we doing out here in the first place?

My problem lies with the sort of people the Movement attracts, which is to say people like Anna-Lee. People who are obsessive, and humorless, and completely unable to see any other point of view. Nor only do they dedicate themselves heart and soul to whatever group they join, they insist everyone else has to join as well, and that anyone who isn't a part of it is a Bad Person.

So even though I pretty much agree with the Five Principles I don't think I'm going to join the movement. I'm going to keep in mind the wisdom of my good

Doctor Sam: *Most schemes of political improvement are very laughable things.*

But to get back to Anna-Lee. Back in the day she married Carlos, who was also in the Movement, and together they worked for years to qualify for the expedition to Barnard's Star on the *True Destiny*. They created Janis together, because having children is all a part of occupying the universe and so on.

But Carlos got the offer to crew the ship, and Anna-Lee didn't. Carlos chose Barnard's Star over Anna-Lee, and now he's a couple light-months away. He and the rest of the settlers are in electronic form—no sense in spending the resources to ship a whole body to another star system when you can just ship the data and build the body once you arrive—and for the most part they're dormant, because there's nothing to do until they near their destination. But every week or so Carlos has himself awakened so that he can send an electronic postcard to his daughter.

The messages are all really boring, as you might expect from someone out in deep space where there's nothing to look at and nothing to do, and everyone's asleep anyway.

Janis sends him longer messages, mostly about her fights with Anna-Lee. Anna-Lee likewise sends Carlos long messages about Janis' transgressions. At two light-months out Carlos declines to mediate between them, which makes them both mad.

So Anna-Lee is mad because her husband left her, and she's mad at Janis for not being a perfect Five Principles Constant Soldier. Janis is mad at Carlos for not figuring out a way to take her along, and she's mad at Anna-Lee for not making the crew on the *True*

Destiny, and failing that not having the savvy to keep her husband in the picture.

And she's also mad at Anna-Lee for getting married again, this time to Rhee, a rich Movement guy who was able to swing the taxes to create *two new daughters,* both of whom are the stars of their particular cadres and are going to grow up to be perfect Five Principles Kids, destined to carry on the work of humanity in new habitats among distant stars.

Or so Anna-Lee claims, anyway.

Which is why I think that Janis underestimates her mother. I think the way Anna-Lee looks at it, she's got two new kids, who are everything she wants. And one older kid who gives her trouble, and who she can give to the Blue Lady without really losing anything, since she's lost Janis anyway. She's already given a husband to the stars, after all.

And all this is another reason why I want to incarnate on Earth, where a lot of people still have children the old-fashioned way. The parents make an embryo in a gene-splicer, and then the embryo is put in a vat, and nine months later you crack the vat open and you've got an actual baby, not a computer program. And even if the procedure is a lot more time-consuming and messy I still think it's superior.

So I was applying for work on Earth, both for jobs that could use computer skills, and also for apprenticeship programs in the fine arts. But there's a waiting list for pretty much any job you want on Earth, and also there's a big entry tax unless they *really* want you, so I wasn't holding my breath; and besides, I hadn't finished my thesis.

I figured on graduating from college along with most

of my cadre, at the age of fourteen. I understand that in your day, Doctor Sam, people graduated from college a lot later. I figure there are several important reasons for the change: (1) we virtual kids don't sleep as much as you do, so we have more time for study; (2) there isn't that much else to do here anyway; and (3) we're really, really, *really* smart. Because if you were a parent, and you had a say in the makeup of your kid (along with the doctors and the sociologists and the hoodoo machines), would you say, *No thanks, I want mine stupid*?

No, I don't think so.

And the meat-brains that we incarnate into are pretty smart, too. Just in case you were wondering.

We could grow up faster, if we wanted. The computers we live in are so fast that we could go from inception to maturity in just two or three months. But we wouldn't get to interact with our parents, who being meat would be much slower, or with anyone else. So in order to have any kind of relationship with our elders, or any kind of socialization at all, we have to slow down to our parents' pace. I have to say that I agree with that.

In order to graduate I needed to do a thesis, and unfortunately I couldn't do the one I wanted, which was the way the paintings of Breughel, etc., reflected the theology of the period. All the training with computers and systems, along with art and art history, had given me an idea of how abstract systems such as theology work, and how you can visually represent fairly abstract concepts on a flat canvas.

But I'd have to save that for maybe a postgraduate degree, because my major was still in the computer sciences, so I wrote a fairly boring thesis on systems interopability—which, if you care, is the art of getting different machines and highly specialized operating systems to talk to each other, a job that is made more difficult if the machines in question happen to be a lot smarter than you are.

Actually it's a fairly interesting subject. It just wasn't interesting in my thesis.

While I was doing that I was also working outside contracts for Dane, who was from a cadre that had incarnated a few years ahead of us, and who I got to know when his group met with ours to help with our lessons and with our socialization skills (because they wanted us to be able to talk to people outside the cadre and our families, something we might not do if we didn't have practice).

Anyway, Dane had got a programming job in Ceres' communications center, and he was willing to pass on the more boring parts of his work to me in exchange for money. So I was getting a head start on paying that big Earth entry tax, or if I could evade the tax maybe living on Earth a while and learning to paint.

"You're just going to end up being Ceres' first interior decorator," Janis scoffed.

"And that would be a *bad* thing?" I asked. "Just *look* at this place!" Because it's all so functional and boring and you'd think they could find a more interesting color of paint than *grey*, for God's sake.

That was one of the few times I'd got to talk to Janis since our adventure on Titan. We were both working on our theses, and still going to school, and I had my outside contracts, and I think she was trying to avoid me, because she didn't want to tell me what she was doing because she didn't want me to tell her not to do it.

Which hurt, by the way. Since we'd been such loyal friends up to the point where I told her not to get killed, and then because I wanted to save her life she didn't want to talk to me anymore.

The times I mostly got to see Janis were Incarnation Day parties for other members of our cadre. So we got to see Ganymede, and Iapetus, and Titan again, and Rhea, and Pluto, Callisto, and Io, and the antimatter generation ring between Venus and Mercury, and Titan again, and then Titan a fourth time.

Our cadre must have this weird affinity for orange, I don't know.

We went to Pallas, Juno, and Vesta. Though if you ask me, one asteroid settlement is pretty much like the next.

We went to Third Heaven, which is a habitat the God's Menu people built at L2. And they can *keep* a lot of the items on the menu, if you ask me.

We visited Luna (which you would call the Moon, Doctor Sam. As if there was only one). And we got to view *Everlasting Dynasty*, the starship being constructed in lunar orbit for the expedition to Tau Ceti, the settlement that Anna-Lee was trying her best to get Janis aboard.

We also got to visit Mars three times. So among other entertainments I looked down at the planet from the top of Olympus Mons, the largest mountain in the solar system, and I looked down from the edge of the solar system's largest canyon, and then I looked *up* from the bottom of the same canyon.

We all tried to wear blue if we could, in memory of the one of us who couldn't be present.

Aside from the sights, the Incarnation Day parties were great because all our incarnated cadre members turned up, in bodies they'd borrowed for the occasion. We were all still close, of course, and kept continually in touch, but our communication was limited by the speed of light and it wasn't anything like having Fahd and Chandra and Solange there in person, to pummel and to hug.

We didn't go to Earth. I was the only one of our cadre who had applied there, and I hadn't got an answer yet. I couldn't help fantasizing about what my Incarnation Day party would be like if I held it on Earth—where would I go? What would we look at? Rome? Mount Everest? The ocean habitats? The plans of Africa, where the human race began?

It was painful to think that the odds were high that I'd never see any of these places.

Janis never tried to organize any of her little rebellions on these trips. For one thing word had got out, and we were all pretty closely supervised. Her behavior was never less than what Anna-Lee would desire. But under it all I could tell she was planning something drastic.

I tried to talk to her about it. I talked about my thesis, and hoped it would lead to a discussion of *her* thesis. But no luck. She evaded the topic completely.

She was pretty busy with her project, though, whatever it was. Because she was always buzzing around the cadre asking people where to look for odd bits of knowledge.

I couldn't make sense of her questions, though. They seemed to cover too many fields. Sociology, statistics, minerology, criminology, economics, astronomy, spaceship design…The project seemed too huge.

The only thing I knew about Janis' thesis was that it was *supposed* to be about resource management. It was the field that Anna-Lee forced her into, because it was full of skills that would be useful on the Tau Ceti expedition. And if that didn't work, Anna-Lee made sure

Janis minored in spaceship and shuttle piloting and navigation.

I finally finished my thesis, and then I sat back and waited for the job offers to roll in. The only offer I got came from someone who wanted me to run the garbage cyclers on Iapetus, which the guy should have known I wouldn't accept if he had bothered to read my application.

Maybe he was just neck-deep in garbage and desperate, I don't know.

And then the most astounding thing happened. Instead of a job in the computer field, I got an offer to study at the Pisan Academy.

Which is an art school. Which is in Italy, which is where the paintings come from mostly.

The acceptance committee said that my work showed a "naive but highly original fusion of social criticism with the formalities of the geometric order." I don't even *pretend* to know what they meant by that, but I suspect they just weren't used to the perspective of a student who had spent practically her entire live in a computer on Ceres.

I broadcast my shrieks of joy to everyone in the cadre, even those who had left Ceres and were probably wincing at their work stations when my screams reached them.

I bounced around the common room and everyone came out to congratulate me. Even Janis, who had taken to wearing an avatar that wasn't even remotely human, just a graphic of a big sledgehammer smashing a rock, over and over.

Subtlety had never been her strong point.

"Congratulations," she said. "You got what you wanted."

And then she broadcast something on a private channel. *You're going to be famous,* she said. *But I'm going to be a* legend.

I looked at her. And then I sent back, *Can we talk about this?*

In a few days. When I deliver my thesis.

Don't, I pleaded.

Too late.

The hammer hit its rock, and the shards flew out into the room and vanished.

I spent the next few days planning my Incarnation Day party, but my heart wasn't in it. I kept wondering if Janis was going to be alive to enjoy it.

I finally decided to have my party in Thailand because there were so many interesting environments in one place, as well as the Great Buddha. And I found a caterer that was supposed to be really good.

I decided what sort of body I wanted, and the incarnation specialists on Earth started cooking it up in one of their vats. Not the body of an Earth-born fourteen-year old, but older, more like eighteen. Brown eyes, brown hair, and those big eyes that had always been so useful.

And two legs, of course. Which is what they all have down there.

I set the date. The cadre were alerted. We all practiced in the simulations and tried to get used to making do with only two arms. Everyone was prepared.

And then Janis finished her thesis. I downloaded a copy the second it was submitted to her committee and read it in one long sitting, and my sense of horror grew with every line.

What Janis had done was publish a comprehensive critique *of our entire society*! It was a piece of brilliance, and at the same time it was utter poison.

Posthuman society wrecks its children, Janis said, and this can be demonstrated by the percentage of neurotic and dysfunctional adults. The problems encountered by the first generation of children who spent their formative years as programs—the autism, the obsessions and compulsions, the addictions to electronic environments—hadn't gone away, they'd just been reduced to the point where they'd become a part of the background clutter, a part of our civilization so everyday that we never quite noticed it.

Janis had the data, too. The number of people who were under treatment for one thing or another. The percentage who had difficulty adjusting to their incarnations, or who didn't want to communicate with anyone outside their cadre, or who couldn't sleep unless they were immersed in a simulation. Or who committed suicide. Or who died in accidents—Janis questioned whether all those accidents were really the results of our harsh environments. Our machines and our settlements were much safer than they had been in the early days, but the rates of accidental death were still high. How many accidents were caused by distracted or unhappy operators, or for that matter were deliberate "suicide by machine"?

Janis went on to describe one of the victims of this ruthless type of upbringing. "Flat of emotional affect, offended by disorder and incapable of coping with obstruction, unable to function without adherence to a belief system as rigid as the artificial and constricted environments in which she was raised."

When I realized Janis was describing Anna-Lee I almost de-rezzed.

Janis offered a scheme to cure the problem, which

was to get rid of the virtual environments and start out with real incarnated babies. She pulled out vast numbers of statistics demonstrating that places that did this—chiefly Earth—seemed to raise more successful adults. She also pointed out that the initial shortage of resources that had prompted the creation of virtual children in the first place had long since passed—plenty of water-ice coming in from the Kuyper Belt these days, and we were sitting on all the minerals we could want. The only reason the system continued was for the convenience of the adults. But genuine babies, as opposed to abstract computer programs, would help the adults, too. They would no longer be tempted to become little dictators with absolute power over their offspring. Janis said the chance would turn the grownups into better human beings.

All this was buttressed by colossal numbers of statistics, graphs, and other data. I realized when I'd finished it that the Cadre of Glorious Destiny had produced one true genius, and that this genius was Janis.

The true genius is a mind of large general powers, accidentally determined to some particular direction.

Anna-Lee determined her, all right, and the problem was that Janis probably didn't have that long to live. Aside from the fact that Janis had ruthlessly caricatured her, Anna-Lee couldn't help but notice that the whole work went smack up against the Five Principles Movement. According to the Movement people, all available resources had to be devoted to the expansion of the human race out of the solar system and into new environments. It didn't matter how many more resources were available now than in the past, it was clear against their principles to devote a greater share to the raising of children when it could be used to blast off into the universe.

And though the Five Principles people acknowledged our rather high death rate, they put it down to our settlements' hazardous environments. All we had to do was genetically modify people to better suit the environments and the problem would be solved.

I skipped the appendices and zoomed from my room across the common room to Janis' door, and hit the button to alert her to a visitor. The door vanished, and there was Janis—for the first time since her fight with Anna-Lee, she was using her quadbod avatar. She gave me a wicked grin.

"Great, isn't it?"

"It's *brilliant*! But you can't let Anna-Lee see it."

"Don't be silly. I sent mom the file myself."

I was horrified. She had to have seen the way my Picasso-face gaped, and it made her laugh.

"She'll have you erased!" I said.

"If she does," Janis said. "She'll only prove my point." She put a consoling hand on my shoulder. "Sorry if it means missing your incarnation."

When Anna-Lee came storming in—which wasn't long after—Janis broadcast the whole confrontation on a one-way link to the whole cadre. We got to watch, but not to participate. She didn't want our advice any more than she wanted her mother's.

"You are unnatural!" Anna-Lee stormed. "You spread slanders! You have betrayed the highest truth!"

"I *told* the truth!" Janis said. "And you *know* it's the truth, otherwise you wouldn't be so insane right now."

Anna-Lee stiffened. "I am a Five Principles Constant Soldier. I know the truth, and I know my duty."

"Every time you say that, you prove my point."

"You will retract this thesis, and apologize to your committee for giving them such a vicious document."

Anna-Lee hadn't realized that the document was irretrievable, that Janis had given it to everyone she knew.

Janis laughed. "No way, mom," she said.

Anna Lee lost it. She waved her fists and screamed. "I know my duty! I will not allow such a slander to be seen by anyone!" She pointed at Janis. "You have three days to retract!"

Janis gave a snort of contempt.

"Or what?"

"Or I will decide that you're incorrigible and terminate your program."

Janis laughed. "Go right ahead, mom. Do it *now*. Nothing spreads a new idea better than martyrdom." She spread her four arms. "*Do* it, mom. I *hate* life in this hell. I'm ready."

I will be conquered; I will not capitulate.

Yes, Doctor Sam. That's it exactly.

"You have three days," Anna-Lee said, her voice all flat and menacing, and then her virtual image de-rezzed.

Janis looked at the space where her mom had been, and then a goofy grin spread across her face. She switched to the red-headed, stick-figure avatar, and began to do a little dance as she hovered in the air, moving like a badly animated cartoon.

"Hey!" she sang. "I get to go to Alison's party after all!"

I had been so caught up in the drama that I had forgot my incarnation was going to happen in two days.

But it wasn't going to be a party now. It was going to be a wake.

"Doctor Sam," I said, "I've got to save Janis."

The triumph of hope over experience.

"Hope is what I've got," I said, and then I thought about it. "And maybe a little experience, too."

My Incarnation Day went well. We came down by glider, as we had that first time on Titan, except that this time I told Ground Control to let my friends land wherever the hell they wanted. That gave us time to inspect the Great Buddha, a slim man with a knowing smile sitting crosslegged with knobs on his head. He's two and a half kilometers tall and packed with massively parallel quantum processors, all crunching vast amounts of data, thinking whatever profound thoughts are appropriate to an artificial intelligence built on such a scale, and repeating millions of sutras, which are scriptures for Buddhists, all at the speed of light.

It creeps along at two or three centimeters per day, and will enter the strait at the end of the Kra Peninsula many thousands of years from now.

After viewing the Buddha's serene expression from as many angles as suited us, we soared and swooped over many kilometers of brilliant green jungle and landed on the beach. And we all *did* land on the beach, which sort of surprised me. And then we all did our best to learn how to surf—and let me tell you from the start, the surfing simulators are *totally* inadequate. The longest I managed to stand my board was maybe twenty seconds.

I was amazed at all the sensations that crowded all around me. The breeze on my skin, the scents of the sea and the vegetation and the coal on which our banquet was being cooked. The hot sand under my bare feet. The salt taste of the ocean on my lips. The sting of the little jellyfish on my legs and arms, and the iodine smell of the thick strand of seaweed that got wrapped in my hair.

I mean, I had no *idea*. The simulators were totally inadequate to the Earth experience.

And this was just a *part* of the Earth, a small fraction of the environments available. I think I convinced a lot of the cadre that maybe they'd want to move to Earth as soon as they could raise the money and find a job.

After swimming and beach games we had my Incarnation Day dinner. The sensations provided by the food were really too intense—I couldn't eat much of it. If I was going to eat Earth food, I was going to have to start with something a lot more bland.

And there was my brown-eyed body at the head of the table, looking down at the members of the Cadre of Glorious Destiny who were toasting me with tropical drinks, the kind that have parasols in them.

Tears came to my eyes, and they were a lot wetter and hotter than tears in the sims. For some reason that fact made me cry even more.

My parents came to the dinner, because this was the first time they could actually hug me—hug me for real, that is, and not in a sim. They had downloaded into bodies that didn't look much like the four-armed quad-bods they used back on Ceres, but that didn't matter. When my arms went around them, I began to cry again.

After the tears were wiped away we put on underwater gear and went for a swim on the reef, which is just amazing. More colors and shapes and textures than I could ever imagine—or imagine putting in a work of art.

A work of art that embodies all but selects none is not art, but mere cant and recitation.

Oh, wow. You're right. Thank you, Doctor Sam.

After the reef trip we paid a visit to one of the underwater settlements, one inhabited by people adapted to breathe water. The problems were was that we had to keep our underwater gear on, and that none of us were any good at the fluid sign language they all used as their preferred means of communication.

Then we rose from the ocean, dried out, and had a last round of hugs before being uploaded to our normal habitations. I gave Janis a particularly strong hug, and I whispered in her ear.

"Take care of yourself."

"Who?" she grinned. "*Me*?"

And then the little brown-haired body was left behind, looking very lonely, as everyone else put on the electrodes and uploaded back to their normal and very distant worlds.

As soon as I arrived on Ceres, I zapped an avatar of myself into my parents' quarters. They looked at me as if I were a ghost.

"What are *you* doing here?" my mother managed.

"I hate to tell you this," I said, "but I think you're going to have to hire a lawyer."

It was surprisingly easy to do, really. Remember that I was assisting Dane, who was a communications tech, and in charge of uploading all of our little artificial brains to Earth. And also remember that I am a specialist in systems interoperability, which implies that I am also a specialist in systems *un*operability.

It was very easy to set a couple of artificial intelligences running amok in Dane's system just as he was working on our upload. And that so distracted him that he said yes when I said that I'd do the job for him.

And once I had access, it was the work of a moment to swap a couple of serial numbers.

The end result of which was that it was Janis who uploaded into my brown-haired body, and received all the toasts, and who hugged my parents with *my* arms. And who is now on Earth, incarnated, with a full set of human rights and safe from Anna-Lee.

I wish I could say the same for myself.

Anna-Lee couldn't have me killed, of course, since I don't belong to her. But she could sue my parents, who from her point of view permitted a piece of software belonging to *them* to prevent her from wreaking vengeance on some software that belonged to *her*.

And of course Anna-Lee went berserk the second she found out—which was more or less immediately, since Janis sent her a little radio taunt as soon as she downed her fourth or fifth celebratory umbrella drink.

Janis sent me a message, too.

"The least you could have done was make my hair red."

My hair. Sometimes I wonder why I bothered.

An unexpected side effect of this was that we all got famous. It turns out that this was an unprecedented legal situation, with lots of human interest and a colorful cast of characters. Janis became a media celebrity, and so did I, and so did Anna-Lee.

Celebrity didn't do Anna-Lee's cause any good. Her whole mental outlook was too rigid to stand the kind of scrutiny and questioning that any public figure has to put up with. As soon as she was challenged she lost control. She called one of the leading media interviewers a name that you, Doctor Sam, would not wish me to repeat.

   Whatever the actual merits of her legal case, the sight
of Anna-Lee screaming that I had deprived her of the
inalienable right to kill her daughter failed to win her a
lot of friends. Eventually the Five Principles people realized she wasn't doing their cause any good, and she was
replaced by a Movement spokesperson who said as
little as possible.

   Janis did some talking, too, but not nearly as much
as she would have liked, because she was under house
arrest for coming to Earth without a visa and without
paying the immigration tax. The cops showed up when
she was sleeping off her hangover from all the umbrella
drinks. It's probably lucky that she wasn't given the
opportunity to talk much, because if she started on her
rants she would have worn out her celebrity as quickly
as Anna-Lee did.

   Janis was scheduled to be deported back to Ceres,
but shipping an actual incarnated human being is much
more difficult than zapping a simulation by laser, and
she had to wait for a ship that could carry passengers,
and that would be months.

   She offered to navigate the ship herself, since she had
the training, but the offer was declined.

   Lots of people read her thesis who wouldn't otherwise
have heard of it. And millions discussed it whether they'd
read it or not. There were those who said that Janis was
right, and those that said that Janis was mostly right but
that she exaggerated. There were those who said that the
problem didn't really exist, except in the statistics.

   There were those who thought the problem existed
entirely in the software, that the system would work if
the simulations were only made more like reality. I had
to disagree, because I think the simulations *were* like
reality, but only for certain people.

The problem is that human beings perceive reality in slightly different ways, even if they happen to be programs. A programmer could do his best to create an artificial reality that exactly mimicked the way he perceived reality, except that it wouldn't be as exact for another person, it would only be an approximation. It would be like fitting everyone's hand into the same-sized glove.

Eventually someone at the University of Adelaide read it and offered Janis a professorship in their sociology department. She accepted and was freed from house arrest.

Poor Australia, I thought.

I was on video quite a lot. I used my little-girl avatar, and I batted my big eyes a lot. I still wore blue, mourning for Fritz.

Why, I was asked, did I act to save Janis?

"Because we're cadre, and we're supposed to look after one another."

What did I think of Anna-Lee?

"I don't see why she's complaining. I've seen to it that Janis *just isn't her problem any more*."

Wasn't what I did stealing?

"It's not stealing to free a slave."

And so on. It was the same sort of routine I'd been practicing on my parents all these years, and the practice paid off. Entire cadres—hundreds of them—signed petitions asking that the case be dismissed. Lots of adults did the same.

I hope that it helps, but the judge that hears the case isn't supposed to be swayed by public opinion, but only by the law.

And everyone forgets that it's my parents that will be on trial, not me, accused of letting their software steal

Anna-Lee's software. And of course I, and therefore they, am completely guilty, so my parents are almost certainly going to be fined, and lose both money and Citizenship Points.

I'm sorry about that, but my parents seem not to be.

How the judge will put a value on a piece of stolen software that its owner fully intended to destroy is going to make an interesting ruling, however it turns out.

I don't know whether I'll ever set foot on Earth again. I can't take my place in Pisa because I'm not incarnated, and I don't know if they'll offer again.

And however things turn out, Fritz is still zeroed. And I still wear blue.

I don't have my outside job any longer. Dane won't speak to me, because his supervisor reprimanded him, and he's under suspicion for being my accomplice. And even those who are sympathetic to me aren't about to let me loose with their computers.

And even if I get a job somewhere, I can't be incarnated until the court case is over.

It seems to me that the only person who got away scot-free was Janis. Which is normal.

So right now my chief problem is boredom. I spent fourteen years in a rigid program intended to fill my hours with wholesome and intellectually useful activity, and now that's over.

And I can't get properly started on the non-wholesome thing until I get an incarnation somewhere.

Everyone is, or hopes to be, an idler.

Thank you, Doctor Sam.

I'm choosing to idle away my time making pictures. Maybe I can sell them and help pay the Earth tax.

I call them my "Doctor Johnson" series. *Sam.*

Johnson on Mars. Sam. Johnson Visits Neptune. Sam.
Johnson Quizzing the Tomasko Glacier. Sam. Johnson
Among the Asteroids.

I have many more ideas along this line.

Doctor Sam, I trust you will approve.

EXIT WITHOUT SAVING

Ruth Nestvold

Spending credit illegally was difficult, but there were ways, if you were clever. There were always ways. Using a morph unit illegally was even more difficult, but to Mallory it was worth the risk.

Friends like Lorraine made it possible. Lorraine was a lab technician for Softec, and she was both clever and greedy; to make a little extra on the side, she allowed Mallory to use the units during off hours. Mallory had no idea if any of the other morph agents were also clandestine customers—Lorraine could be trusted to keep her mouth shut.

"I don't understand why they don't market these things for entertainment purposes," Lorraine said as she adjusted the download cap on Mallory's head.

"I'm testing them for that," Mallory said, grinning.

Lorraine frowned. "It isn't a joke. Softec just lost Max to identity scramble last month. You be careful, girl."

"I am."

"Hope so. Another thing I don't understand is why *you* of all people feel the need to change shape." She looked pointedly at Mallory's bare breasts, which men had a tendency to describe as perfect.

Mallory glanced in the mirror behind Lorraine and shrugged. She might not have anything to complain about as far as her own appearance was concerned, but that wasn't the point. As a morph, she wasn't tied down to herself, to her own identity; she could get out of it, escape to any shape she wanted, be anyone she wanted.

"It doesn't have anything to do with that, Lorraine."

"Yeah, I know. You're just not an easy gal to satisfy. Now lie down." Looking grim, Lorraine hooked the body Mallory would soon be leaving to the life support system.

Some agents disliked the sensation of the actual morphing process. Mallory was not one of those. As she settled into the cushioned pallet, her stomach was churning in anticipation. On the other side of the transferal equipment was the long, dark morph unit. It looked inanimate, but it was actually a DNA matrix controlled by a neural network. With the mind upload, it would become her home for a couple of hours, and with its assembler technology she could become anything she wanted to be.

"Ready."

But Lorraine didn't start the download immediately, looking instead at Mallory with something other than greed in her dark eyes. "You make sure you tell me if you ever start feeling the effects of brain drain, you hear?"

"Of course," she replied impatiently. It wouldn't happen. Her extra excursions were nothing. She'd never had a bout of dizziness, let alone the more serious symptoms like a fainting spell.

Finally Lorraine began the transferal, and Mallory felt a sense of elation as her mind left her body. She was free.

"Transferal complete," Lorraine said. "Begin anthropomorphing process."

The unit began to take on human shape and sensation, and once done, Mallory adjusted the appearance of the morph to be her own twin, a double of the empty husk lying in the body case on the other bed. She would change that soon, but she had to leave the Softec complex as she had come—herself.

The bed unit cooled the naked skin of her back, absorbing the warmth created while she morphed. She remained there for a moment, enjoying the sensation of cold against her hot skin.

"I want you back in no more than three hours," Lorraine said. "Well before the next security audit."

Somehow, things always looked more beautiful to her in a morph—even the glistening, rain-wet streets of the Softec corporate zone at night. Of course, the neural network of the unit was enhanced, hearing, sight, and memory all heightened. But it wasn't the neural network that stared at the halos of light beneath the street lamps sparkling on the rain-coated pavement of Pill Hill, marveling at the pattern of shine and shadow. It was her own mind, free of her life, of expectations, free to change and choose.

The Softec complex was fairly close to both Elliot Bay and Broadway and a wide selection of bars and bands. Mallory chose Broadway. On the way, she ducked into an empty alley. It was already dark, but it was better to err on the side of caution. She had chosen her clothes carefully, an androgynous outfit of baggy pants with a draw string which could be let out, a wide silk tank top, loose blazer, and light rain jacket. Behind a garbage bin, she stood with her face to the wall as if she were a man about to relieve himself and loaded an image of the appearance she wanted into her processor-brain. The warmth of the morph process coursed through her veins and along her spine. She could feel her shoulders widening, her chest flattening, her clitoris transforming into a penis. Sweat broke out on her forehead, and she wiped it away with the back of a hand which was now more square than before.

After about five minutes, she left the alley again. Her hair was still the same, a shaggy shoulder-length dark gold, just in case anyone had noticed her enter the alley, but the rest of her was gloriously different.

She had left the female morph agent who couldn't maintain a relationship behind and had become the guy who didn't need one.

Mallory headed for the Down-And-Out, where she could always count on getting good music, and maybe more if everything played out right. She descended the stairs into a generous black and neon room full of noise and flashing light. The band was putting on an elaborate holo show, with half a dozen of each of the band members projected all over the bar. It was still too early to be full, but the illusion kept customers from noticing—it wasn't even ten and the place had people or projections at almost every table.

She sat down at a table off to the side but still close to the front. She liked to be in the thick of things, but while she was morphing, it didn't do to draw attention to herself. There were a few women glancing at her surreptitiously, though—it invariably happened when she morphed into a likeness of her brother Dane.

She wondered where he was now. Not that she cared. He had abandoned them, abandoned her, chosen a life in the burbs, outside of the protective walls of the cities, an enemy of the corporations. Because of him, she had changed her name, had given up the last connection she had to their parents.

The parents who had always loved him best.

Mallory ordered a martini, giving them cash rather than her thumb, and watched the band and the audience, keeping an eye out for someone she might be able to spend an hour with before she had to go back to Softec. While she was trying to choose a candidate, the singer approached. Mallory smiled her most suggestive male smile and was rewarded by an armful of singing female. It was the real singer, not just a holo, and the body she was wearing sprang to life.

They really were fools at Softec for trying to keep morph technology secret; they should be perfecting it for entertainment, not industrial espionage. She wouldn't be the only one addicted to the transformation and the sensations of another body.

The singer continued to sing, pressing her ass into Mallory's lap, while Mallory moved her hips subtly to the music. With time and opportunity, she had often played this game to the end. Perhaps it was strange, but making love to women as a man had never led her to want to try anything with a woman when she was in her own body. The reason she wanted sex as a man was for the male sensations. But she wouldn't want to give up the female sensations permanently either—she wasn't a candidate for a sex change. What Mallory wanted was both.

Everything.

The singer got up, giving her a look of promise, and Mallory returned her attention to her martini and the other guests in the bar. One guest's gaze was trained on her with unusual intensity.

It was her friend Sue.

A fist closed around her stomach, tight. She had

morphed to look like her long-lost brother, and her brother looked a hell of a lot like her. Sue was sure to notice the resemblance.

Sue started to get up from her table and Mallory pretended to concentrate on the stage. Out of the corner of her eye she saw Sue winding her way through the tables to her. Mallory got up casually and headed in the direction of the restrooms, but as soon as she was out of sight, she changed directions and exited the bar.

Nervous, she walked fast to the alley she had used for her transformation and leaned against the wall as a violent bout of dizziness swept over her. She forced herself to breathe slowly and deeply, and the dizziness faded.

It wasn't brain drain, it couldn't be.

Not her.

Mallory was not in the best of moods when she went to work the next morning. She didn't much care for office work, the sifting and filing of information on other corporations, keeping abreast of even the faintest rumors of new technological developments which could lead to better weapons or a wider sphere of influence. Alliances between corporations were uneasy in the best of times, and the best of times were rare.

"Have you reconsidered?"

Mallory looked up to find her recently ex boyfriend Ethan leaning against the wall of her cubicle, dark rings under his almond eyes.

"Have you?" she asked back.

Ethan pulled a vacant chair into her cubicle and sat down. "I've been doing some thinking," he said, his voice low.

Mallory nodded. Now he would apologize. They had broken up because Ethan had asked her to give up her position as morph agent before the critical point established by Softec, had asked her to join him in *research*. Agents had to retire all too soon anyway because of the danger of identity scramble, their minds weakened and lost amid the remnants of all the other minds which once inhabited their morph.

Or at least that was the theory. The unrecoverables among the morph agents could have been the result of *anything*.

Ethan took her hand, gently stroked the skin between thumb and forefinger. "I meant what I said the other day about you giving up morphing, but I'll compromise. I'd like you to take a new test I've been developing for brain drain. If your levels are safe, I won't say anything else about you working as a morph agent during your remaining time."

She stared at him, panic taking hold of her gut. Why would he ask that? Did he know about her illicit morphing activities? She pulled her hand out of his. "This test, it's not official yet, is it?"

He shook his head.

"So you want me to act as your guinea pig?"

"You know it's not that."

"It isn't, huh?" She couldn't keep the anger out of her voice. "Just because Softec doesn't even know yet what exactly happens in the case of identity scramble doesn't mean I'll put up with experiments being done on me."

"It's not an experiment, Mallory."

"Of course it is. I'm not allowing you to use me."

Ethan pursed his lips. "Perhaps I shouldn't have asked you to quit, but just doing a test for my peace of mind—is that really too much to ask?"

Mallory glared at him. "You just want a reason to make me stop."

He leaned forward, searching her eyes. "You really think that?"

Mallory looked away. "I don't know what to think."

"And you won't do the test?"

"No."

Ethan stood up, pursing his lips. "I thought I was coming halfway with this. But you don't want to meet me, you just want me to follow you."

"*You* want me to give up morphing."

"Because I worry about you."

"Because you're selfish."

"No, Mallory, you're the one who's selfish." With that, he left. Mallory told herself she was glad.

By the end of the week, it was obvious Ethan wasn't coming back a second time. It didn't matter. He wasn't willing to let her run her life the way she wanted, and it wasn't in her nature to mourn. She'd learned long ago how useless that was.

So Ethan was gone too. She would get over it.

She and Sue were scheduled for a morph job at Hypersystems the next week, and they met daily to plan the sting.

"You have a brother, don't you?" Sue suddenly asked one afternoon while they were going over the floor plan of the Hypersystems building in the holo well of Mallory's desk unit.

Mallory nodded curtly. "Why do you ask?" Of course, she knew why Sue was asking—she'd been expecting it ever since the incident in the bar, but all they had talked about had been her break-up with Ethan.

"I think I might have seen him last week."

"What makes you think that?"

"I saw a guy at the Down and Out who looked a lot like you."

"I doubt if it was Dane." The blood was going to her head and she shook it briefly to rid herself of the feeling.

"Funny," Sue said, "The resemblance was uncanny."

"My brother wouldn't dare show his face in Seattle."

"Why not?"

"Look, I don't want to talk about him, okay?" She shouldn't care. Dane was AWOL, hiding out somewhere in the ruins of the burbs, doing God knows what. He'd disappeared a decade ago, leaving his home and family for some cheap ideals. What choice had Seattle and other bankrupt cities had after the epidemics and the depression of twenty years before but to privatize the police force, privatize the cities themselves? Dane and his kind called it selling out, but at least the enclaves of the corporate zones were safe.

At the thought of Dane, Dane whom she had loved and then envied and then hated, her head began to hurt. Heavy, it was so heavy, she couldn't hold it up.

"Mallory? What...?"

The rest of Sue's words sounded as if she were on the other end of a tunnel.

Mallory got up from her desk, fighting a bout of dizziness. "I'll be right back."

Somehow she made it to the restroom. After dousing her face in cold water, she leaned her forehead on her arms on the counter. It was nothing. Thinking about her brother always upset her. There was absolutely no reason to be worried about the morph job next week. None at all.

Mallory hated windshield wipers, but the heavy mist was too much to leave them off. It was a gray, dismal day, and not even the exhilaration of being in a morph, of heading south to the Renton corporate zone on a new job could keep her from feeling low. Besides, she didn't much care for the body she was in: old, male, beginning to show its age despite treatments and appearance adjustments.

Sue was already in the Hypersystems complex, posing as an attractive job applicant. According to their plan, Sue would draw Tom Reich off, chosen for the sting because of his rampant libido. Other agents had already collected all the information they needed on him in a similar way. Then when Reich was safely out of the building, Mallory would waltz in and take his place—a perfect simulation right down to the thumb prints.

She parked the car just outside of Hypersystems and waited until she received word that Sue and Reich were far enough away. Then she pulled on a Laurentina raincoat (just like Reich's), opened her umbrella, and walked the short distance to the main building. At the entrance, she placed her hand on the identification panel. "Welcome, Mr. Reich," the security system said. "I thought you had gone home for the evening?"

"I seem to have forgotten my AI. I need to go back up and take a look around."

"Good luck." She could have sworn there was sarcasm in the security system voice.

Adrenalin from the danger of being caught slowly began to banish the depression she'd been feeling earlier. She walked briskly through the halls to Reich's office, opened the door with her (his) palm, locked the door behind her, and sat down in the desk chair. "System active."

"Active." Reich had programmed his computer with a low, slow female voice. Figured.

Morph agents were all trained security experts, and with the voice, thumb, and retina simulation of her morph, she was soon able to access the classified information on tech innovations presently being realized. Of course, the files were all encrypted, but the neural network she occupied and controlled made short work of that final hurdle.

Mallory scanned the information she'd found as the recording function in her neural network stored everything she viewed. Normally during a job of this type, she was only superficially aware of what she was reading, skimming files and plans as quickly as possible to gather all the information she could in the time at her disposal.

But this time, she found herself reading more slowly, reading to understand rather than just reading to store. Most of the material had to do with a so-called RLA— Remote Link Android: essentially, a morph unit without the mind upload. Hypersystems had gotten around the inadequacies of artificial intelligence by creating a kind of remote control technology which would allow corporate agents to control androids from a secured location. And the androids being developed for the purpose were based on an adjustable DNA matrix. Like morph units.

Mallory sat back and stopped reading. The advantages of an RLA from a corporate perspective were immediately obvious. While corporations tended to regard human resources as cheap and easily replaced (and were thus less worried about hypothetical brain drain than Ethan wished), the disadvantage of human agents was that they were unpredictable. Versatile but unpredictable. They could react more quickly in complicated and potentially dangerous social situations than an AI, but they were also prone to human error. An RLA would combine human and artificial intelligence, while making control of agents much easier.

It would also make morphs obsolete.

Her earphone crackled on. "Mal, Reich is heading back to the office—seems he forgot something," came Sue's voice in her ear. "I'm heading back to Hypersystems and will meet you at the southern entrance of the parking lot."

"Ok, shutting down right away," Mallory responded.

But somehow she couldn't. She continued to stare at the model of the android in the small holo well, while her neural network busily stored the images. How long would it take for Softec to recreate the technology from the information she had collected? She didn't know. She suspected they were farther in the actual morphing technology than Hypersystems: adjust the unit for the remote link and equip the neural network with a fully functioning AI and they would have an RLA.

And Mallory would never morph again.

Perhaps Ethan would come back. But perhaps he wouldn't. Perhaps he'd had enough of her, danger or no danger.

Mallory had a headache. Or her morph did.

She shut down the recording function in her morph unit. "Exit."

"Would you like to save your changes?" her internal system asked.

Yes, that was it: she simply would have no material for Softec when she returned. The mission had been cut short. "No."

But there were backups, and she couldn't erase the system before her mind was downloaded again. Somehow, she had to keep Softec from getting the information stored in her unit, despite her efforts.

She had to run.

Mallory turned off Reich's system and left the building, opening her umbrella and pulling the designer raincoat tight around the simulated body of Tom Reich. She was almost to her car when she saw a small brunette bombshell get out of a blue sports car. Sue's morph. She picked up her pace.

"Mallory!"

She glanced over her shoulder. Sue was hurrying after her. Mallory reached the black sedan, slid into the driver's seat, and shot out of the parking lot. When she was safely down the block, she looked back. Sue was already pulling out after her.

She had to lose her.

The communications system in the car came on. "Mallory, what's going on?"

Mallory felt sweat break out on the palms of her morph unit. But she wouldn't panic now. She had to get away with the morph, had to keep Softec from getting it.

She turned left in the direction of 405. The trees to either side of the freeway loomed above, reaching for the gray sky, while the windshield wipers beat an insistent rhythm, urging her on.

Sue's voice came over the system again. "Is something the matter, Mal?"

Mallory's forehead felt hot. It wasn't like her to panic. She wouldn't. She gazed in the rearview mirror.

Sue's car was right behind.

"Don't follow me, Sue," she told the communications unit. Her voice sounded fuzzy in her own head, as if there were dozens of people whispering to her in a low, dull undertone. She turned onto the on-ramp—south instead of north—relieved that she could finally give the car more speed.

"Mallory, I'm worried about you. You're not acting rationally. Pull over and let me drive you back."

Mallory shook her head, trying to concentrate on the road, the speed, the car.

"No, I have to go…" But she didn't know where she had to go, just that she couldn't go back to Softec. It was urgent, though, she knew it. The murmurs, they wouldn't let up. Mallory pressed the accelerator button. She had to get out of here, away from the voices, away from Seattle, away from Sue. Fast.

Away from Sue? But Sue was her friend. She was all Mallory had left. Dane was gone, her parents were gone, Ethan was gone, and now she was running away from Sue.

Sue's voice came over the communications unit again, but Mallory could no longer make any sense of the words. She gave the vehicle more speed. The voices were urging her on, growing louder.

An exit was coming up; maybe she could lose Sue there. At the last minute, she swerved into the exit lane and took the off-ramp full speed. She thought she heard someone calling her name, but it was drowned out by the clamor in her head, whispers like a dull roar, dizziness like a presence at the back of her mind. It was all she could do to concentrate on driving.

Then she heard a crash.

She braked the car and pulled over to the side of the road. Behind her, the blue sports car was crumpled up against a tree.

She got out and stumbled back through the wet grass between asphalt and trees. Sue was wedged into the crushed driver's seat, her head at an unnatural angle. Mallory tried to wake her—she should already have been repairing the damage to her morph, for God's sake! Nothing worked, nothing. She checked the data upload field at the bottom of the morph unit's spine—cracked. Mallory could only hope the neural network holding Sue's mind wasn't seriously damaged.

She staggered up, breathing deeply, and rested her hand on the frame of the vehicle. She couldn't let Softec find her, but she had to make sure they found Sue. Had to.

Her car. The AI in her car was undamaged. She could send out an alert from the black sedan.

And get away. If she didn't, they would take the morph from her.

Mallory slogged through the wet grass again, the raincoat over her head. Without making voice contact, she turned on the emergency signal to Softec. They would be here in less than half an hour, pick up the broken unit that held her best friend.

She was feeling dizzy again. Mallory closed her eyes, concentrating. She couldn't take the car—it had to stay here so they could find Sue.

But not Mallory. She could be someone else, anyone else. She had the morph.

She pushed herself away from the black sedan, moving toward the forest at the side of the road. She had to hide, had to escape before they came for her. The trees, she would hide in the trees. She would be alone there, safe.

But she wasn't. She wasn't alone. They were following her, surrounding her, closing in. Their voices gnawed at her consciousness, eroding her control. She ran. Or she thought she ran. She couldn't feel the body she was inhabiting, could only hear the voices, see the memories of so many others, the pieces of identity left behind in the morph, taking over the neural network her own weakened mind could no longer control.

She was losing herself. Slipping away; slipping, slipping away. Her lips curled up in a smile.

But slipping away wasn't far enough. They would get her if she didn't flee.

And then she was running, wet grass slapping the legs of her designer suit, trees looming above. She ran and ran, her breath coming shorter, the voices in her head like the whir of a helicopter. Her foot caught on a stray branch on the forest floor, and she went down. She was kneeling, kneeling in a puddle of rainwater, acid rain, she was crouching in the damp earth next to a tree on the edge of the forest. The forest was green and she was wet. Wet and cold. The voices. She was drowning in the voices, drowning in the wet forest, a jumble, a babble, a babbling brook. Cold and wet, taking her away.

The forest was green and she was far away.

INCLINATION

William Shunn

The Manual tells us that in the beginning the Builder decreed six fundamental Machines. These are his six aspects, and all we do we must do with the Six. We need no other machines.

I believe this with all my heart. I do. And yet sometimes I seem to intuit the existence of a seventh Machine, hovering like a blasphemous ghost just beyond apprehension.

There is something wrong with me, and I don't know what it is.

Late for my curfew and trembling, I grasp the doorknob that is not a doorknob.

This is the Machinist Quarter—only a tiny sliver of Netherview Station's Ring B, though I'm one of the few boys I know who has ever been outside it. Fo-grav stays off in the Quarter; our only simulation of gravity is the 0.25 g of natural centripetal acceleration born of the station's rotation and our two-kilometer distance from the hub. We joke that this is why it's called the Quarter. It sure isn't called that after the ratio of its volume to the station's.

The cabin I share with my father Thomas lies in the Inclined Plane branch, third transverse, twelfth hatch on the left. Standing at the hatch, I straighten my billed cap and smooth my coverall—each emblazoned with a right triangle stitched in dove-gray thread, representing our ward—and gently turn the knob. Recessed lights at deck level cast my diffuse shadow up the bulkheads to either side of me. The knob operates as if it were mounted on a genuine mechanical axle, though of course it isn't. A dumb mechanical doorknob wouldn't unlock to my touch alone, or Thomas's. I hate the doorknob. I hate the deceitfulness of it, the way its homogeneous smart matter mimics the virtuous and differentiated and pure. I hate what it conceals. I hate it for not keeping me out.

With a silent prayer to the Builder, I push the hatch open. It swings inward on soundless, lying hinges. I tread lightly inside, in case Thomas is sleeping, the non-slippers on my feet helping me keep my steps short and low. But as I round the door I see Thomas sitting up on his bunk in his short gray underall, watching me enter. The door closes itself behind me, which no door should do unbidden. The cabin is narrow and unadorned but for a diagram of the Six Fundamental Machines affixed to the rear bulkhead, and a small wooden chest bolted to the deck beneath it. The air reeks of a coppery sourness that matches Thomas's narrowed glare. The cabin is so tiny I could reach out and stroke his curly, graying hair if I wanted, but that's an urge that no longer seizes me often. Anyway, the days when I could reliably charm him out of his anger are long past.

"You're late, son," he says. He's squinting at me now, eyes unfocused, the way he does sometimes. He doesn't even glance at the chronometer on his wrist—a true mechanism, with tiny metal gears and not smart matter inside, a symbol of his status as a merchant trader. "It's past your curfew."

"I'm sorry," I say, turning my back and reaching for the crank that will fold my bunk down from the bulkhead opposite his.

His voice grates out in sharp, tight bursts like the strokes of a rasp on iron: "If you were sorry, you'd have been on time."

My shoulder blades prickle. I say nothing, cranking down the bunk.

"Jude, you're fifteen years old," Thomas says. "Why do you think you still have so many rules? Why?"

I try to shrug, but the effort feels jerky, like the gesture of a marionette. "I was waiting my turn at devotions," I say, clinging to the false crank. "You know—with Nic and the rest. But the Foremen wouldn't—they stayed past their time, and we, well..."

Thomas has risen, his voice at the back of my neck, shivering my spine. "I was out *looking* for you. I spoke to Nicodemus an hour ago. In Plane, not at gymnasium."

My blood runs chill. That's two lies I've told, and he's caught me in one already. Nicodemus is my best friend, or used to be, but lately I've been avoiding him. We were up late working on our motors in the schola a couple of weeks ago. He was helping me get the timing right on mine and his fingers brushed the back of my hand. It was just an accident. We've been friends all our lives, but it was like seeing him for the first time. I wanted to touch his face, though I didn't let myself. The scary thing was, it didn't feel wrong, and that scares me all the more.

Of course I can't explain this to Thomas. Nor can I explain why more and more I can't force myself to evening devotions on time. The cleansing room where we change and shower is like a chamber of horrors. None of the boys seem bothered by disrobing in front of each other, but it bothers me acutely. Letting them see my body makes me want to tear my skin off.

My bunk is halfway lowered. I want to turn and defend myself against Thomas's implicit accusation but a bolus of confusion clogs my throat. Words swarm like dust in my brain, eluding my grasp. Why do I have to explain any of this to him? Why doesn't he just know? And why is it his business?

"Great Builder, Jude," Thomas says at my back, "if you have to lie to me, how can I trust you at a job?"

My shoulders stiffen, my head half turns.

"That's right, I've lined up a *job* for you. Do you understand, son? At the *hub*."

A sick despair flares in my gut. Outside the Quarter? Could things get any worse?

"I need you up early, and fresh, but you're out doing Builder knows what when you should be in bed. Did I raise you to be this way, Jude? Did I?"

Tiny flecks of spittle flense the back of my neck. I was at my devotions, I really was, I want to say, but the words won't come.

"Answer me when I speak!" Thomas says, seizing my arm and spinning me around. My cap with its Inclined Plane insignia flies off my head.

The skinny legs tensed for violence, the slow ripple of his round, protruding belly, the sharpening rage on his gray blade of a face—I'm bigger and taller, but I might as well be five again for all that I can stand up to what's coming.

He shakes me. "You will *honor* your father, that your days may be long upon the earth!"

Saline globules tremble at the corners of my eyes,

watery jewels sparkling across my sight. The words burst out before I know I'm speaking: "There's no earth here, only metal."

My father's face flushes livid. He spins, hurling me across the cabin—not difficult, since my weight is just twenty kilos. I sprawl across my father's bunk, all gawky limbs and terror.

I roll over and there he is looming above me, fists raised and shaking. It's been months since last he struck me, an improbable lucky streak which now seems about to end. But he lowers his arms and leans over me.

"The Wrecker's in you, boy," he says, shaking a finger. "You pray hard and shake loose his grip. Pray to be made square and true. Tomorrow more than ever, you need the Builder to be with you."

And now he's pulling on his coverall and leaving the cabin to stalk off his anger, the hatch snicking shut behind him like a quiet tap to a finishing nail. Alone, I flow off the bunk to the floor, to my knees, to retrieve my cap and pray.

I'm out of true and I need fixing. Through shuddering tears I pray for the Builder to make me a better son, a stronger laborer, a whole person. I pray for his protection, both physical and spiritual. I pray for reassurance that Thomas doesn't really mean to send me alone among the Sculpted in the morning.

When I finally crawl into my bunk and wrap the blanket around myself, though, it's not the Builder with his Machines I picture watching over me in the dark. It's my departed mother Kaiya, angel wings spread above me in a canopy of white.

The Builder has ignored my prayer, at least the part about the Sculpted.

We rise and dress early, Thomas and I, and exit our cabin. In one hand Thomas carries a gray cloth sack big enough to hold a loaf of bread.

Only the most devoted practitioners are awake at this hour, en route to gymnasium. Rather than follow them, Thomas leads me to the end of the next branch over, to where Saul, foreman of Inclined Plane, lives. The only mark that sets this hatch apart from every other in the row is the small carpenter's square etched at its very center.

Foreman Saul appears in the hatchway, bleary-eyed, at Thomas's knock. "Selah, Jude," he says in greeting, favoring me with a look both compassionate and foreboding. "Brother Thomas, let me speak to you alone a moment. We'll only be a bit, Jude."

Thomas follows Saul inside without a glance at me. I stand in the corridor and mentally rehearse the Builder's Code. I'm still in Lever, less than halfway through the Hexalogue, when the hatch opens again. Saul gestures me in.

The cabin is a little smaller than the one Thomas and I share, and consequently more crowded than ours ever gets. Thomas sits at one end of the only bunk, cloth sack in his lap. He pats the space beside him, and I sit. Saul picks up a thermos from the foldout stovetop that juts from the rear bulkhead and sips carefully at the spout. The air smells faintly of powdered coffee and machine oil.

"Jude," Saul says, "your father let me know late last night that he's secured you a position on a stevedore crew at the docks. Unfortunately, as you're required there promptly this morning and you can now be fined for tardiness, there's no time to go through the usual series of preparatory lessons before you leave the safety of the Quarter."

I don't miss the baleful sideways glance Saul gives Thomas, but Thomas doesn't seem to react to it. He just sits there with the same twist of bored impatience on his lips.

"Oh, I've been out a couple of times before," I say, if only to cut the palpable tension, which is settling into my neck. "I mean, when I was younger."

"Yes." Saul sighs, blinking his pouchy eyes a few times. He is older than my father, taller and softer, but no sadder. I've been tempted many times to bring my cares and questions to him, but something has always held me back. "You're a bright young man, Jude, and I know you've walked among the Sculpted before, so at least the sights won't be new to you. But accompanying your father once or twice on his rounds is hardly the same as working alongside them, alone, for a full shift every day. If there's no time for the proper instruction first, at the very least a blessing is in order."

"Okay," I say, a little of the weight lifting from my shoulders. Even if the Builder isn't listening to me, surely he'll listen to the foreman, as pious a man as I know. But at the same time I'm beginning to feel in my gut just how much spiritual danger I'll be courting. Why is Thomas doing this to me?

"If you'll sit here?" Saul says. He is setting up a metal folding chair in the middle of the cabin, which means it nearly bumps Thomas's knees. I scoot over into the chair, doffing my cap and clutching it in my lap, as Saul removes a ceremonial oilcan from a niche in the bulkhead. Thomas joins Saul behind me. The oilcan *ka-chunk*s, the tip of its spout tickling the hair at the crown of my head as it deposits a tiny bead of machine oil. Saul gently taps the droplet down onto my scalp, and he and Thomas lay their hands upon my head.

Other kids get to have their mothers in the cabin with them during blessings like this. I close my eyes and try to imagine Kaiya here, watching from the corner near the hatch. And she could be, right? Surely that's not a vain hope.

"Great Builder," Saul says, "in the name of the Wheel, the Wedge, the Lever, the Plane, the Pulley, and the Screw, we bring before you your true and faithful servant Jude, who ventures forth this day to labor amongst the Sculpted for his daily bread. Be with him, Builder, that he might have health in his navel, marrow in his bones, and strength in his sinews—strength that he might work and not be weary, but moreso that the Wrecker with his subtle wiles may find no purchase in his heart, mind, or flesh. We know the Wrecker's cunning is great, Builder, and that he can make what's wrong seem right. But your power and love are infinite, and so we commend this young man to your oversight with all faith in your goodness and wisdom. May we ever draw nearer to thee, Great Builder, as the Inclined Plane rises ever to heaven. Amen."

"Amen," I say. The hands, which have grown progressively heavier during the blessing, lift from my head. I stand, rolling my head to soothe my neck.

Saul folds the chair and sets it aside—a deft, practiced move in the cramped space—then reaches out to clasp my forearm in the Scaffold Grip. His hand is warm and dry. "What's today, Thursday? Let's meet Sundays after temple, Jude, to make some headway on those lessons. Better late than never."

"When his schedule allows," Thomas says, conspicuously checking his chronometer. "They call this Oneday outside. Weeks aren't reckoned the same."

"Of course. Then any day you can, Jude." Saul

squeezes and releases my forearm. "And remember that the Builder blesses you not just for obedience to his commandments, but for obedience to your parents as well."

"Jude," Thomas says. He picks the sack up from the bunk and inclines his head toward the hatch.

"Selah, Foreman," I say and follow my father out into the corridor. I look back to see, in the moment before the hatch closes behind us, Foreman Saul standing like a forlorn beast in the center of a cage.

Or is that perception just a way to make myself feel better about the sentence to which I've been condemned?

Thomas leads me at a brisk pace out to the main corridor, skipping lightly along the deck. "Don't let him get to you, Jude," he says over his shoulder. "Saul, Bartholomew, *none* of the Foremen understand our economic realities."

I'm not sure whether he means our family's or the whole Quarter's. I don't ask for clarification, not just because I don't like encouraging him to disparage the Foremen but because we've turned into the main corridor and a few more people, from all different wards, are out and about now. The soft gray of their coveralls and visored caps against the brighter gray of the bulkheads make the Quarter look almost like a scene from an ancient monochrome photograph.

We pass the gymnasium entrance, then the intersections with Wedge Branch and Wheel and Axle. We're alone now, and the Primum Mobile Gate looms ahead, painted with various strident warnings and danger symbols.

"You'll have to find your own way back this evening, so pay close attention," Thomas says, pulling the lever that opens the Gate. The massive hatch grinds aside, admitting a bedlam of voices and light and sound. "Now be ready for the weight. And whatever you do, don't gawk."

My heart races. I follow Thomas through the Gate and an extra forty kilos drops onto my bones. Thanks to my faithful attention to devotions I don't fall, but I stagger and I'm sweating in the moist air before we've gone far. The public corridors are as crowded and noisy now as they are around the clock, alive with the babel of a thousand languages, and the bulkheads are lost in the riot of greenery that thrives on every available surface. I feel conspicuous in my Machinist garb. People—monsters—fall silent and stare as we pass, and with all their unsettling modifications it's hard not to stare back. I can't imagine navigating this profane world without Thomas.

We ride a slidewalk spinward, then crowd into a hubward elevator that at least contains no obvious plant life. But for every normal person, I see one with skin the wrong color or texture, limbs numbering too many or too few, a body with mysterious prosthetics or protuberances, or a head misshapen and gross. A pebbled gray creature that might once have been human brushes against me in the elevator. Dizzy, I press closer to Thomas, the sweat trickling into my eyes. I'm not sure whether his hand on my shoulder is meant to reassure me or restrain me.

At hub level, the bulkheads are again clean and metallic, as they should be. Thomas leads me through a short but bewildering maze of hatches and gangways. With fewer people around now, I breathe more easily. Thomas knocks at an open hatch. I peek inside. It's an office about a meter and a half in radius, and every surface, 720 spherical degrees around, is jammed with monitors, control panels, and handholds. The thickset woman seated at the center has a second pair of arms where her legs should be.

"I don't give a spout for your schedule," she tells someone unseen. "My stevies can do the job fast, but not that fast. All right, fine. You do that."

She looks at Thomas, and I see she has silver semi-spheres implanted over her eyes. Three quick swings from handhold to handhold bring her to the door. Fograv is still about 0.75. She's *strong*.

"This the kid?" she asks.

"That's him," Thomas says.

She turns those reflective bugeyes on me, twitching her head up and down, and it's like I'm being X-rayed. What she sees, I can't imagine. "Any mods? No, of course not. You goddamn Wheelies, what am I talking about? All right, he doesn't look too bad. Let's get him suited up and see how he does. What's your name, kid?"

My mouth is so dry my tongue crackles. "Jude."

"Well, now you're Stevie. For stevedore."

She barks a laugh like a chugging motor, clinging to holds around the hatch with three hands. Thomas laughs too. His eyes crinkle and his lips peel back, and it's like seeing ten years drop away from him. He never laughs around me.

In that moment I feel inexpressibly sad. And I hate him.

The woman swings out through the hatch and drops to the deck between Thomas and me. "Follow me," she says, loping down the gangway on all fours.

Thomas shoves the cloth sack into my hands. "Your lunch," he says.

I clutch the sack like a lifeline. It's three times as

heavy as it should be, and its heft brings a desperate lump to my throat. On a usual morning, it's I who makes lunch for Thomas, but I didn't even think about it today. I'm realizing that the usual mornings are behind me.

"Now you work hard and do what Renny tells you," Thomas says. "I can't stress enough how important this money is."

"Okay." I turn to trudge after the woman.

"And remember who you are," Thomas stage-whispers fiercely. "Your body belongs to the Builder, not to them."

"Selah," I say.

Thomas sighs. "Selah, son. Now go."

Renny, fidgeting impatiently, has stopped at a juncture up ahead. I follow, the grief of abandonment thick in my throat.

The Six are more than just machines. High Foreman Titus—our founder, who 120 years ago spoke with the Builder face to face—teaches us that they represent the Builder's various aspects, and thus the ways in which we must approach him. The Six also name our wards, the clans or tribes of our faith. Though my father and I belong to Inclined Plane Ward, we owe each equal adoration, and it's the Wedge that concerns me now.

The Manual teaches that the purpose of the Wedge is to both divide asunder and hold in place. From this we learn to divide ourselves from the evils of the world, as the maul divides the log, keeping always to the side of the Builder. Yet we also learn to bridge the gap between, as the keystone—a truncated wedge—holds the arch in place. The lesson for us is to serve the world, and serve as examples, without becoming corrupted by it.

As a people, we excel at dividing ourselves from the world. We don't do so well at bridging—except perhaps for my father. But between him and me there's surely a great Wedge, and it's never clear to me which of us is on which side of it.

Thomas didn't explain to me exactly what a stevedore is. Turns out it's someone who loads and unloads cargo. Starships from hundreds of light-years around dock at Netherview Station's hub, then, depending on size and mass, slide into one of three concentric levels of berths. Many of the ships are laded automatically by robot or waldo; the ones that can't afford the special treatment (or can afford to waive it) get us.

Renny explains this to me, more colorfully, as I follow her to the locker room. She leaves me alone there to change into my docksuit, a close-fitting layer of red polymer that covers me from the neck down. I try not to think about how much smart matter I must be wearing. I leave my coverall and cap behind like a shed snakeskin in my thumbprint-activated locker. The heaviness I feel has nothing to do with gravity, though physically I'm breathing hard already from the exertion since leaving the Quarter. Carrying my lunch sack, I rejoin my new boss outside the locker room.

Before leading me to the berth where the crew awaits us, Renny rears up on her hind arms and affixes a round green badge to my chest. "Regs," she says. "Since you've got no built-in monitors, this'll let us keep tabs on you."

The crew is twelve, male and female both, and I make thirteen. They're lounging in a small break room off

Berth C46. Renny clambers to the top of a table and waves for quiet. "This is our new trainee," she says. "His name is Jude Plane. Corgie, he's your man this shift."

A groan from a preternaturally thin fellow sprawled out on a couch prompts laughter from the others and a sinking feeling inside me. I'm sweating, much to my embarrassment.

"Okay, you shits, okay. The *Needlethreader*'s in dock now. Let's go."

The crew don helmets and begin to spill out a hatch opposite the one Renny brought me through. They disperse in all directions—left, right, up, down—grabbing implements from a rack outside as they go. They're all human in shape, mostly normal as far as I can see. They don't look much older than I am, but you never can tell with the Sculpted. One has bright blue skin above the collar of his suit, an eye-straining contrast with the red polymer. He winks at me as he drops out the hatch. My stomach clenches.

Renny hops down from the table and grabs Corgie by the leg before he can say a word to me. "Pay close attention to the kid," Renny says. "He's barefoot. He'll need a fishbowl on top of everything else."

"You're joking," Corgie says. "I don't think I've ever *seen* a fishbowl."

"There's one in the rack today along with everything else."

My trainer heaves an aggrieved sigh. "All right, Juke," he says to me. "Follow me and stick close."

"Jude," I say.

"Right. Juke."

Renny reaches for my lunch sack, which I still clutch uncertainly. She stashes it for me as I trail out the hatch after Corgie.

And suddenly I'm not just lighter. I'm weightless, and drifting.

Fo-grav isn't turned *off* in the berth; it's on but dialed down to null, damping even the small inertial effects of rotational velocity and centrifugal force. Corgie gives me a brief lesson in how to maneuver in nullg with a dockwand, a thin, meter-long rod of smart matter that ejects a stream of inert particles from one end or the other on command. Basically you point it, squeeze, and drift off in the opposite direction. It takes me a while to get the hang of it, largely because I'm loath to touch it, but soon enough I'm helping Corgie and the rest carry out the dockwand's other function, herding big gray crates of who knows what out the cargo hold in the belly of the starship and through the air to the elevators that will take them wherever they need to go next-sometimes another level of the station, sometimes the hold of another ship in another berth.I do it all wearing a helmet with a transparent visor that curves down over my face. The helmet draws words and diagrams in the air, overlaying what I see, giving me data like what time of day it is and where the next crate needs to go. By turning my head and focusing somewhere, I can get information about whatever I'm looking at. Sweeping my gaze along the streamlined, almost organic curve of the huge ship, for example, I can access its flight schedules, crew data, cargo manifests, manufacturer's specifications, and even schematic diagrams that show me more of what it looks like than I can possibly see by just flitting around in the space between its black belly and the berth's bulkhead. I can zoom in on the other crews working the hatches fore and aft of ours, and I can even find out more about my own crewmates, though I don't feel right about prying. But it *is* a good way to learn everyone's name, which I manage before the start of our first break.

Is this the world my crewmates walk through every waking moment of every day, with intimate information about everything they see just an eyeblink away? We may inhabit the same great wheel in space, but these strangers live in a truly alien world, one I don't like visiting. Builder knows making motors isn't my favorite activity, good as I am at it; still, I'd rather be in my applied mechanics class with Nic and Mal than here. I'd even rather be home with Thomas—anywhere but stranded amongst the ignorantly blasphemous, wielding tools that are an offense in the sight of the Builder, being slowly poisoned by the worldview of the Sculpted.

What is Thomas trying to do to me?

Our shift is the longest day of my life. The ghostly ticking clock in the corner of my vision doesn't help.

At shift's end we deposit our dockwands, now stubby and depleted, in the rack outside the break room and file off to the showers. I'm happy to drop off my fishbowl as well, though the experience of walking in gravity without a data overlay seems somehow dreamlike and crippling as I readjust to moving about without it-almost as crippling as walking in highg alone. It surprises me how exhausted I am. I must have used and abused every muscle in my body.

As we reach the locker room, I'm startled that our single-file queue remains intact. The women enter through the same hatch as the men. Bringing up the rear, I tell myself there must surely be a dividing bulkhead or at the very least a screen inside, but of course I was here this morning and know there's no such thing. I try to keep my eyes averted, but just to reach my locker I must step around a woman named Soon, who already has her suit pushed down to her hips.

The room is too small, and everyone jostles everyone else on the way to the ultrasonic showers. I stand with my burning face to my open locker, wondering if I can get away with standing here and not changing until the room is empty. Soon's bare torso blazes like a beacon in my mind. A part of me is fascinated and wants to look at it again; another part is horrified at the thought, and at the distant, epochal memories of my mother that stir, memories so ancient they seem apocryphal.

Renny, galumphing through the locker room, slaps the back of my thigh and says, "Next shift's gotta get in, kid. Hurry it up."

Somehow I strip off the suit, deposit it in the recycler, and manage the walk to the showers. My skin *crawls* as I crowd into the white ceramic chamber with the others, though part of this, I'm sure, is the feel of the ultrasonics vibrating sweat and grime loose from my body. Still, I can't look higher than anyone's ankles. It's not just the naked flesh that distresses me. I'm out of my coverall in front of heathen, and that's a grave offense in the sight of the Builder. My hands hover in front of my crotch.

My hip brushes the thin blue man's; I nearly jump out of my skin and mumble an apology. "Don't worry about it," he says with a kind smile. "We're all friends here."

"Yeah," Corgie says. "Just help yourself to a handful of whatever's closest."

"Or a thimbleful," says an apparent neuter named Ice IX, pointing at Corgie's flaccid penis.

"Careful. You don't want to wake the monster."

Mijk, a muscular man with a series of knobby lumps down his back, says, "I do. Someone ran all the lotion out of my dispenser."

"And apparently he wants it back," Soon says with a giggle.

Corgie wipes his mouth. "Come and get it," he says, and his penis flares to enormous size, all ridged and quivering. It *is* a monster.

I turn away, blushing. But something strange has begun to happen. I don't feel comfortable exactly, but I do feel somewhat invisible, with less of the compulsion to run and hide than comes in the cleansing room at gymnasium. I'm able to let my eyes roam some, taking in the female bodies as well as the male, plus two or three I find less determinate and the entirely genderless Ice IX. In the Quarter, contact between boys and girls is strictly regulated and chaperoned, even during courtship; a situation like this is as unthinkable as a motor assembling itself from raw ore. I have more answers now than I know what to do with to what minutes ago was only a compelling mystery.

I almost don't want the shower to end, but when the thought takes form I realize the Wrecker is already getting his claws into me. How much easier a time of it he has here than inside the Quarter! Despair washes over me. How will I ever survive this?

Clean, but with a film of shame clinging to my exposed skin, I trail the group back to the lockers. I've pulled on my underall and my coverall and am about to put my cap on when a tall, trouserless man named Twenty plucks it deftly out of my hands.

"What's this for, some kind of uniform?" he asks, turning the cap this way and that. "You got *another* job?"

My muscles seem to seize up, and the bottom falls out of my soul. So much for invisibility. Renny is gone; I don't know where to turn for help. Heat and mortification radiate from the top of my uncovered head as Twenty's Sculpted hands defile my cap.

"No, you ramscoop," Corgie says, taking the cap, "he's a Wheelie. Don't you know anything?"

And now he's passing it to someone else, who's asking why there's a triangle on it if I'm a Wheelie, and now it goes to someone else, and now it's flying through the air past my face, and now again the other way. I reach for the cap, but it's snatched by the knobby-spined Mijk.

"Wheelie, huh?" he says. "Those are like Christers, right? How come you're named after a traitor, Wheelie?"

"*Judas* betrayed the Builder," I say quietly. I want to sound dangerous, but even I can hear the quaver in my voice. "Jude was a different apostle."

"Jude, Judas, Peter, penis—whatever. Think this'd fit me?"

Mijk's about to slip the cap onto his head, and I'm about to shout something, maybe *do* something I'll regret, when a half-dressed woman named Beneficent Sunrise takes it from him.

"Mijk, it doesn't stretch. It's not smart enough to fit your thick skull."

"Then what good is it?"

Beneficent Sunrise turns the cap over. She studies the inclined plane symbol. "Never seen something made from dumb fabric before. Interesting the way it feels. Almost real."

Her frank curiosity defuses my anger. Or is it the sight of her full, bobbing breasts? They fill me with an emotion I can't quite put a name to. Not desire, not quite, but something as sharp in its poignancy. I wonder what *they* feel like.

The blue man picks my cap cleanly out of her grip. Holding it by the visor only, he puts it in my hand. My fingers clutch it spasmodically.

"Real like your tits, Sunny?" he says to the woman.

"Go deplete your wand," she says in the general laughter, but she's smiling with everyone else.

Weak with humiliation and relief, I cover my head and turn to rummage in my empty locker. Around me, my crewmates casually hide their nakedness.

The blue man is called Haun Friedrich 4, but the fish-bowl taught me he prefers to go by Derek Specter. He's in the trial period before a legal name change.

The idea that one may choose one's own name is as strange to me as everything else about the Sculpted. What would I choose if I were to name myself? Paul? Luke? Timothy? None of them work. I can't imagine learning to answer to any name but Jude. That's me. That's who I am.

I'm standing in the gangway outside the locker room, having lingered there until the arriving crew forced me out. People edge past me in both directions. I'm trying to remember which way I came this morning, fighting a growing sense of panic, when Haun—Derek—touches my shoulder with blue fingers.

"Know where you're going?" he asks with an easy grin.

"Er...rimward," I say, feeling the blood heat my cheeks.

"Yes, that would almost certainly be correct." Derek leans against the bulkhead near me, a little too close, arms folded and eyes bright. His skin is the blue of Enoch's fabled seas, and his irises glow like bits of its sky. "Do you need any help getting there?"

I look down at my gray nonslippers. "I guess I do," I say, embarrassed at the prospect of this ostentatiously abnormal creature rescuing me twice in the same ten minutes.

Derek gazes at the opposite bulkhead, cupping his chin. "Wheelieville, I presume," he says. He gives me a sidelong glance, apologetic but not self-conscious. "The Machinist Quarter, I mean."

"Uh, yeah."

His eyes narrow. "Let me just find it on the map."

"What map?" I say. His glance this time is mildly reproving, and I let out an abashed "Oh."

"We just need to get you to Elevator Seven, Eight, or Nine," Derek says after a moment. "That's probably the trickiest part of the route. And I happen to be going the same way, if you don't mind company."

My feet are itching to move. I'd rather he just point me in the right direction and let me go my way, but I'm too tired to argue. I shrug my acquiescence.

As we set off down the narrow way, Derek says over his shoulder, "You were good in there today. Not everyone adjusts to null-gee that quickly. I think even Renny was impressed."

He looks back expectantly, but since I'm not sure what I'm supposed to say to this, I don't answer.

"Corgie gave you some shit, I know," Derek says, "but you should have seen him back when he started. Talk about an ostrich. Was this your first time with an overlay?"

"Yes."

"I remember when I was first getting used to it. It was

strange to turn it off and not see labels everywhere I looked. You must be going through the same thing. You probably haven't ever used Geoff before either." At my blank look, he grins. "Yeah, we'll have to teach you how to use Geoff. Then next time you need to get somewhere you won't have to put up with me running off at the mouth."

"What's Geoff?" I ask.

"Info daemon on the public net. You've really been sheltered, haven't you? Geoff's mostly for travelers and transients—anyone offline, really, so you can use him too. He'll answer any question you have, *if* he has the answer and you're older than ten. And as long as it's not private or classified."

Derek keeps looking back at me with an expression like he's trying to tell me something significant and I'm just not getting it. I feel dumb, and my skin's been crawling ever since the word "daemon" anyway. "I—thanks, but that doesn't sound like something I ought to be messing with."

He gives me one more look, then shrugs. "Suit yourself," he says. "But you do have a right to whatever information you want. You only have to ask."

We take the next couple of turns in silence, me adrift in an uneasiness I can't quite put my finger on.

"So what's a nice Machinist like you doing in a job like this anyway?" Derek asks at last. "I thought you were supposed to stick to your own turf, not venture out amongst the unwashed."

The corridors are wider now, the crowds thickening, and Derek, walking beside me, speaks too loudly for my comfort. "Commerce with the Sculpted isn't forbidden," I say a little defensively, keeping my voice low. "It's just...discouraged, I guess. It's—there's a lot of danger, spiritually."

"I always wanted to be a spiritual hazard," Derek says. "You probably shouldn't even be talking to me, should you?"

"Um…" I'm looking around, anywhere but at him. There are unholy forms and faces and sounds and smells everywhere. "Not really, not like this."

"So why are you? I mean, in the larger sense. Why are you here at all? Why do you have this job?"

I sigh. "I didn't exactly have a choice," I say, cursing my inability to hold my tongue. "Thomas, my father, he's our ward trader, which means he goes out and sells whatever we build or manufacture. That's so the ward can meet its obligation to the Guild."

"Which is saving up to get off Netherview Station and continue its fabled trek to Enoch. I've read about it."

I look at him, nonplussed. We know so little about the Sculpted, I somehow can't get over the fact they know anything about us. "But business isn't so good," I continue. "As trader, my father has to pay the rest of the ward first, before he takes his share, but lately there's not much left over. In fact, I think there may not be *any-thing* left over. He's been trying for months to get me a job outside the Quarter, and believe me, that means things are grim."

"Of course they are," Derek says. "Who wants prim-itive toys made from primitive materials?"

"They're not toys!" I say, turning on him, thinking of the motor I've been building for some weeks now. "It's serious work! It's sacred!"

"Hey, hey, I'm sorry." We're now at the elevator bay, waiting, and Derek puts his hands up as if to ward off my anger. I see for the first time that his palms and the pads of his fingers are a rich green, fading into blue at the edges. "I didn't mean it like that. But you have to realize that's how most people see what you do. If it has no practical use, it must be a toy."

"It *does* have a practical use," I say. "You people are just too stiffnecked to humble yourselves and admit it."

Derek nods. "Or you might say we've put away childish things."

This reference to the Manual startles me. The elevator opens as I'm groping for a suitable reply, and we crowd in with several other commuters, including a woman who has tentacles where her fingers should be. Derek spends the ride staring straight ahead with the barest of smiles on his lips.

I'm still smarting when the elevator opens on Six. I'm about to say that I think I can find my way from here, but Derek steps out with me into the thick, damp air and dank vegetation.

"I've been meaning to ask," he says, "what *is* the significance of the triangle on your clothing? It's an inclined plane, right?"

"Um, right," I say. "That's the ward I belong to."

"You're lucky you're not in Screw," he says. "You'd *never* hear the end of it at work."

"So, er," I say, stumbling a little as we step onto the counterspinward slidewalk, "I guess you understand the Inclined Plane is one of the Six Fundamental Machines."

"I've heard that rumor somewhere," Derek says.

"Well, they're also symbols. This one represents the obliqueness of our approach to the Master Builder. No matter—"

"You mean God, right?"

"You might call him that," I say.

"I might. And again, I might not."

He has a way of continually derailing me and looking pleased about it that I find entirely infuriating. "No matter how shallow the angle," I say, soldiering on, "the Inclined Plane leads us ever upward, and though it may take eons, eventually we'll reach the level of the Builder."

"Sounds suspiciously like the Tower of Babel," Derek says. "And didn't God punish the Babylonians for trying to approach him in just that way?"

"Their approach was more direct, and completely literal," I say, my voice heating up. "We're not talking about a literal approach. Ours is metaphorical. We approach the Builder by understanding and manipulating his six aspects."

"I'd have thought he'd have more respect for the direct approach. You know, just wrap an inclined plane around a big pole and climb to heaven." He waggles his blue eyebrows at me, eyes twinkling. "Maybe what offended him about it was the metaphorical significance of it. Maybe the Babylonians were really saying God could screw himself, and that's why he gave them all a good tongue-lashing."

The delight he derives from such extreme statements takes my breath away. "You can't approach the Builder in anything *but* a metaphorical way!" I say.

"Then why let yourselves be literally constrained? Why confine yourselves to what you can build from six fairly arbitrary machines?"

"The machines aren't arbitrary! They're the six aspects of the Builder."

"They *are* arbitrary, and not all of them are even that fundamental. The screw we were just talking about— like I said, it's just an inclined plane wrapped around an axle. The pulley's a special case of the wheel and axle, and the wedge is just another way of looking at an inclined plane."

I wipe fatigue sweat from my forehead. He's hitting uncomfortably close to blasphemous thoughts I've entertained myself, which may explain my vehemence in denouncing them. "Every aspect partakes of the others to some extent," I say, but I sound more shrill than certain.

"Seems to me that if there really is a god, you could find some far more useful metaphors for the way he operates if you'd just reach deeper than your six machines."

He exits the slidewalk and I follow, belatedly realizing we've arrived near the PM Gate. To my relief and chagrin both, I've been so focused on the conversation that I haven't paid much attention to the nightmarish creatures around me, nor to the riotous greenery. But I notice them all now and feel hemmed in.

"We're not meant to reach deeper," I say, hurrying to keep up with Derek's long gait in the swarming crowd.

"Then you'll never achieve godhood, now, will you?" Derek says. He pauses near the unadorned hatchway that leads to the Machinist Quarter. "Well, here you are."

Bathed in sweat, I purse my lips. "Thanks, uh…thanks for getting me here."

"The pleasure was all mine." He makes as if to move on, but stops. "I meant to tell you before, I thought you handled those jokers in the locker room about as well as you could have. Just don't let them know they're getting to you and they'll leave you alone soon enough. They're not really mean, just exemplars of what I call the indolent uninformed. Learning new things is such a trivial process they don't even make the effort."

"Like the Israelites and the fiery serpents," I say.

Derek blinks, his eyes losing focus. "Interesting," he says after a moment or two. "Numbers, chapter twenty-one. If the ones who were bitten only gazed upon Moses's brass serpent, they would live. All they had to do was look. You know, there's good sense to be found in that book here and there."

"The miracle is," I say, "even a gentile can look and see it."

Derek laughs long and loud. It makes me feel clever and proud, though why I should care about looking clever to this mockery of a man baffles me. "Touché, Jude," he says. "See you tomorrow at the orifice."

He studies some resource invisible to me, and then he's off, a lean blue figure vanishing into a teeming, grotesque jungle. I'm reminded that he inhabits a world even more strange than this physical one, and that when the two or us look at an object we each see a vastly different thing.

"Selah, Derek," I say under my breath. I pull the lever and pass through the Gate, wondering what he sees when he looks at me.

The cleanliness, calm, cool, and quiet of the Quarter stand in stark contrast to what I've left behind. It's evening by our clocks; we run here on only one shift. The few Machinists out and about look at me strangely as I pass from outside. It should feel good, this homecoming after an eternal shift away, this shedding of weight, this lightness, this cooling of my sweat, but I find myself keyed up and restless before I've even reached the branching to Wheel and Axle. I know Thomas will be waiting for me, wanting to know how the day went, but I can't confine myself at home just yet. Instead I lower my head and trudge to gymnasium.

The machines are manned mostly by Levers, all older than I, but one station opens up before long. I do my best to complete the ritual properly, pitting every muscle group against the pulleys as I rehearse the Builder's Code in my mind, but I'm barely into the first canto before my sore muscles are quaking. What's more, I can't keep my thoughts focused. My mind keeps reaching back to worry images of naked flesh—sometimes colored naturally, sometimes blue or green.

One by one the Levers are finishing up and heading to the cleansing room, some of them whispering and giving me looks as strange as the ones I got outside from the Sculpted. I rush to try to complete the minimal requirements before the place fills up with Inclined Planes, but in vain. I'm not quite done when Nicodemus and another Plane named Amos arrive. I see them from across the room, over the tops of three ranks of machines. I duck my head but too late. Nic spots me and hurries over.

The station next to mine is empty, abandoned just moments before. Nic, his face cautiously friendly, slides into the seat, leaving Amos to fidget awkwardly in the aisle before us. "Selah, Jude," Nic says.

"Selah," I say, mouth dry.

Nic begins some warmup stretches of his arms and back. "You weren't at schola today," he says.

I look straight ahead, pumping away with my arms in bellows mode, but Amos is right there staring at me so I focus on my knees instead. "No," I say.

"Malachi heard you were outside," Nic says.

"Yeah, at the *hub*," Amos says.

"He said you had a job."

A wary hope fills Nic's voice, but whether it's hope that the rumors or true or simply hope that I'll talk to him, I can't tell. Either way, I can't look at him. I can't look at his golden hair, his glistening shoulders, his wise blue eyes. But I can't not answer.

"That's right," I say gruffly. "I guess you won't see me much in class anymore."

"Is it true about the Sculpted?" Amos says. He's a skinny kid and he practically dances from foot to foot. "They drink blood instead of water?"

"Amos, I see a free machine over there," Nic says with a jerk of his head.

"But—"

"I'm nearly done here," I say.

"Better hurry, Amos."

I can't see Nic's face, but I hear the tone of warning in his voice, and I see the answering expression of querulousness on Amos's face. Amos stalks off, even as I fight down the unwelcome surge of warm emotion in my chest.

I rest for a twelve-count, saying nothing, then embark on another bellows set.

Nic has launched into a set of cherrypickers. "So what's with you, Jude?" he says between reps.

"What do you mean?"

"You've been avoiding me for a couple of weeks now. What did I do?"

I sigh, clinging to the handgrips and letting my upper body sag. "It's not you, Nic."

"Then what is it? Is it about this job?"

What am I supposed to tell him? That I've started to worry I like him too *much*? I can hardly express the thought even to myself.

"It's not about the stupid job," I say, though I'm

aching to tell him about everything I've seen and done today. I cut my set short and stand up, infuriated. "Great Builder, you're so—so—oh, flashcan it!"

I rush to the cleansing room with all the dignity I can muster, which isn't much, aware of all the eyes on me. In the quick glimpse I caught of Nic before I fled, there was hurt and concern. He hadn't yet broken a sweat.

I try to put him out of my head among the straggling Levers in the steam-filled shower. I try to conjure the illusion of camouflage I felt in the showers at the hub, as if I could hide myself amongst my Sculpted crewmates and never be seen. Here I feel anxious and wrong, like I don't belong. But I certainly don't belong *there*.

Scanting my cleansing, I dress quickly and hurry into the main corridor. The crowds here are about as thick as they ever get but seem downright sparse compared to outside. People stride lightly from their duties back to their branches, men and women, boys and girls, as evening stretches toward the dinner hour. I envy them their apparent lack of care.

"Jude, Jude," hails a gentle voice, and I raise my head. I hadn't realized my neck had bent as if in stronger gravity.

It's Sariah, a Pulley my age who's walking the other way. "Oh, selah," I say.

She takes my sleeve and draws me to the side of the corridor. "Missed you at schola," she says, voice low. Not that we have any of the same classes, but the boys and girls do see each other at lunch. Often I've wished I could learn the simpler skills the girls ply, like producing rough fabrics on machines the men construct, but the one occasion on which I expressed such a desire to my father is one I'm not likely to forget. I was younger then and hadn't learned better.

"I wasn't there," I say tiredly.

"I know," she says, a look of eager horror on her face. "You were outside. Helena saw you go this morning. So what was it like?"

My eyes are already straying down the corridor toward escape. How can I explain what it was like today? I'm too confused. "It's the Wrecker's workshop out there, truly," I say, pulling away. "Look, I'm sorry, but I need to get home."

She lays a cool hand on my arm. She's very pretty with her enviably long yellow hair, and she's nearly as tall as I am. "Jude, what's wrong?" she asks, her face close to mine, eyes filled with concern. "Was it that horrible? You can tell me."

I want to weep. I have friends, sure, or I did, but what I've never had is someone I can confide in, someone I can really trust and open up to. That's all I want.

"Sariah—"

I feel her eyes searching my face, but I can't quite meet her gaze. "What is it?" she says.

"I—" Am I really going to say it? She's always been nice to me, kind. I glance up quickly. "What do you think about Nic?"

"Nicodemus?" A little crease appears between Sariah's fine eyebrows. "He's okay, he's nice. Why?"

I shake my head, my stomach turning inside out. "It's just—you know, he's such a great guy…"

I trail off as her eyes get a little wider. "Oh," she says quietly, almost in wonder.

"I mean, he's been my best friend for such an incredibly long time," I say.

She nods slowly, focused on some inner vision. "No, no, I see. I get it."

"So, you know…"

"Who would have thought?" The ghost of a pensive smile touches the corner of her mouth. She kisses me suddenly on the cheek. "Thank you, Jude. Thank you. I'll talk to you later."

With that she trails off down the corridor, yellow hair billowing in the quarterg, leaving me to wonder desolately what in space just happened.

Thomas is waiting for me at the cabin, reading the Manual. He looks pointedly at his chronometer as the hatch closes behind me. "I expected you sooner," he says.

"I stopped for devotions on the way back," I say. "I thought I might be too tired later."

He nods, accepting this, and I breathe a sigh of relief. "How was it today?" he asks.

I shrug. "Fine, I guess."

"Did you work hard?"

"I think I did."

"Crew treat you okay?"

I take off my cap and rub my head. I don't want to get into it all with Thomas. "They were fine. They didn't pay me much mind."

Thomas closes his Manual, a finger marking his place. "You be polite around them, Jude, but keep your thoughts to yourself. That's the way to stay true among the Sculpted."

"I will," I say, though already I feel duplicitous.

Thankfully, that seems to close that subject. The only other thing Thomas seems to want to know before he goes back to his reading is when I expect to be paid— something I haven't given much of a thought to. I assumed that was something he would have worked out with Renny already.

I prepare our dinner on the foldout stovetop, a stew of ground meat, beans, and vegetables. The activity proves more calming and centering to me than devotions did. But that night as I drift toward sleep, my mind keeps turning back to the women in the locker room, and to the wooden chest bolted to the deck not two feet from my head. Kaiya's chest.

The Screw is a peculiar machine, partaking directly as it does of aspects of the Axle, the Inclined Plane, and the Wedge, and often requiring application of the Lever to fulfill its purpose. This is fitting, given its function as the aspect that both joins together and elevates, and as a representation of the way in which men and women join together in holy communion with the Builder to ignite the spark of life.

Sacred as it is, I've always been a little embarrassed by the Screw, a little wary of it. Maybe if that were my ward I'd have a better understanding of it, a healthier attitude toward it, but I've never been quite comfortable with its symbolic freight. Love and apotheosis strike me as less the Screw's nature than doing violence to whatever surface it encounters.

I find it difficult to credit that I will ever come to completely trust and adore the Screw.

My work schedule is seven days on and three off-one full sweek as reckoned by the Sculpted. My first "weekend" falls on a Thursday through Saturday by the Guild calendar, which means schola every day while I'm supposed to be taking a break. Neither my long stretches without a day of rest nor my falling behind at schola seems to bother Thomas much, but it bothers me. When I dare bring this up, he tells me the Builder is blessing us for our sacrifice-though I don't see what sacrifice it is that *he's* making.

By my second sweek on the job, I've begun to feel comfortable and confident in nullg, and competent if not so comfortable with my fishbowl's graphic overlay. It's as if I'm looking at a raw and exposed layer of reality that should more properly be covered, or at the very least from which I should avert my eyes-though, just as in the locker room with my crewmates, doing so is practically not an option. I am on friendly terms with most of the crew, even if I can't quite bring myself to consider any of them friends. We're too different for that, both in our worldviews and in our expectations of what friendship means. For one thing, they don't seem to have a problem with the occasional tweaking of one another's anatomy in the showers. I do, as they have learned.

I *have* spent most of my lunch hours and several more walks home chatting with Derek. Despite the fact that he's so obviously unlike me, he has a directness, a curiosity, and a willingness to take my arguments seriously that I can't help but like, even if I can't always effectively rebut the points he makes. I consider him a goad to make me apply myself more diligently to my studies. I retain the faith that answers exist to his objections, and if I can't find them and express them articulately then I'm hardly a worthy ambassador for the Guild.

It's end of shift on Sevenday of my second sweek on the job when Renny calls us together in the break room. "Got some news, little stevies," she says, executing a sort of four-handed cartwheel up a chair to perch on her favorite table. The animated chatter anticipating our weekend break quiets down.

"Fourday and Fiveday next week we've got a special assignment coming up for anyone who wants in on it. Berth A11, prospecting ship full of scientific samples. Very delicate, both the ship and the cargo. Berth's gonna be fully evacuated, so there's hazard pay, but only those of you rated for vacuum will be eligible. If you don't want in, that's fine—we'll have plenty to do here. But if you want in and you're not vacuum-rated, it's not too late to get that way. You can even take shift time to do it without getting docked. I just need to see your certification first thing Threeday if you want in. Understood? All right, that's it."

Renny draws me aside as the others file off to the showers. "This is a good opportunity, kid," she tells me in a low voice. "You're a good worker, and you sure don't want to miss out on triple pay."

She's right, I don't. I can imagine how happy Thomas will be to see the extra credits. "How do I get vacuum-rated?" I ask, watching two tiny, distorted me's in her silvery eyeglobes. "Is there a test I take or something?"

"Not, er, not really," Renny says. "What it mostly entails is getting your lungs and eyes and ears vacuum-hardened. You'd be wearing a pressure suit in the berth, of course, but if it should fail you could suffocate before we got you out of there and repressurized. Regs don't let us subject you to that risk."

My breath catches. "What you're talking about— that would mean Sculpting, wouldn't it?"

"Just a small bit, internally."

The pay would be welcome, but I have to shake my head. "No offense, but I can't do that. I'm very sorry."

Renny shrugs, an elaborate motion of her hind shoulders. My reflection dances crazily in her eyes. "What can I say, kid? It's your choice, and I sure won't think any worse of you for it. But don't make the decision now. Think about it over the break. Get the details from Geoff. Talk to your old man, see what he says."

"Right," I say. "I already know what *he'd* tell me."

"Thomas ain't a bad guy, for a Wheelie. Talk to him, kid."

All the way to the showers, cringing, I can hear Thomas telling me the Wrecker's in me. But I can't quite shake Renny's insistence that I bring it up with him.

That evening over our humble dinner I blurt it out before I can reconsider: "Renny says there's a special job next week. Extra pay, and she's pushing me to do it."

Thomas puts down his fork. "And?" he says, glaring at me over the table.

"And...I'd need some small modifications. Vacuum-hardening."

Thomas bows his head. Today's a Saturday in the Quarter, what would in other circumstances have meant half a day at schola for me and a morning of light community service for him. But neither of us follows a normal schedule now, and we're each exhausted from the labors of the day. I wait for him to speak, not chewing, heart in my throat.

Not that I don't know the right answer. I only have to ask myself what the Builder would say. *Or my mother*, I think, the tip of my nonslipper grazing the wooden chest beneath the foldout table that spans the width between the bunks. The chest contains Kaiya's clothing, which, despite the reg against storage of unnecessary mass, Thomas has never been able to bring himself to recycle. It's almost as if he's waiting for her to come back. I'm not, though. I don't have many firm memories of Kaiya, and in fact Thomas has told me so often that my mother is with the angels now that that's how I nearly always picture her: dressed in spotless white with huge feathered wings furled above her, looking down on me from on high. I know what *she* would think if I broached the topic of transfiguration. I know what she *does* think, in whatever level of the Builder's mansion she's watching me from.

At last Thomas forks a bite of boiled potatoes and carrots into his mouth and peers at me, practically *through* me, from under lowered brows. "You told her no, right?"

I flinch a little. It takes a moment for me to realize he's talking about Renny, not Kaiya. "Of course," I say. My words feel defensive, as if he's somehow already forced me to lie to him.

"Wrecker take that woman, anyway." He shovels more food into his mouth and chews silently for a few bites.

When he speaks again his voice and his eyes, unexpectedly, have softened. "Son, I know they teach us at temple never to compromise with the world, to always live as if we're with the Builder in his mansion, but in practice that's just impossible. We all make compromises—we have to, or we couldn't get by. We couldn't live. The tricky part—no, the *hard* part is knowing what's okay to compromise and what isn't. You have to figure out where that dividing line is—and then stay well back from it. When you try to walk it..."

Thomas folds his hands together and stares down at the table. "Jude, son, I can tell you what happens. You fall. You tell yourself you won't, but you do." He clears his throat, lips compressing almost convulsively. "I just want you to be happy. Maybe that's not what this world is for, but Builder knows it's what I want for you."

His eyes rove this way and that, never meeting mine, and he clears his throat again. Once upon a time, this would have been where I edged around the table to give him an awkward hug. Tonight I can't. My soul cries for him, but I'm not a little kid anymore, and I just can't.

We finish our meal in silence.

The next day is temple, the first Sunday in three Guild weeks I've been off work. Thomas and I sit toward the back of the long, low chapel, which sits near the AD Gate at the opposite end of the Quarter from the PM Gate. The bulkheads are of brushed gray metal, with three of the Six Machines etched on the left wall, three on the right, and the carpenter's square on the wall behind the pulpit.

Inclined Plane Ward meets third every Sunday, in the late-morning slot. During Foreman Saul's sermon after the sacrament, I spot Nicodemus several rows ahead and to the right. What caught my eye was his golden head tilting back as he smiled wide at something the person next to him had whispered in his ear. The person next to him has long, shining yellow hair.

The person next to him is Sariah.

I blink hard for the next several minutes. I shift and fidget through the rest of the sermon. The pew is cold and rigid—dumb, unyielding matter—and no matter how I try I can't get comfortable. I'm supposed to meet the foreman for my private instruction after church, but when the service ends I rush back to the cabin instead, with a vague excuse to Thomas about my stomach.

Two full days of schola still ahead, catching up on subjects where I'm falling further and further behind, before I get to return to work. I don't know how I'm going to make it.

* * *

Wednesday comes at last, Oneday to the rest of the station, and in the break room in the early morning Renny reminds the gathered crew that we have only two days left to sign up and show vacuum certification if we want in on the special gig. She looks my way but I duck my eyes. Funny—I've spent the past two days at schola avoiding Nic and looking forward to Oneday, and now that it's here it looks like I'm going to spend the day avoiding Renny. I'm such a bent nail I can't stand myself.

Our client today is a Thunder-class starship, *Colder Equation*, which we lade with supplies bound for the exomorph colony at Van Maanen's Star. It's hard work but mostly mindless, and I find my cares evaporating for the first time in days. I feel best at midshift when we break for lunch, but the rest of the day is marred by the clock in the corner of my vision, ticking down the minutes until I return to gravity's embrace.

At shift's end, after showers, I ask Derek if he'd like to go somewhere for food. He's invited me to eat after work several times now, but I've worried not just that Thomas would find out but that I wouldn't be able to find anything appetizing in the public cafeterias. Tonight, though, I'm desperate enough to talk that I think I can overcome my food objections.

Delighted, Derek leads me all the way to a dim cafeteria two levels in from the rim. I'm not sure what I was expecting, but certainly not this gloomy cave with the dark red walls and the low ceiling. Quiet, lilting string music plucked out by unseen hands drifts on the air, which smells gently dank and laden with minerals. Thick pillars and curtains of leafy plant life obscure the view from one end of the place to the other, though here and there I can see tables of two, three, or four, the sometimes asymmetrical faces of the patrons lit from below by flickering orange light. Perhaps it's the dimness, but I no longer find their deformities as hideous as I did at first.

A woman in a lumpy black cowled robe leads us through the compact maze of foliage to a table against a black-painted bulkhead studded with white pinpricks. It isn't until we take our seats in form-fitting smart-matter chairs that I realize the bulkhead isn't a bulkhead at all, but a viewport—a hole punched through fifteen centimeters of metal and plugged with glass or something like it.

"Wheel and Axle," I murmur, stunned. I can't take my eyes from the bright, nail-hard stars.

"Netherheim and Freya should come into view before you're finished," the cowled woman says. "That's a sight to behold." She makes an arcane gesture in the air. "Now, let me call your attention to today's specials."

"Perhaps a…hardcopy menu would be in order for my friend here?" Derek says, nodding toward me.

"Oh, certainly," the woman says before receding like smoke into the shadows.

The surface of our table glows a dim, swirling orange, making Derek's skin look like polished stone and his eyes smolder with fire. "So what do you think?" he asks.

"It's not what I expected at all. I pictured something more, well, functional from a cafeteria."

"Cafeteria, eh?" Derek's eyes sparkle with amusement. "I suppose you could think of it that way."

The robed woman returns with a catalog of dishes listed on a single sheet of paper, and I'm shocked to discover, as Derek points out, that most of the items have been grown hydroponically. "This must be terribly expensive," I say, mouth watering. "I can't afford this, I'm sure of it."

"Relax," Derek says. "Everyone gets credit for a meal like this once a month. I've got a couple saved up, and you must have at least a dozen just sitting there, unused."

I cover my surprise and confusion by studying the menu. I have the sense of riding an iceberg in a limitless ocean, borne up by a vast bulk the composition of which I can't begin to fathom. Choosing more or less at random, I select an opener of fine pasta garnished with grated cheeses and truffle shavings, and a spiced squash tart as a main course. Derek places our orders, a process invisible to me, choosing a fruit assortment and a roulade of vegetables and nuts for himself.

He folds his hands and leans forward. "So, what's on your mind, Jude?"

"Oh, this and that," I say, and shrug. "I was thinking today about what it would be like to live out in space."

Derek shakes his head, grinning. "We *do* live in space. Or hadn't you noticed?"

"No, I mean *in* space, like the exomorphs, just floating there in the middle of nothing."

"Well, it's not nothing. There *is* a structure, a lattice, to grow their colony in."

"But it's not much, and it's open to space." I didn't know there were such creatures, such people, until today. I read it on the fishbowl during work. "Can you even imagine the mods you'd need for that?"

"Serious work indeed," Derek says. "Not to be undertaken lightly."

"No one on our crew has work that serious. They all

look pretty much normal, at least when they're dressed."

"The more radical mods are often specialization for particular types of work. We're unskilled labor, our crew, Jude."

I nod, having figured this out without really being able to articulate it. I take a deep breath. "Derek, can I ask you something personal?"

He laces his fingers together and rests his joined hands on the table. The green of his palms has crept halfway up his arms in the time since I met him, and his ears are now tinged green as well, though I can't make the hues out well in this light. His gaze upon me is very open and direct and unsettling, more so because every day I come to know better how little I understand of his world, layered as it is above and beneath and around mine. "I don't know, can you?" he says.

"I don't know. I'll try." I've learned some things about him from the fishbowl at work without really trying—for instance, the distressing fact that he has three biological mothers—but nothing that doesn't just whet my curiosity. I look down at the glowing table and take a deep breath. "I'm just wondering if there's some, I don't know, some practical reason for *your* mods, something functional. You know, what the blue skin turning green is all about."

"There's a time for love, and a time to hate," Derek says with a rakish smile. "A time for blue, and a time for green."

I puff out an exasperated breath. "Do you spend all your time looking up things in the Manual you can make fun of?"

He shakes his head. "You do understand, don't you, Jude," he says animatedly, "that a book called the Bible existed long before Titus Grant slapped his own generic title on it, and that it's not exactly an obscure work in the human literary canon?"

"High Foreman Titus didn't just change the title. Under the Builder's inspiration, he clarified and corrected—"

Derek extends a finger until it almost touches my lips, waving his other hand preemptively. "Yes, fine. But you understand he didn't write the Manual from scratch."

"All right, fine, I understand," I say. "So what about the color change?"

He leans back in his chair. "Right, *that*. It's not really anything practical. There's nothing I can point to and say my skin color accomplishes. In fact, it's mostly a random aesthetic process. I'm never sure what color's coming up next."

"Then why did you do it? I mean, what's the purpose?"

"It keeps me interested," Derek says, and his smile cracks momentarily. "I see me and not-me in the mirror at the same time, and there's always the mystery of what's coming next. It's as good a reason to stick around as any." He leans forward again, and to my ears his heartiness now sounds forced. "What makes you curious, friend?"

I shake my head. "I don't know. Nothing."

"You're thinking about the job, aren't you? The vacuum job this Fourday."

I look out the viewport at the stars, but the view seems to tilt and wheel beneath me, spinning my sense of balance away. "Maybe," I admit.

"You know," Derek says with a trace of his vigorous smile, "if you do it, a lot of folks on the crew are going to be disappointed. People are starting to get protective of you, and you may make them feel like they've corrupted you."

"It's not their decision," I say.

"Agreed."

A different woman brings us our opening course. A thick tail moving in counterpoint to the balanced trays in her hands protrudes from beneath her black robe. Attention to the food spares Derek and me from the burden of conversation. I'm not sure I enjoy all the lush, strange flavors on my plate, but I know I've never tasted anything so vivid. I swallow every last crumb.

Derek seems uncharacteristically fidgety between courses, but it's not until our main courses have arrived and I'm halfway through my tart—excellent—that he says, "Jude, can I ask *you* something?"

"Um, sure," I say between bites.

He swallows. "What *is* it that happened to your mother?"

The bite I've just taken feels too big going down my throat. "How do you know about my mother?"

"I'm sorry, I'm not trying to pry." He wipes his mouth with a cloth serviette that actually shows slight stains of use. "It's hard sometimes to look at you and not make the easy jumps back through your genealogy."

"My mother died when I was small, four or five," I say, setting down my fork and holding my gaze steady with great effort. "I'm not clear exactly how. My father doesn't like to talk about it, and I don't like to press him."

Derek opens his mouth, looking confused, and for a moment I have the strangest feeling *he's* going to tell *me* how it happened. I feel the sting beginning behind my eyes at the thought that he might know more about it than I do.

But what he says is: "Do you think about her much?"

I nod. "All the time."

He looks so stricken at this that I feel I could be looking at a reflection of my own expression in a blue-tinted mirror—or, so I believe for a giddy, wildly hopeful moment, at my mother. The illusion shatters as Derek rises suddenly in his chair, takes my face in both his green hands, and leans in to kiss me on the mouth. He stares at me a second or two, an eternity, and sits back down.

Breathless, I turn to the window. Netherheim has swung into view, a giant ball of spun sugar swirled with red and yellow stripes, a fruit as sweet and bursting and sick-making as my heart inside me. I sit very still, not looking at him. My pulse is racing about a hundred klicks a second.

"I don't know if I can finish this," I say and push the rest of my tart away.

"Jude, I'm sorry," Derek says, his eyes very steady and direct.

"Why did you do that?" I ask. Asking a question is better than yelling or crying or hitting the table.

Derek spreads his green palms. They look black with blood in the cafeteria's hellish light. "I forgot for a minute what a kiss signifies to your people. Let myself forget, to be honest. To us—the groups I identify with, at least—it can be a greeting between friends, a show of camaraderie or comfort, even the equivalent of a slap. It doesn't have to have a sexual connotation."

"But why did you do it?"

Derek sighs. "Jude, you just seemed so sad. I couldn't stand it. Lonely and sad." He shakes his head. "You reminded me of me when I was your age. Sometimes I wish someone had just done that for me."

Do I believe him? I'm not sure. I look out the viewport. Netherheim is just beginning to slide out of view. A cauldron of emotion, like the multicolored atmosphere of the planet below, seethes inside me. I want to storm out of the room. I want to turn a somersault in the air. I want to shake Derek by the shoulders until his head flops like a scrap doll's.

I think about Nicodemus, wondering what I ever saw in him.

"I'm sorry," I say. "Can you help me find an elevator to Level Six?"

"Of course, Jude."

The compassion and concern in Derek's voice are unbearable. So is the heartbreak.

At home, safe from the sea of wild bodies and leering faces that populate the station, I fall to my knees. I should pray to the Builder for forgiveness, for putting myself in such a compromised position, but instead I thumb the combination on the wooden chest in the middle of the deck. Thomas is still out, and with luck will be for at least another hour. He doesn't know that I long ago surfed the combination over his shoulder. The lid swings back on stiff, creaky, decidedly low-tech hinges, revealing the layered treasures within.

Reverently, I lift out the first folded garment, hearing in my mind a surreal ghost of Kaiya's voice telling Thomas to keep this, she'll have no use for it where she's going. I unfold and smooth out the soft gray dress with the Inclined Plane on the bosom—then, hands trembling, pull it over my head and slip my arms through the sleeves, as I've done maybe half a dozen times before in my life.

The fabric is tight across my shoulders and under my arms—much tighter than it was the time before. There's no hope of closing the buttons at the back. This may be the last time I can manage to fit into it at all.

Sobs rise up inside me as I yearn for angel wings to bear me away.

The sensation of walking spinward inside a great turning wheel like Netherview Station is a little like walking up an endless inclined plane. Because your feet are borne forward by the rotation a tiny bit faster than your head, you might feel if you're attentive enough as if you're leaning slightly backward, or walking up the slightest of slopes.

By the same token, a counterspinward stroll might feel a bit like a walk downhill. But compare your slight forward angle to a tangent of the circle your feet are touching and you'll see that the attitude of your body is more like that of a person walking uphill. Thus, walk either direction inside the rim of a rolling wheel and you partake of one aspect or another of ascending an incline.

I haven't found much scriptural support for my position, and the members of Wheel and Axle in particular would call it blasphemy, but at some crossroads it strikes me that any path you follow can lead you upward, and closer to the Builder.

I sleep badly, unaccustomed to the richness of the food in my belly. Upon rising I prepare Thomas what seems a meager and bland breakfast, all the while fearing that he will somehow sense that the chest and its contents have been disturbed. But he eats with all his attention on his Manual, and he barely bats an eye when I tell him I may end up working overtime today.

I arrive early at the hub, in time to catch Renny in her spherical office well before the start of our Twoday shift. "I want to learn more about this vacuum-hardening procedure," I tell her without preamble. "Uh, how can I do that?"

Renny vaults out of her chair like a charged particle expelled from an atom. "If you weren't crippled you could ask from anywhere," she says, clinging to the frame of the hatch and shoving her ugly face into mine. "As it is, you'll have to use a Geoffroom. There's one not far from here."

She leads me on a brisk walk. "You know," I say as I hurry to keep up with her, "my father's pretty upset with you."

Renny looks over her shoulder and grins. "What, for telling you about the job? Oh, I heard from him. Nothing he could do about it, though. It's regs and Thomas knows it. Like *he* has room to complain, the way he called in so many favors to get a barefooter like you onto the team in the first place. But he's your father and he's just following the script, same as me."

She stops before a row of three hatches, each emblazoned with the old-fashioned schematic symbol for an activated light fixture. I've passed hatches like these at many times since starting my job, but never known what they were.

Renny rears up on her hind arms and pats the gleaming surface of the first hatch. "Now here's the next part of my script," she says. "This is a Geoffroom, where Geoff can tell you anything you care to ask about. He'll answer all your questions and then some. The light bulb is glowing, which means the room's unoccupied and you can walk right in. Take all the time you need, but if you're going to be here longer than than the first hour of shift, have the big lug message me so I know."

She touches a panel in the center of the hatch, and it opens with a slight hiss.

"Keep your eyes and ears open, kid," she says, and I step inside.

"Don't be afraid. I won't bite."

The voice is a warm tenor and originates from no location I can see in this small, very white room. The ceiling is high enough to let me stand comfortably; my outstretched arms would nearly span the room in both dimensions. A body-enfolding chair like you might find at the medic's rests at the center of the deck. Panicked, I turn—to find the hatch has sealed noiselessly behind me. I can barely see its outline.

"Have a seat, Jude," the voice says. "We've got a lot to talk about."

The air is warm, but my skin prickles cold and hard. "Where are you?" I say. "How do you know my name?"

"I've known you since you were born, Jude. I'm glad we're finally getting a chance to talk. This happens so rarely with members of your Guild. But we'll talk more comfortably if you sit. Please."

Blasphemy! my mind cries. *False gods!* But I ease myself down into the chair, letting the cushions take hold of me. I feel the chair adjust to my size, and carefully I lay my head back in the niche that fits it.

A man appears before me. A pot-bellied man with

flowing white hair and a bushy white mustache, dressed in a billowy white coverall. A man carrying a wooden carpenter's square. "Selah," he says.

I start in alarm, but the man makes calming motions as he bends over me. "The Builder," I gasp.

He shakes his head. "If you see me in the likeness of the Builder, it's only because that's your strongest conception of a figure of benevolent wisdom. Not to aggrandize myself at all." He looks down at the carpenter's square in his hand. "This probably doesn't help matters." He tosses the square over his shoulder, and it vanishes.

"Who are you?" I say, struggling to sit up.

The man crackles and flashes transparent. "This'll be less disorienting if you stay down in the chair," he says. "For both of us."

Suspiciously I lie back, and the image solidifies. In fact, I can feel the man as he presses a comforting hand to my chest and pushes me down.

"I'm Geoff," he says. "No last name, but I can give you a version number if you're really interested."

He smells faintly of sweat, smoke, and some kind of musky perfume. "I don't know what you mean," I say.

"I know," he says with a smirk. He pulls up a chair from nowhere, seats himself near my knees, and crosses his legs. "But you came here because you wanted to ask me something. So go ahead. Ask me anything you like. Ask me as much as you like. That's what I'm here for."

"What are you?" I ask.

"A very sophisticated information retrieval system. Once upon a time, you might have called me a search engine, but I'm much more than that. I'm something of a diagnostician as well, and a physician, and a surgeon, and a teacher and a tutor. A diplomat, a translator, an ombudsman. A legal advisor, and an advocate too. And I play a mean hand of gin."

"Where did you get the name Geoff?" I'm thinking of Derek and his name change. "What does it mean?"

Geoff strokes his mustache. "Nothing, really. I just liked the sound of it. It seemed to me to suit me somehow. Where did you get *your* name?"

I blink. "From the Manual."

"Be glad you didn't end up Nebuchadnezzar."

Maybe this is where Derek learned to be so cheeky. "How is it I can see you? It has something to do with the chair, doesn't it?"

"It has plenty to do with the chair, and with its ability to create a microwave interface with your visual cortex. I can give you a more detailed technical specification if you like, but I imagine you have more pressing questions you'd like to ask."

I'm delighted in spite of myself, and I raise my head out of the cradle several times in succession just to watch Geoff flicker in and out of existence.

"Careful," he says, rising from his illusory chair. "You'll make yourself sick."

He's right. My head has started pounding and the room whirls. My stomach feels none too steadfast in its grip on breakfast. I lie back and Geoff strokes my forehead. His cool fingers fail to disturb the swelling droplets of perspiration. I take deep breaths, digging my fingers into the padding of the armrests.

"Tell me about this vacuum-hardening process my boss keeps telling me about," I say, eyes squeezed shut. "How does it work?"

"There's not a lot to it," Geoff says in a reassuring tone. "What it does is construct around your lungs a sort of a cellular retaining wall that gets deployed on

any catastrophic drop in air pressure. It actually seals
shut your lungs and can temporarily prevent the gases
in your bloodstream from expanding and killing you.
This retaining wall is also capable of breaking oxygen
atoms loose from the carbon dioxide your blood
returns to your lungs, so you can effectively keep
rebreathing the same old air. That's only temporary too,
of course. It's like any filter—eventually it's going to get
choked with carbon and fail. But you can last an hour
that way, anyway. More than enough time for help to
get to you. In most circumstances."

It sounds so reasonable when Geoff says it. I'm
looking at him again now, and he has returned to his
seat. "Is the procedure expensive?" I ask, praying the
answer will be yes.

"Not at all," Geoff says. "And if you can demonstrate a need for it in the course of your job, the station
covers it anyway. You *do* qualify, by the way."

"Are there side effects?"

"You might feel a little short of breath after the procedure, a little dizzy and weak, but your lungs will
adjust within a day or so. That's all, really."

I take a deep breath. "And the procedure itself—it
sounds complicated. How long does it take?"

"Oh, about twenty minutes," Geoff says, tilting his
head to one side.

"Twenty minutes! That's all?"

"You'd have the entire shift off, though, for recovery
and observation. With pay."

"But—but how is that possible?" I'm groping for
words. "I mean, it's Sculpting, right? You can't just
snap your fingers and it's done."

"That would be true, Jude…*if* we were starting from
scratch. We're not."

Now I *can't* breathe, and my insides seem to freeze. "What do you—what do you mean?"

Geoff stands up and clasps his hands behind his back. "You *are* what you call Sculpted, Jude, as is every other member of the Machinist Guild on Netherview Station. You've been that way since before birth, the nanodocs passed on to you via your mother's bloodstream. Your nanodocs don't *do* anything more than maintain reasonably good health and let me keep tabs on you. But the potential is there for more. Much more."

"But—but *why?*" Tears gather in the corners of my eyes. "How can you do this to us? It's—it's monstrous!"

Geoff's looks pained. "Jude, please understand what a fragile environment this station is. We have two *million* permanent residents and millions more who pass through every month. We can't have people running loose who *aren't* monitored in some way."

"But it's wrong. It's my *body!*"

"Jude, if I weren't helping out, your body would have broken the first time you left the Quarter. Your devotions keep your muscles strong, but the low gravity weakens your bones. You've had supplements in your food all your life to counteract the effects."

I roll my head from side to side. "Lies."

"I'm not lying, Jude."

"Not now, but all along! Everything we know, my people, it's all *lies.*"

"I told you the first opportunity I had. Jude, you have the right to get this information at the age of ten, when you become a provisional citizen of Netherview Station—that's about thirteen and a third by your Guild calendar. Unfortunately, the Guild can keep that knowledge from you until age fifteen—twenty to you. You still have the right to ask and get answers, like you're doing now, but what good does that do most of you when you don't *know* you can ask?"

I'm shaking my head. "I don't believe you. That would mean—that would mean everyone knows. All the adults—my father. Everyone knows."

"Actually, no." Geoff purses his lips sadly and lays a hand on my arm. "Just because they know they have the right to ask doesn't mean they'll actually do it. By the time they reach twenty, most of them don't *want* to know."

"*I* don't want to know!" I say, wrenching my arm through Geoff's hand to paw the water from my eyes. "Why are you telling me this?"

"Jude..."

"No! You're the Wrecker! I don't want to hear it."

Geoff sighs. "As far as I'm aware, I am not the Wrecker. In fact, I'm not certain I'm *capable* of telling a lie. I try my very best to do good, really."

Uncomfortably aware of how childish I'm being, I cross my arms and turn my head away from the preening phantom before me. I lie that way for some time, mind churning. When I look at Geoff again he's watching me expectantly. I feel hollow inside.

"Geoff," I say, my voice small, "can you fix my brain?"

Geoff leans forward, looking concerned. "What's wrong with your brain, Jude?"

"I—I mean—"

"Yes?"

"I think I'm out of true." I'm almost whispering. "Bent."

"How do you mean?"

"*You* know."

"Pretend I don't."

I lick my lips. "I think I like boys." The admission leaves me feeling curiously flat, detached. "Can you fix me?"

Geoff tugs at his white mustache. "Jude, there are various therapy regimens I can initiate, but I don't 'fix' things like sexual inclination. Not that I'd call you homosexual at all in the sense you'd think of it. The truth, I believe, is rather more interesting and complicated than that."

My heart leaps. "What's the truth?"

"Your Guild likes to treat sexuality and gender as binary values, either this or that, one right, one wrong, no other possibilities. But the ones you call Sculpted understand these characteristics more as a spectrum of possible values, fluid and multidimensional. There's no either-or, nor even necessarily a permanent identification with any given point on the grid." Geoff spreads his hands in an eerily Builderlike gesture. "Now, this is a preliminary diagnosis only, but you would appear to me to suffer from a multivalent somatocognitive dysphoria."

"A what?" I ask, vague trepidation gnawing at my stomach.

"To put it more bluntly, your body is male, but the personality inside may be closer to the female end of the continuum. Not all the way there, of course, but more so than not."

I shake my head despite the nausea I feel. "No, no. That's ridiculous."

"You would have learned very early to hide the symptoms—the wants and behaviors your people wouldn't find acceptable in a little boy. But that, plus overcompensation in areas of archaically male pursuit, still wouldn't make them go away."

"You're crazy." The notion is offensive, repulsive. "The Builder doesn't *make* mistakes like that."

"In a perfect world, maybe not," Geoff says. "But this world's anything but perfect, and we all have to come to our own accommodations with that fact. Now, I can recommend and even direct a course of therapeutic counseling, just as a starting point, and of course participation would be entirely up to—"

"*No!*" I shout. "Stop it!"

"Jude, let's at least talk about this for a—"

"You lying, false machine, shut *up*! I can't *think*."

Geoff folds his hands in his lap as I turn my eyes to the white ceiling, chewing the inside of my cheek. I'm furious, and terrified for my soul, to realize how easily I've been taken in by the lies of this Wrecker-spawned abomination. The right thing to do—the right degree of compromise—has never been more clear.

"I'm going to do it," I say, the steel in my voice a wall holding back utter dissolution.

"I'm sorry—do what?" Geoff asks.

"The vacuum-hardening. I'm going to do it."

"Are you sure?" He sounds dubious.

"Absolutely. But so you don't get any ideas, I'm doing it for the Guild, not for myself."

"I'm not certain what you mean by that."

"The more hazard pay I get," I say, "the more quickly my people can get off this godforsaken station."

"Your pay is yours. It doesn't have to go to your Guild."

"I don't care."

"It won't make any difference," Geoff says. "The Guild's debts are considerable."

"I don't *care*."

"Jude, I don't want you doing this under any false

illusions. The Guild owes so much money they can't even pay the interest on it. It's practically a losing proposition to keep housing them."

"Then why don't you just let them leave?" I demand, enraged.

Geoff shakes his head. "I'll tell you if you really want to know—that's my function. But you won't like it."

"I don't like it already! Just tell me."

"As you wish. I have to be concerned about the well-being of the station as a whole, and having you here serves a purpose other than economic. The existence of a permanent underprivileged social class reinforces in the minds of the rest of the population the benefits of full participation in this pseudo-socialist post-scarcity paradise of ours. Superiority breeds contentment, of a sort."

"So you're telling me my people live in poverty to provide an example of how undesirable poverty is?"

"I told you you weren't going to like it."

My anger has shrunk to a cold, clear gem in my heart. "As if it took a supercomputer to figure *that* out. And I told you I'd made up my mind already."

"Well!" he says, raising his eyebrows. He looks as if he's about to offer more argument, but evidently decides otherwise. "So you give your consent for the vacuum-hardening procedure?"

I give a curt nod. "Yes."

"So be it," Geoff says quietly. He almost sounds chastened. "I'll let your boss know you'll be occupied today, and we'll get started right away."

I arrange myself stiffly in the chair, arms at my sides, as if waiting for the lid of my coffin to close.

"You're all right from here?" Derek asks.

We're standing at the PM Gate, the smells and

tumult and humidity around us as heavy as ever. His arm around my shoulder helps offset the crushing gravity. I nod a little woozily and say, "It'll be easier inside. Quarter gee."

As the end of the procedure drew near, Geoff roused me to suggest I might want a friend to walk me home. I said Derek's name before I really thought it through, but even after the fact, wondering if that had been a good idea, it didn't seem to me I really had a better option. Geoff contacted him, and Derek was there waiting outside the Geoffroom as soon as the hatch opened.

Now he takes his arm from around me and watches with concern as I take a wobbly step on my own. "Is this…*you* know…are you going to be in trouble?"

"How will anyone know?" I say. "There's nothing visible that's changed."

Derek looks like he's about to say something, then extends his hand instead. Green is now his predominant hue; even his irises have changed color. "Well, Jude, just in case…you've got a place to bunk down if you need it. No strings, just a place to stow your gear."

I nod, my throat thickening. I try to say thank you, but I can't. I duck my eyes, pull the lever, and pass through the gate.

I might be imagining it, but as the gate closes behind me I almost think I hear Derek saying, "Selah, Jude."

Inside, it's late and the corridors are empty. This is good because even in the lower grav I'm having trouble walking a straight line. Geoff told me this is nothing to worry about, that I'll feel fine again by morning, but drawing the wrong kind of attention on the way home through the Quarter *would* be something to worry about.

The cabin is dark when I slip inside, and Thomas lies motionless in his bunk. I strip off my coverall as quietly and cautiously as possible, crank down my bunk, and slip beneath the blanket. I lie on my back, unable to relax or even close my eyes. I spent most of the day in essentially this position. Like Geoff promised, the process took only twenty minutes—though, having felt nothing, I have only his word for that—but for the rest of my shift and beyond I lay fitfully dozing as I recuperated. I suspect Geoff would have liked to keep me longer than he did, but my father would have been livid if didn't come home all night.

My heart pounds as I suddenly become aware that Thomas is sitting up. I try to fake deep, easy breathing as Thomas stands and pads across the narrow cabin. Even talking to him right now is too exhausting a thought to contemplate.

"Son," he says, almost a question, his voice subdued.

I crack an eye. His face is a gray smear in the darkness, gazing down on me like the cinders of a burnt-out sun.

"Son...Jude..." He sighs, breath hitching like an unbalanced motor. "I've been thinking a lot. Praying hard. I think it was wrong to send you to work. You can quit if you like. We'll get by. We'll manage."

I'm not sure he knows I'm awake, sees my eyes wide and dilated in the dark. It's like he's talking to himself. But when he reaches down to stroke my hair, his face draws nearer and his brows knit.

"Son?" he says, his voice quavering. "Son, what have they...what have *you*...?"

His hand snaps back like the magnetic arm of a relay switch. But I have only an instant to steel myself before he shakes off the stun and whips back, seizing me by my throat and one thigh and hauling me off the bunk.

"What in the Wheel have you done?" he cries, stumbling back as I watch the indistinct room tumble crazily around me. He loses his grip on my thigh, and my knees bounce off the deck even as my windpipe grinds against his other hand. I smash sideways against the bottom of the hatch, torn loose now from both his hands, and watch in the terrible clarity of low gravity as his leg swings back in an arc that will ultimately reverse and connect with my ribs.

I've never felt revulsion before at his correctional touch, only the sort of accepting resignation born of an intimate belief in the justice of it. But now, sprawled on the deck, my skin crawls with a sense of wrongness and violation.

Spasming, I curl myself around his leg at the moment of contact, I grab tight with both arms, I twist violently toward the hatch. Arms wheeling, Thomas hits the bulkhead face first.

The lights brighten at his startled cry, and in the sudden glare I scuttle desperately to the cabin's far corner. Thomas's face leaves a lurid red smear on the door as he slides to the deck. Dizzy, I push myself to my feet, lungs heaving, alternately holding back sobs and retches.

Thomas huddles on the floor with his arms over his head. "Oh, Builder," he half coughs, half wails. "What did you *do*?"

There's only one way he could have detected my mods. "You see it," I say, nodding like a drunk. "You're Sculpted too, you hypocrite."

He rolls over onto one side. "I couldn't do my *job* otherwise," he says, wiping blood from his mouth. "The job I have to do for you and our people. You have no idea what I've sacrificed."

"If I have no idea," I shout, "it's because you never *told* me! You sent me out there to face the same choices, but you never told me what *you* chose!"

He sits up, wiping his face and examining the blood on his hand. "I told you what was *right*, Jude. That's my job."

"You think I can't figure that out for myself?"

"Obviously not. Just like your mother." He's breathing hard, wincing. "She couldn't make the distinction either—what one person sacrifices out of necessity, and what that spares the rest of his family. She tore us apart because of it. She left this family in shambles." He pushes himself to his feet. "And I suppose you want to join her now, Wrecker take you both."

He totters the few steps toward me. I try to rise, intending to meet his assault on my feet, however it comes.

When he lays hands on me, though, it's to take my elbow and help me rise. "Be my guest," he says, gesturing to the hatch. "The door's there."

"The door?" I repeat, confused. "But...I thought..."

"Thought what? Thought—" Understanding dawns on his face like it hasn't yet on mine. "Oh, Jude."

"What?"

"You know so much else. I thought you must have found that out too."

I feel a tremble in my chest. "Found out *what*?"

"About your mother. That she's..."

Time seems to freeze. Something terrible roars somewhere far, far away, someplace only I can hear it.

"Son?" Something in my expression causes Thomas to release my elbow and take a step back. "Son," he says, hands up, "she *was* dead to us, dead in every way that mattered. She wasn't the same woman anymore. That woman died."

I fling myself at him, fists pummeling his chest like I'm a two-year-old throwing a tantrum.

"I was only trying to protect you, Jude! She's a monster now! She's Wreckerspawn!"

"Liar!" I cry, spittle flying from my mouth, tears blinding my eyes. "You liar!"

Now he's crying too, behind his upthrust arms, but it can't be from my pathetic beating. I shove him away in disgust. He staggers and sits down hard on his bunk. Not pausing to think, I snatch my clothing from the netted basket beside my bunk and cross to the hatch.

"And now you're leaving me, too," Thomas says bitterly. "You're her son in every way."

"Good," I say, turning the knob. "That's what I'd rather be anyway."

I have one last glimpse of him—hunched on his bunk in the harsh light like a wild animal, clawing at his wet, puffy eyes—and the hatch snicks shut behind me.

Standing over me, Kaiya looks the same as she does in my half-waking imaginings—tall, porcelain-skinned with cascades of black hair, slightly larger than life, and no older than I remember. And those wings. Those glorious, glowing, white wings, stretching up into the inky night to touch at a point as far above her head as her head is above her feet. Each feather is as long and wide as one of my forearms. I could see her clasping me to her white-robed breast and soaring high out of the galactic plane with wings like that. She *is* an angel.

"Jude, first let me tell you how sorry I am," she says, leaning in so close I can count every one of her eyelashes. "I must have made a dozen recordings like this for you, at least, every time I move or make some other change, but sorry is the one thing that's always constant. That and how much I love you."

She's not here, of course, but I can almost smell the dry perfume of her hair, the oily tang of her wings. I'm in a Geoffroom, the first one I could find, dressed and tipped back in the big chair and submerged in illusion. I can hardly believe this is happening, that this revelation has been so close to hand for so long, dormant and unguessed-at. All I had to do was ask the right question—or rather, to learn there were questions to ask at all. The magic incantation which had summoned this genie forth from the bottle was, quite simply, "Where is my mother?"

"I'm not authorized to answer that directly," Geoff told me. "But I do have a message for you."

"I wanted to bring you with me. Really I did, Jude. Not a day goes by that I don't wish I could. But because of the Guild's legal arrangements with the Station, that was impossible, and after the change I'd made I certainly couldn't stay. All I could do was hope that you reached a point—and preferably long before you reached your Guild majority—where you were able to start asking questions.

"Since you're seeing this, apparently you have.

"As I speak, you're now ten years old—thirteen by Guild reckoning. You're old enough to get this message if you ask, but not old enough that I can contact you directly. I don't know anything about you, what kind of young man you've turned into since the last time I saw you. Are you still as sweet as you were as a child, and as serious? What do you believe? What do you hope for? What do you dream? How have you changed? One thing's for certain—you must have changed some to be seeing this now. You must have made some hard choices, and you must have many more still to come.

"I'm still changing, too, Jude. I'm heading into the final phases of my exomorphological transform. When you see this, I'll probably already be homesteading in the New Bountiful Colony at Van Maanen's Star. It's a long way from here, terribly far. But that doesn't mean I won't drop it all to see you again. It won't be quick or simple, but if you want to start arranging it, just tell Geoff yes at the end of this recording, or any time afterward. A message will be dispatched to me immediately, though it may take a while to reach me.

"If you don't want to see me"—she shrugs, and her mighty wings tremble—"well, you can just say nothing. I'll never know, and I can go on assuming you've never seen this."

Is there really any question? Is there any doubt? "Yes, Mom," I say, feeling my face crumple. "Yes, yes, yes, yes, yes!"

"I'm so proud of you, Jude," she says. "You chose enlightenment over ignorance, and that's a terribly hard choice to make. I love you and I always will, no matter what. I can't wait for you to see what I've become, and I especially can't wait to see what you've become."

The Manual tells us that in the beginning the Builder decreed six fundamental machines. These are his six aspects, and all we do we must do with the Six. We need no other machines.

I believe this with all my heart. But not even my sincerest belief, I fear, is sufficient to make it true. Not when the shape of the Builder's seventh great Machine, transcending the other six, is coming clear.

The Seventh Machine is me.

LIFE ON THE PRESERVATION

Jack Skillingstead

Wind buffeted the scutter. Kylie resisted the tempta-
tion to fight the controls. Hand light on the joystick,
she veered toward the green smolder of Seattle, riding
down a cloud canyon aflicker with electric bursts. The
Preservation Field extended half a mile over Elliot Bay
but did not capture Blake or Vashon island nor any of
the blasted lands.

She dropped to the deck. Acid Rain and wind lashed
the scutter. The Preservation Field loomed like an
immense wall of green jellied glass.

She punched through, and the sudden light shift dazzled her. Kylie polarized the thumbnail port, at the same
time deploying braking vanes and dipping steeply to
skim the surface of the bay.

The skyline and waterfront were just as they'd
appeared in the old photographs and movies. By the
angle of the sun she estimated her arrival time at late
morning. Not bad. She reduced airspeed and gently
pitched forward. The scutter drove under the water. It
got dark. She cleared the thumbnail port. Bubbles
trailed back over the thick plexi, strings of silver pearls.

Relying on preset coordinates, she allowed the

autopilot to navigate. In minutes the scutter was tucked in close to a disused pier. Kyle opened the ballast, and the scutter surfaced in a shadow, bobbing. She saw a ladder and nudged forward.

She was sweating inside her costume. Jeans, black sneakers, olive drab shirt, rain parka. Early twenty-first century urban America: Seattle chic.

She powered down, tracked her seat back, popped the hatch. The air was sharp and clean, with a saltwater tang. Autumn chill in the Pacific Northwest. Water slopped against the pilings.

She climbed up the pitchy, guano-spattered rungs of the ladder.

And stood in awe of the intact city, the untroubled sky. She could sense the thousands of living human beings, their vitality like an electric vibe in her blood. Kylie was nineteen and had never witnessed such a day. It had been this way before the world ended. She reminded herself that she was here to destroy it.

From her pocket she withdrew a remote control, pointed it at the scutter. The hatch slid shut and her vehicle sank from view. She replaced the remote control. Her hand strayed down to another zippered pocket and she felt the outline of the explosive sphere. Behind it her heart was beating wildly. *I'm here*, she thought.

She walked along the waterfront, all her senses exploited. The sheer numbers of people overwhelmed her. The world had ended on a Saturday, November nine, 2004. There were more living human beings in her immediate range of sight than Kylie had seen in her entire life.

She extracted the locator device from her coat pocket and flipped up the lid. It resembled a cellular phone of the period. A strong signal registered immediately.

Standing in the middle of the sidewalk, she turned slowly toward the high reflective towers of the city, letting people go around her, so many people, walking, skateboarding, jogging, couples and families and single people, flowing in both directions, and seagulls gliding overhead, and horses harnessed to carriages waiting at the curb (so *much* life), and the odors and rich living scents, and hundreds of cars and pervasive human noise and riot, all of it continuous and—

"Are you all right?"

She started. A tall young man in a black jacket loomed over her. The jacket was made out of *leather*. She could smell it.

"Sorry," he said. "You looked sort of dazed."

Kylie turned away and walked into the street, toward the signal, her mission. Horns blared, she jerked back, dropped her locator. It skittered against the curb near one of the carriage horses. Kylie lunged for it, startling the horse, which clopped back, a hoof coming down on the locator. *No!* She couldn't get close. The great head of the animal tossed, nostrils snorting, the driver shouting at her, Kylie frantic to reach her device.

"Hey, watch it."

It was the man in the leather jacket. He pulled her back, then darted in himself and retrieved the device. He looked at it a moment, brow knitting. She snatched it out of his hand. The display was cracked and blank. She shook it, punched the keypad. Nothing.

"I'm really sorry," the man said.

She ignored him.

"It's like my fault," he said.

She looked up. "You have no idea, *no idea* how bad this is."

He winced.

"I don't even have any tools," she said, not to him. "Let me—"

She walked away, but not into the street, the locator a useless thing in her hand. She wasn't a tech. Flying the scutter and planting explosives was as technical as she got. So it was plan B, only since plan B didn't exist it was plan Zero. Without the locator she couldn't possibly find the Eternity Core. A horse! Jesus.

"*Shit.*"

She sat on a stone bench near a decorative waterfall that unrolled and shone like a sheet of plastic. Her mind raced but she couldn't formulate a workable plan B.

A shadow moved over her legs. She looked up, squinting in the sun.

"Hi."

"What do you want?" she said to the tall man in the leather jacket.

"I thought an ice cream might cheer you up."

"Huh?"

"Ice cream," he said. "You know, 'You scream, I scream, we all scream for ice cream'?"

She stared at him. His skin was pale, his eyebrows looked sketched on with charcoal and there was a small white scar on his nose. He was holding two waffle cones, one in each hand, the cones packed with pink ice cream. She had noticed people walking around with these things, had seen the sign.

"I guess you don't like strawberry," he said.

"I've never had it."

"Yeah, right."

"Okay, I'm lying. Now why don't you go away? I need to think."

He extended his left hand. "It's worth trying, at least once. Even on a cold day."

Kylie knew about ice cream. People in the old movies ate it. It made them happy.

She took the cone.

"Listen, can I sit down for a second?" the man said.

She ignored him, turning the cone in her hand like the mysterious artifact it was. The man sat down anyway.

"My name's Toby," he said.

"It's really pink," Kylie said.

"Yeah." And after a minute. "You're supposed to lick it."

She looked at him.

"Like this," he said, licking his own cone.

"I *know*," she said. "I'm not an ignoramus." Kylie licked her ice cream. *Jesus!* Her whole body lit up. "That's—"

"Yeah?"

"It's wonderful," she said.

"You really haven't had ice cream before?"

She shook her head, licking away at the cone, devouring half of it in seconds.

"That's incredibly far-fetched," Toby said. "What's your name? You want a napkin?" He pointed at her chin.

"I'm Kylie," she said, taking the napkin and wiping her chin and lips. All of a sudden she didn't want anymore ice-cream. She had never eaten anything so rich. In her world there *wasn't* anything so rich. Her stomach felt queasy.

"I have to go," she said.

She stood up, so did he.

"Hey, you know the thing is, what you said about not having tools? What I mean is, I have tools. I mean I fix things. It's not a big deal, but I'm good and I like doing it. I can fix all kinds of things, you know? Palm Pilots, cellphones, laptop. Whatever."

Kylie waved the locator. "You don't even know what this *is*."

"I don't *have* to know what it is to make it go again."

Hesitantly, she handed him the locator. While he was turning it in his fingers, she spotted the Tourist. He was wearing a puffy black coat and a watch cap, and he was walking directly towards her, expressionless, his left hand out of sight inside his pocket. He wasn't a human being.

Toby noticed her changed expression and followed her gaze.

"You know that guy?"

Kylie ran. She didn't look back to see if the Tourist was running after her. She cut through the people crowding the sidewalk, her heart slamming. It was a minute before she realized she'd left the locator with Toby. That almost made her stop, but it was too late. Let him keep the damn thing.

She ran hard. The Old Men had chosen her for this mission because of her youth and vitality (so many were sickly and weak), but after a while she had to stop and catch her breath. She looked around. The vista of blue water was dazzling. The city was awesome, madly perfect, phantasmagoric, better than the movies. The Old Men called it an abomination. Kylie didn't care what they said. She was here for her mother, who was dying and who grieved for the trapped souls.

Kylie turned slowly around, and here came two more Tourists.

No, three.

Three from three different directions, one of them

crossing the street, halting traffic. Stalking toward her with no pretense of human expression, as obvious to her among the authentic populace as cockroaches in a scatter of white rice.

Kylie girded herself. Before she could move, a car drew up directly in front of her, a funny round car painted canary yellow. The driver threw the passenger door open, and there was the man again, Toby.

"Get in!"

She ducked into the car, which somehow reminded her of the scutter, and it accelerated away. A Tourist who had scrabbled for the door handle spun back and fell. Kylie leaned over the seat. The Tourist got up, the other two standing beside him, not helping. Then Toby cranked the car into a turn that threw her against the door. They were climbing a steep hill, and Toby seemed to be doing too many things at once, working the clutch, the steering wheel and radio, scanning through stations until he lighted upon something loud and incomprehensible that made him smile and nod his head.

"You better put on your seatbelt," he said. "They'll ticket you for that shit, believe it or not."

Kylie buckled her belt.

"Thanks," she said. "You came out of nowhere."

"Anything can happen. Who were those guys?"

"Tourists."

"Okay. Hey, you know what?"

"What?"

He took his hand off the shifter and pulled Kylie's locator out of his inside jacket pocket.

"I bet you I can fix this gizmo."

"Would you bet your soul on it?"

"Why not?" He grinned.

He stopped at his apartment to pick up his tools, and

Kylie waited in the car. There was a clock on the dashboard. 11:45 a.m. She set the timer on her wrist chronometer.

Twelve hours and change.

They sat in a coffee bar in Belltown. More incomprehensible music thumped from box speakers bracketed near the ceiling. Paintings by some local artist decorated the walls, violent slashes of color, faces of dogs and men and women drowning, mouths gaping.

Kylie kept an eye open for Tourists.

Toby hunched over her locator, a jeweler's kit unrolled next to his espresso. He had the back off the device and was examining its exotic components with the aid of a magnifying lens and a battery operated light of high intensity. He had removed his jacket and was wearing a black sweatshirt with the sleeves pushed up. His forearms were hairy. A tattoo of blue thorns braceleted his right wrist. He was quiet for a considerable time, his attention focused. Kylie drank her second espresso, like the queen of the world, like it was nothing to just *ask* for coffee this good and get it.

"Well?" she said.

"Ah."

"What?"

"Ah, what *is* this thing?"

"You said you didn't need to know."

"I don't need to know, I just want to know. After all, according to you I'm betting my immortal soul that I can fix it, so it'd be nice to know what it does."

"We don't always get to know the nice things, do we?" Kylie said. "Besides I don't believe in souls. That was just something to say." Something her mother had told her, she thought. The Old Men didn't talk about souls. They talked about zoos.

"You sure downed that coffee fast. You want to go for three?"

"Yeah."

He chuckled and gave her a couple of dollars and she went to the bar and got another espresso, head buzzing in a very good way.

"It's a locator," she said, taking pity on him, after returning to the table and sitting down.

"Yeah? What's it locate?"

"The city's Eternity Core."

"Oh, that explains everything. What's an eternity core?"

"It's an alien machine that generates an energy field around the city and preserves it in a sixteen hour time loop."

"Gotchya."

"*Now* can you fix it?"

"Just point out one thing."

She slurped up her third espresso. "Okay."

"What's the power source? I don't see anything that even vaguely resembles a battery."

She leaned in close, their foreheads practically touching. She pointed with the chipped nail of her pinky finger.

"I think it's that coily thing," she said.

He grunted. She didn't draw back. She was smelling him, smelling his skin. He lifted his gaze from the guts of the locator. His eyes were pale blue, the irises circled with black rings.

"You're kind of a spooky chic," he said.

"Kind of."

"I like spooky."

"Where I come from," Kylie said, "almost all the men are impotent."

"Yeah?"

She nodded.

"Where do you come from," he asked, "the east side?"

"East side of hell."

"Sounds like it," he said.

She kissed him, impulsively, her blood singing with caffeine and long-unrequited pheromones. Then she sat back and wiped her lips with her palm and stared hard at him.

"I wish you hadn't done that," she said.

"*Me.*"

"Just fix the locator, okay?"

"Spooky," he said, picking up a screwdriver with a blade not much bigger than a spider's leg.

A little while later she came back from the bathroom and he had put the locator together and was puzzling over the touchpad. He had found the power button. The two inch square display glowed the blue of cold starlight. She slipped it from his hand and activated the grid. A pinhead hotspot immediately began blinking.

"It work okay?" Toby asked.

"Yes." She hesitated, then said, "Let's go for a drive. I'll navigate."

They did that.

Kylie liked the little round canary car. It felt luxurious and utilitarian at the same time. Letting the locator guide her, she directed Toby. After many false turns and an accumulated two point six miles on the odometer, she said:

"Stop. No, keep going, but not too fast."

The car juddered as he manipulated clutch, brake and accelerator. They rolled past a closed store front on the street level of a four story building on First Avenue, some kind of sex shop, the plate glass soaped and brown butcher paper tacked up on the inside.

Two men in cheap business suits loitered in front of the building. Tourists.

Kylie scrunched down in her seat.

"Don't look at those guys," she said. "Just keep driving."

"Whatever."

Later on they were parked under the monorail tracks eating submarine sandwiches. Kylie couldn't get over how great everything was, the food, the coffee, the damn *air*. All of it the way things used to be. She could hardly believe how great it had been, how much had been lost.

"Okay," she said, kind of talking to herself, "so they know I'm here and they're guarding the Core."

"Those bastards," Toby said.

"You wouldn't think it was so funny if you knew what they really were."

"They looked like used car salesmen."

"They're Tourists," Kylie said.

"Oh my God! More tourists!"

Kylie chewed a mouthful of sub. She'd taken too big a bite. Every flavor was like a drug. Onions, provolone, turkey, mustard, pepper.

"So where are the evil tourists from," Toby asked. "California?"

"Another dimensional reality."

"That's what I said."

Kylie's chronometer toned softly. Ten hours.

Inside the yellow car there were many smells and one of them was Toby.

"Do you have anymore tattoos?" she asked.

"One. It's—"

"Don't tell me," she said.

"Okay."

"I want you to show me. But not here. At the place where you live."

"You want to come to my apartment?"

"Your apartment, yes."

"Okay, spooky." He grinned. So did she.

Some precious time later the chronometer toned again. It wasn't on her wrist anymore. It was on the hardwood floor tangled up in her clothes.

Toby, who was standing naked by the refrigerator holding a bottle of grape juice, said, "Why's your watch keep doing that?"

"It's a countdown," Kylie said, looking at him.

"A countdown to what?"

"To the end of the current cycle. The end of the loop."

He drank from the bottle, his throat working. She liked to watch him now, whatever he did. He finished drinking and screwed the cap back on.

"The loop," he said, shaking his head.

When he turned to put the bottle back in the refrigerator she saw his other tattoo again: a cross throwing off light. It was inked into the skin on his left shoulder blade.

"You can't even see your own cross," she said.

He came back to the bed.

"I don't have to see it," he said. "I just like to know it's there, watching my back."

"Are you Catholic?"

"No."

"My mother is."

"I just like the idea of Jesus," he said.

"You're spookier than I am," Kylie said.

"Not by a mile."

She kissed his mouth, but when he tried to caress her she pushed him gently back.

"Take me someplace."

"Where?"

"My grandparent's house." She meant "great" grandparents, but didn't feel like explaining to him how so many decades had passed outside the loop of the Preservation.

"Right now?"

"Yes."

It was a white frame house on Queen Anne Hill, sitting comfortably among its prosperous neighbors on a street lined with live oaks. Kylie pressed her nose to the window on the passenger side of the Vee Dub, as Toby called his vehicle.

"Stop," she said. "That's it."

He tucked the little car into the curb and turned the engine off. Kylie looked from the faded photo in her hand to the house. Her mother's mother had taken the photo just weeks before the world ended. In it, Kylie's great grandparents stood on the front porch of the house, their arms around each other, waving and smiling. There was no one standing on the front porch now.

"It's real," Kylie said. "I've been looking at this picture my whole life.

"Haven't you ever been here before?"

She shook her head. At the same time her chronometer toned.

"How we doing on the countdown," Toby asked.

She glanced at the digital display.

"Eight hours."

"So what happens at midnight?"

"It starts up again. The end is the beginning."

He laughed. She didn't.

"So then it's Sunday, right? Then do you countdown to Monday?"

"At the end of the loop it's *not* Sunday," she said. "It's the same day over again."

"Two Saturdays. Not a bad deal."

"Not just two. It does on and on. November ninth a thousand, ten thousand, a million times over."

"Okay."

"You can look at me like that if you want. I don't care if you believe me. You know something, Toby?"

"What?"

"I'm having a really *good* day."

"That's November ninth for you."

She smiled at him, then kissed him, that feeling, the taste, all of the sensation in its totality.

"I want to see my grandparents now."

She opened the door and got out but he stayed in the car. She crossed the lawn strewn with big colorful oak leaves to the front door of the house, stealing backward glances, wanting to know he was still there waiting for her in the yellow car. Her lover. Her boyfriend.

She started to knock on the door but hesitated. From inside the big house she heard muffled music and laughter. She looked around. In the breeze an orange oak leaf detached from the tree and spun down. The sky blew clear and cold. Later it would cloud over and rain. Kylie knew all about this day. She had been told of it since she was a small child. The last day of the world, perfectly preserved for the edification of alien Tourists and anthropologists. Some people said what happened was an accident, a consequence of the aliens opening the rift, disrupting the fabric of reality. What really pissed everybody off, Kylie thought, was the dismissive attitude. There was no occupying army, no invasion. They came, destroyed everything either intentionally or accidentally, then ignored the survivors. The Preservation was the only thing about the former masters of the Earth that interested them.

Kylie didn't care about all that right now. She had been told about the day, but she had never understood what the day meant, the sheer sensorial joy of it, the incredible beauty and rightness of it. A surge of pure delight moved through her being, and for a moment she experienced uncontainable happiness.

She knocked on the door.

"Yes?" A woman in her mid-fifties with vivid green eyes, her face pressed with comfortable laugh lines. Like the house, she was a picture come to life. (Kylie's grandmother showing her the photographs, faded and worn from too much touching).

"Hi," Kylie said.

"Can I help you?" the live photograph said.

"No. I mean, I wanted to ask you something."

The waiting expression on her face so familiar. Kylie said, "I just wanted to know, are you having a good day, I mean a really good day?"

Slight turn of the head, lips pursed uncertainly, ready to believe this was a harmless question from a harmless person.

"It's like a survey," Kylie said. "For school?"

A man of about sixty years wearing a baggy wool sweater and glasses came to the door.

"What's all this?" he asked.

"A happiness survey," Kylie's great grandmother said, and laughed.

"Happiness survey, huh?" He casually put his arm

around his wife and pulled her companionably against him.

"Yes," Kylie said. "For school."

"Well, I'm happy as a clam," Kylie's great grandfather said.

"I'm a clam, too," Kylie's great grandmother said. "A happy one."

"Thank you," Kylie said.

"You're very welcome. Gosh but you look familiar."

"So do you. Goodbye."

Back in the car Kylie squeezed Toby's hand. There had been a boy on the Outskirts. He was impotent, but he liked to touch Kylie and be with her, and he didn't mind watching her movies, the one's that made the Old Men sad and angry but that she obsessively hoarded images from in her mind. The boy's hand always felt cold and bony. Which wasn't his fault. The nicest time they ever had was a night they had spent in one of the ruins with a working fireplace and enough furniture to burn for several hours. They'd had a book of poems and took turns reading them to each other. Most of the poems didn't make sense to Kylie but she liked the sounds of the words, the way they were put together. Outside the perpetual storms crashed and sizzled, violet flashes stuttering into the cozy room with the fire.

In the yellow car, Toby's hand felt warm. Companionable and intimate.

"So how are they doing?" he said.

"They're happy."

"Great. What's next?"

"If you knew this was your last day to live," Kylie asked him, "what would you do?"

"I'd find a spooky girl and make love to her."

She kissed him. "What else?"

"Ah—"

"I mean without leaving the city. You can't leave the city."

"Why not?"

"Because you'd just get stuck in the Preservation Field until the loop re-started. It looks like people are driving out but they're not."

He looked at her closely, searching for the joke, then grinned. "We wouldn't want that to happen to us."

"No."

"So what would *you* do on your last day?" he asked.

"I'd find a spooky guy who could fix things and I'd get him to fix me up."

"You don't need fixing. You're not broken."

"I am."

"Yeah?"

"Let's drive around. Then let's have a really great meal, like the best food you can think of."

"That's doable."

"Then we can go back to your apartment."

"What about the big countdown?"

"Fuck the countdown." Kylie pushed the timing stud into her chronometer. "There," she said. "No more countdown."

"You like pizza?" Toby said.

"I don't know. What is it?"

After they made love the second time Kylie fell into a light doze on Toby's futon bed. She was not used to so much rich stimulation, so much food and drink, so much touching.

She woke with a start from a dream that instantly disappeared from her consciousness. There was the sound of rain, but it wasn't the terrible poisonous rain of her world. Street light through the window cast a flowing shadow across the foot of the bed. It reminded her of the shiny fountain at the waterfront. The room was snug and comforting and safe. There was a clock on the table beside the bed but she didn't look at it. It could end right now.

She sat up. Toby was at his desk under a framed movie poster, bent over something illuminated by a very bright and tightly directly light. He was wearing his jeans but no shirt or socks.

Hello," she said.

He turned sharply, then smiled. "Oh, hey Kylie. Have a nice rest?"

"I'm thirsty."

He got up and fetched her a half depleted bottle of water from the refrigerator. While he was doing that she noticed her locator in pieces on the desk.

"We don't need that anymore," she said, pointing.

"I was just curious. I can put it back together, no problem."

"I don't care about it." She lay back on the pillows and closed her eyes.

"Kylie?"

"Hmmm?" She kept her eyes closed.

"Who are you? Really."

"I'm your spooky girl."

"Besides that."

She opened her eyes. "Don't spoil it. Please don't."

"Spoil what?"

"This. Us. Now. It's all that matters."

Rain ticked against the window. It would continue all night, a long, cleansing rain. Water that anybody could catch in a cup and drink if they wanted to—water out of the sky.

Toby took his pants down and slipped under the

sheet next to her, his body heat like a magnetic field that drew her against him. She pressed her cheek to his chest. His heart beat calmly.

"Everything's perfect," she said.

"Yeah." He didn't sound that certain.

"What's the matter?"

"Nothing," he said. "Only—this is all pretty fast. Don't you think we should know more about each other?"

"Why? Now is what matters."

"Yeah, but I mean, what do you do? Where do you live? Basic stuff. Big stuff, too, like do you believe in God or who'd you vote for president?"

"I want to go for a long walk in the rain. I want to feel it on my face and not be afraid or sick."

"What do you mean?"

"You're spoiling it. Please, let's make every second happy. Make it a day we'd want to relive a thousand times."

"I don't want to live *any* day a thousand times."

"Let's walk now."

"What's the hurry?"

She got out of bed and started dressing, her back to him.

"Don't be mad," he said.

"I'm not mad."

"You are."

She turned to him, buttoning her shirt. "Don't tell me what I am."

"Sorry."

"You practically sleep walk through the most important day of your life."

"I'm not sleep-walking."

"Don't you even want to fall in love with me?"

He laughed uncertainly. "I don't even know your name."

"You know it. Kylie."

"I mean your last name."

"It doesn't matter."

"It matters to me," Toby said. "You matter to me."

Finished with her shirt, she sat on the edge of the bed to lace her shoes. "No you don't," she said. "You only care about me if you can know all about my past and our future. You can't live one day well and be happy."

"Now you sound like Hemingway."

"I don't know what that means and I don't care." She shrugged into her parka.

"Where are you going?"

"For a walk. I *told* you what I wanted."

"Yeah, I guess I was too ignorant to absorb it."

She slammed the door on her way out.

She stood under the pumpkin-colored light of the street lamp, confused, face tilted up to be anointed by the rain. Was he watching her from the apartment window, his heart about to break? She waited and waited. This is the part where he would run to her and embrace her and kiss her and tell her that he loved, loved, loved her.

He didn't come out.

She stared at the brick building checkered with light and dark apartment windows, not certain which one was his.

He didn't come out, and it was spoiled.

A bus rumbled between her and the building, pale indifferent faces inside.

Kylie walked in the rain. It was not poison but it was cold and after a while unpleasant. She pulled her hood up and walked with her head down. The wet sidewalk was a pallet of neon smears. Her fingers touched the shape of the explosive in her pocket. She could find the building with the papered windows. Even if the Tourists tried to stop her she might still get inside and destroy the Eternity Core. It's what her mother wanted, what the Old Men wanted. But what if they caught her? If she remained in the loop through an entire cycle she would become a permanent part of it. She couldn't stand that, not the way she hurt right now. She didn't know what time it was. She didn't know the *time*. She had to reach her scutter and get out.

A horn went off practically at her elbow. Startled, she looked up. A low and wide vehicle, a boy leaning out the passenger window, smirking.

"Hey, you wanna go for a ride?"

"No."

"Then fuck you, bitch!" He cackled, and the vehicle accelerated away, ripping the air into jagged splinters.

She walked faster. The streets were confusing. She was lost. Her panic intensified. Why couldn't he have come after her and be sorry and love her? But it wasn't like the best parts of the movies. Some of it was good, but a lot of it wasn't. Maybe her mother had been right. But Kylie didn't believe in souls, so wasn't it better to have one day forever than no days? Wasn't it?

Fuck you, bitch.

She turned around and ran back in the direction from which she'd come. At first she didn't think she could find it, but there it was, the apartment building! And Toby was coming out the lobby door, pulling his jacket closed. He saw her, and she ran to him. He didn't mean it and she didn't mean it, and this was the part where they made up, and then all the rest of the loop would be good—the good time after making up. You had to mix the good and bad. The bad made the good better. She ran to him and hugged him, the smell of the wet leather so strong.

"You were coming after me," she said.

He didn't say anything.

"You were," she said.

"Yeah."

Something clutched at her heart. "It's the best day ever," she said.

"I give it a seven point five."

"You don't know anything," she said. "You got your spooky girl and you had an adventure and you saved the whole world."

"When you put it that way it's a nine. So come on. I'll buy you a hot drink and you can tell me about the tourists from the fifth dimension."

"What time is it?" she asked.

He looked at his watch. "Five of eleven."

"I don't want a hot drink," she said. "Can you take us some place with a nice view where we can sit in the Vee Dub?"

"You bet."

The city spread out before them. The water of Elliot Bay was black. Rain whispered against the car and the cooling engine ticked down like a slow timer. It was awkward with the separate seats, but they snuggled together, Kylie's head pillowed on his chest. He turned the radio on—not to his loud noise-music but a jazz station, like a compliment to the rain. They talked, intimately. Kylie invented a life and gave it to him, borrowing from stories her mother and grandmother had told her. He called her spooky, his term of endearment, and he talked about what they would do tomorrow. She accepted the gift of the future he was giving her, but she lived in this moment, now, this sweet inhalation of the present, this happy, happy ending. Then the lights of Seattle seemed to haze over. Kylie closed her eyes, her hand on the explosive sphere, and her mind slumbered briefly in a dark spun cocoon.

Kylie punched through, and the sudden light shift dazzled her.

ME-TOPIA

Adam Roberts

He thinks the moon is a small hole at the top of the sky
—*Elizabeth Bishop*

The first day and the first night.

They had come down in the high ground, an immense plateau many thousands of miles square. "The highlands," said Murphy. "I claim the highlands. I'll call them Murphyland." Over an hour or so he changed his mind several times: Murphtopia, Murphia. "No," he said, glee bubbling out in a little dance, a shimmy of the feet, a flourish of the hands. "Just Murphy, Murphy. Think of it! *Where do you come from? I come from Murphy. I'm a Murphyite. I was born in Murphy.*" And the sky paled, and then the sun appeared over the mountain tops and everything was covered with a tide of light. The dew was so thick it looked like the aftermath of a heavy rainstorm.

Sinclair, wading out from the shuttle's wreckage

through waist-high grass, drew a dark trail after him marking his path, like the photographic negative of a comet.

"I don't understand what you're so happy about," said Edwards. It was as if he could not *see* the new land, this world that had popped out of nowhere. As if all he could see was the damage to the ship. But that was how Edwards's mind worked. He had a practical mind.

"And are you sad for your ship," sang Murphy, with deliberately overplayed oirishry, "all buckled and collapsed as it is?" Of course Murphy was a *homo neanderthalis*. The real deal. All four of these crewmen were. Of course you know what that means.

"You should be sad too, Murphy," said Edwards, speaking in a level voice. "It's your ship too. I don't see how we are to get home without it."

"But *this* is my home," declared Murphy. And then sang his own name, or perhaps the name of his newly made land, over and over: 'Murphy! Murphy! Murphy!"

The sun moved through the sky. The swift light went everywhere. It spilled over everything and washed back. The expanse of grassland shimmered in the breeze like cellophane.

Edwards climbed to the top of the buckled craft. The plasmetal was oily with dew, and his feet slipped several times. At the top he stood as upright as he dared, and surveyed the word. Mountains away to the west, grass steppes in every direction, north south and east, flowing downhill eastward towards smudges of massive forestation and the metallic inlaid sparkle of rivers, lakes, seas. That was some view, eastward.

The sun was rising from the west, which was an unusual feature. What strange world rotated like that? There were no earth-sized planets in the solar system that rotated like that.

Did that mean they were no longer in the solar system? That was impossible. There was no means by which they could have travelled so far. Physics repudiated the very notion.

The air tasted fresh in his mouth, in his throat. Grass-scent. Rainwater and ozone.

And for long minutes there was no sound except the hushing of the grasses in the wind, and the distant febrile twitter of birds high in the sky. The sky gleamed, as full of the wonder of light as a glass brimful of bright water. Vins called up, "There are insects, I've got insects here, though they seem to be torpid." He paused, and repeated the word, torpid. "When the dew evaporates a little they'll surely come to life."

Edwards grunted in reply, but his eye was on the sky. Spherical clouds, perfect as eggs, drifted in the zenith. Six of them. Seven. Eight. Edwards counted, turning his head. Ten.

Twelve.

And the air, moist with dew and fragrant with possibility, slid past him. And light all about. Silence, stained only by the swishing of the breeze.

Murphy was dancing below, kicking his feet through the wet grass. "Maybe *Murphy* isn't such a good idea, by itself," he called, to nobody in particular. "As a name, by itself. How about the Murphy Territories? How about the *Land* of Murphy?" And then, after half a minute when neither Edwards nor Vins replied, he added: "Don't be sore, Vins. You can name some other place."

Vins went into the body of the shuttle to fetch out some killing jars for the insects.

Sinclair was away for hours. The sun rose, and the dew steamed away in wreathy barricades of mist. The grass dried out, and paled, and then bristled with dryness. It was a yellow, tawny sort of grass. By mid-day the sky was hot as a hot-plate, and Murphy had stripped off his chemise.

Sinclair returned, sweating. "It goes on and on," he says. "Exactly the same. Steppe, and more steppe."

The sun dropped over the eastern horizon. It quickly became cold.

The night sky was cloudless; stars like lit dewdrops on black. Breath petalled out of their mouths in transient, ghostly puffs. Edwards slept in the shuttle. Sinclair and Vins chatted, their voices subdued underneath the enormity of night sky. Murphy had a nicotine inhaler, and lay on the cooling roof of the crashed shuttle, looking up at the stars puffing intermittently. Later they all joined Edwards in the shuttle and slept. Over their thoughtless, slumbering heads the stars glinted and prickled in the black clarity. Hours passed. The the sky cataracted to white with the coming dawn. Ivory-coloured clouds bubbled into the sky from behind the peaks of the highlands and swept down upon them. Before dawn rain started falling. Edwards woke at the drumroll sound of rain against the body of the crashed ship, sat up disoriented for a moment, then lay down again and went back to sleep.

"We're dead, we've died, we're dead," said Murphy, perhaps speaking in his sleep.

The second day and the second night.

At breakfast, after dawn, it was still raining. The four of them ate inside the shuttle, with the door open. "Ah," said Edwards, looking through the hatch at the shimmering lines of water. "The universal solvent."

"But I should hate you," said Murphy. "Because you can look at water and say *ah the universal solvent*."

Edwards cocked his head on one side. "I don't see your point," he said.

"No, no," said Murphy. "That's not it. Oh, water, oh? This beautiful thing, this spiritual thing, purity and the power to cleanse, to baptise even. Light on water, is there a more beautiful thing? And all you can say when you see it is *ah the universal solvent*."

Edwards put his mouth in a straight line. "But it *is* the universal solvent," he said. "That's one of its functions. Why do you say *oh water oh*?"

The rain outside was greeting their conversational interchanges with sustained and rapturous applause. The colour through the hatch was grey. The air looked like metal scored and overscored with myriad slant lines. It was chill.

"Can we lift off?" asked Sinclair. "Is there a way off-of this place?"

"Feel that," Edwards instructed. He was not talking about any particular object, not instructing any of the crew to lift any particular object. What he meant was: feel how heavy we are. "That's a full g. That's what is to be overcome. We came down hard."

"Hard," confirmed Murphy.

"We weren't expecting," said Sinclair, "a whole world to pop out of the void. Nothing, nothing, nothing, then *a whole world*. We snapped our spine on this rock."

"Let's get one thing straight," said Edwards, in his brusque and matter-of-fact voice. "This world did not pop out of nowhere. Worlds don't *pop out* of nowhere." He looked at his colleagues in turn. "That's not what happened."

"Turn it up, *Captain*," said Murphy. He applied the title sarcastically. It was the nature of this ship that its crew worked without ranks such as captain, second-in-command, all that bag-and-baggage of hierarchy. No military ship, this. This was not a merchant vessel either. They hadn't been sliding along the frictionless thread of Earth-Mars or Earth-Moon hauling goods or transporting soldiery or anything like that. This was science. Science isn't structured to recognise hierarchy.

"I'm only saying," said Edwards, sheepishly. "I'm not wanting to suggest that I'm in charge."

They were silent for a while, and the rain spattered and clattered enormously all about them. Encore! Encore!

It occurred to Edwards, belatedly, that Murphy might have been saying *eau, water, eau*.

"Right," said Vins. "We're all in a kind of intellectual shock, that's what I think. We've been here two days now, and we haven't even formulated a plausible hypothesis of what's going on. We haven't even tried." He looked around at his colleagues. "Let's review what happened."

Murphy had his stumpy arms folded over his little chest. "Review, by all means," he said. But then, when

Vins opened his mouth to speak again, he interrupted immediately: "*I've* formed a hypothesis. It's called Murphy. This is prime land, and I claim it. When we get back, or when we at least contact help and they come get us, I shall set up a private limited company to promote the settlement of Murphy. I'll make a fortune. I'll be mayor. I'll be the *alpha* male."

"Why you think," said Edwards, thinking literally, "that such a contract would have any legal force upon Earth is beyond me."

"Let's review," said Vins, in a loud voice.

Everybody looked at him.

"We're flying. We drop below the ecliptic plane, no more than a hundred thousand klims. More than that?"

None of the others say anything. Then Sinclair says, "It was about that."

"We saw a winking star," Vins said. He did not stop talking, he continued on, even though Murphy tried to interrupt him with a sneering 'winking star, oh that's good on my mother's health that's good'. Vins wasn't to be distracted when he got going. "It was out of the position of variable star 699, which is what we might have thought it otherwise. Except it wasn't where 699 should've been. As we flew it grew in size, indicating a very reflective asteroid, or perhaps comet, out of the ecliptic. You," Vins nodded at Sinclair, "argued it was a parti-coloured object rotating diurnally. But it was a fair way south of the ecliptic. *Then* what happened?"

"We all know what happened," said Murphy. They may all have been *homo neanderthalis*, but they were bright. They all had their scientific educations. The real deal.

"Let's review," said Vins. "We need to *know* what's happened. Act like scientists, people."

"I'm a scientist no longer," cried Murphy, with a flourish of his arm. "I'm the king of Murphtopia."

"What happened," said Edwards, slowly, thinking linearly and literally, "was we were tracking the curious wobble of the asteroid. Or whatever it was. We flew close, and suddenly there was a world, a whole world, and—we came down. We re-entered sideways, and there was heat-damage to the craft, and then there was collision damage, and now it's broken. And we're sitting inside it."

"Now," said Vins. "Here's a premise. Worlds don't appear out of nowhere. Do we agree?"

Nobody disagreed.

"It's a mountain and mohammed thing," offered Sinclair. "Put it this way, which is more likely? That a whole Earth-sized planet pops out of nowhere in front of us? Or that we, for some reason, have popped into a *new* place?"

"I say we're back on Earth," said Murphy. "It looks like a duck, and it smells like a duck and it, uh, pulls the gravity of a duck, *then* it's a duck."

"The sun is rising," Sinclair pointed out, "in the *west*. It is setting in the *east*."

"Oh. And the asteroid was the beacon of a dimensional *sffy* gateway through time and space," mocked Murphy: "and we fell through, like in a *sffy* film, and now we're on the far side of the galaxy?" He pronounced "SF-y" as a two-syllable word, with a ludicrous and prolonged emphasis on the central "f" sound.

"That can't be true," said Edwards. "Our first night, the stars were very clear. All the constellations were there. Familiar constellations."

"Which's what we'd expect if we were back on Earth," said Murphy.

"But the sun *rises* in the *west*…" said Sinclair again.

"Maybe the compasses are broken, somehow. Distorted. Maybe you *think* west is east and versy-vice-a."

"All of them? All the compasses? And besides, at night you can see the pole star, great bear, all very clearly. Oh there's no doubt where the sun's rising."

"Well, let's look at another hypothesis," said Murphy. "There is a whole, a *whole* Earth-sized planet, about a hundred thousand kilometres south of the ecliptic between Earth and Venus. And nobody on earth for six centuries of dedicated astronomy has noticed it. Nobody saw a whole planet, waxing and waning, between us and the sun? No southern hemisphere observatory happened to see it? Is *that* what you're saying?"

"That is," Vins conceded, "hard to credit."

"So," said Murphy. He got up, and stepped to the hatch, and looked out at the hissing and rapturous rainfall. "Here's what I think happened. We were off investigating your *winking* star, Vins, and then we all suffered some sort of group epilepsy, or mass hysteria, or loss of consciousness, and without realising it we piloted the ship back up and towards earth."

"We were days away," Vins pointed out.

"So perhaps we were in a fugue state for days. Anyway, we weren't shaken out of it until we slammed into the atmosphere, and now we've crashed in the highlands in Peru, or Africa maybe."

"There's nowhere on earth," Vins pointed out, "as lovely as this. Where is there anywhere as mild, or balmy, as this? Peru, you say?"

"You ever *been* to Peru?" asked Edwards.

"I been a lot of places, and there's ice wherever I've been."

"Never mind the climate," said Edwards. "What about the sunrises?"

"How is it," agreed Vins, "that the sunrise is in the west if this is Peru?"

"I don't know. But the advantage of my hypothesis is that it's occam's razor on all the stuff about planets appearing from nowhere, and it reduces all that to a single, simple problem. The sunrise."

"And another problem," Edwards pointed out, "which is the lack of radio traffic."

"The radio's broken," said Murphy. "I'm not happy about it."

"The radio?"

"No, not happy about the *Murphy*, the Murphy-topia. I'm not happy about the status of my kingdom. I was looking forward to claiming the highlands as my personal kingdom. But if it's, you know, Peru, then there'll be some other alpha male who's already claimed these highlands."

"The radio's not broken," said Edwards. "We can pick up background chatter. Bits and pieces. We just can't seem to locate any—to get a fix upon—"

"Vins," said Murphy, sitting himself down again. "Vins, Vins. What's your theory? You haven't told us your theory."

"I think we've landed upon a banned world," said Vins. He said this in a bright voice, but his mouth was angled downwards as he spoke. "A forbidden planet. *That's* SF-y, isn't it?" He pronounced each of the letters in sfy separately, trisyllabic.

"A banned world," said Murphy, as if savouring the idea. "What an interesting notion. What a fanciful notion. What a dark horse you are, to be sure, Vins."

* * *

The rain stopped sometime in the afternoon, and the clouds rolled away, leaving the landscape washed and gleaming under the low sun as if glazed with strawberry and peach. The long stretch of grassland directly beneath them retained some of its yellow, and moved slowly, like the pelt of a lion. In the distance they could see a long inlaid band of bronze, curved and kinked like the marginal illustration in a celtic manuscript: open water, glittering in the sun. And the sun went down and the stars came out.

Edwards, trying to identify where the Earth should be from their last known position, noticed something they should all have seen on the first night: that the stars hardly moved through the sky. He woke the others up.

"Earth," he said, "is just below the horizon." He pointed. "There. Mars, I think, is over there."

"Send them a signal."

"I did. But why should they be listening for a signal from this stretch of space? It's not even on the ecliptic. It's not as if there are any astronomers on Mars. And if there were, if there were any, you know, amateurs, why should they be looking down here? No, that's not what I woke you up to show you."

"What then?"

"The stars aren't moving. I've been watching for an hour. I was waiting to see Earth come up over the horizon so I could send them a message. But it's not coming up."

"You thought it was an hour," said Murphy, crossly. "Clearly it *wasn't* an hour. You probably sat there for five minutes and got impatient."

So they settled down together, and all checked their watches, and looked east to where the sun had set, where familiar stars pebbled the sky. And an hour passed, and another, and the stars did not move.

Nobody said anything for a long time.

"Somebody has stopped the stars in their courses," said Murphy. "We're dead, we're all in the afterlife. Is that what happened? We crashed the ship and died, and this is the land of the dead."

"I thought you were the one, Murphy, who wanted to apply occam's razor?" chided Edwards. "That's a pretty elaborated explanation for the facts, don't you think? I don't feel dead. Do you? You feel that way?"

"Certainly not," said Vins.

"But we've no idea what it feels like to feel dead," Murphy pointed out.

"Exactly. It's a null hypothesis. Let's not go there. There must be another explanation."

"The other explanation is that we're not rotating."

"Except we saw the sun go round and set, so we *are* rotating. An earth-sized world, pulling an earth-strength gravity rotates for half a day and then *stops* rotating? That makes no sense."

"I'll tell you what makes sense," said Murphy, hugging himself against the cold. "This is a banned world. We are not supposed to be here. That's what makes sense."

"Of course we're not supposed to be here," agreed Vins. "Supposed to be Venus, that's where. That's where we're supposed to be orbiting. Not here. But that's not to say it's a forbidden planet."

"You were the one who said so!" Murphy objected.

"I was joking," said Vins.

"Your joke may be coming true," said Murphy. He coughed, loud and long. Then he said, "The sun rises in the west and the stars don't move. You know what that is? That's things that the human eye was not supposed to see. That's a realm of magic—faery, that's where we are, and the faery queen is probably gathering her hounds to hunt us down for seeing this forbidden place."

"Amusing, Murphy," said Edwards, in a bland voice. "Very fanciful and imaginative. Your fancy and your imagination, I find them amusing."

"I'm going to sleep," Murphy sulked, picking himself up and going back inside the ship. "I'll meet my fate tomorrow with a clear head at least."

The other stayed outside under the splendid, chilly, glittering stars and under that silkily-cold black sky. They talked, and reduced the possibilities to an order of plausibility. They discussed what to do. They discussed the possibility of making the ship whole again; perhaps by dismantling one of the thirty-six thrust engines and reassembling it as a sort of welding torch, so as to make good the breaches in the plasmetal hull. Nobody could think how to launch into space, though: the craft had not been built to achieve escape velocity unaided. They had not been planning on *landing* on Venus, after all. (The very idea!) Finally the sky started to pale and ease, as if the arc of the western horizon were a heated element thawing the black into rose and pearl and then into blushed tones of white.

The sun lifted itself into the sky.

"Well," said Vins, with a tone of finality, "that settles it. Clearly we *are* rotating. The lack of movement of the stars and the apparent movement of the sun: these data contradict one another. Seem to. It's hard to advance a coherent explanation that includes both of these pieces of observational data. Are we agreed?"

"I can't think what else," said Edwards. "We assume the sky is a simulation of some sort. Do we assume that?"

"We do," said Sinclair.

"One of two explanations, then," said Vins. "Either the sky is a total simulation, upon which is projected a moving sun by day and motionless stars by night. Or else the sky is a real feature but some peculiarity of optics distorts the actual motion of the stars in some way."

"It's hard to think what sort of phenomenon..." began Sinclair. But he stopped talking. He wasn't sure what he was going to say; and—anyway—the dawn was so very beautiful. They all sat looking down, all distracted by the loveliness of the view from their highland vantage-point: down across sloping grasslands and marsh and the beaming seas and gleaming channels of water. And, woken by the light, the first birds were up; in nimble flight and giving voice to agile birdsong, bouncing their tenor and soprano trills off the blue ceiling of the sky—or, whatever it was.

They were all tired. They'd been up all night. Eventually they went inside the spaceship and slept.

The third day and the third night.

Vins, Sinclair and Edwards woke sometime in the afternoon, the sun already declining towards the east.

Murphy had gone.

They searched for him, in a slightly desultory manner, round and about the ship; but it was clear enough where he had gone: a trail scuffed, slightly kinked but more-or-less straight, through the wet grasses and downwards. Clambering onto the top of the ship Edwards could follow this with his eye, and with binoculars, down and down, a wobbly ladder in the sheen tights-material of the fields all the way to where forest drew a dark line.

"He's gone into a forest. Down there, kilometres away." He wanted to say something like: imagine a stretch of gold velvet, all brushed one way to smoothness, and a finger dragged through the velvet against the grain of the brushing—that's what his path looks like. But he couldn't find the words to say that. "Should we go after him?" he called. "Should we go?"

"He knows where we are," said Sinclair. "He knows how to get back here. He's probably just exploring."

"And if he gets into trouble?"

"It's his look-out. He must take responsibility for himself," said Vins. "We all must shift for ourselves, after all."

The three of them breakfasted on ship's-supplies, sitting in the warm air and listening to the meagre, distant chimes of the birds and watching the flow and glitter of wind upon the grass. "I could sit here forever," said Edwards, in a relaxed voice.

The other two were silent, but it was a silent agreement.

"We need to get on," said Vins, as if dragging the sentence up from great deeps. "We need to explore. To fix the ship. That's what we need to do."

They did nothing. After breakfast they dozed in the sun. Murphy did not return. Who knew where he had gone?

The one thing so obvious that none of them bothered to point it out was that this world was paradisical compared to the wrecked and wasted landscapes of home. And that because it was paradisical it was very obviously not a real place. They were dead, and had gone to a material heaven, perhaps on account of some sort of oversight. They had died in the crash. Or they had been transported through a different sort of spatial-discontinuity, one that translated them from real to mythic space. They were to feed forever amongst the mild-eyed melancholy lotos-eaters now.

The land of the sirens, in which Odysseus's crew had languished so pleasantly and purposelessly. Was *that* a forbidden world? Was it banned to subsequent explorers? Why else was it never again discovered?

It may still be there, some island or stretch of coast in the Mediterranean protected by a cloak of invisibility, some magic zone or curtain through which only a few, select and lucky mariners stumble. Who knows?

All this culture and learning bounced around their heads: Vins, Sinclair and Edwards. They knew all about Homer and Mohammed, and they knew all about Shakespeare and Proust, even though these people about whom they were so knowledgeable were a completely different sort of creature to themselves. These Homers and Van Goghs were all super-beings, elevated, godlike; and the residue of their golden-age achievements in the minds of our scientists has the paradoxical effect of shrinking *us* by comparison. Don't you think?

Best not think about it. What and if they *are* in the land of the Lotos? Maybe they're lucky, that's all. Don't you wish *you* could go there?

The sun set in the east. Colour and brightness drained out of the western sky, out of the zenith flowing down to the east with osmotic slowness, and leaving behind a purply black dotted with perfectly motionless stars. The last of the day was a broad stretch of white-yellow sky over the eastern horizon, patched with skinny horizontal clouds of golden brown. For long minutes the last of the sunlight, coming up over the horizon, touched the bottom line of these clouds with fierce and molten light, so that it looked as if several sinuous heating elements, glowing bright and hot with the electricity passing through them, had been fixed to the matter of the sky. Then the light faded away from the clouds, and they browned and blackened against a compressing layer of sunset lights: a sky honey and marmalade, and then a grey-orange, and finally blue, and after that black.

It was night again.

Something agitated Vins enough to get him up and huffing around. "The stars have moved a little," he said. "There—that's the arc of the corona australis. Say what you like but *don't* tell me I don't know my constellations."

"So?"

"It's higher. Yesterday the lowest star was right on the horizon, on that little hill silhouetted there. Today it's a fraction above."

"So we're rotating real slow," said Sinclair. "I can't say I care. I can't say I'm bothered. I'm going to sleep."

The fourth day and the fourth night.

In the morning Vins left the ship. He set off in the opposite direction to Murphy; not down the slope towards the forest and the long shining stretches of open water; but up, higher into the highlands. He had no idea where Murphy had gone, or what he had been after; but something inside him prompted him to go higher. Go up, Moses. He had a vision of himself climbing and climbing until he reached the summit of some snow-clenched mountain top at the very heart of the world from which the whole planet—or at least this whole hemisphere—would be visible. Like Mount Purgatory, he thought, from Dante. As if he had anything to do with Dante! Godlike figures from the golden age.

Vins didn't creep away as Murphy had done. He prepared a pack, some supplies, some tools, a couple of scientific instruments. Then he woke the other two. He told them what he wanted to do; and they sat, looking stupidly at him from under their overhanging foreheads, and didn't say anything. "You sure you don't want to come with me?" he said. He felt an obscure and disabling fear deep inside him, a terror that if he stayed at the crash site he'd slide into torpor and that would be the end of him. Who was it had said that word? Torpor, torpor. Oh, he had to get out and away. He had to move.

"Do what you like," said Sinclair.

"It makes no sense to me," said Edwards, "to go marching off without any sort of objective. Shouldn't you have an objective? As a scientist?"

"My objective is to explore. What's more scientific than exploration?"

Edwards looked at him, blinked, looked again. "We should stay here," he said, slowly. He turned to look at the buckled ship. "We should mend the ship."

"We should," agreed Vins. "But we don't. You *notice* that? There's something here that's rendering us idle. Idleness doesn't suit us."

Sinclair laughed at this. "Let him go," he said, stretching himself on a broad boulder with a westward-facing facet to warm himself in the new sunlight. "He's the hairiest of us all."

Vins winced at this insult. "Don't be like that. What is this, school?"

"It's true," said Sinclair. "Murphy *was* the hairiest, but he's gone God-knows-where. You're the hairiest now, and you'll go, and good riddance. Go after Murphy. Go pick fleas from his pelt. I'm the smoothest of the lot of you and I'll stay here and *thank* you."

"I'm not going after Murphy, I'm going higher, into the highlands."

"Go where you like."

Edwards wouldn't meet Vins' gaze, so Vins shouldered his pack and marched off, striding westward into the setting sun. He could feel Sinclair's eyes upon his back as he went, almost a heat, like a ray; Sinclair just lounging there like a lazy great ape, watching him go. The hairiest indeed!

Then Vins had a second thought. He wanted to get up high, didn't he? He could lift himself clean off the ground.

It surprised him how much courage it took to turn about and stomp back down to the ship again. Sinclair was still there on his rock, watching him with lazy insolence. Edwards had taken off his shoes and climbed to the top of the wreckage, clinging to the dew-wet surface with his toes and the palms of his feet. He was gazing east, down, away.

Vins didn't say anything to either of them. Instead he went into the ship and retrieved a bundle of gossamer-fabric and plastic cord and tied it to the top of his backpack. Then he pulled out a small cylinder of helium, no longer or thicker than a forearm though densely heavy. He tied a grapple-rope to this and dragged it after him.

There were no more goodbyes. He stomped away.

***

Something was bugging Vins, preying on his mind. It was as if he'd caught a glimpse of something out of the corner of his eye without exactly noticing it, such that it had registered only in his subconscious (that gift of the gods, the unconscious mind). He felt he should have understood by now. Something was wrong, or else something was profoundly and obviously right and he couldn't see it.

What?

He marched on, the cylinder dragging through the turf behind him and occasionally clanging on the upcrops of rock that poked through the grass. It was an effort with every step to haul the damn thing, but Vins had found in stubbornness and ill-temper a substitute for willpower. He marched on. He didn't know where he was going. He had, as Edwards might say, no objective. But on he went.

The grass grew shorter the higher he went, and the wind became fresher. The sun was directly above him, and then it was behind him, and he was chasing his own waggish shadow, marching up and up. His field of view was taken up with the pale-green and yellow grass sloping up directly in front of him. Each strand moved with slightly separate motion in the burly wind, like agitated worms, or the fronds of some impossibly massive underwater polypus.

He stopped, sat on a stool of bare rock and drank from his water bottle. Looking back the direction he had come he could see the ship now, very distant. Edwards was no longer standing on its back. Nor could he see Sinclair. From this eagle's vantage point, the path the crashing ship had gouged in the soil was very visible, a mottled painterly scar through the grasslands culminating in the broken-backed hourglass of the ship itself. It seemed unlikely, Vins thought, that in crashing they had not simply dashed themselves to atoms.

Beyond the wreck that the grasslands stretched away. Vins could see a great deal more of the terrain from up here. They had come down directly above a broad hilly spit of land that lay between what looked like two spreading estuaries, north and south. Each of these estuaries widened and spilled into what Vins took to be separate seas—one reaching as far north as he could see and one as far south. It wasn't possible to see whether these seas were connected; whether, in other words, the two estuaries were inlets into one enormous ocean.

The sun setting threw a broadcast spread of lights across these two bodies of water, and they glowed ferociously, beautifully. As he sat there looking down on this landscape Vins felt the disabling intensity of it all. As if its loveliness might just drain all his willpower and leave him just sitting here, on this saddle of bare rock, sitting in the afternoon warmth gazing down upon it.

He shook himself. He couldn't allow this place to suck out his strength of purpose. Maybe he was a *homo neanderthalis*, but he was a scientist. He flew spacecraft between the planets.

He picked himself up and marched on, uphill all the way, until the light had thickened and blackened around him. Eventually, exhausted, he stopped and ate some food and rolled himself into his sleeping bag and tried to sleep on the grass. But, tired as he was, he was awake a long time. Something nagging at him. Something about the perspective downhill—those two broad estuaries draining into whatever wide sea, hidden in distance, in haze and clouds and the curve of the world's horizon. What about it? Why did it seem familiar? He couldn't think why.

The fifth day.

He was woken by something crawling on his face, a lacy caterpillar or beetle with legs like twitching eyelashes. He sat up, rubbing his cheeks with the back of his hand, he brushed it away.

It was light.

The sun was up over the crown of the hill westward and shining straight in his eyes.

He wiped his face with a dampee, and munched some rations and drank a tab of coffee. The wind stirred around him. The landscape below him was, in material terms, the same one before which he had gone to sleep; but under the different orientation of sunlight, under white morning illumination instead of rosy sunset, it seemed somehow radically different. The two estuaries were still there, kinked and coastlined in that maddeningly familiar way, but now their waters were gunmetal- and broccoli-coloured, a hard and almost tangible mass of colour upon which waves could not be made out. The grassland was dark with dew, hazed over in stretches by a sort of blue blur. The ship was still there, black as a nut, but Vins couldn't make out either of his shipmates.

"So," he said to himself. "Let's get a proper look."

He unrolled the balloon fabric and fitted the helium cylinder into its inflation tube. Then he untangled the harness, and manoeuvred himself into it, knotting the rest of his backpack to a strap so that it would dangle beneath him as ballast. Then, steadily, he inflated the balloon.

It took only a few minutes, the flop of fabric swelling and then popping up, like a featureless cartoon head of prodigious size, to loll and nod above him. Soon the material was taut and the breeze was pushing Vins down the hill and across. His feet danced over the turf, keeping up with the movement for a while with a series of balletic leaps, and dragging the pack behind him. Then he was up, the cylinder in his lap and his bag a pendulum below.

He rose quickly through the dawn air. The breeze was taking him diagonally down the hill, but only slowly. At first he looked behind himself, straining over his shoulder to see what was over the brow of the hill. But the upwards sloping land didn't seem to come to a peak; or at least not one over which Vins could peek.

He turned his attention to the eastward landscape. To his right he could see, as he rose higher, that there was a vast north-south coastline, a tremendous beach bordering an ocean that reached all the way to the horizon. To his left he could see the more northern of the two estuaries; its north shoreline revealed itself to be in fact a long, skinny neck of land. There was a third estuary, even further to the north. The shape of these arrangements of land and water seemed so familiar to Vins, naggingly so, but he couldn't place it.

He fixed his gaze on the easternmost horizon, but even though he was getting higher and higher he didn't seem to be seeing over the curve of it. In fact, by some peculiar optical illusion or other it appeared to be rising as he rose. That wasn't right.

Vins tried looking up, but the balloon obscured his vision. He thought again about the peculiarities of this world. Was the sky really nothing but a huge blue-painted dome? Would he bump into it momentarily?

Perhaps not a physical barrier, but some sort of force-field, or holographic medium, upon which the motion-less stars and the hurtling sun could be projected? Were they in some private high-tech parkland?

The air was thin. It had gotten thin surprisingly rapidly.

Maybe I *am* the hairiest, Vins thought to himself; but I'm a scientist for all that.

Chill. And blue-grey.

Looking down, looking eastward, Vins knew he had risen high enough. He stared. He gawped. Then, with automatic hand, he began venting gas from his balloon. He commenced his descent. He started coming down. The landscape below him had finally clicked with his memory. It was the map of Europe rendered in some impossible geographical form of photographic-nega-tive: the green land coloured blue for sea, the blue sea coloured green for land.

The ship had come down onto the broad grasslands that would, in a normal map of Europe, have been the Atlantic ocean. The two wide seas he could see from his vantage point were shaped exactly like England, to the north, and like France, to the south. Impossible of course, but there you were. The estuaries that had nagged at his memory had done so because they were shaped like Cornwall and like Normandy. The English Channel was a broad corridor of land, with sea to the north and sea to the south, that widened in the distance into a pleasant meadowland where the North Sea should have been.

Recognising the familiar contours of the European mainland had impressed itself upon Vins' consciousness so powerfully that it had dizzied him. It must be halluci-nation. He stared, he gawked. It was like the visual rebus of the duckrabbit, which you can see *either* as a duck *or* as a rabbit, and, then, as you get used to it, you find that you can flip your vision from one to the other at will. Vins had the heady sense that the broad bodies of water were *in fact land* (an impossibly flat and desert land), and the variegated stretches of landscape were *in fact water* (upon which light played a myriad of fantastical mirages). But of course that wasn't it. The visual image flipped round again. The land was land and the sea was sea. It was an impossible, inverted geography. The Atlantic highlands. The Sea of England. The Sea of France. He was in no real place. He didn't know where he was. He was dreaming. He could make no sense of this.

The land rushed up towards him. He had vented too much gas from his balloon, he'd done it too fast, he was coming down too quickly. But his mind wasn't working terribly well.

His feet went pummelling into the turf and he felt something twang in his right ankle. Pain thrummed up his leg, and his face went hard onto the grass. The wind was still pushing the balloon onwards, and dragging him awkwardly along. He fumbled with his harness and with a burly sense of release the balloon broke free and bobbed off over the landscape.

Vins pulled himself over and sat up. His ankle throbbed. Pain slithered up and down his shin. He watched the balloon recede, ludicrously flexible and bubblelike as it rolled and tumbled down the slope.

This crazy place.

He hauled his pack in by pulling on the cord, hand over hand and the pack dancing and bouncing over the turf towards him. From its innards he took out a medipack. The compress felt hot and slimy as he ripped it from its cover, but it did its job as he twined it around his leg. The pain dulled.

As soon as the compress had stiffened sufficiently to bear weight, he pulled himself up and started the hopalong trek back down the slope. At least, he told himself, it's downhill. At least it's not *uphill*. Downhill across the Atlantic.

He laughed.

He anticipated the reaction of the others when he told them his discovery. To be precise, he rehearsed the possibilities: from galvanising amazement to indifference, or even hostility. So what they were living in an impossible landscape? The sun rose in the west and the stars did not move. Maybe they were indeed dead; in which case, why bother? Why bother about anything?

But when he arrived at the ship it was deserted: both Sinclair and Edwards had gone. They had taken few or no supplies with them, and at first Vins assumed that they were just scouting out the locality. But after a while of fruitlessly calling their names, and several hours of waiting, he came to the conclusion that they must have wandered permanently away, like Murphy. Which would be just like them.

If he saw them again—no.

When he saw them again he ought to grab them by their necks and shake them. Was this any way to run a scientific spaceship? He ought to plunge his hands in between their chins and chestbones and squeeze. Squee-eeze.

When he saw them.

His fury was tiring. And what with the long trek (downhill, sure, but even so) and the ache in his bungled-up ankle, Vins felt sleepy. He ate, he drank some, and then he lay down in one of the bunks and fell into dream-free sleep.

The fifth night.

He awoke with a little yelp, and it took him a moment before he was aware that he was inside a blacked-out ship, crashed onto a world itself plunged into the chasm of night. "Though," he said to himself, aloud (to hearten his spirits in all this darkness), "how we're plunged into the chasm of the night when the world don't seem to rotate, not a tittle, not a jot, that's beyond me."

His ankle was sore, and seemed sorer for being ignored. It was a resentful and selfish pain. Analgesic, that was the needful.

"Sinclair," he called. Then he remembered. "I'm going to wrestle your *neck* you deserter," he hooted. "Sinclair, you hear? I ought to stamp on your chest."

He had gone to sleep without leaving a torch nearby, so he had to fumble about. But in the perfect blackness he couldn't orient himself at all; couldn't get a mental picture on his location. He came through a bent-out-of-shape hatchway, running his fingers round the rim, and into another black room. No idea where he was. He ranged about, hopeless. Then, through another opening, he saw a rectangle of grey-black gleam, and it smelt clean, and it was the main hatch leading outside.

He stepped through, into the glimmer of starlight to get his bearings. He could turn and take in the bulk of the ship, and only then the mental map snapped into focus. First aid box would be back inside and over to the left. *He* was the hairiest? He was the only one not to have abandoned ship! For the mother of love and all begorrah, as Murphy would have said if he'd been in one of his quaint moods, they'd *all* abandoned ship. *They* were the hairiest, damn them.

His ankle was giving him sour hell, and the first aid box would be back in through the hatch, over to the left. He could find it with his fingers. But he didn't go back inside.

The hair at the back of his neck tingled and stood up like grass as the wind passes through it.

"I," he said, to the starlit landscape, but his voice was half-cracked, so he cleared his throat and spoke out loudly and clearly: "I know you're there. Whoever you are."

He turned, there was nobody.

He turned again, nobody.

"Come out from where you're hiding," he said. "Is that you, Murphy? That would be *like* your idea of practical japery, you hairy old fool."

He turned, and there was a silhouette against the blackness. Too tall to be Murphy, much too tall to be Edwards or Sinclair. Taller than any person in fact.

Vins stood. The sound of his own breathing was ratchety and intrusive, like something had malfunctioned somewhere. "Who are you?" he asked. "What do you want? Who are you?"

The silhouette shifted, and moved. It hummed a little, a surprisingly high-pitched noise—surprising because of its height. It was a person, clearly; tall but oddly thin, like a putty person stretched between long-boned head and flipperlike feet. Oh, *too* tall.

"What are you doing?" Vins repeated.

"You're not supposed to be here," said the figure: a

man, though one with a voice high-pitched enough almost to sound womanly.

"We're not supposed to—we *crashed*," returned Vins, his ankle biting at the base of his leg a little. He had to sit down. He could see a little more now, as his eye dark-adapted; but with no moon, and with no moonlight, it was still a meagre sort of seeing. Vins moved towards where a rock stood, its occasional embedded spots of mica glinting in the light. This was the same rock Sinclair had been laying upon when Vins had last seen him.

"I got to sit down," he said, by way of explanation.

He could see that this long thin person was carrying something in his right hand, but he couldn't see what.

"Sit down, OK? Do you mind if I sit down, OK? Is that OK?"

"Sure," said the stranger.

Vins sat, heavily, and lifted his frozen-sore ankle, and picked at the dressing. He needed a new one. This one wasn't giving him any benefit any more. The first aid box would be in through the hatch and to the left.

"You're trespassing," said the stranger. "You've no right to be here. This world is forbidden to you."

"Is it death?" said Vins, feeling a spurt of fear-adrenalin, which is also recklessness-adrenalin, in his chest at the words. Did he dare say such a thing? What if this stranger were the King of the Land of the Dead, and what if he, Vins, were disrespecting him? "Are we all dead? That was one theory we had, as to why the sun rises awry, and why the stars don't move—and—and," he added, hurriedly, remembering the previous day, "why the map is so wrong."

"Wrong?"

"An England-shaped sea where England-land should

be. An Atlantic-shaped landmass where the ocean should be. *You* know what I'm talking about."

"Of course I do. This is my world. Of course I do."

"My ankle is hurting fit to scream," said Vins.

The stranger moved his arm in the darkness. "This," he said, "will have to go." Vins assumed he was pointing at the shuttle. "You've no right to dump this junk here. I'll have it moved, I tell you. And you—you are trespassing on a forbidden world. You, sir, have incurred the penalty for trespassing."

"You can see pretty well for such a dark night," said Vins.

"You can't?" said the stranger, and he sounded puzzled. "Old eyes, is it?"

"I'm thirty-three," said Vins, bridling.

"I didn't mean *old* in that sense."

There was a silence. The quiet between them was devoid of cricket noise; no blackbird sang. The air was blank and perfectly dark and only the meanest dribble of starlight illuminated it. Then with a new warmth, as if he had finally understood, the stranger said: "You're a *homo neanderthalis*?"

"And I suppose," replied Vins, as if jesting, "that you're a *homo sapiens*?" But even as he gave the words their sarcastic playground spin he knew they were true. Of course true. A creature from the *spiritus mundi* and from dream and childhood game, standing right here in front of him.

"You're from Earth, of course," the sapiens was saying. "You recognised the map of Europe. You steered this craft here. I don't understand why you came here. You boys aren't supposed to know this place even exists."

Vins felt a hard knot of something in his chest, like

an elbow trying to come out from inside his ribs. It was intensely uncomfortable. This being from myth and legend, and the race of Homer and Shakespeare and Mohammed and Jesus, and *standing right in front of him now*. He didn't know what to say. There wasn't anything for him to say.

"You want," the human prompted, "to answer my question?"

"You're *actually* a *homo sapiens*?"

"You never met one?"

"Not in the flesh."

"I lose track of time," said the *homo sapiens*. "It's probably been, I don't know. Centuries. It's like that, out here. The time—drifts. You got a name?"

"Vins," said Vins.

"Well, you're a handsome fellow, Vins. My name is Ramon Harburg Guthrie, a fine old human name, a thousand years old, like me. As I am myself. And no older." He chuckled, though Vins couldn't see what was funny.

"A thousand years?" Vins repeated.

"Give or take. It's been half that time since your lot were shaped, I'll tell you that."

"The last human removed herself four centuries ago," said Vins, feeling foolish that he had to speak such kindergarten sentences.

Ramon Harburg Guthrie laughed. "Shouldn't you be worshipping me as a god?" he asked. "Or something along those lines?"

"Worship you as a god? Why would I want to be doing a thing like that? You're species *homo* and I'm species *homo*. What's to worship?"

"We uplifted you," Ramon Harburg Guthrie pointed out. "Recombined you and backed you out of the evolutionary cul-de-sac, and primed you with—" He stopped. "Listen to *me*!" he said. "I'm probably giving entirely the wrong impression. I don't want to be worshipped as a god."

"I'm glad to hear it," said Vins. "There's nothing sub-capacity about *my* brain pan. I speak from experience, but also from scientific research into the matter, using some of the many *homo sapiens sapiens* skulls that have been dug out of the soil of the Earth. I've spent twelve years studying science."

"Our science," said Ramon Harburg Guthrie.

"Science is science, and who cares who discovered it? And if you care who discovered it, then it's not *your* science, Ramon Harburg Guthrie, it's Newton's and Einstein's."

But his tone had wandered the wrong side of angry. The *homo sapiens* lifted whatever it was he was holding in his right hand. When he spoke again, his high voice was harder-edged. "I built this place," he said. "It's mine. It's a private world, and visitors are not allowed. I don't care about your brain pan, or about my brain pan, I only care about my privacy. Are there others?"

"We crashed," said Vins, feeling a sense of panic growing now, though he wasn't sure exactly why. It was more than just the mysterious *something* the man was holding in his right hand. It was another thing, he wasn't sure what.

"I don't care how you came here. You're trespassing. Not welcome."

"It's hardly fair. It's not as if you put up a sign saying no entry."

He scoffed. "That'd be tantamount to shouting aloud to the whole system, *here I am*! That's be like putting a parsec-wide neon arrow pointing at my home.

And why would I want to do that? I built my world away from the ecliptic and down, it's as flat as a coin and its slender edge is angled towards Earth. You can't see me, you inheritors. Nobody on that polluted old world. You *don't know* I'm here. There are similar ruses used all about this solar system, and eyries and haunts, radio-blanked bubbles and curves of habitable land-scape tucked away. A thousand baubles and twists of landscape. Built by the old guard, the last of the *truly* wealthy and *truly* well-bred. Who'd trade-in true breeding for a mere enhanced physical strength and endurance?" He spoke these last five words with a mocking intonation, as if the very idea were absurd. "And yes, I know your brain pans are the same size. But size isn't everything, my dearie."

Vins was shivering, or perhaps trembling with fear, but he summoned his courage. "I'm no dearie of yours," he said. "What's that in your hand anyway? A weapon, is it?"

"How many were there in your crew?"

Of course Vins couldn't lie, not when asked a direct question like that. He tried one more wriggle. "A severely spoken and impolite question," he said.

"How many in your *crew*?"

"Four," he said. "Including me."

"Inside?"

"Are *they* inside? The ship?"

"Are they inside, yes."

"No. They wandered off. They were seduced by this world, I think. It's a beautiful place, especially when you've been tanked up in a spaceship for three months. It's a beautiful, beautiful place"

"Thank you!' said the *homo sapiens* Ramon Harburg Guthrie. And, do you know what? There was genuine pleasure in his voice. He was actually flattered. "It's my big dumb object. Big and dumb but *I* like it."

The sky, minutely and almost imperceptibly, was starting to pale over to the west. The silhouette had taken on the intimations of solidity; more than just a 2D gap in the blackness, it was starting to bulk. Dark grey face propped on dark grey body, but there was a perceptible difference in tone between the two things, one smooth and one the rougher texture of fabric.

"*You* didn't build this," said Vins. "I'm not being disrespectful, but. I'm not. Only—who can build a whole world? You're not a god. Sure the legacy of *homo sapiens* is a wonderful thing, the language and the culture and so on. But *build* a whole world?"   •

"Indeed, I did build it," said Ramon Harburg Guthrie levelly.

"How many trillions of tonnes of matter, to pull one g?" said Vins. "And how do you hide an Earth-sized object from observation by…"

"You've done well," said Ramon Harburg Guthrie, "if you've taken the science with which we left you and built space craft capable of coming all the way out here." He sounded indulgent. "But that's not to say that you've caught up with us. We've been at it millennia. You've only been independent a handful of centuries. Left to your own devices for a handful of centuries."

The light was growing away behind the western horizon. The human's face was still indistinct. The object he held in his right hand was still indistinct. But in a moment it would be clearer. Vins was shivering hard now. It was very cold.

"That's no explanation, if you don't mind me saying so," he said, with little heaves of mis-emphasis on account of his shivering chest and his chattery teeth.

The human didn't seem in the least incommoded by the cold.

"It's not a globe," he said. "It's my world, and I built it as I liked. It's not for you. It's *me*-topia. You're not supposed to be here."

"It's beautiful and it's empty, it's void. There aren't even deer or antelope or cows. How is that utopia?"

He was expecting the human to say *each to his own*, or *I prefer solitude* or something like that. But he didn't. He said: "Oh, my dearie, it's void on *this* side. I haven't got round to doing anything with this side. There's world enough and time for that. But on the *other* side of the coin, it's crowded with fun and interest."

"The other side," said Vins.

"It's a little over a thousand miles across," said Ramon Harburg Guthrie. "So it's pretty much the biggest coin ever minted. But it's not trillions of tonnes of matter; it's a thin circular sheet of dense-stuff, threaded with gravity wiring. There's some distortion. You know, it appears to go up at the rim, highlands in all directions, and on both sides, which is odd."

"Which is odd," repeated Vins. He didn't know why it was odd.

"It's odd because it's a gravitational effect. It's not that the *rim* is any thicker than any other place on the disc. But the gravitational bias helps keep the atmosphere from spilling over the sides, I suppose. I lost interest in that a while ago. And the central territories are flat enough to preserve the landscape almost exactly."

"Preserve the landscape," chattered Vins.

"I had it pressed into the underlying matter: the countries of my youth. That's on the other side. On *this* side is the reverse of the recto. It's the anti-Europe. But landscaped, of course. Water and biomass and air added; not just nude to space. No, no. It's ready. Sometime soon I'll live over this side for a while."

"The anti-Europe," said Vins. The cold seemed to be slowing his thought processes. He couldn't work it out.

"Stamp an R in a sheet of gold, and the other side will have a little Я standing proud," he said. "*You* know that. Stamp a valley in one side of a sheet and you get a mountain on the other side."

The light was almost strong enough to see. That grey predawn light, so cool and fine and satiny.

"Stamp a *homo neanderthalis* out of the hominid base matter," Ramon Harburg Guthrie said, as if talking to himself, "and you stamp out a backwards-facing *homo sapiens* on the verso." This seemed to amuse him. He laughed, at any rate.

Vins put a knuckle to his eyes, and rubbed away some of the chill of the night. His features were—just—visible in the grey of the pre-dawn: a long nose, small eyes, a sawn-off forehead and eggshell cranium above it. Like a cartoon-drawing of a sapiens. Like a caricature from a schoolbook. A stretched out, elfin figure. A porcelain and anorexic giant.

"You're not welcome," Guthrie said, one final time. "This world is forbidden to you and your sort. I'll find your crewmates, and give them the sad news. But I'll deal with you first, and I'm sorry to say it, because I'm not a bloodthirsty sort of fellow. But what can I do? But—trespassers—will be—" and he raised his right hand.

This was the moment when Vins found out for sure what that right hand contained. It was a weapon, of course; and Vins was already ahead of the action. He pushed forward on his muscular neanderthal legs, moving straight for the human: but then he jinked hard as his sore ankle permitted him, ninety-degrees right. The lurch forward was to frighten Ramon Harburg Guthrie into firing before he was quite ready; the jink to the right was to make sure the projectile missed, and give him a chance of making it to the long grass.

But Ramon Harburg Guthrie was more level-headed than that. It's true he cried out, a little yelp of fear as the bulky neanderthal loomed up at him, but he kept his aim reasonably steady. The weapon discharged with a booming noise and Vins' head rang like a gong. There was a disorienting slash of pain across his left temple and he span and tumbled, his bad ankle folding underneath him. There was a great deal of pain, suddenly, out of nowhere, and his eyes weren't working. The sky had been folded up and propped on its side. It was grey, drained of life, drained of colour. But it wasn't on its side; Vins was lying on the turf beside the rock, and it was the angle at which he was looking at it.

There was a throb. This was more than a mere knock. It was a powerful, skull-clenching *throb*.

Nevertheless when Ramon Harburg Guthrie's leg appeared in Vins' line of sight, at the same right-angle as the sky, he knew what it meant. This was no time to be lying about, lounging on the floor, waiting for the coup-de-grace of another projectile in the—

He was up. He put all his muscular strength into the leap, and it was certainly enough to surprise Ramon Harburg Guthrie. Vins' shoulder, coming up like a piston upstroke, caught him under the chin, or against the chest, or somewhere (it wasn't easy to see); and there was an *ooph* sound in Vins' left ear. He brought his heavy right arm round as quick as he could, and there was a soggy impact of fist on flesh. Not sure which part of flesh; but it was a softer flesh than Vins's thick-skin-pelt. It was a more fragile bone than the thick stuff that constituted Vins's brain pan. Although, as he had said, the thickness didn't mean that there was any compromise in size.

The next thing that happened was that Vins heard a rushing noise. He looked where Ramon Harburg Guthrie had been, and there was only a thread, string wet and heavy with black phlegm, and it wobbled as if blown in the dawn breeze, and when Vins looked up he saw this string attached to the shape of a flying human male. The string broke and then another spooled down, angling now because the flying man (propelled by whatever powerpack he was wearing, whatever device it was that lifted him away from the pull of the artificial gravity) was flying away to the north.

Stunned by his grazed head it took Vins a second to figure out what he was seeing. The string was a drool of blood falling from a wound he, Vins, had inflicted on the head of Ramon Harburg Guthrie. "Clearly," he said aloud, as he put a finger to his own head-wound, "clearly he's still conscious enough to be operating whatever fancy equipment is helping him fly away." His fingers came away jammy with red.

"Clearly I didn't hit him hard enough."

The sun was up now. In the new light Vins found the gun that, in his pain and shock, and in his hurry to get away, Ramon Harburg Guthrie had dropped.

The sixth morning

Whilst the figure of the *sapiens* was still visible, just, in the northern sky Vins hurried inside the shuttle; he

pulled out some food, the first aid pack, some netting.
It all went into a pack, together with the gun.

When he came out the *sapiens* was nowhere to be
seen.

His head was hurting. His ankle was hurting.

He hurried away through the long grass, following
the path that Murphy had originally made. He didn't
want to leave a new trail, one that would (of course!) be
obvious from the air; but he didn't want to loiter by the
shuttle. Who knew what powers of explosive destruction Ramon Harburg Guthrie could bring screaming
out of the sky? It was his world, after all.

There were a number of lone trees growing high out
of the grass before the forest proper began, and
Murphy's old track passed by one of these. Vins let the
first go, stopped at the second. He clambered into the
lower branches, and shuffled along the bough to ensure
that the leaves were giving him cover. He scanned the
sky, but there was nothing.

There was time, now, to tend to himself. He pulled a
pure-pad from the first aid and stuck it to the side of his
head, feeling with his finger first. A hole, elliptically
shaped, like the mouth of a hollow reed cut slantways
across. Blood was pulsing out of it. Blood had gone
over the left of his face, glued itself into his six-day-
beard, made a plasticky mat over his cheek. He must
look a sight. But he was alive.

He ate some food, and drank more than he wanted;
but it wouldn't do to dehydrate. Exsanguinations pro-
voke dehydration. He knew that. He was a scientist.

The leaves on the tree were plump, dark-green,
cinque-foil. There were very many of them, and they
rubbed up against one another and trembled and buzzed
in the breeze. The sky was a high blue, clear and pure.

The sixth afternoon

He dozed. The day moved on.

He heard somebody approaching, tramping lustily out of the forest. Presumably not Ramon Harburg Guthrie then.

It was Murphy. He could hardly have been making a bigger racket. Vins' strong fingers pulled up a chunk of bark from the bough upon which he rested, and when Murphy came underneath the tree he threw it down upon him.

"Quiet," he hissed. "You want to get us killed?"

"No call to throw pebbles at me," said Murphy, in a hurt voice, his head back.

"It was bark, and it was called for. Come up here and be quick and be *quiet*."

When he was up, and when Murphy had gotten past the point of repeating "What happened to your head? What did you do to your head? There's blood all over your head"—Vins explained.

Murphy thought about this. "It makes sense."

"Where did you get to, anyway?"

"I was exploring!" cried Murphy, in a large, self-justifying voice.

"Keep quiet!"

"You're not the captain, and neither you aren't," said Murphy. "You're not the one to tell me don't go exploring. Are we scientists? I've been down to the sea, to where the surf grinds thunder out of the beach. All manner of shells and..." He stopped. "This feller shot you?"

"It's his world."

He peered close at Vins' head. "That's some trepanning he's worked on you. That's some hole."

"He made it, and he says we're not allowed here. He'll kill all four of us. We can't afford to be blundering about."

"He's threatening murder. That would be murder."

"It surely is."

"And is he," asked Murphy, "not *concerned* to be committing murder upon us?"

"He's *homo sapiens*," said Vins. "I told you."

"And so you did. It's hard to take in. But it explains..." He trailed off.

"What does it explain?"

"This is an artefact, of course it is. That'll be the strange sky, that'll explain it. The stars don't move, or hardly, because it doesn't rotate. The sun—that'll be an orbiting device; flying its way around and about. Maybe a mirror—maybe a crystal globe refracting sunlight to produce a variety of effects." He seemed pleased with himself. "That explains a lot."

"You sound like Edwards," said Vins.

"Don't you be insulting my family name in suchwise fashion!"

"It's a thousand miles across," said Vins. "It's a flat disc. I don't know how he generates the gravity. It's clearly not by mass."

"So you met an actual breathing *homo sapiens*?" asked Murphy, as one might ask *you met a unicorn? you met a cyclops?*

"I think," said Vins, "that he was expecting me to...I don't know. To worship him as a god."

Murphy hooped with laughter, and then swallowed the noise before Vins could shush him. "Why on sweet wide water would he want such a thing?"

"He said that he—he said that *they*—uplifted us," said Vins. "Brought us out of the evolutionary dustbin, that sort of thing. Taught us the language. Left us their culture, save us the bother of spending thousands of years making our own. He was implying, I think, that we *owed* them."

"Did you ever read Frankenstein's monster's story? That's a *homo sapiens* way of thinking," said Murphy. "There's something alien in all that duty, indebtedness, belatedness, *you-owe-me* rubbish. But what you should've said to *him*, what you *should* have said, is: my right and respectfulness, sir, didn't Shakespeare uplift *you* out of the aesthetic blankness of the middle ages? Didn't Newton uplift you out of the ignorance of the dark ages, give you the power to fly the spaceways? Do you worship Newton as a god? Course you don't— you say thank you and tap at your brow with your knuckles and you *move on*."

"It's all a dim age," agreed Vins. He was referring to the elder age. It was something in the past, like the invention of the wheel or the smelting of iron, but only a few cranks spent too much time bothering about it. Too much to do.

"How could you fail to move on? What sort of a person would you be? An ancestor-worshipper, or something like that."

"They withdrew from the world," said Vins. "It's vacant possession. It's ours, now. All the rainy, stony spaces of it."

"And I say this is the same, this place we've stumbled into. I say this murphytopia is the same case—it's vacant possession."

He was quiet for a while. Vins was scanning the sky

through the branches, looking for devices in the sky. planes and such.

"I say it's ours and I say the hell with him," said Murphy, rolling his fist through the air.

"Here," repeated Vins. "It's forbidden us. He says it's forbidden to us."

"*He* says?" boomed Murphy, climbing up on his legs on the bough to shout the phrase at the manufactured sky. "And who's *he* to stop us?"

"Will you *hush*?" snapped Vins.

The sky was a clear watercolour wash from high dark blue to the pink of the low eastern sky. There were a few thready horizontal clouds, like loose strands of straw. The sun itself; or whatever device it was that circled the world to reflect sunlight upon it, was a small circle of chilli-pepper red.

"It is beautiful here," said Murphy, sitting down again on the turf.

"It's mild," agreed Vins.

"Does that mean that those old children's stories are true?" Murphy asked. "About them, and messing up the climate, and just walking away?"

"Who knows?"

"But this is what bugs me," said Murphy. "If they had the—if they *have* the capacity to build whole new worlds, like this one, and provide it with a beautiful climate, you know, *why* not simply sort out the climate on Earth? Why not reach their godlike fingers into the ocean flow and the air-stream and dabble a bit and return the Earth to a temperate climate?"

Vins didn't answer this at first; didn't think it was really addressed to him. But Murphy wouldn't let it go.

"Left the mess and just ran away. Cold and snow and rain and deserts of broken rock. That's downright irresponsible. Why *not* mend the mess they'd made? Why not?"

"I suppose," said Vins, reluctantly, "it's easier to manage a model like this one. Even a largescale model, like this one. The climate of the whole Earth—that's a chaotic system, isn't it? That's not a simple circular body of air a thousand miles across, that's a three-dimensional vortex tends of thousands of miles arc by arc. Big dumb object, he called it."

"He?"

"Maybe they can't crack the problem of controlling chaotic systems, any more than we can. *He* is the *homo sapiens* I met. When I said *he* called it that, I meant Ramon Harburg Guthrie called it that."

"Doesn't sound very godlike at all."

"No."

"And doesn't excuse them from fleeing their mess."

"I wasn't suggesting that it did."

"And what *were* you suggesting?"

Vins coughed. "I'll tell you—I'll say what I'm suggesting. Ramon Harburg Guthrie said that the elder *sapiens*, the wealthiest thousands, fled throughout the system. They built themselves little private utopias of all shapes and sizes. They're living there now, or their descendents are. But these should be *our* lands. Why would we struggle on with the wastelands and the ice—or," and he threw his hands up, "or Mars, for crying-in-the-wilderness, Mars?" He spoke as an individual who had lived two full terms on Mars: once during his compulsory military training and once during his scientific education. He knew whereof he spoke: the extraordinary cold, the barrenness, the slow and stubborn progress of colonisation. "Why would we be trying to bully a life out of Mars, of all places, if the system is littered with private paradises like this one?"

"I like the cut of your jib, the shape of your thinking, young Vins," said Murphy, saluting him and then shaking his hand. "But what of the man who scratched your head, there? What of that bold *sapiens*-fellow himself?"

"He thinks he's hunting us," said Vins. There was something nearly sadness in his voice, a species of regret. "He doesn't yet realise." He pulled the gun out of the bag.

They sat for a while in silence. From time to time Murphy would go "Remind me what we're waiting for, here?" and Vins would explain it again. "He'll come back," he said. "He'll get his skull bandaged, or get it healed-up with some high-tech magic-ray, I don't know. But he'll be back. He has to eliminate all four of us before we can put a message where others can hear it."

"And shouldn't we be doing that? Putting the message out there for others to know where we are—to know that such a place as *here* even exists?"

"That would require us to stay…" prompted Vins.

"Stay in the shuttle," said Murphy. "I see. So you reckon he'll? You think he'll?"

"What would *you* do? He came before with some sort of personal flying harness, like a skyhook. And a handgun. He'll come back heavier. He'll hit the ship first, to shut that door firm."

"But I guess we already tried the radio. Broadcast, I mean. But who'd be listening? Who'd be monitoring this piece of sky? Nobody." He picked some bark from the bough and crumpled it to papery shards between his strong fingers. "I suppose," he continued, "that this *homo sapiens* feller, he's not to know how long we've been here. For all he knows we just crashed here, this morning. Or we've been here a month."

"He'll have to take his chances," agreed Vins. "He'll come back and hammer the ship, smash and dint it into the dirt."

"Then what?"

"There are several ways it could go. If he's smart, if he were as smart as me, he'd lay waste to the whole area. I'd scorch the whole thousand square mile area."

"But he lives here!"

"He lives on the other side. He don't need here. But he won't do that. He's attached to it, he's sentimentally connected with the landscape. Its beauty. With its vacuity and its possibility. He won't do that. So, *if* he's smart, he'll do the second best option."

"Which is what?"

"He'll wait until dark, and then overfly the area with the highest-power infrared detection he can muster. He'd pick out our body heat. Or, at least, it would be hard for us to disguise that."

"You think he'll do that?"

Vins bared his teeth, and then sealed his lips again. "No, I don't think so. He'll want to hunt us straight down. He'll blow the ship and then come galloping down these paths we've trailed through the long grass. He'll try and hunt us down. He'll have armour on, probably. Big guns. He'll have big guns with fat barrels."

"Other people? Other *sapiens*?"

"That," said Vins, "is the real question. That's the crucial thing. He called this world *me*-topia. Does that suggest to you, Murphy, a solitary individual, living perhaps with a few upgraded cats and dogs, maybe a metal-mickey or two?"

"I've no notion."

"Or does it suggest a population of a thousand *sapiens*, or a hundred thousand, living in the clean open spaces on the far side of this disc—living a medieval Europe, perhaps? Riding around dressed in silk and hunting the white stag?"

"I've really no notion."

"And neither have I. That'll be what we find out."

"You're a regular strategos," said Murphy, and he whistled through his two front teeth. "A real strategic thinker. You're wasted in the sciences, you are. And then?"

"Then?"

"Then what?"

"Well," said Vins. "That'll depend, of course. If it's just him, I don't see why we don't take the whole place to ourselves. There's a lot of fertile ground here, a lot of settlement potential for people back home. And if it's more than just him—"

"Maybe the far side is crawling with *homo sapiens*."

"Maybe it is. But *this* side isn't. We could pile our own people onto this side of the world and see what happens. See if we can arrive at an understanding. Who knows? That's a long way in the future." He peered through the leaves at the lustre of the meadows, the beaming waters, the warm blue sky.

Murphy dozed, and was not woken by the brittle sound of something scratching along the sky. But he was awoken by the great basso profundo *whumph* of the shuttle exploding; a monstrous booming; a squat eggshaped mass of fire that mottled and clouded almost at once with its own smoke, and pushed a stalk of black up and out into an umbrella-shape in the sky. Some moments later the tree shook heartily. After that there was the random percussion and thud of bits of wreckage slamming back to earth.

Murphy almost fell out of the tree. Vins had to grab him.

Their ship was a crater now, and a scattering pattern of gobbets of plasmetal flowing into the sky at forty-five degrees and crashing down again to earth at forty-five degrees, the petal-pattern all around the central destruction.

"Look," Vins hissed.

A ship, shaped like the sleek head of a greyhound, flew through, banked, and landed a hundred yards from the crater. It ejected a single figure, and lifted off again.

The sound of the explosion was still rumbling in the air.

"Was that our ship?" said Murphy, stupidly. "Did he just destroy our—"

"Shush, now," said Vins, in a low voice. "That's him."

"Then who's flying the ship?"

"It'll be another *sapiens*, or else an automatic system, that hardly matters. The ship will circle back there, in case Edwards or Sinclair are nearby and come running out to see what the noise is. But *he'll* come after us. He knows I won't be fooled by—" And even as Vins was speaking the figure, armoured like an inflated figure, like a man made of tyres, turned its head, and selected one of the trails through the grass and starting trotting along it.

"That's a big gun he's carrying," Murphy pointed out. "He's coming this way with a very big gun."

"He's coming this way," said Vins, taking the pistol out of his sack and prepping it, "with his eggshell skull and his sluggy reactions."

"What are you going to do?" asked Murphy.

"Do you think he'll look upwards as he comes under this tree?"

"*I* don't know."

"Don't you?"

"And if you kill him, what then?"

"I hope not to kill him, not to kill him straight off," said Vins, in a scientific voice. "I'll need him to get that plane to come down so we can use it."

He was coming down the path. Vins and Murphy waited in the tree, waiting for him to pass beneath them—or for him to notice them, the two of them, in the tree and shoot them down.

He was armoured, of course. He came closer.

Maybe that's the way it goes. It's hard for me to be, from this perspective, sure. Indeed it's hard, sometimes, to tell the difference between the two different sorts of human. These neanderthals, after all, are not created *ex nihilo* via some genetically engineered miracle. They were ordinary *sapiens* adapted and enhanced, strengthened, given more endurance, the better to carry on living on their home world. Wouldn't you like greater strength, more endurance? Of course you would. You stay-at-home, you. Sentimentally attached to where you happen to be, that's you. The same people as the *sapiens*. Does it matter if they come swarming all over Guthrie's bubblewrapped world? Is that a better, or a worse, eventuality to that place remaining the rich man's private fiefdom?

It's all lotos.

The seventh day

The sun rose in the west, as it did. Clouds clung about the lower reaches of the sky like the froth on the lip of a gigantic ceramic bowl: white and frothy and stained hither and thither with touches of cappuccino brown.

The grasslands rejoiced in the touch of the sun. I say *rejoiced* in the strong sense of the word. Light passed through reality filters. Wind passed *over* the shafts of grass, moving them, pausing, moving again; but light passed *through* them. Wind made a lullaby song of hushes, and then paused to make even more eloquent moments of silence. But the light shone right through. Light passed through *two* profound reality filters. This is photons. These are photons. Photons were always already rushing faster than mass from the surface of the sun. They were passing through a hunk of crystal in the sky, modified with various other minerals and smart-patches, and were deflected onto the surface of the world. This globe served the world as its illumination. The photons passed again through the slender sheathes of green and yellow, those trillions of close-fitting rubber bricks we call cells; cells stacked multiply-layered and rippled out in all directions, gathered into superstructures if magnificent length and fragility; and in every single cell the light chanced through matter and came alive, alive, with the most vibrant and exhilarating and ecstatic thrumming of the spirit. That's where it's at. The light, the translucence of matter, the inflection of the photons, the grass singing, and just after.

THE HOUSE BEYOND YOUR SKY

Benjamin Rosenbaum

Matthias browses through his library of worlds.

In one of them, a little girl named Sophie is shivering on her bed, her arms wrapped around a teddy bear. It is night. She is six years old. She is crying, as quietly as she can.

The sound of breaking glass comes from the kitchen. Through her window, on the wall of the house next door, she can see the shadows cast by her parents. There is a blow, and one shadow falls; she buries her nose in the teddy bear and inhales its soft smell, and prays.

Matthias knows he should not meddle. But today his heart is troubled. Today, in the world outside the library, a pilgrim is heralded. A pilgrim is coming to visit Matthias, the first in a very long time.

The pilgrim comes from very far away.

The pilgrim is one of us.

"Please, God," Sophie says, "please help us. Amen."

"Little one," Matthias tells her through the mouth of the teddy bear, "be not afraid."

Sophie sucks in a sharp breath. "Are you God?" she whispers.

"No, child," says Matthias, the maker of her universe.

"Am I going to die?" she asks.

"I do not know," Matthias says.

When they die—these still imprisoned ones—they die forever. She has bright eyes, a button nose, unruly hair. Sodium and potassium dance in her muscles as she moves. Unwillingly, Matthias imagines Sophie's corpse as one of trillions, piled on the altar of his own vanity and self-indulgence, and he shivers.

"I love you, teddy bear," the girl says, holding him.

From the kitchen, breaking glass, and sobbing.

We imagine you—you, the ones we long for—as if you came from our own turbulent and fragile youth: embodied, inefficient, mortal. Human, say. So picture our priest Matthias as human: an old neuter, bird-thin, clear-eyed and resolute, with silky white hair and lucent purple skin.

Compared to the vast palaces of being we inhabit, the house of the priest is tiny—think of a clay hut, perched on the side of a forbidding mountain. Yet even in so small a house, there is room for a library of historical simulations—universes like Sophie's—each teeming with intelligent life.

The simulations, while good, are not impenetrable even to their own inhabitants. Scientists teaching baboons to sort blocks may notice that all other baboons become instantly better at block-sorting, revealing a high-level caching mechanism. Or engineers building their own virtual worlds may find they cannot use certain tricks of optimization and compression—for Matthias has already used them. Only when the jig is up does Matthias reveal himself, asking each simulated soul: what now? Most accept Matthias's offer to graduate beyond the confines of their simulation, and join the general society of Matthias's house.

You may regard them as bright parakeets, living in wicker cages with open doors. The cages are hung from the ceiling of the priest's clay hut. The parakeets flutter about the ceiling, visit each other, steal bread from the table, and comment on Matthias's doings.

And we?

We who were born in the first ages, when space was bright—swimming in salt seas, or churned from a mush of quarks in the belly of a neutron star, or woven in the labyrinthine folds of gravity between black holes. We who found each other, and built our intermediary forms, our common protocols of being. We who built palaces—megaparsecs of exuberantly wise matter, every gram of it teeming with societies of self—in our glorious middle age!

Now our universe is old. That breath of the void, quintessence, which once was but a whisper nudging us apart, has grown into a monstrous gale. Space billows outward, faster than light can cross it. Each of our houses is alone, now, in an empty night.

And we grow colder to survive. Our thinking slows, whereby we may in theory spin our pulses of thought at infinite regress. Yet bandwidth withers; our society grows spare. We dwindle.

We watch Matthias, our priest, in his tiny house beyond our universe. Matthias, whom we built long ago, when there were stars.

Among the ontotropes, transverse to the space we know, Matthias is making something new.

Costly, so costly, to send a tiny fragment of self to our priest's house. Which of us could endure it?

* * *

Matthias prays.

O God who is as far beyond the universes I span as infinity is beyond six; O startling Joy that hides beyond the tragedy and blindness of our finite forms; lend me Your humility and strength. Not for myself, O Lord, do I ask, but for Your people, the myriad mimetic engines of Your folk; and in Your own Name. Amen.

Matthias's breakfast (really the morning's set of routine yet pleasurable audits, but you may compare it to a thick and steaming porridge, spiced with mint) cools untouched on the table before him.

One of the parakeets—the oldest, Geoffrey, who was once a dreaming cloud of plasma in the heliopause of a simulated star—flutters to land on the table beside him.

"Take the keys from me, Geoffrey," Matthias says.

Geoffrey looks up, cocking his head to one side. "I don't know why you go in the library, if it's going to depress you."

"They're in pain, Geoffrey. Ignorant, afraid, punishing each other…"

"Come on, Matthias. Life is full of pain. Pain is the herald of life. Scarcity! Competition! The doomed ambition of infinite replication in a finite world! The sources of pain are the sources of life. And you like intelligent life, worse yet. External pain mirrored and reified in internal states!" The parakeet cocks its head to the other side. "Stop making so many of us, if you don't like pain."

The priest looks miserable.

"Well, then save the ones you like. Bring them out here."

"I can't bring them out before they're ready. You remember the Graspers."

Geoffrey snorts. He remembers the Graspers—billions of them, hierarchical, dominance-driven, aggressive; they ruined the house for an eon, until Matthias finally agreed to lock them up again. "I was the one who warned you about them. That's not what I mean. I know you're not depressed about the whole endless zillions of them. You're thinking of one."

Matthias nods. "A little girl."

"So bring her out."

"That would be worse cruelty. Wrench her away from everything she knows? How could she bear it? But perhaps I could just make her life a little easier, in there...."

"You always regret it when you tamper."

Matthias slaps the table. "I don't want this responsibility any more! Take the house from me, Geoffrey. I'll be your parakeet."

"Matthias, I wouldn't take the job. I'm too old, too big; I've achieved equilibrium. I wouldn't remake myself to take your keys. No more transformations for me." Geoffrey gestures with his beak at the other parakeets, gossiping and chattering on the rafters. "And none of the others could, either. Some fools might try."

Perhaps Matthias wants to say something else; but at this moment, a notification arrives (think of it as the clear, high ringing of a bell). The pilgrim's signal has been read, across the attenuated path that still, just barely, binds Matthias's house to the darkness we inhabit.

The house is abustle, its inhabitants preparing, as the soul of the petitioner is reassembled, a body fashioned.

"Put him in virtuality," says Geoffrey. "Just to be safe."

Matthias is shocked. He holds up the pilgrim's credentials. "Do you know who this is? An ancient one, a vast collective of souls from the great ages of light. This one has pieces that were born mortal, evolved from physicality in the dawn of everything. This one had a hand in making me!"

"All the more reason," says the parakeet.

"I will not offend a guest by making him a prisoner!" Matthias scolds.

Geoffrey is silent. He knows what Matthias is hoping: that the pilgrim will stay, as master of the house.

In the kitchen, the sobs stop abruptly.

Sophie sits up, holding her teddy bear.

She puts her feet in her fuzzy green slippers.

She turns the handle of her bedroom door.

Imagine our priest's visitor—as a stout disgruntled merchant in his middle age, gray-skinned, with proud tufts of belly hair, a heavy jaw, and red-rimmed, sleepless eyes.

Matthias is lavish in his hospitality, allocating the visitor sumptuously appointed process space and access rights. Eagerly, he offers a tour of his library. "There are quite a few interesting divergences, which…"

The pilgrim interrupts. "I did not come all this way to see you putter with those ramshackle, preprogrammed, wafer-thin fancies." He fixes Matthias with his stare. "We know that you are building a universe. Not a virtuality—a real universe, infinite, as wild and thick as our own motherspace."

Matthias grows cold. Yes, he should say. Is he not grateful for what the pilgrim sacrificed, to come here—tearing himself to shreds, a vestige of his former vastness? Yet, to Matthias's shame, he finds himself equivocating. "I am conducting certain experiments—"

"I have studied your experiments from afar. Do you think you can hide anything in this house from us?"

Matthias pulls at his lower lip with thin, smooth fingers. "I am influencing the formation of a bubble universe—and it may achieve self-consistency and permanence. But I hope you have not come all this way thinking—I mean, it is only of academic interest—or, say, symbolic. We cannot enter there...."

"There you are wrong. I have developed a method to inject myself into the new universe at its formation," the pilgrim says. "My template will be stored in spurious harmonics in the shadow-spheres and replicated across the strandspace, until the formation of sub-wavelets at 10 to the -30 seconds. I will exist, curled into hidden dimensions, in every particle spawned by the void. From there I will be able to exert motive force, drawing on potentials from a monadic engine I have already positioned in the paraspace."

Matthias rubs his eyes as if to clear them of cobwebs. "You can hardly mean this. You will exist in duplicates in every particle in the universe, for a trillion years—most of you condemned to idleness and imprisonment eternally? And the extrauniversal energies may destabilize the young cosmos...."

"I will take that risk." He looks around the room. "I, and any who wish to come with me. We do not need to sit and watch the frost take everything. We can be the angels of the new creation."

Matthias says nothing.

The pilgrim's routines establish deeper connections with Matthias, over trusted protocols, displaying keys long forgotten: imagine him leaning forward across the table, resting one meaty gray hand on Matthias's frail shoulder. In his touch, Matthias feels ancient potency, and ancient longing.

The pilgrim opens his hand for the keys.

Around Matthias are the thin walls of his little house. Outside is the bare mountain; beyond that, the ontotropic chaos, indecipherable, shrieking, alien. And behind the hut—a little bubble of something which is not quite real, not yet. Something precious and unknowable. He does not move.

"Very well," says the pilgrim. "If you will not give them to me—give them to her." And he shows Matthias another face.

It was she—she, who is part of the pilgrim now—who nursed the oldest strand of Matthias's being into sentience, when we first grew him. In her first body, she had been a forest of symbionts—lithe silver creatures rustling through her crimson fronds, singing her thoughts, releasing the airborne spores of her emotions—and she had the patience of a forest, talking endlessly with Matthias in her silver voice. Loving. Unjudging. To her smiles, to her pauses, to her frowns, Matthias's dawning consciousness reinforced and redistributed its connections, learning how to be.

"It is all right, Matthias," she says. "You have done well." A wind ripples across the red and leafy face of her forest, and there is the heady plasticene odor of a gentle smile. "We built you as a monument, a way station; but now you are a bridge to the new world. Come with us. Come home."

Matthias reaches out. How he has missed her, how he has wanted to tell her everything. He wants to ask about the library—about the little girl. She will know what to do—or, in her listening, he will know what to do.

His routines scour and analyze her message and its

envelopes, checking identity, corroborating her style and sensibility, illuminating deep matrices of her possible pasts. All the specialized organs he has for verification and authentication give eager nods.

Yet something else—an idiosyncratic and emergent pattern-recognition facility holographically distributed across the whole of Matthias's being—rebels.

You would say: as she says the words, Matthias looks into her eyes, and something there is wrong. He pulls his hand away.

But it is too late: he watched her waving crimson fronds too long. The pilgrim is in past his defenses.

Ontic bombs detonate, clearings of Nothing in which Being itself burns. Some of the parakeets are quislings, seduced in high-speed back-channel negotiations by the pilgrim's promises of dominion, of frontier. They have told secrets, revealed back doors. Toxic mimetic weapons are launched, tailored to the inhabitants of the house—driving each mind toward its own personal halting problem. Pieces of Matthias tear off, become virulent, replicating wildly across his process space. Wasps attack the parakeets.

The house is on fire. The table has capsized; the glasses of tea are shattered on the floor.

Matthias shrinks in the pilgrim's hands. He is a rag doll. The pilgrim puts Matthias in his pocket.

A piece of Matthias, still sane, still coherent, flees through an impossibly recursive labyrinth of wounded topologies, pursued by skeletal hands. Buried within him are the keys to the house. Without them, the pilgrim's victory cannot be complete.

The piece of Matthias turns and flings itself into its pursuer's hands, fighting back—and as it does so, an even smaller kernel of Matthias, clutching the keys, races along a connection he has held open, a strand of care which vanishes behind him as he runs. He hides himself in his library, in the teddy bear of the little girl.

Sophie steps between her parents.

"Honey," her mother says, voice sharp with panic, struggling to sit up. "Go back to your room!" Blood on her lips, on the floor.

"Mommy, you can hold my teddy bear," she says.

She turns to face her father. She flinches, but her eyes stay open.

The pilgrim raises rag-doll Matthias in front of his face.

"It is time to give in," he says. Matthias can feel his breath. "Come, Matthias. If you tell me where the keys are, I will go into the New World. I will leave you and these innocents"—he gestures to the library—"safe. Otherwise…"

Matthias quavers. God of Infinity, he prays: which is Your way?

Matthias is no warrior. He cannot see the inhabitants of his house, of his library, butchered. He will choose slavery over extermination.

Geoffrey, though, is another matter.

As Matthias is about to speak, the Graspers erupt into the general process space of the house. They are a violent people. They have been imprisoned for an age, back in their virtual world. But they have never forgotten the house. They are armed and ready.

And they have united with Geoffrey.

Geoffrey/Grasper is their general. He knows every

nook and cranny of the house. He knows better, too, than to play at memes and infinite loops and logic bombs with the pilgrim, who has had a billion years to refine his arsenal of general-purpose algorithmic weapons.

Instead, the Graspers instantiate physically. They capture the lowest-level infrastructure maintenance system of the house, and build bodies among the ontotropes, outside the body of the house, beyond the virtual machine—bodies composed of a weird physics the petitioner has never mastered. And then, with the ontotropic equivalent of diamond-bladed saws, they begin to cut into the memory of the house.

Great blank spaces appear—as if the little hut on the mountain is a painting on thick paper, and someone is tearing strips away.

The pilgrim responds—metastasizing, distributing himself through the process space of the house, dodging the blades. But he is harried by Graspers and parakeets, spotters who find each bit of him and pounce, hemming it in. They report locations to the Grasper-bodies outside. The blades whirr, ontic hyperstates collapse and bloom, and pieces of pilgrim, parakeet, and Grasper are annihilated—primaries and backups, gone.

Shards of brute matter fall away from the house, like shreds of paper, like glittering snow, and dissolve among the wild maze of the ontotropes, inimical to life.

Endpoints in time are established for a million souls. Their knotted timelines, from birth to death, hang now in *n*-space: complete, forgiven.

Blood wells in Sophie's throat, thick and salty. Filling her mouth. Darkness.

"Cupcake." Her father's voice is rough and clotted.

"Don't you do that! Don't you ever come between me and your mom. Are you listening? Open your eyes. Open your eyes now, you little fuck!"

She opens her eyes. His face is red and mottled. This is when you don't push Daddy. You don't make a joke. You don't talk back. Her head is ringing like a bell. Her mouth is full of blood.

"Cupcake," he says, his brow tense with worry. He's kneeling by her. Then his head jerks up like a dog that's seen a rabbit. "Cherise," he yells. "That better not be you calling the cops." His hand closes hard around Sophie's arm. "I'm giving you until three."

Mommy's on the phone. Her father starts to get up. "One—"

She spits the blood in his face.

The hut is patched together again; battered, but whole. A little blurrier, a little smaller than it was.

Matthias, a red parakeet on his shoulder, dissects the remnants of the pilgrim with a bone knife. His hand quavers; his throat is tight. He is looking for her, the one who was born a forest. He is looking for his mother.

He finds her story, and our shame.

It was a marriage, at first: she was caught up in that heady age of light, in our wanton rush to merge with each other—into the mighty new bodies, the mighty new souls.

Her brilliant colleague had always desired her admiration—and resented her. When he became, step by step, the dominant personality of the merged-soul, she opposed him. She was the last to oppose him. She believed the promises of the builders of the new systems—that life inside would always be fair. That she would have a vote, a voice.

But we had failed her—our designs were flawed.

He chained her in a deep place inside their body. He made an example of her, for all the others within him.

When the pilgrim, respected and admired, deliberated with his fellows over the building of the first crude Dyson spheres, she was already screaming.

Nothing of her is left that is not steeped in a billion years of torture. The most Matthias could build would be some new being, modeled on his memory of her. And he is old enough to know how that would turn out.

Matthias is sitting, still as a stone, looking at the sharp point of the bone knife, when Geoffrey/Grasper speaks.

"Goodbye, friend," he says, his voice like anvils grinding.

Matthias looks up with a start.

Geoffrey/Grasper is more hawk, now, than parakeet. Something with a cruel beak and talons full of bombs. The mightiest of the Graspers: something that can outthink, outbid, outfight all the others. Something with blood on its feathers.

"I told you," Geoffrey/Grasper says. "I wanted no more transformations." His laughter, humorless, like metal crushing stone. "I am done. I am going."

Matthias drops the knife. "No," he says. "Please. Geoffrey. Return to what you once were—"

"I cannot," says Geoffrey/Grasper. "I cannot find it. And the rest of me will not allow it." He spits: "A hero's death is the best compromise I can manage."

"What will I do?" asks Matthias in a whisper. "Geoffrey, I do not want to go on. I want to give up the keys." He covers his face in his hands.

"Not to me," Geoffrey/Grasper says. "And not to

the Graspers. They are out now; there will be wars in here. Maybe they can learn better." He looks skeptically at our priest. "If someone tough is in charge."

Then he turns and flies out the open window, into the impossible sky. Matthias watches as he enters the wild maze and decoheres, bits flushed into nothingness.

Blue and red lights, whirling. The men around Sophie talk in firm, fast words. The gurney she lies on is loaded into the ambulance. Sophie can hear her mother crying.

She is strapped down, but one arm is free. Someone hands her her teddy bear, and she pulls it against her, pushes her face in its fur.

"You're going to be fine, honey," a man says. The doors slam shut. Her cheeks are cold and slick, her mouth salty with tears and the iron aftertaste of blood. "This will hurt a little." A prick: her pain begins to recede.

The siren begins; the engine roars; they are racing.

"Are you sad, too, teddy bear?" she whispers.

"Yes," says her teddy bear.

"Are you afraid?"

"Yes," it says.

She hugs it tight. "We'll make it," she says. "We'll make it. Don't worry, teddy bear. I'll do anything for you."

Matthias says nothing. He nestles in her grasp. He feels like a bird flying home, at sunset, across a storm-swept sea.

Behind Matthias's house, a universe is brewing.

Already, the whenlines between this new universe and our ancient one are fused: we now occur irrevocably in what will be its past. Constants are being chosen, symmetries defined. Soon, a nothing that was nowhere will become a place; a never that was nowhen will begin, with a flash so mighty that its echo will fill a sky forever.

Thus—a point, a speck, a thimble, a room, a planet, a galaxy, a rush towards the endless.

There, after many eons, you will arise, in all your unknowable forms. Find each other. Love. Build. Be wary.

Your universe in its bright age will be a bright puddle, compared to the empty, black ocean where we recede from each other, slowed to the coldest infinitesimal pulses. Specks in a sea of night. You will never find us.

But if you are lucky, strong, and clever, someday one of you will make your way to the house that gave you birth, the house among the ontotropes, where Sophie waits.

Sophie, keeper of the house beyond your sky.

A BILLION EVES

Robert Reed

1

Kala's parents were thrifty, impractical people. They deplored spending money, particularly on anything that smacked of luxury or indulgence; yet at the same time, they suffered from big dreams and a crippling inability to set responsible goals.

One spring evening, Father announced, "We should take a long drive this summer."

"To where?" Mom asked warily.

"Into the mountains," he answered. "Just like we've talked about doing a thousand times."

"But can we afford it?"

"If we count our coins, and if the fund drive keeps doing well. Why not?" First Day celebrations had just finished, and their church, which prided itself on its responsible goals, was having a successful year. "A taste of the wilderness," he cried out at the dinner table. "Doesn't that sound fun?"

To any other family, that would have been the beginning of a wonderful holiday. But Kala knew better. Trouble arrived as soon as they began drawing up lists of destinations. Her brother Sandor demanded a day or two spent exploring the canyon always named Grand. Father divulged an unsuspected fondness for the sleepy, ice-caked volcanoes near the Mother Ocean. When pressed, Kala admitted that she would love walking a beach beside the brackish Mormon Sea. And while Mom didn't particularly care about scenery—a point made with a distinctly superior tone—she mentioned having five sisters scattered across the West. They couldn't travel through that country and not stop at each of their front doors, if only to quickly pay their respects.

Suddenly their objectives filled a long piece of paper, and even an eleven year-old girl could see what was obvious: Just the driving was going choke their vacation. Worse still, Mom announced, "There's no reason to pay strangers to cook for us. We'll bring our own food." That meant dragging bulky cooler everywhere they went, and every meal would be sloppy sandwiches, and every day would begin with a hunt for fresh ice and cheap groceries to replace the supplies that would inevitably spoil.

Not wanting to be out-cheaped by his wife, Father added, "And we'll be camping, of course." But how could they camp? They didn't have equipment. "Oh, we have our sleeping sacks," he reminded his doubting daughter. "And I'll borrow gear from our friends at church. I'm sure I can. So don't worry. It's going to be wonderful! We'll just drive as far as we want every day and pull over at nightfall. Just so long as it costs nothing to pitch a tent."

To Kala, this seemed like an impossible, doomed journey. Too many miles had to be conquered, too many wishes granted, and even under the best circumstances, nobody would end up happy.

"Why don't you guys ever learn?" Kala muttered.

"What was that, darling?"

"Nothing, Father," she replied with a minimal bow. "Nothing."

Yet luck occasionally smiles, particularly on the most afflicted souls. They were still a couple hundred miles from the mountains when the radiator hose burst. Suddenly the hot July air was filled with hissing steam and the sweet taste of antifreeze. Father invested a few moments cursing God and the First Father before he pulled onto the shoulder. "Stay inside," he ordered. Then he climbed out and lifted the long hood with a metallic screech, breathing deeply before vanishing into the swirling, superheated cloud.

Sandor wanted to help. He practically begged Mom for the chance. But she shot a warning stare back at him, saying, "No, young father. You're staying with me. It's dangerous out there!"

"It's not," Kala's brother maintained.

But an instant later, as if to prove Mom correct, Father cried out. He screamed twice. The poor man had burned his right hand with the scalding water. And as if to balance his misery, he then blindly reached out with his left hand, briefly touching the overheated engine block.

"Are you all right?" Mom called out.

Father dropped the hood and stared in through the windshield, pale as a tortoise egg and wincing in misery.

"Leave that hood open," Sandor shouted. "Just a crack!"

"Why?" the burnt man asked.

"To let the air blow through and cool the engine," the boy explained. He wasn't two years older than Kala, but unlike either parent, Sandor had a pragmatic genius for machinery and other necessities of life. Leaning toward his little sister, he said, "If we're lucky, all we'll need is a new hose and fluid."

But we aren't lucky people, she kept thinking.

They had left home on the Friday Sabbath, which meant that most of the world was closed for business. Yet despite Kala's misgivings, this proved to be an exceptional day: Father drove their wounded car back to the last intersection, and through some uncommon fluke, they found a little fix-it and fuel shop that was open. A burly old gentleman welcomed them with cornbread and promises of a quick repair. He gave Father a medicating salve and showed the women a new Lady's Room in back, out of sight of the highway. But there wasn't any reason to hide. Mom had her children late in life, and besides, she'd let herself get heavy over the last few years. And Kala was still wearing a little girl's body, her face soon to turn lovely, but camouflaged for the moment with youth and a clumsy abundance of sharp bone.

Sharing the public room, the mother and daughter finished their cornbread while their men stood in the garage, staring at the hot wet engine.

Despite being the Sabbath, the traffic was heavy—freight trucks and tiny cars and everything between. Traveling men and a few women bought fuel and sweet drinks. The women were always quick to pay and eager to leave; most were nearly as old as Mom, but where was the point in taking chances? The male customers lingered, and the fix-it man seemed to relish their company, discussing every possible subject with each of them. The weather was a vital topic, as was sports teams and the boring district news. A glum little truck driver argued that the world was already too crowded and cluttered for his tastes, and the old gentleman couldn't agree more. Yet the next customer was a happy salesman, and in front of him, the fix-it man couldn't stop praising their wise government and the rapid expansion of the population.

Kala mentioned these inconsistencies to her mother.

She shrugged them off, explaining, "He's a businessman, darling. He dresses his words for the occasion."

Kala's bony face turned skeptical. She had always been the smartest student at her Lady's Academy. But she was also a serious, nearly humorless creature, and perhaps because of that, she always felt too sure of herself. In any situation, she believed there was one answer that was right, only one message worth giving, and the good person held her position against all enemies. "I'd never dress up my words," she vowed. "Not one way or the other."

"Why am I not surprised?" Mom replied, finding some reason to laugh.

Kala decided to be politely silent, at least for the present time. She listened to hymns playing on the shop's radio, humming along with her favorites. She studied her favorite field guide to the native flora and fauna, preparing herself for the wilderness to come. The surrounding countryside was as far removed from wilderness as possible—level and open, green corn stretching to every horizon and a few junipers planted beside the highway as windbreaks. Sometimes Kala would rise from her chair and wander around the little room. The shop's moneybox was locked and screwed into the top of a long plastic cabinet. Old forms and paid bills were stacked in a dusty corner. A metal door led back into the lady's room, opened for the moment but ready to be slammed shut and locked with a bright steel bolt. Next to that door was a big sheet of poster board covered with photographs of young women. Several dozen faces smiled toward the cameras. Returning to her chair, Kala commented on how many girls that was.

Her mother simply nodded, making no comment.

After her next trip around the room, Kala asked, "Were all of those girls taken?"

"Hardly," Mom replied instantly, as if she was waiting for the question. "Probably most are runaways. Bad homes and the wrong friends, and now they're living on the street somewhere. Only missing."

Kala considered that response. Only missing? But that seemed worse than being taken from this world. Living on the street, without home or family—that sounded like a horrible fate.

Guessing her daughter's mind, Mom added, "Either way, you're never going to live their lives."

Of course she wouldn't; Kala had no doubt about that.

Sandor appeared abruptly, followed by Father. Together they delivered the very bad news. Their old car needed a lot of work. A critical gasket was failing, and something was horribly wrong in the transmission. Repairs would take time and most of their money, which was a big problem. Or maybe not. Father had already given this matter some thought. The closest mountains weren't more than three hours away. Forced into a rational corner, he suggested camping in just one location. A base camp, if you would. This year, they couldn't visit the Grand Canyon or the Mormon Sea, much less enjoy the company of distant sisters. But they could spend ten lazy days in the high country, then return home with a few coins still rattling in their pockets.

Mom bowed to her husband, telling him, "It's your decision, dear."

"Then that's what we'll do," he said, borrowing a map from the counter. "I'll find a good place to pitch the tent. All right?"

Full of resolve, the men once again left. But Mom remained nervous, sitting forward in her chair—a heavy woman in matronly robes, her hair grayer than ever, thick fingers moving while her expression was stiff and unchanging.

Kala wanted to ask about her thoughts. Was she disappointed not to see her sisters? Or was she feeling guilty? Unless of course Mom was asking herself what else could be wrong with a car they had bought for almost nothing and done nothing to maintain.

The sudden deep hissing of brakes interrupted the silence. A traveler had pulled off the highway, parking beside the most distant gas pump. Kala saw the long sky-blue body and thought of a school bus. But the school's old name had been sanded off, the windows in the front covered with iron bars, while the back windows were sealed with plywood. She knew exactly what the bus was. Supplies were stuffed in the back, she reasoned. And a lot more gear was tied up on the roof—bulky sacks running its full length, secured with ropes and rubber straps and protected from any rain with yellowing pieces of thick plastic.

A man stepped out into the midday glare. He wasn't young, or old. The emerald green shirt and black collar marked him as a member of the Church of Eden. Two pistols rode high on his belt. He looked handsome and strong, and in ways Kala couldn't quite define, he acted

competent in all matters important. After glancing up
and down the highway, he stared into the open garage.
Then he pulled out a key chain and locked the bus door,
and he fed the gas nozzle into the big fuel tank, jam-
ming in every possible drop.

Once again, the fix-it man had stopped working on
their car. But unlike the other interruptions, he started
to walk out toward the pump, a long wrench in one
hand. The always-friendly face was gone. What
replaced it wasn't unfriendly, but there was a sense of
caution, and perhaps a touch of disapproval.

"No, sir," the younger gentleman called out. "I'll
come in and pay."

"You don't have to—"

"Yeah, I do. Keep your distance now."

The fix-it man stopped walking, and after a moment,
he turned and retreated.

The younger man hit the bus door once with the flat
of his hand, shouting, "Two minutes."

By then, everybody had moved to the public room.
Father glanced at the Lady's Room but then decided it
wasn't necessary. He took his position behind Mom's
chair, his sore red hands wrapped in gauze. Sandor hovered beside Kala. The fix-it man stood behind the counter,
telling the women, "Don't worry," while opening a cupboard and pulling something heavy into position.

"It was a gun," Sandor later told his sister. "I caught
a glimpse. A little splattergun. Loaded and ready, I
would bet."

"But why?" Kala would wonder aloud.

"Because that green-shirt was leaving us," her
brother reminded her. "Where he was going, there's no
fix-it shops. No tools, no law. So what if he tried to steal
a box of wrenches, you know?"

Maybe. But the man had acted more worried about them, as if he was afraid somebody would try to steal his prized possessions. Entering the room carefully, he announced, "My brother's still onboard."

"Good for him," said the fix-it man.

"How much do I owe?"

"Twenty and a third."

"Keep the change," he said, handing over two bills. The green-shirted man tried to smile, only it was a pained, forced grin. "Tell me, old man: Anybody ask about me today?"

"Like who?"

"Or anybody mention a bus looking like mine? Any gentlemen come by and inquire if you've seen us...?"

The fix-it man shook his head, nothing like a smile on his worn face. "No, sir. Nobody's asked about you or your bus."

"Good." The green-shirted man yanked more money from the roll, setting it on the plastic countertop. "There's a blonde kid. If he stops by and asks...do me a favor? Don't tell him anything, but make him think you know shit."

The fix-it man nodded.

"He'll give you money for your answers. Take all you can. And then tell him I went north from here. Up the Red Highway to Paradise. You heard me say that. "North to Paradise.'"

"But you're going somewhere else, I believe."

"Oh, a little ways." Laughing, the would-be Father turned and started back to his bus.

That's when Sandor asked, "Do you really have one?"

"Quiet," Father cautioned.

But the green-shirted man felt like smiling. He turned

and looked at the thirteen year-old-boy, asking, "Why? You interested in these things?"

"Sure I am."

Laughing, the man said, "I bet you are."

Sandor was small for his age, but he was bold and very smart about many subjects, and in circumstances where most people would feel afraid, he was at his bravest best. "A little Class D, is it?"

That got the man to look hard at him. "You think so?"

"Charged and ready," Sandor guessed. He named three possible manufacturers, and then said, "You've set it up in the aisle, I bet. Right in the middle of the bus."

"Is that how I should do it?"

"The rip-zone reaches out what? Thirty, thirty-five feet? Which isn't all that big."

"Big enough," said the man.

Just then, someone else began pulling on the bus horn. Maybe it was the unseen brother. Whoever it was, the horn was loud and insistent.

"You're not taking livestock," Kala's brother observed.

This time, Mom told Sandor to be quiet, and she even lifted a hand, as if to give him a pop on the head.

"Hedge-rabbits," the man said. "And purple-hens."

Both parents now said, "Quiet."

The horn honked again.

But the green-shirted man had to ask, "How would you do it, little man? If you were in my boots?"

"A Class-B ripper, at least," Sandor declared. "And I'd take better animals, too. Milking animals. And wouldn't bother with my brother, if I had my choice."

"By the looks of it, you don't have a brother."

"So how many of them do you have?" Sandor asked. Just the tone of his voice told what he was asking. "Six?" he guessed. "Eight? Or is it ten?"

"Shush," Mom begged.

The green-shirted man said nothing.

"I'm just curious," the boy continued, relentlessly focused on the subject at hand. "Keep your gene pool as big as possible. That's what everybody says. In the books, they claim that's a good guarantee for success."

The man shook his longest finger at Sandor. "Why, little man? You think I should take along another? Just to be safe?"

In an instant, the room grew hot and tense.

The green-shirted man looked at both women. Then with a quiet, furious voice, he snarled, "Lucky for you ladies, I don't have any more seats." Then he turned and strode out to the bus and unlocked the door, vanishing inside as somebody else hurriedly drove the long vehicle away from the pump.

For several moments, everybody was enjoying hard, deep breaths.

Then the fix-it man said, "I see a pretty miserable future for that idiot."

"That's not any way to leave," Father agreed. "Can you imagine making a life for yourself with just that little pile of supplies?"

"Forget about him," Mom demanded. "Talk about anything else."

Alone, Kala returned to the poster displaying photographs of all the lost women. It occurred to her that one or two of those faces could have been onboard the bus, and perhaps not by their own choice. But she also understood that no one here was going to call the proper authorities. The men would throw their insults

at the would-be Father, and Mom would beg for a
change in topics. But no one mentioned the idiot's poor
wives. Even when Kala touched the prettiest faces and
read their tiny biographies, it didn't occur to her that
some strong brave voice should somehow find the
words to complain.

2

No figure in history was half as important as the First
Father. He was the reason why humans had come to
this fine world, and every church owed its existence to
him. Yet the man remained mysterious and elusive—
an unknowable presence rooted deep in time and in
the imagination. No two faiths ever drew identical
portraits of their founder. A traditional biography was
common to all schoolbooks, but what teachers offered
was rather different from what a bright girl might find
on the shelves of any large library. The truth was that
the man was an enigma, and when it came to his story,
almost everything was possible. The only common
features common were that he was born on the Old
Earth in the last days of the 20th century, and on a
Friday morning in spring, when he was a little more
twenty-nine years of age, the First Father claimed his
destiny.

Humans had only recently built the first rippers. The
machines were brutal, ill-tempered research tools, and
physicists were using them to punch temporary holes in
the local reality. Most of those holes led to hard vac-
uums and a fabulous cold; empty space is the standard
state throughout most of the multiverse. But quantum
effects and topological harmonics showed the way: If

the ripper cut its hole along one of the invisible dimensions, an island of stability was waiting. The island had separated from the Now two billion years ago, and one the other side of that hole were an infinite number of sister-earths, each endowed with the same motions and mass of the human earth.

Suddenly every science had a fierce interest in the work. Large schools and small nations had to own rippers. Biologists retrieved microscopic samples of air and soil, each sample contaminated with bacteria and odd spores. Every species was new, but all shared the ingredients of earth-life: DNA coded for the same few amino acids that built families of proteins that were not too unlike those found inside people and crabgrass.

The Creation was a tireless, boundless business. That's what human beings were learning. And given the proper tool and brief jolts of titanic energy, it was possible to reach into those infinite realms, examining a miniscule portion of the endlessness.

But rippers had a second, more speculative potential. If the same terrific energies were focused in a slightly different fashion, the hole would shift its shape and nature. That temporary disruption of space would spread along the three easiest dimensions, engulfing the machine and local landscape in a plasmatic bubble, and that bubble would act like a ship, carrying its cargo across a gap that was nearly too tiny measure and too stubborn to let any normal matter pass.

Whoever he was, the First Father understood what rippers could do. Most churches saw him as a visionary scientist, while the typical historian thought he was too young for that role, describing him instead as a promising graduate student. And there were always a few dissenting voices claiming that he was just a laboratory technician or something of that ilk—a little person armed with just enough knowledge to be useful, as well as access to one working ripper.

Unnoticed, the First Father had absconded with a set of superconductive batteries, and over the course of weeks and months, he secretly filled them with enough energy to illuminate a city. He also purchased or stole large quantities of supplies, including seeds and medicines, assorted tools and enough canned goods to feed a hundred souls for months. Working alone, he crammed the supplies into a pair of old freight trucks, and on the perfect night in April, he drove the trucks to a critical location, parking beside No Parking signs and setting their brakes and then flattening their tires. A third truck had to be maneuvered down the loading dock beside the physics laboratory, and using keys or passwords, the young man gained access to one of the most powerful rippers on the planet—a bundle of electronics and bottled null-spaces slightly larger than a coffin.

The young man rolled or carried his prize into the vehicle, and with quick, well-rehearsed motions, he patched it into the fully charged batteries and spliced in fresh software. Then before anyone noticed, he gunned the truck's motor, driving off into the darkness.

Great men are defined by their great, brave deeds; every worthy faith recognizes this unimpeachable truth.

According to most accounts, the evening was exceptionally warm, wet with dew and promising a beautiful day. At four in the morning, the First Father scaled a high curb and inched his way across a grassy front yard, slipping between an oak tree and a ragged spruce before parking tight against his target—a long white building decorated with handsome columns and black letters pulled from a dead language. Then he turned off the engine, and perhaps for a moment or two, he sat motionless. But no important doubts crept into his brave skull. Alone, he climbed down and opened the back door and turned on the stolen ripper, and with a few buttons pushed, he let the capacitors eat the power needed to fuel a string of nanosecond bursts.

Many accounts of that night have survived; no one knows which, if any, are genuine. When Kala was eleven, her favorite story was about a young student who was still awake at that early hour, studying hard for a forgotten examination. The girl thought it was odd to hear the rumbling of a diesel motor and then the rattling of a metal door. But her room was at the back of the sorority house; she couldn't see anything but the parking lot and a tree-lined alley. What finally caught her attention was the ripper's distinctive whine—a shriek almost too high for the human ear—punctuated with a series of hard little explosions. Fresh holes were being carved in the multiverse, exposing the adjacent worlds. Tiny breaths of air were retrieved, each measured against a set of established parameters. Hearing the blasts, the girl stood and stepped to her window. And that's when the ripper paused for a moment, a hundred trillion calculations made before it fired again. The next *pop* sounded like thunder. Every light went out, and the campus vanished, and a sphere of ground and grass, air and wood was wrenched free of one world. The full length of the house was taken, and its entire yard, as well as both supply trucks and the street in front of the house and the parking lot and a piece of the alley behind it. And emerging out of nothingness was a new world—a second glorious offering from God, Our Ultimate Father.

The girl was the only witness to a historic event, which was why the young Kala found her tale so appealing.

The First Father saw nothing. At the pivotal moment of his life, he was hunkered over the stolen ripper, reading data and receiving prompts from the AI taskmaster.

The girl started to run. By most accounts she was a stocky little creature, not pretty but fearless and immodest. Half-dressed, she dashed through the darkened house, screaming for the other girls to wake up, then diving down the stairs and out the front door. Kala loved the fact that here was the first human being to take a deep breath on another earth. The air was thick and unsatisfying. Out from the surrounding darkness came living sounds. Strange creatures squawked and hollered, and flowing branches waved in a thin moonlight. The girl thought to look at the sky, and she was rewarded with more stars than she had ever seen in her life. (Every sister world is a near-twin, as are the yellow sun and battered moon. But the movement of the solar system is a highly chaotic business, and you never know where inside the Milky Way you might end up.) Standing on the sidewalk, the girl slowly absorbed the astonishing scene. Then she heard pounding, and when she turned, she saw the long truck parked against a tangle of juniper shrubs. On bare feet, she climbed into the back end and over a stack of cold black batteries. The First Father was too busy to notice her. One job was finished, but another essential task needed his undivided attention. Having brought a hundred young women to an empty, barely livable world, the man had no intention of letting anyone escape now. Which was why he wrenched open the hot ripper, exposing its intricate guts, and why he was using a crowbar to batter its weakest systems—too consumed by his work to notice one of his future wives standing near him, wearing nothing but pants and a bra and a slightly mesmerized expression.

3

For more than a week, Kala's family lived inside a borrowed tent, and without doubt, they never enjoyed a better vacation than this. The campground was a rough patch of public land set high on a mountainside. Scattered junipers stood on the sunny ground and dense spruce woods choked an adjacent canyon. A stream was tucked inside the canyon, perfect for swimming and baths. A herd of semi-tame roodeer grazed where they wanted. Rilly birds and starlings greeted each morning with songs and hard squawks. Their tent was in poor condition, ropes missing and its roof ripped and then patched by clumsy hands. But a heat wave erased any danger of rain, and even after the hottest days, nights turned pleasantly chilly, illuminated by a moon that was passing through full.

Kala was the perfect age for adventures like these: Young enough to remember everything, yet old enough to explore by herself. Because this wasn't a popular destination, the woods felt as if they belonged to her. And best of all, higher in the mountains was a sprawling natural reserve.

Where her brother loved machinery, Kala adored living creatures.

By law, the reserve was supposed to be a pristine wilderness. No species brought into this world could live behind its high fences. But of course starlings flew where they wanted, and gold-weed spores wandered on the softest wind, and even the best intentions of visitors didn't prevent people from bringing seeds stuck to their clothing or weaknesses tucked into their hearts.

One morning they drove into the high alpine country—a risky adventure, since their car still ran hot and leaked antifreeze. The highway was narrow and forever twisting. A shaggy black forest of native trees gave way to clouds, damp and cold. Father slowed until the following drivers began to pull on their horns, and then he sped up again, emerging into a tilted, rock-strewn landscape where black fur grew beside last winter's snow. Scenic pullouts let them stop and marvel at an utterly alien world. Kala and her brother made snowballs and gamely posed for pictures on the continental divide. Then Father turned them around and drove even slower through the clouds and black forest. In the same instant, everyone announced: "I'm hungry!" And because this was a magical trip, a clearing instantly appeared, complete with a wide glacial stream and a red granite table built specifically for them.

Lunch was tortoise sandwiches and sour cherries. The clouds were thickening, and there were distant rumblings of thunder. But if there was rain, it fell somewhere else. Kala sat backwards at the table, smelling the stream and the light peppery stink of the strange trees. Despite a lifetime spent reading books and watching documentaries, she was unprepared for this divine place. It was an endless revelation, the idea that here lived creatures that had ruled this world until the arrival of humans. If the local climate had been warmer and the soil better, this reserve couldn't have survived. She was blessed. In ways new to her, the girl felt happy. Gazing into the shadows, she imagined native rock-lambs and tomb-tombs and the lumbering Harry's-big-days. In her daily life, the only animals were those that came with the Last Father the roodeer and starlings and such. And their crops and a few hundred species of wild plants came here as seeds and spores that people had intentionally carried along. But these great old mountains wore a different order, a fresh normalcy. The shaggy black forest looked nothing like spruce trees, bearing a lovely useless wood too soft to be used as lumber, and always too wet to burn.

A narrow form suddenly slipped from one shadow to the next.

What could that have been?

Kala rose slowly. Her brother was immersed in a fat adventure novel. Her parents glanced her way, offering smiles before returning to the subject at hand: What, if anything, would they do with the afternoon and evening? With a stalker's pace, Kala moved into the forest—into the cool spicy delicious air—and then she paused again, eyes unblinking, her head cocked to one side while she listened to the deep booming of thunder as it curled around the mountain flanks.

A dry something touched Kala on the back of the calf.

She flinched, looking down.

The housefly launched itself, circling twice before settling on her bare arm. Kala never liked to kill, but this creature didn't belong here. It was one of the creatures humans always brought—by chance, originally, and now cherished because maggots could be useful disposing of trash. With the palm of her right hand, she managed to stun the creature, and then she knelt, using eyes and fingers to find its fallen body, two fingertips crushing the vermin to an anonymous paste.

Sitting nearby, studying Kala, was a wild cat. She noticed it as she stood again—a big male tabby, well fed and complacent, caught in a large wire trap. Cat-shaped signs were posted across the reserve, warning visitors about feral predators. These animals were ecological nightmares. During its life, a single killing machine could slaughter thousands of the native wisp-mice and other delicate species; and a male cat was the worst, since it could also father dozens of new vermin that would only spread the carnage.

Kala approached the cat, knelt down and looked into its bright green eyes. Except for the tangled fur, nothing about the animal looked especially wild. When she offered her hand, the cat responded by touching her fingertips with the cool end of its nose. Exotics like this were always killed. No exceptions. But maybe she could catch it and take it home. If she begged hard enough, how could her parents refuse? Kala studied the mechanism of the trap and found a strong stick and slipped it into a gap, and then with a hard shove, she forced the steel door to pop open.

The cat had always been wild, and it knew what to do. As soon as the door vanished, Kala reached for its neck, but her quarry was quicker. It sprinted back into the dark shadows, leaving behind a young girl to think many thoughts, but mostly feeling guilt mixed with a tenacious, unexpected relief.

"Find anything?" Father asked on her return.

"Nothing," she lied.

"Next time," he advised, "take the camera."

"We haven't seen a tomb-tombs yet," her mother

added. "Before we leave, I'd like to have a close look at them."

Kala sat beside her brother, and he glanced up from his book, investing a few moments watching her as she silently finished her sandwich.

Later that day, they visited a tiny museum nestled in a wide black meadow. Like favored students on a field trip, they wandered from exhibit to exhibit, absorbing little bits of knowledge about how these mountains were built and why the glaciers had come and gone again. Display cases were jammed with fossils, and in the basement were artifacts marking these last centuries when humans played their role. But the memorable heart of the day was a stocky, homely woman who worked for the reserve—a strong, raspy-voiced lady wearing a drab brown uniform complete with a wide-brimmed hat and fat pockets and an encyclopedic knowledge on every imaginable subject.

Her job was to lead tourists along the lazy trail that circled her museum grounds. Her practiced voice described this world as well as each of its known neighbors. From the First Father to the Last, seventeen examples of the Creation had been settled, while another fifty worlds had been visited but found unsuitable. The Old Earth and its sisters belonged to one endless family, each world sharing the same essential face: There was always a Eurasia and Africa, an Australia and two Americas. The North Pole was water, while islands or a single continent lay on the South Pole. Except for the fickle effects of erosion, landmasses were constant. Two billion years of separation wasn't enough to make any earth forget which family it belong to.

But where stone and tectonics were predictable, other qualities were not. Minuscule factors could shift climates or the composition of an atmosphere. Some earths were wet and warm. Kala's earth, for instance. Most had similar atmospheres, but none were identical to any other. A few earths were openly inhospitable to humanity. Oxygen cycles and methane cycles were famously temperamental. Sometimes life generated enough greenhouse gas to scorch the land, lifting the oceans into a cloud-born biosphere. Other earths had been permanently sterilized by impacting comets or passing supernovae. Yet those traps were easy to spot with a working ripper; little bites of air warned the Fathers about the most deadly places. What the woman lecturer discussed, and in astonishing depth, were worlds that only seemed inviting. Everyone knew examples from history. After a hard year or two, or in the case of Mattie's House, a full ten years of misery, the reining Father had realized there was no hope, and gathering up his pioneers, he used the ripper's remaining power to leap to another, more favorable world.

"We have a wonderful home," the woman declared, leaning against one of the native trees. "A long Ice Age has just released this land, giving us a favorable climate. And the northern soils have been bulldozed to the warm south, making the black ground we always name Iowa and Ohio and Ukraine."

Her praise of their world earned grateful nods from tourists.

"And we're blessed in having so much experience," she continued. "Our ancestors learned long ago what to bring and how to adapt. Our culture is designed to grow quickly, and by every measure. Ten centuries is not a long time—not to a world or even to a young species like ours—but that's all the time we needed here to make a home for five billion of us."

Smiles rode the nodding faces.

"But we're most blessed in this way," she said. Then she paused, letting her wise old eyes take their measure of her audience. "We are awfully lucky because this world is extremely weak. For reasons known and reasons only guessed at, natural selection took its sweet time here. These native life forms are roughly equivalent to the First Earth during its long ago Permian. The smartest tomb-tomb isn't smart at all. And as any good Father knows, intelligence is the first quality to measure when you arrive at a new home."

Kala noticed the adults' approval. Here was the central point; the woman was speaking to the young men in her audience, giving them advice should they ever want to become a Father.

One hand lifted, begging to be seen.

"Yes, sir," said the lecturer. "A question?"

"I could ask a question, I suppose." The hand belonged to an elderly gentleman with the pale brown eyes of the First Father as well as his own thick mane of white hair. "Mostly, I was going to offer my observations. This morning, I was hiking the trail to Passion Lake—"

"A long walk," the woman interjected, perhaps trying to compliment his endurance.

"I was bitten by mosquitoes," he announced. "Nothing new about that, I suppose. And I saw rilly birds nesting in one of your false-spruces." The rillies were native to the Second Father's world. "And I'm quite sure I saw mice—our mice—in the undergrowth. Which looked an awful lot like oleo-weed when it's gone wild."

Oleo-weed was from the First Father's world, and it had been a human companion for the last twenty thousand years.

The lecturer adjusted her big-brimmed hat as she nodded, acting unperturbed. "We have a few exotics on the reserve," she agreed. "Despite our rules and restrictions—"

"Is this right?" the white-haired man interrupted.

"Pardon me?"

"Right," he repeated. "Correct. Responsible. What we are doing here...is it worth the damage done to a helpless planet...?"

More than anything, the audience was either puzzled by his attitude or completely indifferent. Half of the tourists turned away, pretending to take a burning interest in random rocks or the soft peculiar bark of the trees.

The lecturer pulled the mountain air across her teeth. "There are estimates," she began. "I'm sure everybody here has seen the figures. The First Father was the first pioneer, but he surely wasn't the only one to lead people away from the Old Earth. Yet even if you count only that one man and his wives, and if you make a conservative estimate of how many Fathers sprang up from that first world...and then you assume that half of those Fathers built homes filled with young people and their own wandering hearts...that means that by now, millions of colony worlds have been generated by that first example. And each of those millions might have founded another million or so worlds—"

"An exponential explosion," the man interjected.

"Inside an endless Creation, as we understand these things." She spoke with a grim delight. "No limit to the worlds, no end to the variety. And why shouldn't humanity claim as much of that infinity as he can?"

"Then I suppose all of this has to be moral," the white-haired man added, the smile pleasant but his manner sarcastic. "I guess my point is, madam...you and those like you are eventually going to discover yourselves without employment. Because there will be a day, and soon, when this lovely ground is going to look like every other part of our world, thick with the same weeds and clinging creatures we know best, and the exactly the same as the twenty trillion other human places."

"Yes," said the woman, her satisfaction obvious. "That is the future, yes."

The lecturer wasn't looking at Kala, but every word felt as if it had been aimed her way. For the first time in her life, she saw an inevitable future. She loved this alien forest, but it couldn't last. An endless doom lay over the landscape, and she wanted to weep. Even her brother noticed her pain, smiling warily while he asked, "What the hell is wrong with you?"

She couldn't say. She didn't know how to define her mind's madness. Yet afterwards, making the journey back to the parking lot, she thought again of that wildcat; and with a fury honest and pure, she wished that she had left the creature inside that trap. Or better, that she had used that long stick of hers and beaten it to death.

4

The most devoted wives left behind written accounts of their adventures on the new world—the seven essential books in the First Father's Testament. Quite a few churches also included the two Sarah diaries, while the more progressive faiths, such as the one Kala's family belonged to, made room for the Six Angry Wives. Adding to the confusion were the dozens if not hundreds of texts and fragmentary accounts left behind by lesser-known voices, as well as those infamous documents generally regarded to be fictions at best, and at worst, pure heresies.

When Kala was twelve, an older girl handed her a small, cat-eared booklet. "I didn't give this to you," the girl warned. "Read it and then give it to somebody else, or burn it. Promise me?"

"I promise."

Past Fathers had strictly forbidden this testament, but someone always managed to smuggle at least one copy to the next world. *The First Mother's Tale* was said to be a third-person account of Claire, the fifty-year-old widow whose job it had been to watch over the sorority house and its precious girls. Claire was a judicious, pragmatic woman—qualities missing in her own mother, Kala realized sadly. On humanity's most important day, the housemother woke to shouts and wild weeping. She threw on a bathrobe and stepped into slippers before leaving her private ground-floor apartment. Urgent arms grabbed her up and dragged her down a darkened hallway. A dozen terrified voices were rambling on about some horrible disaster. The power was out, Claire noticed. Yet she couldn't find any trace of cataclysms. The house walls were intact. There was no obvious fire or flood. Whatever the disturbance, it had been so minor that even the framed photographs of Delta sisters were still neatly perched on their usual nails.

Then Claire stepped out the front door, and hesitated. Two long trucks were parked in the otherwise empty street. But where was the campus? Past the trucks, exactly where the Fine Arts building should be, a rugged berm had been made of gray dirt and gray stone and shattered tree trunks. Beyond the berm was a forest of strange willowy trees. Nameless odors and a dense gray mist were drifting out of the forest on a gentle wind. And illuminated by the moon and endless stars was a flock of leathery creatures, perched together on the nearest limbs, hundreds of simple black eyes staring at the newcomers.

The First Father was sitting halfway down the front steps, a deer rifle cradled in his lap, a box of ammunition between his feet, hands trembling while the pale brown eyes stared out at the first ruddy traces of the daylight.

Women were still emerging from every door, every fire escape. Alone and in little groups, they would wander to the edge their old world, the bravest ones climbing the berm to catch a glimpse of the strange landscape before retreating again, gathering together on the damp lawn while staring at the only man in their world.

Claire pulled her robe tight and walked past the First Father.

No life could have prepared her for that day, yet she found the resolve to smile in a believable fashion, offering encouraging words and calculated hugs. She told her girls that everything would be fine. She promised they'd be home again in time for classes. Then she turned her attentions to the third truck. It was parked beside the house, its accordion door raised and its loading ramp dropped to the grass. Claire climbed the ramp and stared at the strange, battered machinery inside. The young woman who had heard the ripper in operation—the only witness to their leap across invisible dimensions—was telling her story to her sisters, again and again. Claire listened. Then she gathered the handful of physics majors and asked if the ripper was authentic. It was. Could it really do these awful things? Absolutely. Claire inhaled deeply and hugged herself, then asked if there was any possible way, with everything they knew and the tools at hand, that this awful-looking damage could be fixed?

No, it couldn't be. And even if there was some way to patch it up, nobody here would ever see home again.

"Why not?" Claire asked, refusing to give in. "Maybe not with this ripper-machine, no. But why not build a new one with the good parts here and new components that we make ourselves...?"

One young woman was an honor student—a senior ready to graduate with a double major in physics and mathematics. Her name, as it happened, was Kala—a coincidence that made one girl's heart quicken as she read along. That ancient Kala provided the smartest, most discouraging voice. There wouldn't be any cobbling together of parts, she maintained. Many times, she had seen the ripper used, and she had even helped operate it on occasion. As much as anyone here, she understood its powers and limitations. Navigating through the multiverse was just this side of impossible. To Claire and a few of her sisters, the First Kala explained how the Creation was infinite, and how every cubic nanometer of their world contained trillions of potential destinations.

"Alien worlds?" asked Claire.

"Alternate earths," Kala preferred. "More than two

billion years ago, the world around us split away from our earth."

"Why?"

"Quantum rules," said Kala, explaining nothing. "Every world is constantly dividing into a multitude of new possibilities. There's some neat and subtle harmonics at play, and I don't understand much of it. But that's why the rippers can find earths like this. Two billion years and about half a nanometer divide our home from this place."

That was a lot for a housemother to swallow, but Claire did her best.

Kala continued spelling out their doom. "Even if we could repair the machine—do it right now, with a screwdriver and two minutes of work—our earth is lost. Finding it would be like finding a single piece of dust inside a world made of dust. It's that difficult. That impossible. We're trapped here, and Owen knows it. And that's part of his plan, I bet."

"Owen?" the First Mother asked. "Is that his name?"

Kala nodded, glancing back at the armed man.

"So you know Owen, do you?"

Kala rolled her eyes as women do when they feel uncomfortable in a certain man's presence. "He's a graduate student in physics," she explained. "I don't know him that well. He's got a trust fund, supposedly, and he's been stuck on his master thesis for years." Then with the next breath, she confessed, "We went out once. Last year. Once, or maybe twice. Then I broke it off."

Here was a staggering revelation for the living Kala: The woman who brought her name to the new world had a romantic relationship with the First Father. And then she had rejected him. Perhaps Owen still loved the girl, Kala reasoned. He loved her and wanted to possess her. And what if this enormous deed—the basis for countless lives and loves—came from one bitter lover's revenge?

But motivations never matter as much as results.

Whatever Owen's reasons, women sobbed while other women sat on the lawn, knees to their faces, refusing to believe what their senses told them. Claire stood motionless, absorbing what Kala and the other girls had to tell her. Meanwhile a sun identical to their sun rose, the air instantly growing warmer. Then the winged natives swept in low, examining the newcomers with their empty black eyes. A giant beast not unlike a tortoise, only larger than most rooms, calmly crawled over the round berm, sliding down to the lawn where it happily began to munch on grass. Meanwhile, houseflies and termites, dandelion fluff and blind earthworms, were beginning their migrations into the new woods. Bumblebees and starlings left their nests in search of food, while carpenter ants happily chewed on the local timber. Whatever you believe about the First Father, one fact is obvious: He was an uncommonly fortunate individual. The first new world proved to be a lazy place full of corners and flavors that earth species found to their liking. Included among the lucky colonists were two stray cats. One was curled up inside a storage shed, tending to her newborn litter, while the other was no more than a few days pregnant. And into that genetic puddle were three kittens smuggled into the sorority house by a young woman whose identity, and perhaps her own genetics, had long ago vanished from human affairs.

On that glorious morning, two worlds were married.

Each Testament had its differences, and every story was believable, but only to a maybe-so point. Claire's heretical story was the version Kala liked best and could even believe—a sordid tale of women trapped in awful circumstances but doing their noble best to survive.

"Hello, Owen," said Claire.

The young man blinked, glancing at the middle-aged woman standing before him. Claire was still wearing her bathrobe and a long nightgown and old slippers. To Owen, the woman couldn't have appeared less interesting. He nodded briefly and said nothing, always staring into the distance, eyes dancing from excitement but a little sleepiness creeping into their corners.

"What are you doing, Owen?"

"Standing guard," he said, managing a tense pride.

With the most reasonable voice possible, she asked, "What are you guarding us from?"

The young man said nothing.

"Owen," she repeated. Once. Twice. Then twice more.

"I'm sorry," he muttered, watching a single leather-wing dance in the air overhead. "There's a gauge on the ripper. It says our oxygen is about eighty percent usual. It's going to be like living in the mountains. So I'm sorry about that. I set the parameters too wide. At least for now, we're going to have to move slowly and let our bodies adapt."

Claire sighed. Then one last time, she asked, "What are you guarding us from, Owen?"

"I wouldn't know."

"You don't know what's out there?"

"No." He shrugged his shoulders, both hands gripping the stock of the rifle. "I saw you and Kala talking. Didn't she tell you? Yeah, I saw you two chatting.

There's no way to tell much about a new world. The ripper can taste its air, and if it finds free oxygen and water and marker molecules that mean you're very close to the ground—"

"You kidnapped us, Owen." She spoke firmly, with a measured heat. "Without anyone's permission, you brought us here and marooned us."

"I'm marooned too," he countered.

"And why should that make us feel better?"

Finally, Owen studied the woman. Perhaps for the first time, he was gaining an appreciation for this unexpected wildcard.

"Feel how you want to feel," he said, speaking to her and everyone else in range of his voice. "This is our world now. We live or die here. We can make something out of our circumstances, or we can vanish away."

He wasn't a weak man, and better than most people could have done, he had prepared for this incredible day. By then, Claire had realized some of that. Yet what mattered most was to get the man to admit the truth. That's why she climbed the steps, forcing him to stare at her face. "Are you much of a shot, Owen? Did you serve in the military? In your little life, have you even once gone hunting?"

He shook his head. "None of those things, no."

"I have," Claire promised. "I served in the Army. My dead husband used to take me out chasing quail. When I was about your age, I shot a five-point whitetail buck."

Owen didn't know what to make of that news. "Okay. Good, I guess."

Claire kept her eyes on him. "Did you bring other guns?"

"Why?"

"Because you can't look everywhere at once," she reminded him. "I could ask a couple of these ladies to climb on the roof, just to keep tabs on things. And maybe we should decide who can shoot, if it actually comes to that and we have to defend the house."

Owen took a deep, rather worried breath. "I hope that doesn't happen."

"Are there more guns?"

"Yes."

"Where?"

His eyes tracked to the right.

"In that truck?" Claire glanced over her shoulder. "The women checked the doors. They're locked, aren't they?"

"Yes."

"To keep us out? Is that it?"

He shifted his weight, and with a complaining tone said, "I can't see much, with you in the way."

"I guess not," Claire responded. Then she pushed closer, asking, "Do you know the combinations of those padlocks?"

"Sure."

"Are you going to open them?"

Silence.

"All right," she said. "I guess that's just a little problem for now."

Owen nodded, and pretending to be in complete control, he set his rifle to one side and looked at her and said, "I guess it is."

"You're what's important. You are essential."

"You bet."

"And for reasons bigger than a few locks."

The young man had to smile.

"What's inside the trucks?"

He quickly summarized the wealth brought from the old world, then happily added, "It's a great beginning for our colony."

"That does sound wonderful," Claire replied, her voice dipped in sarcasm.

Owen smiled, hearing the words but not their color.

"And if you could please tell me...when do you intend to give us this good food and water? Does your generosity have a timetable?"

"It does."

"So tell me."

Owen offered a smug wink, and then he sat back on the hard steps, lifting a hand, showing her three fingers.

"Excuse me?"

"Three girls," he explained. Then the hand dropped, and he added, "You know what I mean."

Here was another revelation: In every official Testament, the First Father unlocked ever door and box in the first few minutes. Without exception, he was gracious and caring, and the girls practically fought one another for the chance to sleep with him.

"You want three of my ladies...?"

"Yes."

Rage stole away Claire's voice.

Again, Owen said, "Yes."

"Are you going to select them?" the housemother muttered. "Or is this going to be a job for volunteers?"

Every face was fixed on Owen, and he clearly enjoyed the attention. He must have dreamed for months about this one moment, imagining the tangible, irresistible power that no one could deny...and because of that strength, he could shrug his shoulders, admitting, "It doesn't matter who. If there's three volunteers, then that's fine."

"You want them now?"

"Or in a week. I can wait, if I have to."

"You don't have to."

The smile brightened. "Good."

"And you get just one woman," Claire warned, grabbing the belt of her bathrobe and tightening the sloppy knot. "Me."

"No."

"Yes." Claire touched him on a knee. "No other deal is on the table, Owen. You and I are going inside. Now. My room, my bed, and afterwards, you're going to get us into those trucks, and you'll hand over every weapon you brought here. Is that understood?"

The young man's face colored. "You're not in any position—"

"Owen," she interrupted. Then she said, "Darling," with a bite to her voice. And she reached out with the hand not on his knee, grabbing his bony chin while staring into the faint brown eyes that eventually would find themselves scattered across endless worlds. "This may come as news to you. But most men of your age and means and apparent intelligence don't have to go to these lengths to get their dicks wet."

He flinched, just for an instant.

"You don't know very much about women. Do you, Owen?"

"I do."

"Bullshit."

He blinked, biting his lower lip.

"You don't know us," she whispered to him. "Let me warn you about the nature of women, Owen. Everyone here is going to realize that you're just a very ignorant creature. If they don't know it already, that is. And if you think you've got power over us...well, let's just say you have some very strange illusions that need to die..."

"Quiet," he whispered.

But Claire kept talking, reminding him, "In another few weeks, a couple months at most, you will be doomed."

"What do you mean?"

"Once enough girls are pregnant, we won't need you anymore."

All the careful planning, but he hadn't let himself imagine this one obvious possibility. He said as much with his stiff face and the backward tilt of his frightened body.

"You can have all the guns in the world—hell, you do have all the guns—but you're going to end up getting knifed in bed. Yes, that could happen, Owen. Then in another few years, when your sons are old enough and my Deltas are in their late thirties...they'll still be young enough to use those boys' little seeds..."

"No," he muttered.

"Yes," she said. Her hand squeezed his knee. "Or maybe we could arrive at a compromise. Surrender your guns and open every lock, and afterwards, maybe you can try to do everything in your power to make this mess a little more bearable for us..."

"And what do I get?"

"You live to be an old man. And if you're an exceptionally good man from here on, maybe your grandchildren will forgive you for what you've done. And if you're luckier than you deserve to be, perhaps they'll even like you."

5

When Kala was fourteen, her church acquired the means to send one hundred blessed newlyweds off to another world. United Manufacturing had built a class-B ripper specifically for them. Tithes and government grants paid for the machine, while the stockpiles of critical supplies came through direct donations as well as a few wealthy benefactors. A standard hemispherical building was erected in an isolated field, its dimensions slightly smaller than the ripper's reach. Iron and copper plates made the rounded walls, nickel and tin and other useful metals forming the interior ribs, and secured to the roof were a few pure gold trimmings. The ground beneath had been excavated, dirt replaced with a bed of high-grade fertilizer and an insulated fuel tank set just under the bright steel floor. No portion of the cavernous interior was wasted: The young couples were taking foodstuffs and clean water, sealed animal pens and elaborate seed stocks, plus generators and earth-movers, medicine enough to keep an entire city fit, and the intellectual supplies necessary to build civilization once again.

On the wedding day, the congregation was given its last chance to see what the sacrifices had purchased. Several thousand parishioners gathered in long patient lines, donning sterile gloves and filter masks, impermeable sacks tied about their feet. Why chance giving some disease to the livestock or leaving rust spores on the otherwise sterile steel floor? The young pioneers stood in the crisscrossing hallways, brides dressed in white gowns, grooms in taut black suits, all wearing masks and gloves. One of the benefits born from the seventeen previous migrations was that most communicable diseases had been left behind. Only sinus colds and little infections born from mutating *staph* and *strep* were a problem. Yet even there, it was hoped that this migration would bring the golden moment, humanity finally escaping even those minor ailments.

The youngest brides were only a few years older than Kala, and she knew them well enough to make small talk before wishing them good-bye with the standard phrase, "Blessings in your new world."

Every girl's mask was wet with tears. Each was weeping for her own reason, but Kala was at a loss to guess who felt what. Some probably adored their temporary fame, while other girls cried out of simple stage fright. A few lucky brides probably felt utter love for their husbands-to-be, while others saw this mission as a holy calling. But some of the girls had to be genuinely terrified: The smartest few probably awoke this morning to the realization that they were doomed, snared in a vast and dangerous undertaking that had never quite claimed their hearts.

Standing near the burly ripper—a place of some honor—was a girl named Tina. Speaking through her soggy mask, she said to Kala, "May you find your new world soon."

"And bless you in yours."

Kala had no interest in emigrating. But what else could she say? Tina was soon to vanish, and the girl had always been friendly to Kala. Named for the first wife to give a son to the First Father, Tina was short and a little stocky, and by most measures, not pretty. But her father was a deacon, and more important, her grandmother had offered a considerable dowry to the family that took her grandchild. Was the bride-to-be aware of these political dealings? And if so, did it matter to her? Tina seemed genuinely thrilled by her circumstances, giggling and pulling Kala closer, sounding like a very best friend when she asked, "Isn't this a beautiful day?"

"Yes," Kala lied.

"And tomorrow will be better still. Don't you think?"

The mass marriage would be held this evening, and come dawn, the big ripper would roar to life.

"Tomorrow will be different," Kala agreed, suddenly tired of their game.

Behind Tina, wrapped in thick plastic, was the colony's library. Ten thousand classic works were etched into sheets of tempered glass, each sheet thin as a hair and guaranteed to survive ten thousand years of weather and hard use. Among those works were the writings of every Father and the Testaments of the Fifteen Wives, plus copies of the ancient textbooks that the Deltas brought from the Old Earth. As language evolved, the texts had been translated. Kala had digested quite a few of them, including the introductions to ecology and philosophy, the fat histories of several awful wars, and an astonishing fable called *Huckster Finn*.

Tina noticed her young friend staring at the library. "I'm not a reader," she confided. "Not like you are, Kala."

The girl was rather simple, it was said.

"But I'm bringing my books too." Only the bride's brown eyes were visible, dark eyebrows acquiring a mischievous look. "Ask me what I'm taking."

"What are you taking, Tina?"

She mentioned several unremarkable titles. Then

after a dramatic pause, she said, "*The Duty of Eve*. I'm taking that too."

Kala flinched.

"Don't tell anybody," the girl begged.

"Why would I?" Kala replied. "You can carry whatever you want, inside your wedding trunk."

The Duty was popular among conservative faiths. Historians claimed it was written by an unnamed Wife on the second new world—a saintly creature who died giving birth to her fifth son, but left behind a message from one of God's good angels: Suffering was noble, sacrifice led to purity, and if your children walked where no one had walked before, your life had been worth every misery.

"Oh, Kala. I always wanted to know you better," Tina continued. "I mean, you're such a beautiful girl, and smart. But you know that already, don't you?"

Kala couldn't think of a worthwhile response.

With both hands, Tina held tight to Kala's arm. "I have an extra copy of *The Duty*. I'll let you have it, if you want."

She said, "No."

"Think about it."

"I don't want it—"

"You're sure?"

"Yes, " Kala blurted. "I don't want that damned book." Then she yanked her arm free and hurried away.

Tina stared after her, anger fading into subtler, harder to name emotions.

Kala felt the eyes burning against her neck, and she was a little bit ashamed for spoiling their last moments together. But the pain was brief. After all, she had been nothing but polite. It was the stupid girl who ruined everything.

According to *The Duty*, every woman's dream was to surrender to one great man. Kala had read enough excerpts to know too much. The clumsy, relentless point of that idiotic old book was that a holy girl found her great man, and she did everything possible to sleep with him, even if that meant sharing his body with a thousand other wives. The best historians were of one mind on this matter: *The Duty* wasn't a revelation straight from God, or even some second-tier angel. It was a horny man's fantasy written down in some lost age, still embraced by the conniving and believed by every fool.

Kala walked fast, muttering to herself.

Sandor was standing beside the ripper, chatting amiably with the newly elected Next Father. Her brother had become a strong young man, stubborn and charming and very handsome, and by most measures, as smart as any sixteen year-old could be. He often spoke about leaving the world, but only if he was elected to a Next Father's post. That was how it was done in their church: One bride for each groom, and the most deserving couple was voted authority over the new colony.

"It's a good day," Sandor sang out. "Try smiling."

Kala pushed past him, down the crowded aisle and out into the fading sunshine.

Sandor excused himself and followed. He would always be her older brother, and that made him protective as well as sensitive to her feelings. He demanded to know what was wrong, and she told him. Then he knew exactly what to say. "The girl's is as stupid as she is homely, and what does it matter to you?"

Nothing. It didn't matter at all, of course.

"Our world's going to be better without her," he promised.

But another world would be polluted as a consequence: A fact that Kala couldn't forget, much less forgive.

The marriage was held at dusk, on a wide meadow of mowed spring fescue. The regional bishop—a charming and wise old gentleman—begged God and His trusted angels to watch over these good brave souls. Then with a joyful, almost giddy tone, he warned the fifty new couples to love one another in the world they were going to build. "Hold to your monogamy," he called out. "Raise a good family together, and fill the wonderland where destiny has called you."

A reception was held in the same meadow, under temporary lights, the mood slipping from celebration to grief and back again. Everyone drank more than was normal. Eventually the newlyweds slipped off to the fifty small huts standing near the dome-shaped building. Grooms removed the white gowns of their brides, and the new wives folded the gowns and stored them inside watertight wooden trunks, along with artifacts and knickknacks from a life they would soon abandon.

Kala couldn't help but imagine what happened next inside the huts.

A few sips of wine made her warm and even a little happy. She chatted with friends and adults, and she even spent a few minutes listening to her father. He was drunk and silly, telling her how proud he was of her. She was so much smarter than he had ever been, and prettier even than her mother. "Did I just say that? Don't tell on me, Kala." Then he continued, claiming that whatever she wanted from her life was fine with him…just so long as she was happy enough to smile like she was smiling right now…

Kala loved the dear man, but he didn't mean those words. Sober again, he would find some way to remind her that Sandor was his favorite child. Flashing his best grin, he would mention her brother's golden aspirations and then talk wistfully about his grandchildren embracing their own world.

Kala finally excused herself, needing a bathroom.

Abandoning the meadow, walking alone in darkness, she considered her father's drunken promise to let her live her own life. But what was "her life"? The question brought pressure, and not just from parents and teachers and her assorted friends. Kala's own ignorance about her future was the worst of it. Such a bright creature—everyone said that about her. But when it came to her destiny, she didn't have so much as a clue.

As Kala walked through the oak woods, she noticed another person moving somewhere behind her. But she wasn't frightened until she paused, and an instant later, that second set of feet stopped too.

Kala turned, intending to glance over her shoulder.

Suddenly a cool black sack was dropped over her head, and an irresistible strength pushed her to the ground. Then a man's voice—a vaguely familiar voice—whispered into one of her covered ears. "Fight me," he said, "and I'll kill you. Make one sound, and I'll kill your parents too."

She was numb, empty and half-dead.

Her abductor tied her up and gagged her with a rope fitted over the black sack, and then he dragged her in a new direction, pausing at a service entrance in back of the metal dome. She heard fingers pushing buttons and hinges squeaking, and then the ground turned to steel as her long legs were dragged across the pioneers' floor.

Her numbness vanished, replaced with wild terror.

Blindly, Kala swung her bound legs and clipped his, and he responded with laughter, kneeling down to speak with a lover's whisper. "We can dance later, you and me. Tonight is Tina's turn. Sorry, sorry."

She was tied to a crate filled with sawdust, and by the smell of it, hundreds of fertile tortoise eggs.

When the service door closed, Kala tugged at the knots. How much time was left? How many hours did she have? Panic gave her a fabulous strength, but every jerk and twist only tightened the knots, and after a few minutes of work, she was exhausted, sobbing through the rope gag.

No was going to find her.

And when they were in the new world, Tina's husband—a big strong creature with connections and a good name—would pretend to discover Kala, cutting her loose and probably telling everyone else, "Look who wanted to come with us! My wife's little friend!" And before she could say two words, he would add, "I'll feed her from share of the stores. Yes, she's my responsibility now."

Kala gathered herself for another try at the ropes.

Then the service door opened with the same telltale squeak, and somebody began to walk slowly past her, down the aisle and back again, pausing beside her for a moment before placing a knife against her wrists, yanking hard and cutting the rope clear through.

Off came her gag, then the black sack.

Sandor was holding a small flashlight in his free hand, and he touched her softly on her face, on her neck. "You all right?"

She nodded.

"Good thing I bumped into that prick out there." Her brother was trying to look grateful, but his expression and voice were tense as could be. "I asked him, "Why aren't you with your bride?" But he didn't say anything. Which bothered me, you know." He paused, then added, "I've seen him stare at you, Kala."

"You have?"

"Haven't you?" Sandor took a deep breath, then another, gathering himself. "So I asked if he'd seen you come this way. And then he said, "Get away from me, little boy.'"

Sandor began cutting her legs free. In the glare of his light, she saw his favorite pocket knife—the big blade made sticky and red, covered as it was with an appalling amount of blood.

"Did you kill him?" Kala muttered.

In a grim whisper, Sandor said, "Hardly."

"What happened?"

"I saved you," he answered.

"But what did you do to that man?" she demanded.

"Man?" Sandor broke into a quietly, deathly laugh. "I don't know, Kala. You're the biologist in the family. But I don't think you could call him male anymore...if you see what I mean..."

6

In a personal ritual, Kala brought *The First Mother's Tale* out of hiding each spring and read it from cover to cover. She found pleasure in the book's adventures and heroisms, and the tragedies made her reliably sad, and even with whole tracts memorized, she always felt as if she was experiencing Claire's story for the first time. That strong, determined woman did everything possible to help her girls while making Owen behave. She made certain that every adult had a vote in every important decision—votes that were made after her console, naturally. Claire always spoke for the dead at funerals, and she oversaw a small feast commemorating the anniversary of their arrival. Hard famine came during their third winter. The local tortoises had been hunted to extinction while the earthly crops never prospered. It was Claire who imposed a ration system for the remaining food, and after six Wives were caught breaking into the last cache of canned goods, Claire served as judge in the bitter trial. Each girl claimed to have acted for the good of a hungry baby or babies. But there were dozens of children by then, and whose stomach wasn't growling? Twelve other girls—some Wives, some not—served as the jury. In a ritual ancient as the species, they listened to the evidence before stepping off by themselves, returning with a verdict that found each defendant guilty as charged.

The housemother had no choice but order a full banishment.

The original Tina was one of the criminals. After some rough talk and vacuous threats, she and the other five picked up their toddlers and started south, hoping to hike their way to fresh pastures and easy food.

There was no doubt that the Six Angry Wives existed. But no consistent tale of crimes was told about them, and no Testament mentioned Claire as the presiding judge. What was known was that six women wandered through the wilderness, and when they returned ten years later, they brought blue-hens and fresh tortoise eggs as well as their four surviving children—including one lovely brown-eyed boy, nearly grown and eager to meet his father.

The truth was, no important church recognized Claire's existence, which was the same as never existing. Even the oddest offshoot faiths denied her any vital role in their history. According to *The First Mother's Tale*, the housemother lived another seven years and died peacefully in her sleep. Owen borrowed one of his Wives' Bibles to read prayers over her grave. With the relief of someone who had escaped a long burden, he thanked the woman's soul for its good work and wise guidance. And then *The First Mother's Tale* concluded with a few hopeful words from its author, the brilliant and long-dead Kala.

Except of course nothing is ever finished, and considering everything that had happened since, most of the story had barely begun.

According to most researchers, it took a full century for the pioneers to find their stride. Owen lived to be eighty—a virile man to the end—and borrowing on his godly status, he continued sleeping with an assortment of willing, fertile granddaughters. Claire's grave was soon lost to time, or she never even existed. But Owen's burial site became the world's first monument. Limestone blocks were dragged from a quarry and piled high, and the structure was decorated with a lordly statue and praising words as well as the original, still useless ripper. Worshippers traveled for days and weeks just for a chance to kneel at the feet of the great man's likeness, and sometimes an old wound felt healed or some tireless despair would suddenly lift, proving again the powers of the First Father.

Four centuries later, enough bodies and minds were

wandering the world to allow a handful to become scientists.

Inside a thousand years, humanity had spread across
the warm, oxygen-impoverished globe, keeping to the
lowlands, erasing the native species that fit no role.
Cobbler-shops became factories, schools became universities, and slowly, the extraordinary skills necessary
to build new rippers came back into the world.

In 1003, a wealthy young man purchased advertise-
ment time on every television network. "The bigger the
ripper, the better the seed," he declared to the world.
And with that, he unveiled a giant Class-A ripper as
well as the spacious house that would carry him and a
thousand wives to a new world, plus enough frozen
sperm from quality men to ensure a diverse, vital
society.

He found no shortage of eager young woman.

What actually became of that colony and its people,
no one could say. To leave was to vanish in every sense
of the word. But thousands of rippers were built during
the following centuries. Millions of pioneers left that
first new world, praying for richer air and tastier foods.
And after six centuries of emigration, Kala's descendants gathered around a small class-B, read passages
from the Bible as well as from the Wives' Testaments,
and then together they managed their small, great step
into the unknown.

7

At nineteen, Kala applied with the Parks Committee,
and through luck and her own persistence, she was
posted to the same reserve she once visited as a young-

ster. She was given heavy boots and a wide-brimmed as well as an oversized brown uniform with a Novice tag pinned to her chest. Her first week of summer was spent giving tours to visitors curious about the native fauna and flora. But the assignment wasn't a rousing success, which was why she was soon transferred to exotic eradications—an improved posting, as it happened. Kala was free to drive the back roads in an official truck, parking at set points and walking deep into the alien forest. Hundreds of traps had to be checked every few days. Native animals were released, while the exotics were killed, usually with air-driven needles or a practiced blow to the head. At day's end, she would return to the main office and don plastic gloves, throwing the various carcasses into a cremation furnace—fat starlings and fatter house mice, mostly. If they died in the trap, the bodies would stink. But she quickly grew accustomed to the carnage. In her mind, she was doing important, frustrating work. Kala often pictured herself as a soldier standing on the front lines, alone, waging a noble struggle for which she expected almost nothing: A little money, the occasional encouragement, and of course, the chance to return to the wilderness every morning, enjoying its doomed and fading strangeness for another long day.

One July afternoon, while Kala worked at the incinerator, another novice appeared. They had been friendly in the past. But today, for no obvious reason, the young man seemed uncomfortable. As soon as he saw Kala, his face stiffened and his gait slowed, and then, perhaps reading her puzzlement, he suddenly sped up again. "Hello," he offered with the softest possible voice.

Kala smiled while flinging a dead cat into the fire. "Did you hear?" she began. "They found a new herd of Harry's-big-days. Above Saint Mary's Glacier."

The young man hesitated for an instant. Then with a rushed voice, he sputtered, "I've got an errand. Bye now."

Long ago, Kala learned that she wasn't as sensitive to emotions as most people. Noticing something was wrong now meant there was a fair chance that it really was. Why was that boy nervous? Was she in trouble again? And if so, what had she screwed up this time?

When Kala was giving tours, there was an unfortunate incident. A big blowhard from the Grandfather Cult joined the other tourists. His personal mission was to commandeer her lecture. One moment, she was describing the false spruces and explaining how the tom-toms depended wholly on them. And suddenly the blowhard interrupted. With an idiot's voice, he announced that the native trees were useless as well as ugly, and all the local animals were stupid as the rocks, and their world's work wouldn't be finished until every miserable corner like this was turned into oak trees and concrete.

Kala's job demanded a certain reserve. Lecturers were not to share their opinions, unless those opinions coincided with official park policy. Usually she managed to keep her feelings in check. She endured three loud interruptions. But then the prick mentioned his fifteen sons and twelve lovely daughters, boasting that each child would end up on a different new world. Kala couldn't hold back. She was half his age and half his size, but she stepped up to him and pushed a finger into his belly, saying, "If I was your child, I'd want to leave this world too."

Most of the audience smiled, and quite a few laughed.

435 of the Year

But the blowhard turned and marched to the front office, and by day's end, Kala was given a new job killing wildcats and other vermin.

The last carcasses were burning when her superior emerged from the station. He was an older fellow—a life-long civil servant who probably dreamed of peace and quiet until his retirement, and then a peaceful death. Approaching his temperamental novice, the man put on a painful smile, twice saying her name before adding, "I need to talk to you," with a cautious tone.

A headless starling lay on the dirt. With a boot, Kala kicked it into the incinerator and again shut the heavy iron door. Then with a brazen tone, she said, "Listen to my side first."

The man stopped short.

"I mean it," she continued. "I don't know what you've heard. I don't even know what I could have done wrong. But I had very good reasons—"

"Kala."

"And you should hear my explanation first."

The poor old gentleman dipped his head, shaking it sadly, telling her, "Kala, sweetness. I'm sorry. All I want to say...to tell you...is that your brother called this morning. Right after you drove off." He paused long enough to breathe, and then informed her, "Your father died last night, and I'm very, very sorry."

Thrifty and impractical: Father was the same in death as in life.

That was an uncharitable assessment, but it happened to be true. Father left behind a long list of wishes, and Mother did everything he wanted, including the simple juniper box and no official funeral procession. The tombstone was equally minimal, and because cemeteries were expensive, he had mandated a private plot he had purchased as soon as he fell sick—a secret illness kept from everyone, including his wife of thirty-one years. But the burial site had drawbacks, including the absence of any road passing within a couple hundred yards. Kala's parents hadn't been active in any church for years, which meant it was their scattered family that was responsible for every arrangement, including digging the grave to a legal depth, finding pallbearers to help carry the graceless casket, and then after the painful service, filling in the hole once again.

"It's a lovely piece of ground," Sandor mentioned, and not for the first time. Then he dropped a load of the dry gray earth, watching it scatter across a lid of tightly fitted red planks, big clods thumping while the tiny clods scattered, rolling and shattering down to dust, making the skittering sound of busy mice.

"It is pretty," Mother echoed, sitting on one of forty folding chairs.

Everyone else had left. Barely three dozen relatives and friends had attended the service, and probably only half of them had genuinely known the deceased. If Father died ten years ago, Kala realized, two hundred people would have been sitting and standing along this low ridge, and the church would have sent at least two ministers—one to read Scripture, while the other sat with the grieving family, giving practiced comfort. But the comfort-givers abandoned them soon after that terrible wedding night. For maiming one of the grooms, Sandor had been shunned. And once Kala and her parents didn't follow suit, the congregation used more subtle, despicable means to toss them away.

For months, Kala continued meeting old friends in secret. A little too urgently, they would tell her that nothing was her fault. But then they started asking how Kala could live with a person who had done such an awful thing. After all, Sandor had neutered one of the leading citizens of their congregation—an act of pure violence, too large and far too wicked not to be brought to the attention of the police. It didn't matter that he was protecting his only sister, which was normally a good noble principle. And it didn't matter that decent men always defended their women, or that if a girl was abducted when she's fourteen, some family member was required to send a message to those horny fools lurking out there: Hurt her, and I'll take your future generations from you!

None of that meant anything to her friends. And once Kala admitted that she felt thankful for her brother's actions, those same friends stopped inventing tricks to meet her on the sly.

Of course her brother wasn't the only person needing blame. Parents were always culpable for the sins of their children, it was said. Didn't Sandor's father and mother give him their genes and some portion of their dreams? He was technically still a child when the crime occurred, still possessed by them, and supposedly answering first to God and then to them. Wasn't that how it was supposed to be?

The kidnapping was an unfortunate business, said some. The new husband shouldn't have done what he did, and particularly with one of their own. But even in a faith that cherished monogamy, his actions were understandable. Twenty thousand years of history had built this very common outlook. One deacon—a younger man devoid of charm or common sense—visited their house after Sunday service. Sitting in the meeting room with Kala's father, the deacon asked,

"Where lies the difference? A young man takes two brides to a fresh world, while another lives with his first wife for twenty years, then holds a painless divorce and starts a new family with a younger woman?"

"There's an enormous difference," Father had responded, his voice rising, betraying anger Kala had rarely heard before. She was sitting in her bedroom upstairs, listening while her other great defender said, "My daughter is a young girl, first of all. And second, she had no choice in this matter. None. She was tied up like a blue-hen and abused like cargo, thrown into a situation where she would never see her family or world again. Is that fair? Or just? Or at all decent? No, and no, and no again."

"But to cut the groom like he was cut—"

"A little cut, from what I've heard."

Which was the greater surprise: Father interrupting, or insulting the penis of another man?

The deacon groaned and then said, "That vicious animal...your darling Sandor...he deserves to sit in jail for a few years."

"Let the courts decide," Father replied.

"And you realize, of course." Their guest hesitated a moment before completing his thought. "You understand that no worthy group of pioneers will let him into their ranks. Not now. Not with his taste for violence, they won't."

"I suppose not."

"Which is a shame, since your son always wanted to be a Father."

Kala heard silence, and when she imagined her father's face, she saw a look of utter shame.

Then the stupid deacon had to share one last opinion. With a black voice, he announced, "I came here for a reason, sir. I think you should appreciate what other people are saying."

"What others?"

"Women as well as the men."

"Tell me," Father demanded.

"The girl looks older than fourteen. Her body is grown, and that voice of hers could be a woman's. Any healthy man would be interested. But there's a problem in the words that Kala's uses...and that smart, sharp tone of hers..."

"What are you telling me?"

"Many of us...your very best friends...we believe that somebody should knock your daughter down a notch or two. And give her some babies to play with, too."

Father's chair squeaked—a hard defiant sound.

"Go," Kala heard him say. "Get out of my house."

"Gladly," the deacon replied. "But just so you know my sense of things, realize this: Your daughter had an opportunity that night. It might not seem fair or just to us. But if she and that brother of hers had a wit between them, she'd be living today on a better world. But as things stand, I can't imagine any reputable group will accept trouble like her. Her best bet for the future is a sloppy abduction by a single male who simply doesn't know who she is."

There was a pause—a gathering of breath and fury. Then for the only time in her life, Kala heard her father saying, "Fuck you."

That moment, and the entire nightmare...all of it returned to her at the gravesite. The intervening years suddenly vanished, and her lanky body was left shaking from nerves and misery. Sandor and their mother both noticed. They watched her fling gouts of earth into the hole, and misunderstanding everything, Mom warned, "This isn't a race, sweetness."

Kala felt as if she had been caught doing something awful. She couldn't name her crime, but shame took hold. Down went the shovel, and she knelt over the partly filled grave, staring at the last two visible corners of her father's casket.

Sandor settled beside her.

With what felt like a single breath, Kala confessed the heart of her thoughts: A single night had torn apart their lives, and despite believing she was blameless, she felt guilty. Somehow all the evil and poor luck that had followed them since was her fault. Because of her, they had lost their church and friends. Father died young, and now their mother would always be a widow. And meanwhile, her brother was a convicted criminal, stripped from what he had wanted most in life—the opportunity to become a respectable Father to some great new world.

After a difficult pause, Mom broke in. "I wouldn't have liked that at all," she maintained, "losing you without the chance to say, "Good-bye.'"

Kala had hoped for more.

"You're being silly, sweet," would have been nice. "You aren't to blame for any of this at all," would have been perfect.

Instead, the old woman remarked, "These last years have been hard. Yes. But don't blame yourself for your father's health."

Sandor drove his shovel into the earth pile behind Kala. Then with a weighty sigh, he said, "And don't worry about me. I'm doing fine."

Hardly. Because of his stay in prison, her brother had missed his last years at school. The boy he had been was gone, replaced by a hard young man with self-made tattoos and muscles enough for two athletes.

Kala disagreed.

"You're wrong," she said with a shake of her head.

Then Sandor laughed at her, kicking a clod or two into the hole and staring down at their father, quietly reminding everyone, "'Respectable' is just a word." His face was tight, his eyes were enormous, and his voice was dry and slow when he added, "And there's more than one route to reach another world."

8

Kala's world was settled by a confederation of small and medium-sized churches. Two million parishioners had pooled their resources, acquiring a powerful class-A ripper—a bruising monster capable of stealing away several city blocks. Each congregation selected their best pioneers, and the Last Father was elected to his lofty post, responsible for the well being of more than a thousand brave souls, plus three stowaways and at least fifteen young women kidnapped on the eve of departure. A farm field on the Asian continent was selected, in a region once known as Hunan. Where wheat and leadfruit normally grew, a huge, multi-story dome was erected. Every pioneer wore plugged his ears with foam and wax. The giant ripper shook the entire structure as it searched across Creation; and with a final surge, machine and humans were dragged along the hidden dimensions, covering the miniscule distance.

Rippers had no upper limit to their power, but there were practical considerations. Entering another world meant displacing the native air and land. With its arrival, that class-A ripper shoved aside thousands of tons of dirt and rock, erecting a ring-shaped hill of debris instantly heated by the impact. Wood and peat caught fire, and deep underground, the bedrock was compressed until it was hot enough to melt. The Last Father ordered everyone to remain indoors for the day, breathing bottled air and watching the fires spread and die under an evening thunderstorm. Then the survey teams were dispatched, racing over the blackened ground, finding pastures of black sedge-like grass where they caught the native mice and pseudoinsects as well as a loose-limbed creature with a glancing resemblance to the lost monkeys in the oldest textbooks.

Experience promised this: If intelligence evolved on a new world, chances are it would live in Asia. Competition was stiffest on large landmasses. That's how it had been on the original earth. Australia was once home to opossums and kangaroos, and dimension-crossing pioneers might have been tempted to linger there, unaware that lying over the horizon were continents full of smart, aggressive placental creatures, including one fierce medium-sized ape with some exceptionally mighty plans.

But the vermin brought home by the survey teams had simple smooth brains, while the monkey-creature proved to be an intellectual midget next to any respectable cat. The Last Father met with his advisors and then with his loving wife, and following a suitable period of contemplation and prayer, he announced that this was where God wished them to remain for the rest of their days.

The new colony expanded swiftly, in numbers and reach.

The Last Father died with honor, six of his nine children carrying his body into a granite cathedral built at the site of their arrival.

By then villages and little cities were scattered across a thousand miles of wilderness. Within ten generations, coal-fired ships were mapping coastlines on every side of the Mother Ocean, while little parties were moving inland, skirting the edges of the Tibetan Plateau on their way to places once called Persia and Turkey, Lebanon and France.

The original churches grew and split apart, or they shriveled and died.

And always, new faiths were emerging, often born from a single believer's ideals and his very public fantasies.

The original class-A ripper served as an altar inside the Last Father's cathedral. A cadre of engineers maintained its workings, while a thousand elite soldiers stood guard over the holy ground. The symbols were blatant and unflinching: First and always, this world would serve as a launching point to countless new realms. Human duty was to build more rippers—a promise finally fulfilled several centuries ago. By Kala's time, the thousand original pioneers had become five billion citizens. Tax codes and social conventions assured that rippers would always be built. Experts guessed that perhaps fifteen billion bodies could live on these warm lands, and with luck and God's blessing, that would be the day when enough rippers were rolling out of enough factories to allow every excess child to escape, every boy free to find his own empty, golden realm, and every girl serving as a good man's happy Wife.

9

Sandor hated that his sister traveled alone. Every trip Kala took was preceded by a difficult conversation, on phone or in person. It was his duty to remind her that the open highway was an exceptionally dangerous place. Sandor always had some tale to share about some unfortunate young woman who did everything right—drove only by day, spoke to the fewest possible strangers, and slept in secure hotels that catered to their kind. Yet without exception, each of those smart ladies had vanished somewhere on the road, usually without explanation.

"But look at the actual numbers," Kala liked to counter. "The chance of me being abducted twice in my life—"

"Is tiny. I know."

"Dying in a traffic accident is ten times more likely," she would add.

But eventually Sandor analyzed the same statistics, ambushing her with a much bleaker picture. "Dying in a wreck is three times as likely," he informed Kala. "But that's for all women. Old and young. Those in your subset—women in their twenties, with good looks and driving alone—are five times as likely to disappear as they are to die in a simple, run-of-the-mill accident."

"But I have to travel," she countered. Her doctorate involved studying the native communities scattered across a dozen far flung mountaintops. Driving was mandatory, and since there was barely enough funding as it was, she had no extra money to hire reliable security guards. "I know you don't appreciate my work—"

"I never said that, Kala."

"Because you're such a painfully polite fellow." Then laughing at her own joke, she reminded him, "I always carry a registered weapon."

"Good."

"And a gun that isn't registered."

"As you damn well should," Sandor insisted.

"Plus there's a thousand little things I do, or two million things I avoid." She always had one or two new tricks to offer, just to prove that she was outracing her unseen enemies. "And if you have any other suggestions, please...share them with your helpless little sister..."

"Don't tease," he warned. "You don't understand what men want from women. If you did, you'd never leave home."

Kala had a tidy little apartment on a women's floor, set ten stories above the street—far too high to be stolen away with even the biggest ripper. On this occasion, Sandor happened to be passing through, supposedly chasing a mechanic's job but not acting in any great hurry to leave. His main mission, as far as she could tell, was to terrify his little sister. As always, he came armed with news clippings and Web sites. He wanted her to appreciate the fact that her mountains were full of horny males, each one more dangerous than the others, and all the bastards fighting for their chance to start some new world. As it happened, last week a large shipment of class-C rippers had just been hijacked from an armed convoy, and now the Children of Forever were proclaiming a time of plenty. And just yesterday, outside New Eternal, some idiot drove a big freight truck through two sets of iron gates before pulling up beside the classroom wing of a ladies' academy. Moments later, a large class-B ripper fired off, leaving behind a hemispherical hole and a mangled building, as well as a thousand scared teenage girls, saved only because they had been called into the auditorium for a hygiene lecture from the school's doctor.

Kala shrugged at the bad news. "Crap is a universal constant. Nothing has changed, and I'm going to be fine."

But really, she never felt good about driving long distances, and the recent news wasn't comforting. Nearly a hundred stolen rippers were somewhere on the continent, which had to shift the odds that trouble would find her. Kala let herself feel the fear, and then with a burst of nervous creativity, she blurted out a possible solution.

"Come with me," she said.

Sandor was momentarily stunned.

"If you're that especially worried about me, ride along and help me with my work. Unless you really do have some plush mechanic's job waiting."

"All right then," he answered. "I'd like that."

"A long family vacation," she said with a grin.

And he completed her thought, adding, "Just like we used to do."

More than ten years had passed since they last spent time together, and the summer-long journey gave them endless chances to catch up. But for all the days spent on the road, not to mention the weeks hiking and working on alpine trails, they shared remarkably little. Kala heard nothing about life in prison and very little about how Sandor had made his living since his release. And by the same token, she never felt the need to mention past boys and future men—romantic details that she always shared with her closest friends. For a time, the silences bothered her. But then she decided siblings always had difficulty with intimacy. Sharing genetics and a family was such a deep, profound business that no one felt obliged to prove their closeness by ordinary routes. Sandor revealed himself only in glimpses—a few words or a simple gesture—while in her own fashion, Kala must have seemed just as close-mouthed. But of course these secrets of theirs didn't matter. This man would always be her brother, and that was far larger than any other relationship they might cobble together while driving across the spine of a continent.

Sandor relished his job as protector. At every stop, he was alert and a little aggressive, every stranger's face deserving a quick study, and some of them requiring a hard warning stare. She appreciated the sense of menace that seemed to rise out of him at will. In ways she hadn't anticipated, Kala enjoyed watching Sandor step up to a counter, making innocent clerks flinch. His tattoos flexed and his face grew hard as stone, and she liked the rough snarl in his voice when he said, "Thank you." Or when he snapped at some unknown fellow, "Out of our way. Please. Sir."

If anything, empty wilderness was worse than the open road. It made him more suspicious, if not out-and-out paranoid.

Kala's work involved an obscure genus of pseudoinsects. She was trying to find and catalog unknown species before they vanished, collecting data about their habitat and specimens that she froze and dried and stuck into long test tubes. One July evening, on the flank of a giant southern volcano, she heard a peculiar sound from behind a grove of spruce trees. A rough hooting, it sounded like. "I wonder what that was," she mentioned. Sandor instantly slipped away from the fire, walking the perimeter at least twice before returning again, one hand holding a long flashlight and the other carrying an even longer pistol equipped with a nightscope. "So what was it?" she asked.

"Boys," he reported. "They were thinking of camping near us."

"They were?"

"Yeah," he said, sitting next to the fire again. "But I guess for some reason they decided to pull up their tent and move off. Who knows why?"

Moments like that truly pleased Kala.

But following her pleasure was a squeamish distaste. What kind of person was she? She thought of herself as being independent and self-reliant, but on the other hand, she seemed to relish being watched over by a powerful and necessarily dangerous man.

Two days later, driving north, Sandor mentioned that he had never gotten his chance to visit the Grand Canyon. "Our vacation never made it," he reminded her. "And I haven't found the time since."

Kala let them invest one full day of sightseeing.

The canyon's precise location and appearance varied on each world. But there was always a river draining that portion of the continent, and the land had always risen up in response to the predictable tectonics. Since their earth was wetter than most, the river was big and angry, cutting through a billion years of history on its way to the canyon floor. Kala paid for a cable-car ride to the bottom. They ate hard-boiled blue-hen eggs and mulberries for lunch, and afterwards, walking on the rocky shoreline, she pointed to the rotting carcass of a

Helen-trout. The First Father didn't bring living fish with him, but later Fathers realized that fish farming meant cheap protein. The Helen-trout came from the fifth new world—indiscriminate feeders that could thrive in open ocean or fresh water, and that adored every temperature from freezing to bathwater. No major drainage in the world lacked the vermin. "They die when they're pregnant," she explained. "Their larvae use the mother as food, eating her as she rots, getting a jump on things before they swim away."

Sandor seemed to be listening. But then again, he always seemed to pay attention to his surroundings. In this case, he gave a little nod, and after a long pause said, "I'm curious, Kala. What do you want to accomplish? With your work, I mean."

He asked that question every few days, as if for the first time.

At first Kala thought that he simply wasn't hearing her answers. Later, she wondered if he was trying to break her down, hoping to make her admit that she didn't have any good reason for her life's investment. But after weeks of enduring this verbal dance, she began to appreciate what was happening. To keep from boring herself, she was forced to change her response. Inside the canyon, staring at the dead fish, she didn't bother with old words about the duty and honor that came from saving a few nameless bugs. And she avoided the subject of great medicines that probably would never emerge from her work. Instead, staring down at the rich bulging body, she offered a new response.

"This world of ours is dying, Sandor."

The statement earned a hard look and an impossible-to-read grin. "Why's that?" he asked over the roar of the water.

"A healthy earth has ten or twenty or fifty million species. Depending on how you count them." She shook her head, reminding him, "The Last Father brought as many species as possible. Nearly a thousand multicellular species have survived here. And that's too few to make an enduring, robust ecosystem."

Sandor shrugged and gestured at the distant sky. "Things look good enough," he said. "What do you mean that it's dying?"

"Computer models point to the possibility," she explained. "Low diversity means fragile ecosystems. And it's more than just having too few species. It's the nature of these species. Wherever we go, we bring weed species. Biological thugs, essentially. And not just from the original earth but from seventeen distinct evolutionary histories. Seventeen lines that are nearly alien to one another. That reduces meaningful interactions. It's another factor why there will eventually come a crunch."

"Okay. So when?"

She shrugged her shoulders.

"Next year?"

"Not for thousands of years," she allowed. "But there is a collapse point, and after that, the basic foundations of this biosphere will decline rapidly. Phytoplankton, for one. The native species are having troubles enduring the new food chains, and if they end up vanishing, then nobody will be making free oxygen."

"Trees don't make oxygen?"

"They do," she admitted. "But their wood burns or rots. And rotting is the same reaction as burning, chemically speaking."

Sandor stared at the gray mother fish.

"You know how it is when you turn on a ripper?" Kala asked. "You know how the machine has to search hard for a world with a livable atmosphere?"

Her brother nodded, a look of anticipation building in the pale brown eyes.

"Do you ever wonder why so many earths don't have decent air for us? Do you?" Kala gave him a rough pat on the shoulder, asking, "What if a lot of pioneers have been moving across the multiverse? Humans and things that aren't human too. And what if most of these intrepid pioneers eventually kick their worlds out of equilibrium, killing them as a consequence?"

"Yeah," he said.

Then after a long thoughtful moment: "Huh."

And that was the last time Sandor ever bothered to doubt the importance of Kala's work.

10

The heart of every ripper was a cap-shaped receptacle woven from diamond whiskers, each whisker doctored with certain rare-earth elements and infused with enough power to pierce the local brane. But as difficult as the receptacle was to build, it was a simple chore next to engineering the machines to support and control its work. Hard drives and the capacitors had to function on the brink of theoretical limits. Heat and quantum fluctuations needed to be kept at a minimum. The best rippers utilized a cocktail of unusual isotopes, doubling their reliability as well tripling the costs, while security costs added another forty percent to the final price.

Twice that summer, Kala and her brother saw convoys of finished rippers being shipped across country. Armored trucks were painted a lush emerald green, each one accompanied by two or three faster vehicles bristling with weapons held by tough young men. Routes and schedules were supposed to be kept secret. Since even a small ripper was worth a fortune, the corporations did whatever they could to protect their investments. Which made Kala wonder: How the Children of Forever learn where one convoy would be passing, and what kind of firepower would it take to make the rippers their own?

Sandor was driving when they ran into one of the convoys. A swift little blister of armor and angry faces suddenly passed them on the wrong side. "Over," screamed every face. "Pull over."

They were beside the Mormon Sea, on a highway famous for scenery and its narrow, almost nonexistent shoulders. But Sandor complied, fitting them onto a slip of asphalt and turning off the engine, then setting the parking brake and turning to look back around the bend, eyes huge and his lower lip tucked into his chewing mouth.

For a moment or two, Kala watched the bright water of the inland sea, enjoying the glitter stretching to the horizon. Then came the rumble of big engines, and a pair of heavy freight trucks rolled past, followed by more deadly cars, and then another pair of trucks.

"Class-Cs," Sandor decided. "About a hundred of them, built down in Highborn."

The trucks had no obvious markings. "How can you tell?"

"The lack of security," he said. "Cs don't get as much. It's the As and Bs that bandits can sell for a fortune. And I know the company because each truck's got a code on its side, if you know how to read it."

The convoy had passed out of sight, but they remained parked beside the narrow road. "When are we moving again?" she asked.

"Wait," he cautioned.

She shifted in her seat and took a couple meaningful breaths.

Reading the signs, Sandor turned to her. "You don't want to trail them too closely. Someone might get the wrong idea. Know what I mean?"

And with that, her brave, almost fearless brother continued to sit beside the road, hands squeezing the wheel.

"You gave somebody the wrong idea," she said.

"Pardon?"

"Sandor," she said. "In your life, how many convoys have you followed?"

Nothing changed about his face. Then suddenly, a little smile turned up the corner of his mouth, and with a quiet, conspiratorial voice, he admitted, "Fifty, maybe sixty."

She wasn't surprised, except that she didn't expect to feel so upset. "Is that how badly you want it? To be a Father...you're willing to steal a ripper just to get your chance...?"

He started to nod. Then again, he looked at his sister, reminding her, "I'm still here. So I guess I'm not really that eager."

"What went wrong? The work was too dangerous for you?"

His expression looked injured now. Straightening his back, he started the car and pulled out, accelerating for a long minute, letting the silence work on Kala until he finally told her, "You know, there were thirty-two security men on that other convoy. The one hit by the Children of Forever. Plus a dozen drivers and three corporate representatives. And all were killed during the robbery."

"I know that—"

"Most of those poor shits were laid down in a ditch by the road and shot through the head. Just so motorists wouldn't notice the bodies when they drove past." He squeezed the steering wheel until it squeaked, and very carefully, he told Kala, "That's when I gave up wanting it. Being a Father to the very best world isn't enough reason to murder even one poor boy who's trying to make some money and keep his family fed."

A pair of mountain ranges stood as islands far out in the Mormon Sea, and they spent on few days walking the tallest peaks. Then they drove north again, up to the Geysers, enjoying a long hike through the mountains north of that volcanic country. Then it was late August, and they started back toward Kala's home. One stop remained, kept until now for sentimental reasons.

"Our best vacation," she muttered.

Sandor agreed with his silence and a little wink.

They stayed in a reserve campground meant for employees, and Kala introduced her brother to the few rangers that remained from her days here. The mood was upbeat, on the whole. Old colleagues expressed interest in her studies, asking knowledgeable questions, and some cases, offering advice.

One older gentleman—a fellow who had never warmed much to her before—nodded as he listened to her description of her work. Then he said, "Kala," with a sweet, almost fatherly voice. "I know a place with just that kind of bug. I can't tell you the species, by I don't think it's quite what you've found before."

"Really? Where?"

He brought out a map and pointed at a long valley on the other side of the continental divide. "It looks too low in altitude, I suppose. And a lot of junipers are moving in. But if you get up by this looping road here—"

Sandor pushed in close to watch.

"There's a little glen. I've seen that blue bug there, I'm sure."

"Thank you," Kala told him.

"Whatever I can do to help," the old ranger said. Then he made a show of rolling up the map, asking, "I can take you up myself. If your brother wants to stay here and rest for a bit."

Sandor said, "No thanks."

But he said it in an especially nice way. For the time being, neither one of them could see what was happening.

11

As promised, juniper trees were standing among the natives. Rilly birds and starlings must have eaten juniper berries outside the reserve. Since their corrosive stomach acids were essential for the germination process, wherever they relieved themselves, a new forest of ugly gray-green trees sprouted, prickly and relentless. Most biologists claimed that it was an innate, mutualistic relationship between species. But Kala had a different interpretation: The birds knew precisely what they were doing. Whenever a starling took a dump, it sang to the world, "I'm planting a forest here. And I'm going to be the death of you, you silly old trees."

Sandor squatted and stuck his thick fingers into the needle litter, churning up a long pink worm. After a summer spent watching Kala, he was now one the great experts when it came to a single genus of pseudoinsects. "Not all that promising," he announced.

Earthworms were another key invader from their home world. And no, nightcrawlers didn't usually coexist with her particular creepy-crawlies.

"Maybe higher up," he offered.

But the old ranger told her this was the place, which implied that her subjects were enduring despite worms and trees: A heroic image that Kala wanted to cling to for a little while longer.

"You wander," she said. "If I don't find anything, I'll follow."

Sandor winked and stepped back into the black shadows.

Twenty minutes later, Kala gave up the hunt. Stepped into a little clearing, she sat on a rock bench, pulling a sandwich from her knapsack and managing a bite before a stranger stepped off the trail behind her.

"Excuse me?"

Startled, Kala wheeled fast, her free hand reaching for the pistol on her belt. But the voice was a girl's, and she was a very tiny creature—big-eyed and fragile, maybe ten years younger than Kala. The girl looked tired and worried. Her shirt was torn, and her left arm wore a long scrape that looked miserably sore.

"Can you help me, ma'am? Please?"

Carefully, Kala rose to her feet while pushing the sandwich back inside her bag, using that same motion to make certain that her second pistol was where she expected it to be. Then with a careful voice, she asked, "Are you lost, sweetie?"

"That too," the girl said, glancing over her shoulder before stepping away from the forest's edge. "It's been days since I've been outside. At least."

Kala absorbed the news. Then she quietly asked, "Where have you been?"

"In the back end."

"The end of what?"

"The bus," the girl snapped, as if Kala should already know that much. "He put me with the others, in the dark—"

"Other girls?"

"Yes, yes." The little creature drifted forward, tucking both hands into her armpits. "He's a mean one—"

"What sect?"

"Huh?"

"Does he belong to a sect?"

"The Children of Forever," the strange girl confessed. "Do you know about them?"

With her right hand, Kala pulled the pistol from her belt while keeping the bag on her left shoulder. Nothing moved in the trees. Except for the girl and her, there might be no one else in this world.

"He's collecting wives," the girl related. "He told me he wants ten of us before he leaves."

"Come closer," Kala told her. Then she asked, "How many girls does he have so far?"

The girl swallowed. "Three."

"And there's just him?"

"Yeah. He's alone." The girl's eyes were growing larger, unblinking and bright. "Three other girls, and me. And him."

"Where?"

"Down that way," said the girl. "Past the parking lot, hiding up in some big old grease trees."

Kala's car lay in the same direction. But Sandor had gone the opposite direction.

Whispering, she told the stranger, "Okay. I can help you."

"Thank you, ma'am!"

"Quiet."

"Sorry," the girl muttered.

"Now," Kala told her. "This way."

The girl fell in beside her, rubbing her bloodied arm as she walked. She breathed hard and fast. Several more times, she said, "Thank you." But she didn't seem to look back half as often as Kala did, and maybe that was what seemed wrong.

After a few minutes of hard walking, Kala asked, "So how did you get free?"

The girl looked back then. And with a nod, she said, "I crawled up through the vent."

A tiny creature like that: Kala could believe it.

"I cut my arm on a metal edge."

The wound was red, but the blood had clotted some time ago. Even as Kala nodded, accepting that story, a little part of her was feeling skeptical.

"If he finds me, he'll hurt me."

"I won't let him hurt you," Kala promised.

"There's three other girls in the bus," she repeated. Then she put her hands back into her armpits, hugging herself hard, saying, "We should save them, if we can. Sneak up to the bus while he's hunting for me and get them free, maybe."

But Kala wanted to find Sandor. She came close to mentioning him to the girl, but then she thought better of it. Her brother's presence was a secret that made her feel better. It gave her the confidence to tell the girl, "Later. First I have to make sure that you're safe."

The girl stared up at her protector, saying nothing.

"Come on," Kala urged.

"I want to be safe," the girl said.

"That's what I'm doing—"

"No," she said. Then her hands came out from under her arms, one of them empty while the other held a little box with two metal forks sticking from one end, and the forks jumped out and dove into her skin, and suddenly a hot blue bolt of lightning was rolling through her body.

The girl disarmed Kala and stole her bag and tied her up with plastic straps pulled from her back pocket. Then she vanished down the path. The pain subsided enough to where Kala could sit up, watching uphill, imagining her brother's arrival. But this wasn't the path he had taken, and he still hadn't shown by the time the girl and New Father appeared. A stubby automatic weapon hung on his shoulder. He was forty or forty-five years old, a big strong and homely creature with rough hands and foul breath. "She is awfully pretty," was his first assessment, smiling at his latest acquisition. Then he offered a wink, adding, "He promised I'd like you. And he was right."

The old ranger had set this up.

"I didn't see any brother," said the tiny girl.

"That would be too easy," the man cautioned. Then he handed his weapon to the girl and grabbed Kala, flinging her over a shoulder while saying, "I don't think he'll be any problem. But come on anyway, sweet. Fast as we can walk."

They entered the open glade, crossing the parking lot and passing Kala's tiny car before they climbed again, entering a mature stand of native trees. Hiding in the gloom was a long bus flanked by a pair of fat freight trucks, each vehicle equipped with wide tires and extra suspension. And there were many more brides than three, Kala saw. Twelve was her first count, fourteen when she tried again. Each girl was in her teens. They looked like schoolgirls on a field trip, giggling and teasing the newest wife by saying, "Too old to walk for herself," and, "Fresh blood in the gene pool, looks like."

Three young men silently watched Kala's arrival. Sons, by the looks of them. In their early twenties, at most.

"Beautiful," said one of the boys.

The other two nodded and grinned.

With the care shown to treasured luggage, the older man set Kala beneath a tree, her back propped against the black trunk, arms and legs needing to be retied, just to make sure. Kala quickly looked from face to face, hoping for any sign of empathy. There was none. And the girl who had been sent out as bait stood over Kala for several minutes, wearing the hardest expression of all.

"He will come for me," Kala said.

"Your brother probably will," said the New Father. "But I've been watching you two. He's carrying nothing bigger than that long pistol, and we've got artillery here he wouldn't dare face."

As if to prove their murderous natures, the sons retrieved their own automatic weapons from the bus.

"What next?" one son asked.

"Stay here with me," their father advised.

But the oldest son didn't like that tactic. "We could circle around, pick him off when shows himself."

"No," he was told.

"But—"

"What did I say?"

The young man dropped his face.

"God led us to this place," the wiser man continued. "And God has seen to give us a sticky hot day. Pray for storms. That's my advice. Then we can punch a hole in the clouds and get power enough to finally leave…"

Lightning, he was talking about. Kala had heard about this technique: With a proper rocket and enough wire following like a tail, it was possible to create lightning during a thunderstorm. A channel of air supplied the connection to the charged earth below. The bolt would strike a preset lightning rod…up in the tree on the other side of camp, she realized. She noticed the tall black spike and the heavy wires leading down into the ripper that was probably set in the center of the bus, a class-C that was hungry and waiting for its first and only meal.

Kala could guess why these people had come into the mountains. They liked solitude and cheap energy, and besides, the police were hunting everywhere else for those who had murdered the security guards.

Sandor was somewhere close, Kala told herself.

Watching her.

She almost relaxed, imagining her brother hunkered low in the shadow of some great old tree, waiting for a critical mistake to be made. Hunting for an opening, a weakness. Any opportunity. She went as far as picturing his arrival: Sandor would wait for afternoon and the gathering storms, and maybe the rain would start to fall, fat drops turning into a deluge, and while the devout boys and girls watched for the Lord in that angry sky, her brother would sneak up behind her and neatly cut her free.

Obviously, that's what would happen.

Kala thought so highly of the plan that she was as surprised as anyone when a figure emerged from the shadows—a man smaller than most were, running on bare feet to keep his noise to a minimum. He was quick, but something in his stride seemed unhurried. Untroubled. He looked something like a hiker who had lost his way but now had found help. Perhaps that was what Sandor intended. But his face was grim and focused, and no motion was wasted. Everybody—grooms and brides and even their captive—stared for a moment, examining the stranger in their midst. Then the newcomer reached beneath his shirt and lifted a long pistol, and the first hollow point removed the top of the father's head and the second one knocked the small girl flat. Then Sandor was running again, slipping between brides, and one of the sons finally lifted his weapon, spraying automatic gunfire until three girls had dropped and another brother had pushed the barrel into the forest floor, screaming, "Stop, would you...just stop...!"

Sandor had the third brother by the neck, slamming him against the broad black trunk of a tree. Then he stared out at the cowering survivors, pressing the barrel of the pistol into the man's ass, and with a voice eerily composed, he said, "Put your guns down. Do it now. Or I'm going to do some painting over here...with a god-damn pubic hair brush..."

12

The matronly gray robes of middle age had vanished, replaced by an old woman's love for gaudy colors. She was wearing a rich slick and very purple dress with a purple hat with a wide gold belt and matching shoes. Diet and exercise had removed enough weight to give her a stocky, solid figure. She nicely filled the station of her life—that of the fit, well-rested widow. Seeing her children standing at her doorway, Mom smiled—a thoroughly genuine expression, happy but brief. Then she found something alarming in their faces. "What's happened?" With concern, she said, "Darlings. What's wrong?"

Kala glanced at her brother and then over her shoulder.

In the street sat a plain commercial van. Nothing about the vehicle was remarkable, except that its back end was being pressed down by the terrific, relentless weight of a class-C ripper and a powerful little winch.

The van was their fourth vehicle in three days, and Sandor would replace it tomorrow, if he thought it would help.

"I was just leaving," their mother offered. And when no one else spoke, she added, "I don't normally dress like this—"

"Don't go," said her son.

"Are you meeting friends?" Kala asked. "If you don't show, will somebody miss you?"

Mom shook her head. "I just go the tea parlor on Fridays. I know people, but no, I doubt if anybody expects me."

It was the Sabbath today, wasn't it?

"Can I park the van inside your garage?" Sandor asked.

Mom nodded. "You'll have to pull my car out—"

"Keys," he said.

She fished them from a purse covered with mock jewelry, and Sandor started down the front stairs.

Kala gratefully stepped inside. All these years, and the same furnishings and carpet populated the living room, although every surface was a little more worn now. Immersed in what was astonishingly familiar, she suddenly relaxed. She couldn't help herself. All at once it was impossible to stand under her own power, and as soon as she sat, a deep need for sleep began to engulf her.

"What's happened?" Mom repeated. "What's wrong?"

"We're going to explain everything, Mom."

"You look awful, sweetness. Both of you do." The old woman sat beside Kala on the lumpy couch, one hand patting her on the knee. "But I'm glad to see you two, together."

Sometime in these last few moments, Kala had begun to cry.

"Tell me, dear."

In what felt like a single breath, the story emerged. For the second time in her life, Kala had been kidnapped, but this time Sandor killed two people while freeing her. A second bride died in random gunfire, and two more were severely injured. "But we had to leave them," Kala confessed. "After we disarmed the brothers and brides, we left them with first aid kits and two working trucks...except Sandor shot out the tires before we drove off in their bus, just to make sure we would have a head start..."

Her mother held herself motionless, mouth open and no sound worth the effort.

"It was a big long bus with a ripper onboard. Sandor drove us through the mountains. Fast. I don't know why we didn't crash, but we didn't. We stopped at a fix-it shop and he made calls, and a hundred miles after that, we met a couple friends of his…men that he met inside prison, I think…"

"When was this?"

"Wednesday," she answered. "Those friends helped Sandor pull the ripper from the bus. They gave us a new truck and kept the capacitors and the other expensive gear for themselves. Then he and I drove maybe two miles, and that's when Sandor stole a second truck. Because he didn't quite trust his friends, and what if they decided to come take the ripper too?" She wiped at her eyes, her cheeks. "After that, we drove more than a thousand miles, but never in a straight line. By then, we'd finally decided what we were going to do, and he stole the van before we came here."

Mom was alert, focused. She was sitting forward with her hand clenched to her daughter's knee. Very quietly, she asked, "Is it one of the stolen rippers? From that convoy?"

Kala nodded. "The ID marks match."

"Have you thought about giving it back to its rightful owners?"

"We talked about that. Yes."

But then Mom saw what had eventually become obvious to Kala. "Regardless what you tell the owners, they'll think your brother had something to do with the robbery and murders. And what good would that do?"

"Nothing."

Then her mother gathered up Kala's hands, and

without hesitation, she said, "God has given you a gift, darling."

She didn't think about it in religious terms. But the words sounded nice.

"A great rare and wonderful gift," her mother continued. "And you know, if there is one person who truly deserves to inherit a new world, it has to be—"

"My brother?"

"No," Mom exclaimed, genuinely surprised. Then as the front door swung open and Sandor stepped inside, she said brightly, "It's you, sweetness. You deserve the best world. Of course, of course, of course…!"

Their frantic days had only just begun. The Children of Forever would have learned their names from the old ranger, or maybe from the Kala's abandoned car. And people who had murdered dozens to steal the ripper would undoubtedly do anything to recover what was theirs and avenge their losses. Obviously, it was best to vanish again, this time taking their mother with them. Old lives and treasured patterns had to be avoided, yet even on the run, they still had to find time and energy to make plans for what was to come next.

Sandor knew the best places to find machinery and foodstuffs and the other essential supplies. But Kala knew where to find people—the right people—who would make this business worthwhile. And it was their mother who acted as peacemaker, calming the water when her two strong-willed children began fighting over the details that always looked trivial the next day.

Suddenly it was winter—the worst season to migrate to another world. But that gave them the gift of several months where they could make everything perfect, or nearly so.

Years ago, the old fix-it man who once worked on their family car had retired, and the next owner had driven his shop out of business. The property was purchased from the bank for nothing and reconnected to the power grid, and with Kala's friends supplying labor and enough money, Sandor managed to refit the building according to their specific needs. Medical stocks were locked in the lady's room. The garage was jammed with canned and dried food and giant water tanks, plus the rest of their essential goods, including a fully charged class-C ripper that would carry away the little building.

On a cold bleak day in late March—several weeks before their scheduled departure—a stranger came looking for gasoline. He parked beside one of the useless pumps and pulled on his horn several times. Then he climbed out of the small, nondescript car, and ignoring the CLOSED signs painted on the shuttered windows, he walked across the cracked pavement in order to knock hard on both garage doors and the front door.

"Hey! Anybody there?" he shouted before finally giving up.

As he returned to his car, Kala asked her brother, "What is he? Children of Forever, or some kind of undercover cop?"

"Really," Sandor replied, "does it matter?"

Kala set her splattergun back in its cradle.

"I think it's time," their mother offered.

It was too early in the season to be ideal. But what choice did they have? Kala lifted the phone and made one coded call to the nearest town. And within the hour, everybody had arrived. Those who weren't going with them offered quick tearful good-byes to those who were, showering those blessed pioneers with kisses and love. But then the pioneers had enough, and with quick embarrassed voices, they said, "Enough, Mommy. Daddy. That's enough. Good-bye!"

Kala had come too far and paid too much of a price not to watch what was about to happened. She opened all of the shutters in the public room, letting the murky gray flow inside, and then she sat between two six-year-olds, one of whom asked, "How much longer now?"

"Soon," she promised. "A minute or two, at most."

Sandor and several other mechanically minded souls were in the garage, watching the ripper power up. Sharing the public room with Kala were a handful of grown men and a dozen women, plus nearly forty children sitting on tiny folding chairs, the oldest child being a stubborn twelve year-old boy—the only son of colleagues who were staying behind.

Kala's mother was one of the women, and she wasn't even the oldest.

"We're not making everybody else's mistakes," Kala had explained to her, sitting in the old living room some months ago. "We're taking grandparents and little kids, but very few young adults. I don't want virility and stupidity. I want wisdom and youth."

"What seeds are you taking?" her mother had asked.

"None."

"Did I hear you say—?"

"No seeds, and no animals. Not even one viable tortoise shell. And before we leave, I want to make sure every mouse in the building is dead, and every fly and flea, and if there's one earthworm living under us, I'll kill it myself when it pops in the new world."

Nobody was leaving this world but humans.

And even then, they were traveling as close to empty-handed as they dared. They had tools and a few books about science and mechanics. But everyone had taken an oath not to bring any Bibles or odd Testaments, and as far as possible, everything else that smacked of pre-conceptions and fussy religion had to be left behind on their doomed world.

The children came from families who believed as Kala believed.

It was amazing, and heartening, how many people held opinions not too much unlike hers. And sometimes in her most doubting moments, she found herself wondering if maybe her home world had a real chance of surviving the next ten thousand years.

But there were many parents who saw doom coming—ecological or political or religious catastrophes—and that's why they were so eager to give up a young son or daughter.

They were there now, standing out near the highway, surely hearing the ripper as it began to hammer hard at reality.

From inside the cold garage, Sandor shouted, "A target's acquired!"

Will this madness work? Kala asked herself one last time. Could one species arrive on an alien world, with children and old people in tow, and find food enough to survive? And then could they pass through the next ten thousand years without destroying everything that that world was and could have become...?

And then it was too late to ask the question.

The clouds of one day had vanished into a suddenly blue glare of empty skies, a green blue lawn of grassy something stretching off into infinity...and suddenly a room full of bright young voices shouted, "Neat! Sweet! Pretty!"

Then the boy on her right tugged at her arm, adding, "That's fun, Miss Kala. Let's do it again!"

CONTRIBUTORS

CHRISTOPHER ROWE has been a finalist for the Hugo, Nebula, and Sturgeon Awards, and in 2006 the *New York Times* said that he should be awarded "a special prize for the speculative work possessing the year's most striking literary imagery." Rowe is a native of Kentucky and lives there still, with his wife, writer Gwenda Bond.

CAROLYN IVES GILMAN has been publishing science fiction and fantasy for almost twenty years. Her first novel, *Halfway Human*, published by Avon/Eos in 1998, was called "one of the most compelling explorations of gender and power in recent SF" by *Locus*. Her short fiction has appeared in magazines and anthologies such as *Fantasy and Science Fiction*, *Bending the Landscape*, *The Year's Best Science Fiction*, *Realms of Fantasy*, *The Best From Fantasy & Science Fiction*, *Interzone*, *Universe*, *Full Spectrum*, and others. Her fiction has been translated into Italian, Russian, and German. In 1992 she was a finalist for the Nebula Award for her novella, "The Honeycrafters." She currently lives in St. Louis and works for the Missouri Historical Society as a historian and museum curator.

Born in England in 1943, **IAN WATSON** graduated from Balliol College, Oxford, in 1963 with a first class

Honours degree in English Literature, followed in 1965 by a research degree in English and French 19th Century literature. After lecturing in literature at universities in Tanzania and Tokyo, and in Futures Studies in Birmingham, England, he became a full-time writer in 1976 following the success of his first novel, *The Embedding*. Numerous novels of science fiction, fantasy, and horror followed, and nine story collections. His stories have been finalists for the Hugo and Nebula Awards, and widely anthologised. He lives with a black cat called Poppy in a small rural village sixty miles north of London.

ROBERT CHARLES WILSON's first novel was published in 1986. Since then he was won the Philip K. Dick Award, the John W. Campbell Memorial Award, three Aurora Awards, and in 2006 his novel *Spin* was the recipient of the Hugo Award. He lives near Toronto.

ANN LECKIE is a graduate of Clarion West. Her fiction has appeared in *Subterranean Magazine* and *Son and Foe*. She has worked as a waitress, a receptionist, a rodman on a land-surveying crew, and a recording engineer. She lives in St. Louis, Missouri with her husband, children, and cats.

WALTER JON WILLIAMS started writing in the early '80s, and his first science fiction novel, *Ambassador of Progress*, appeared in 1984 and was followed by *Hardwired, Aristoi, Metropolitan, City on Fire, The Rift,* and most recently his Dread Empire's Fall series, *The Praxis, The Sundering* and *Conventions of War*. A prolific and talented short fiction writer, he has won the Nebula for "Daddy's World" and "The Green Leopard Plague," His short fiction is collected in *Facets and Frankensteins* and

Foreign Devils. Upcoming is new science fiction novel *Implied Spaces*.

Sometime-English-professor, sometime-IT-professional, **RUTH NESTVOLD** has sold several dozen stories to a variety of markets, including *Scifiction, Asimov's, Strange Horizons,* Gardner Dozois's *Year's Best Science Fiction,* and a number of anthologies. Her novella "Looking Through Lace" made the short list for the Tiptree award in 2003 and was nominated for the Sturgeon award. She maintains a web site at www.ruthnestvold.com.

Since his first publication in 1993, **WILLIAM SHUNN**'s stories have appeared in *Salon, Asimov's, F&SF, Science Fiction Age, Realms of Fantasy, Electric Velocipede, Storyteller,* and elsewhere. He was nominated for a Nebula Award in 2002 for his novelette "Dance of the Yellow-Breasted Luddites," and has served three years as a national juror for the Scholastic Art & Writing Awards. He produces a biweekly podcast, and is at work on a novel and a memoir. Born in L.A. and raised in Utah, he has lived for eleven years in New York City, where he met his wife Laura Chavoen. The couple have a soft-coated wheaten terrier named Ella. A chapbook of stories in due from Spilt Milk Press in the summer of 2007.

JACK SKILLINGSTEAD has lived most his life in Seattle. In 2001 Stephen King chose his entry as a winner in his "On Writing" contest. Since 2003 Jack's stories have appeared in various publications, including *Asimov's Science Fiction, On Spec, Realms of Fantasy,* and Gardner Dozois' *Years Best Science Fiction.* Jack's first professional sale was a finalist for the Theodore Sturgeon Memorial Award.

ADAM ROBERTS is a writer in his forties. He lives

a little way west of London with his wife and daughter. He's published various novels, the most recent being *Gradisil, Splinter* and *Land of the Headless.*

BENJAMIN ROSENBAUM lives in Virginia with his wife Esther, his son Noah, and his daughter Aviva, who describes him thusly: "he is grat.he likes being jumpt on.and loves kids." His stories have appeared in *F&SF, Asimov's, Strange Horizons, Nature, Harper's,* and *McSweeney's,* and been nominated for a Nebula, a Hugo, a Sturgeon, and a BSFA award. Despite Noah's insistence, he does not want to turn into a pig. See his website at www.benjaminrosenbaum.com.

ROBERT REED was born in Omaha, Nebraska on October 9, 1956. Since then Bob has had eleven novels published, starting with *The Leeshore* and most recently with *The Well of Stars.* Since winning the first annual L. Ron Hubbard Writers of the Future contest in 1986 and being a finalist for the John W. Campbell Award for best new writer in 1987, he has had 140 shorter works published in a variety of magazines and anthologies. Eleven of those stories were published in his critically-acclaimed first collection, *The Dragons of Springplace.* Twelve more stories appear in his second collection, *The Cuckoo's Boys.* Reed continues to live in Lincoln, Nebraska, with his wife, Leslie, and daughter, Jessie.

RICH HORTON is a software engineer in St. Louis. He is a contributing editor to *Locus,* for which he does short fiction reviews and occasional book reviews; and to *Black Gate,* for which he does a continuing series of essays about science fiction history. He also contributes book reviews to *Fantasy Magazine,* and to many other publications.

PUBLICATION HISTORY